TEN
CREEKS RUN

TEN
CREEKS RUN

···

MILES
FRANKLIN

Eden

EDEN PAPERBACKS
an imprint of Angus & Robertson Publishers

Unit 4, Eden Park, 31 Waterloo Road,
North Ryde, NSW, Australia 2113, and
16 Golden Square, London W1R 4BN,
United Kingdom.

First published 1930
First Angus & Robertson edition 1952
This Eden paperback edition 1988

Copyright Miles Franklin estate 1930

ISBN 0 207 15787 1

Printed in Australia by The Book Printer

AUTHOR'S NOTE

THESE people never were, and the incidents here recorded could not therefore have happened to them. They remain more vivid than reality because of imagination. I ramp impatiently, desirous of progressing to other scenes and souls, but, demonstrating the full scale of human emotions, they crowd about me suffocatingly, craving—nay, demanding—perpetuation. I am faced by a patternless, trackless region out of which I must urgently beat my way like the early explorers, uncertain if I am merely going round and round, or right through, or slipping out the side by a false route.

"You poor old nonentities," I exclaim in the irritation of fatigue and close confinement to their affairs. "What profit in agitating the printing-presses on your behalf! You are not among those who have contributed ideas to human knowledge, nor have you taken the human race one flicker above the mud on that road to super-humanhood for which some of us gape."

"Bah!" they retort. "That stuff's all tommy rot! No matter what airs of spiritual or mental superiority people give themselves, it's all a bottle of smoke in the end, and the end is before you can bally well get your pipe to draw decently. They will all lie down and die and rot like the cows and horses, and, in spite of all the faith and belief, no one knows for a dead cert if they have any more soul, or as much as old 'Flea Creek', who carried the salt-bags out on the Run because the other horses were too flash for the job."

"That's all very well," I contend, "but it does not solve the problem of your inconsequence as material from which to concoct a story. Whatever happened to you but that you were born in your turn, grew up in your turn, were smitten with the procreative urge or scourge—sometimes out of your turn—and tried to marry women who seldom wanted you; whereupon you turned to those more obliging, and who served equally well; whereupon you reproduced your species without male restraint or mercy to the limit of female capacity and endurance; and the reproductions like yourselves mostly, were not worth the women's birth-pangs, nor the women worth any other sort of pangs. Then in due time you were buried, and ordinary funerals are as monotonously alike as infants. One generation of you was but a repetition of a former, with a marriage or a funeral as a highlight—not a single epic adventure to create a hero, nor a hero to engineer an epic adventure in the whole boiling!"

"Hold hard!" says one old philosopher, who has thought much in the solitudes. I see him on the outer edge of the crowd. "Is it real life here in this part of the world you're driven to make this blanky book about, or is it about some strange, unusual, far-away land, with kings and savages, or professors and millionaires, and other kinds of fantastic people?"

"It has to be set bang here in Australia, with none but you kicking up your heels and using bad language in the middle of the natural scenery."

"Well, then, it seems to me that all you have to do is yarn along and make us come alive just as we blooming well were. Let us drivel and meander like life itself. You have nothing to do with the way of our lives or the character of our performances, whether big or little, or dull, or exciting. If a funeral, or a marriage, or a drought, or a flood, or a snake-bite, or a spree, or a broken leg was our greatest experience, that is not your responsibility. Blow it all, you're not the Lord Himself! You have only to show how things were without any squirming about the why or how. You don't need to swell your head with shaping destiny or interpreting life according to those new-fangled blokes who never baked a damper, or felled a tree, or rode a buck-jumper, or killed a snake or a beast, or tanned a hide, or broke in a team of bullocks, or knocked up a coffin for a mate out of stringybark, or drank water out of their hats. You just set us down on paper as we were, without any of your own shenannakin!"

There! Put in my place as simple delineator and comforted by bearing in mind that life is the most discursive and fragmentary experience, I proceed free of misgivings about the flatness of the contours or the duller colours of my material, and concerned only with what I can capture of inevitability, actuality, proportion. My "squirming" shifts to the realization of my own bewildering nescience in face of the task which sucks me down. Why, in a universe revolving upon marvels, magnitudes, and problems, before which the best of human intellects are but as thimbles to conserve or direct Murrumbidgees, and man's day but an ephemeral hazard like that of the horse-fly at Wamgambril swamps snapped by the iridescent kingfisher in his flight, should I be possessed to limn the inconsequent pioneers and horses that have gone?

Howbeit, I must deliver myself of my love and loyalty to them, before my own precarious moment in this consciousness is ended.

If achievement be maddeningly inadequate to conception and inspiration, nevertheless for the sake of peace I must press on. If I do my task only roughly, as the old pioneers knocked up their humpies and blazed their tracks single-handed against untamed nature, well, that cannot be helped. There are hosts to come after me—that is all!

BRENT OF BIN BIN.

NEW SOUTH WALES,
November 1927.

CHAPTER 1

"Stick to him, Jerry! Stick to him!"

"Garn! Stick to your grandmother! He's only pig-rootin'!"

"Ole Flea Creek could do better'n that! You orter seen *him* last spring!"

"Stop that, you —— fool!" commanded an older voice. "What the hell do you mean, kicking the insides out of a horse just to show off? There'll be plenty real riding to take the flashness out of you and the mokes before the muster is done!"

"Ssh! Milly!" said another in honour of a girl verging on teens, balanced on the top rail of the horseyards.

"Blow her! What's she doin' here? Oughter be home learnin' to sew!"

"Milly, you better go home," commanded her uncle, overhearing. "This is no place for you. Your mother wants you."

"Mother's coming herself to see them back Corroboree."

"He's not going to be backed today. Billy's not here."

"Yes, he is. He's coming down from the huts now. Besides, Uncle Bert said I could go to the muster."

"You'll get your neck broken!"

"No fear! I could stick anything in my new saddle, and Uncle Bert is going to take me himself." Milly put out her tongue behind her relative's back. Covert grins. The boss was not popular: Milly was, and in danger of being spoilt. Young Farquharson tweaked her long pigtail. Milly moved closer to Uncle Bert, where there was safety.

A busy time had come for the Run. The professional buyers for the Indian Army were expected, and the usual crowd that would as soon have missed the local agricultural shows as a muster were arriving for the fray. Among the top-rail critics and advisers were neighbouring squatters and station-hands as well as horse-fanciers and touts from Monaro, Queanbeyan, Yass, Goulburn, Tumbarumba, Bool Bool, Tumut, and Gundagai, who had come to look for strays or to pick up a promising colt or filly in advance from the stations celebrated for their products.

There were friends like Curradoobidgee Poole and Ronald Dice of Bookaledgeree, who had ridden from afar to take home

1

their own strays and lend a hand in general: there were the Far-quharsons from farther down the River—the river Murrumbidgee—smart fellows and great on harness horses. There were Billings and Cross-eyed Prendergast from Gundagai, in hopes of securing something for the coach lines, since the Milford brothers of Jinnin-jinninbong, over the river—the river Coolgarbilli—had introduced a coaching strain of late years, and the muster on that station was a joint affair with Ten Creeks Run. There was little Tommy Roper, unattached bachelor and horse-trainer at large, who picked up a living partly by following the shows with his hunters, and by droving, etc., between whiles. He was the man of the hour by reason of his recent epic which had left dead bullocks along the route from Riverina to the Victorian border, and incidentally left Tommy bankrupt, but he hoped to make a fresh start with something likely from the impending muster.

*   *   *   *   *

Old Jack Stanton, boss of Ten Creeks Run, and son of the original Stanton of Stanton's Plains, Bool Bool, before he became old Jack, had gone down the River—the river Murrumbidgee—to Turrill Turrill and started in sheep, where he did well. He had, however, never been weaned from the mountain country and with spare capital started a horse station with some first-class blood at Ten Creeks. In droughty summers he also travelled his sheep up. Friends and neighbours were the Milfords, natives of the other side towards Yass, who had secured Jinninjinninbong and other runs and established permanent homes on the opposite side of the Coolgarbilli, and were known for the uniformly high quality of their mob horses.

Jack Stanton was unmarried. His widowed sister—Milly's mother—kept house for him. She enjoyed the mountains, and often spent half the year in the home-made wooden house on the Cool-garbilli. It was due to her presence, and that of the Mesdames Milford, that there was a sprinkling of women guests among the musterers. The Farquharsons were accompanied by two sisters, and Aileen Healey had come with her brother Larry from Neangen Station adjoining Bookaledgeree. Aily was as pretty as the girls on chocolate-boxes, as her mirror told her any time she looked in it, a pleasant story now being confirmed in the eyes of the muster, and, most enchantingly to her, in the eyes of Ronald Dice.

It was the liveliest time of the year for these inaccessible sta-tions. House and huts were full. Mrs Saunders had an ex-sailor in the kitchen and in the house proper a couple of brumby girls supplemented by intermittent help from as many rouseabouts as could be filched from the pursuits of the Run. They were easy to filch with two such baits as Sarah and Ellen Humphreys, and the girls among such swarms of admirers no sooner felt their affections beginning to root on one desirable than they were uprooted by the intrusion of another.

A fine draft of colts and fillies was expected this season to do credit to the brand "SP over J"—SP standing for the original Stanton's Plains, which each son retained as he set up for himself and added his own initial below. The runs were to be combed from the Wamgambril almost to the Jenningningahama and the head of the Murrumbidgee through to the fringe of the Bimberies and Tidbinbillies and back to Jinninjinninbong and Ten Creeks.

There were forty or fifty saddle horses in the home yards that glorious morning, most of them seasoned stock horses, with a few ladies' hacks and beasts fit for any show, and all in top condition. Some, turned out since last summer, were expected to be collar-proud and more experienced buckers than bewildered colts undergoing their first ordeal. There were several celebrities on rebel count, or for their pedigrees and potentialities. Foremost of these was Corroboree, a glorious four-year-old, sixteen hands, coal black, luxuriant of mane and tail, the spit of his imported sire, owned by the Potters of Cuppinbingle, farther down the river. The Potters were known for their hard riding and hard swearing, with a good deal of carousing and other virility thrown in, and as the best breeders and judges of horse-flesh from the Murrumbidgee to the Murray. One of them was expected on the morrow, and today was represented by a trainer and Mick Muldoon, the latter a horny old boundary-rider, drover, etc., who did not remember learning to ride or when he first camped out on his lone.

Opinion was so in favour of backing Corroboree and others that SP-over-J had to let the morning go in a buck-jumping tourney.

*　　*　　*　　*　　*

William Bowes, known as Flash Billy the Breaker, now approached, and interest shifted to a young man with limbs loosely hung and disproportionately long for his body, like a pair of tongs. His black hair was sleekly greased and grew low above his eyes on his small bullet head. His face was garnished with two black lawns fornent his ears and a slick moustache with coquettish curls at the ends. He had glaringly strapped trousers, a tight short coat, a bright blue-fronted waistcoat, and the light boots of the horsey acolyte. Everything about him was flash, from the ring on his little finger to his long spurs, and the cabbage-tree hat "hanging on three hairs", as his contemporaries expressed it, and coloured the

3

right shade like a meerschaum. He had tested his frame and earned renown breaking for Curradoobidgee, Gowandale, Cuppinbingle, and other stations previously to having all he could do on Ten Creeks. It was never denied that he had earned his sobriquet honestly. He had arrived but a few hours earlier from Queanbeyan and was in holiday apparel. He swung up to the top rail beside Milly and spat with terrific efficiency onto Corroboree as he was being run round the yard with head aloft and the carriage of an emperor.

"He crackles like a bag of rattlesnakes. Golly, just listen to him!" observed Long Billy, the rouseabout.

"What makes him make that noise? Is that good or bad?" inquired Milly. This raised a guffaw. Uncle Bert came to her rescue.

"My old dad, who knew more about a horse than any man I know——"

"Not more than you, Uncle Bert, surely?"

"I can manage to tell a horse from a cow if I'm not too rushed, but my dad knew all that was to be known about the gee-gees, and the more the colts would rattle the better pleased he'd be."

"I reckon he was dead right," confirmed Flash Billy.

"What about ketchin' him, Billy?" inquired Jerry Riddall.

"Wait till mother comes; she and the girls want to see him. I'll catch old Readymoney while we're waiting."

"Don't attempt such a thing!"

"You'll have your eyes kicked out!"

Protest arose from all round the top rail from men with halters or bridles awaiting a propitious moment to drop among the crowd cunning in presenting slickly aimed heels to the enemy.

"If you won't let me ride Romp, I shan't have anything but Readymoney. The others are logs of wood. It would take the polled Angus team to hold or slew them."

"Don't attempt Readymoney till Billy gives him a turn. He bucked like blue murder last spring," said SP-over-J.

Readymoney was a sweater's horse, one taken illegally and ridden till knocked up and turned adrift. His brand was botched, so he had never been claimed. He had been trained down the country and was the delight of Milly and other women riders for his urbane manners. Trained paces set a gap between the stock horse and the saddle horse. High prices were given by Sydney and Melbourne buyers for paced thoroughbreds guaranteed free from vice, with trial permitted. SP-over-J filled this kind of order, and in meeting it Billy Bowes was an artist of importance.

"Flash Billy's like a feller outer a circus. He can learn a horse to do anythink but talk," his admirers proclaimed.

He had been reared in the right atmosphere, his dad having been an old lag who had served his time on Cuppinbingle, and Billy, the last of his litter, was cradled in the Potter stables in which he learnt the more aristocratic methods of horse-training. His mother was a Red Rover lass, which is highly irrelevant, the lass and her old man having been long abed in a grave near their hut where the itching cattle were pushing the palings down, and high grass and thistles on the mound made a home for a pair of fat old goannas what time the Corroboree colt was being tamed. The old hands used the grave as a landmark, but it is obliterated today; the killing of timber alters the face of the ranges, and the old hands—what few of them remain—are growing forgetful.

*　　*　　*　　*　　*

Scornful of warnings, Milly dropped into the crowd with her pretty bridle, its blue forehead-band threaded through a macramé fly-chaser. Poole of Curradoobidgee dropped down behind her, but Readymoney, sneezing his goodwill, allowed the little girl to secure him. She led him out of the ruck in triumph, and when eyes were off her, slipped astride his fat back and cried, "Open the gate while I ride the bucking outlaw through!"

"Get down at once! You ought to be ashamed of yourself," said her uncle.

"Then I'll ride sideways." She changed and Readymoney ambled away without protest.

The ladies were now coming from the house with Ronald Dice and Mr Eustace Blenkinsop in attendance.

"Come on, Billy, shall we put the tackle on the colt?" asked Jerry Riddall.

"Put it on the Wamgambril fust. He'll do yous for a start to warm up," said Flash Billy with consequence.

"Young Dice seems to be stickin' like a fly in tar to the ladies," remarked young Billings to Dan Spires, the overseer.

"You'll see him wherever there's a bit of rag about. He's like me," interposed Flash Billy.

"All the good riders seems to be weak on the skirts," said Jerry Riddall flatteringly. "What have you done with your girl, Billy?"

"Left her in Queanbeyan till next week." Billy was fluttering round a barmaid there.

"I heard a cove from Goulburn was top o' the runnin'," remarked Long Billy, the rouseabout.

"That tin mug with the handle off!" Billy was contemptuous.

"You might git left. You never can tell with females. The ——s

5

seem to pick out the mugs and pass by the likeliest chaps for spite," said Cross-eyed Prendergast.

"Perhaps they think you're looking at someone else all the time," ventured Long Billy.

"Begor', if the faymales didn't pick the culls, some of yez would stand a fat chance of iver getting married at all." This was Mick Muldoon's contribution.

"Is that why you're an old bachelor?"

"Maybe Oi'm wan of the proizes was passed over for the culls by the spoiteful faymales."

"It's Aily Healey!" observed young Billings, as the ladies drew near. "How did she get here?"

"On old Healey's chestnut mare, that's *how*; but if you want to know *why*, go ask Ron Dice," said little Tommy Roper, by reason of his aptitude and peregrinations, so forehanded in other people's affairs that he was credited with eyes in the back of his head.

"Ron Dice! Wotta yer mean?"

"Some fun there, I betcher! Ole Skinny Guts has shown signs of stickin' up to her since the show in Bool Bool," continued Tommy in a whisper.

"Who says that?" demanded Timmy Porter, eager on the track of gossip.

"Anyone with as much gumption as a wall-eyed wombat can see some things for himself," said Tommy.

Further confidences were impossible. Teddy Parsons, Long Billy, Jerry Riddall, and others had the tackle on the Wamgambril colt, so named from the direction of his foaling, and he stood breathing defiance in one of the outer yards. These youths were as tough as greenhide, having been dragged up on cockatoo selections about Bool Bool, but they lacked horse-flesh to squander, so for the present held ambition in leash and waited upon the great.

"Any cove like to show off what he can do fust?" called Billy. "I ain't been outer the saddle for a couple of days, and ain't had any sleep since the night before last."

"Here's a chance for volunteers," cried Ronald Dice gaily from the top rail as he sat between Rose Farquharson and Aily Healey, tenderly helping Aily to balance.

"Surely yous ain't afeared of a buster or two," continued Billy. "I git 'em meself now an' again if I git playin' the goat."

Tim Porter stepped forward. He had a bullet head and a large, loose mouth. He and his dad before him had been brought up on Bookaledgeree, where old Tim Brennan of The Gap had set up Tim, jun., some thirty years before this history takes its rise.

"I'd jist like to try," he said, paling round the gills. Tim would never be a crack. He lacked the intelligence, and a horse-breaker who does not have that needs to be minus a derangeable nervous system. Tim mounted amid copious advice from the top rail. The colt went into action immediately.

"Stick to him, Tim! Hang on a little longer! He's givin' in!"

"*He* can't ride! The colt's only pig-rootin'!"

"Pooh! He's hangin' on by his spurs!"

"The next root will bring him a buster."

Tim was stood on his head, his gymnastics greeted by guffaws. He got up and walked off with a forced grin.

"Well tried, old man!" said Dice kindly. "You only want to grip better with your knees and throw your weight with the movement of the horse—practice will do it."

"Who's next?" called Flash Billy.

"If someone will put my new saddle on him," said Milly, "I could easily stick those bucks."

A gale of laughter greeted this. "You could ride him all right," said Poole quietly, "but sticking a buck is no game for a girl: no game for a man either with any savvy, and it's no good for the horse, and unnecessary."

"Sure, 'tis tin chances to wan the beast wouldn't buck at all if you got on him, missy," said Mick Muldoon. "Only the Creathor Himself knows the way of high-spirited horses with women. A blood horse that would jump out av his hoïde to get rid of a crack rider will let a hoigh-spirited gurrul play circus thricks wid him, him lettin' out snorts of contint. Or he will let a short-witted man put a pack-saddle on him an' climb aboord himself atop of the load. Sure, there's food for the philosophers there. Can ye explain it, Mr Poole, an' ye knowin' more av a horse than annywan aloive?"

"The trouble is, Muldoon, that we drive horses to buck and then break them of it. It would be much better if they were never let buck at all, and never learnt how, but that of course can't be done with so many to handle."

"Gettin' frightened!" whispered Tommy Roper to Dan Spires. "The greatest rider that ever threw a leg over a horse in his young days! I've seen the day when no horse could do nothing with him—not very long ago neither; an' when he'd get tired of buckin', his nibs would rouse him up again—must be losin' his teeth altogether."

"Goin' barmy to talk like that, I reckon. Aw, he's an old geezer now. I hope I'll kick the bucket before ever I get like that. No more good than a —— ole woman!"

"Ye're roight, av coorse, Mr Poole, but ye couldn't git thim young turkey cocks to credit it. But how do ye explain it furder with a horse that has been learnt to buck—take ould Readymoney now with Miss Milly on him bareback, an' she could have taken a tin can on with her to boot and he wouldn't disturb a nest of eggs in a silk hat, but if Flash Billy got aboord him there would have been the Ould Gintleman to pay."

The Breaker was called Flash Billy to his face to avoid confusion with Long Billy. He took no umbrage, considering it a tribute of jealousy to his smart trousers and waistcoats.

"I think it bears out what I have said," replied Poole. "A woman is not allowed on a horse till the buck is out of him, so he has no fear of her as an enemy, and all is friendly from the start."

     ❄   ❄   ❄   ❄   ❄

A traveller was announced by the watch-dogs among the heelers, kangaroo dogs, and mongrels—visiting and resident—that were settling differences by direct action.

"Hogan's ghost! Here's old Teddy O'Mara!" announced the hawk-eyed Billy Bowes. This was disputed, betted upon, and settled by the appearance of a large brindled kangaroo dog followed by a smaller grey one, both in poison muzzles of perforated leather securely strapped on, protecting their lives and robbing them of joy. Behind them on a track down the river a horseman came out of the timber.

"He allus has them old dawgs."

"I never see them used for anything."

"Couldn't use them for nothing but to kill fowls or sheep."

"Keeps 'em for company, I reckon."

"It's a lonely thing to be travellin' without a dawg."

The horseman bent forward in somewhat the posture later introduced by Tod Sloan, and since adopted by all professional jockeys. In that day it was the distinguishing antic of a half-wit.

"Queer ole feller! Always lays on his belly on horseback. Oughter git a bed an' be done with it."

"He turned in at Keba before we left. We wanted him to anchor there, because we have plenty to keep him going," said young Farquharson.

Teddy hitched his horse in the line outside the yards, kicked a few dogs from his path, and beamed upon the company.

"Well, Teddy, are you travelling or only going somewhere?" said Dice.

"I'm goin' as far as I'm goin'," said Teddy. He was a tall man with greying whiskers in unclipped possum formation. His tousled curls protruded through a tattered felt hat: he wore a ragged overcoat despite the warm day, and twine served as bootlaces. Fearless decency shone from his clear blue eyes.

"Have you got married yet, Teddy?"

"No fear, the missus wouldn't let me."

"That's right, Teddy, you listen to what she says," commended Mrs Saunders, and remarked to Flora Farquharson, "I think it's disgusting to talk about marriage to that sort of men—might put dangerous notions in their heads about women."

"Heard you were at Keba for the summer," said Poole, and shook hands with him.

"No fear, that lousy old Farquharson offered me thirty bob a week. 'Keep your lousy thirty bob,' I says to him. 'I never work for less than a pound a week.' Ha! Ha! Ha!"

A kookaburra chorus ensued.

"My word, Teddy! That's the way to treat the blasted bosses!" laughed Dice.

"Your father ought to be ashamed of himself to play a dirty trick like that on poor old Teddy," smiled Poole at Farquharson.

"It was pretty low-down. I must see into it," laughingly agreed Farquharson.

"But I put the bell on him, you bet I did!" maintained Teddy hilariously. Again the guffaws at a primitive type of humour—which persists out of proportion to man's development in other ways—the propensity of the five-eighths-witted to find intense delight in guying the half-witted.

"Where are you bound for now—staying here?" asked SP-over-J.

"No fear! I'm making over the river to my young missus."

Two or three years previously the younger Milford had captured one of the Labosseer girls of Coolooluk, and it was to her that Teddy referred. His beat ran from Coolooluk to Curradoo-bidgee on Monaro and from there to Ten Creeks and Jinninjinnin-bong back to the Mazeres and Stantons of Bool Bool. Now and again a squatter outside the circle tried to entice Teddy with a higher wage, but usually met the fate of the Farquharsons because he could not count higher than a pound. His headquarters were with Mrs Rachel Labosseer. On her estate perfection reigned. Every stray man, Chinese, dog, or horse that came that way received attention. There Teddy returned when destitute and in tatters, and from there he was never allowed to depart without warm clothing and stout boots, and, if it was winter, an overcoat. A steam-roller could not have deflected him from seemliness, but he had to live life on his own terms as one of God's fools. Horse-breaking since he was twelve or fourteen, not even outlaws were untamable by him, but he left them with nature's paces and

9

believed a walk an example of equine debauchery brought about by contact with cities. The cities to him were strange towns like Goulburn, Gundagai, and Wagga Wagga. Bool Bool and Cooma were home paddocks where to diddle Teddy brought upon the miscreant a dragooning from a Mazere, Labosseer, Brennan, or Poole.

Seeing that the dogs were all without muzzles, no baits having been laid for weeks before the muster, Teddy released his pets.

"Well, Teddy, you're in the nick of time," said Dice. "We're going to ride the Corroboree colt and when he's flung us all you can have a turn."

     ✧   ✧   ✧   ✧   ✧

A fresh arrival brought word that the Milford brothers would be over on the morrow to run the Bull Flat Creek mob into trap-yards out that way, so the day was relinquished to recreation. The more immediate sports opened briskly. Half a dozen young fellows with more energy than intelligence were soon raising a dust in the outer yards.

"I don't see any real fun in this bucking business," remarked Lucy Saunders. "It must rack a man."

"Of course it does," agreed Flora Farquharson. "Mother told me . . ." She lowered her voice for a juicy confidence.

"You must tell me tonight."

Men's ribaldries regarding women were mostly obscenities about such basic facts as the procreative functions, and fed a distorted or debased craving for genuine humour, but the remotest men would have been staggered to know what percolated to women of their beings, and as strictly divested of prurience as a surgeon's treatise. There was nothing hidden from a decent full-witted woman concerning a man in those districts if she had a mind to know, and less hidden from the indecent. It has always been so. It will be more so as time goes on, but what men do not know of women is that about which women deceive them, plus what women do not know of themselves.

Flash Billy was genuinely tired from lack of sleep and hard riding consequent upon pursuit of l'amour, and merely kept an eye on the active practitioners. The prince of riders that day was Ronald Dice, elated because Aily Healey was an onlooker and that old SP-over-J seemed to be narked. Larry Healey was not riding, for a recent accident had strained his shoulder and he was resting to be ready for the feats of the muster. Dice's performance was easy and dashing. By sheer high spirits he excited his mounts and was not among those suffering falls. Admiration in Aily's pretty eyes was too much for SP-over-J.

10

"The real rider is the one who can stick Corroboree for five minutes when he really goes to market," said he. "Anyone who can do that can have his pick of the first yard of yearlings run in tomorrow."

"Is that a real offer?" asked Flash Billy. Stanton never flung his money about. "Skinny Guts" had more reference to his parsimony than to his physique.

"A square offer this morning to everyone within hearing, and I'll make it for anything under three years old."

"I wish I was not so thunderin' tired," complained Flash Billy.

"You and Mr Poole can be the timekeepers and judges." This mollified the Breaker. "Besides, there's not much chance of anyone winning—not anyone riding today. They can flop about on ladies' hacks pig-rooting, but let them have a go at Corroboree and they'll find their class."

There was a stir to rope and gear the colt, the snorting beauty, short of rib with barrel splendidly rounded, big in the girth, shoulders well laid in, great legs and quarters, built like a rock to stay, with breeding and intelligence stamped all over him. He came from a proud line of winners on the sire's side and on the other had a strain of Poole's famous Black Belles and Waterfalls.

When he was saddled, Jerry Riddall was the first to step forward. One of the greatest drovers known, young Jerry had never been off the roads till he engaged himself for a change on Ten Creeks. He was a better sprinter than rough rider, but the mob spirit here edged him on.

The colt was deceivingly calm. Equine intelligence pitted against human had so far kept him free from surrender. The flash bravado of horse-breakers could be a tea-party for two. Here was no terrified sufferer with quivering flank, tail tight between the hindquarters, and ears laid back. It was Jerry that trembled and had his tail between his legs.

Milly supported Poole as timekeeper when he took out his watch, a gold repeater presented to him over thirty years before when, single-handed, he had rid the Southern District of a guerrilla band of bushrangers.

Jerry hardly seated himself when a marvellous lurch flung him in the air. Dan Spires, the overseer, the second candidate, speedily met Jerry's fate. Then followed Jim Porter. Paddy Leary, the Cuppinbingle trainer, next had a try, but Corroboree dislodged him with the lightning lurch.

"The trouble with this 'ere colt is vice," said Flash Billy. "He's been at these capers for 'most a year now and it looks like he'll never give over."

"He's got the rale thoroughbred spring in him, an' he's carryin' his tail like a paycock, an' him the spit of his dad. Sure, if he's niver safe but for to pack salt 'tis a pity," observed Muldoon.

"With thorough precautions, I'd like a try," said Alistair Farquharson.

"Me first," said Long Billy. He took no end of precautions. He dampened the saddle amid the jeers of the spectators, and blindfolded the colt. Flash Billy and Dice led him round the ploughed yard before they took off the handkerchief and backed away. The colt merely raised his perfect muzzle and sniffed the morning breeze, honey-sweet with wattle borne down the valley to the music of the Coolgarbilli. Long Billy led off gingerly. Not a buck.

"Touch him up a little!" commanded Stanton. Long Billy dug a heel in his flank, but the horse did not seem to object.

"I don't think he's going to——" One splendid backward lurch onto his hindquarters and Long Billy went onto the wither, another forward and the rouseabout shot off like a pebble from a catapult amid shouts of glee.

There was a rush to recapture the colt lest he should clear the dog-leg fence of the bucking-yard and get away with the saddle, a deep-seated treasure with perfect knee-pads, but the colt only trotted back to the gate of the inner yard to be near his mates, allowing himself to be caught without fuss. Poole noted that he was quite calm, showing no touch of bad temper.

"Great Scott, what a clinker!" exclaimed young Dice, who had not seen him in action till then. "All he needs seems to be a rider. Have you tried him lately, Billy?"

"I'm allers tryin' him."

"Can he get rid of you?"

"I allers tire fust. He's as active as a cat, an' a stayer, an' as cunning as Beelzebub."

"He only needs a rider, though, for all that," said Stanton insinuatingly. "I've seen the day when Poole could have bested him without any fuss at all. Young fellows nowadays can't ride like they used to. They're not *game*!" He slyly watched the effect of his words on Aileen Healey. He half feared that if Dice took the challenge he might win, though Corroboree had not turned a hair yet. Wait till a succession of tormentors got his blood up!

"Oh, Uncle Bert, why don't you try now?" demanded Milly. "I'm sure he couldn't chuck you. Wouldn't you love to see Uncle Bert on him, Aileen?"

"I'd hate to see anyone hurt," said Aileen dubiously.

"She'd rather watch some of the flash young fellows who think they can ride," said Stanton.

12

"The colt ain't in his top form today," said Bowes.

"That's good news," said Alistair Farquharson. "I'll have a go and chance the dux." He had watched the horse's methods and thought he could be ready for his sudden prop.

A few vigorous bucks failed to dislodge him. Alistair stirred him up and was treated to the backward prop. Surviving this he began to feel hopeful, but he could not read the colt's mind for the next move. It was an oblique lunge to the off-side and a swing-back to the left with such terrific speed and strength that Alistair might as well have tried to sit a derrick loose in a southerly. It placed him on the crupper and a bound forward set Corroboree free.

"I managed the prop but that twister did for me," said Alistair, getting up and dusting himself with unruffled amiability. "I'd rather break him to harness with my new-fashioned breast collar."

"That's allers the way with him. You may think you learnt all his moves, but you'll allers find him one ahead of the game."

"I'd like a go just to show I'm not yellow," said Dice, stepping up and examining the tackle. He vaulted to the saddle with strength and grace and spurred the horse into immediate action. His tactics were to put him on the defensive. The onlookers enjoyed an exhibition of every kind of buck with a breather between the efforts—side to side, the sharp swing round, kicking-up and bucking forward at the same time, and compelling the rider to employ two kinds of seat simultaneously. This failed to dislodge young Dice.

"He's the only feller of me own age I'd ever be afeared of taking second place to," said Bowes commendingly, "but he's only been on a couple er minutes yet."

SP-over-J grew uneasy. "You must stir him up. You mustn't camp till the time is up," he called out harshly.

Ronald applied a prick of his heel. The horse was warming up. Terror was stealing into his haughty heart such as no rider had been able to put there since he had dislodged the first impertinence. When first backed he had felt similar terror. Here was one who might be a fixture. A convulsion of rage stirred the horse. Back and forth, up till he was perpendicular as a man! This being unavailing, he finally acted like a dog with a heavily charged bait and in frenzy flung himself clean backwards. A spur high in the glinting sun, the clink of a stirrup, and his tormentor rolled from under with agility and presence of mind.

With a snort of satisfaction Corroboree trotted away.

"You pulled him too far over. Would you like a second try?" inquired Stanton suavely.

"No, Mr Stanton, that wasn't it," interposed Billy. "It's what

I was sayin'; it's vice. That's what he does when he can't get rid of you by fair means."

"Going to take a second shot?" persisted Corroboree's owner.

"Not now, thanks," said Dice, dusting himself and working his limbs to be sure they were uninjured. "He's bested me fairly, but I shouldn't call it vice, would you, Mr Poole?"

"No, Ronnie, I shouldn't. I've never seen a better bit of riding, but when it came to bedrock he was the better warrior. It's not the right way to tackle that beast, if I know anything."

"Teddy! Now's your chance!"

"Come on, Teddy—Teddy O'Mara up!"

"Don't let the poor old fellow on that beast. He might be killed," said Mrs Saunders.

"It's not fair! He's getting too old!" said Rose Farquharson.

"They say it was a fall on his head when he was little left him as he is," said her sister.

"I should say he came short from his mother," said Stanton.

"He's not short on lots of things that others would be better to be a bit longer on," said Poole. "I don't know a decenter old fellow from here to the Upper Murray. No woman has ever had to make a complaint about poor old Teddy, and he works his passage through life."

"It's a shame to barrack him onto an outlaw," said Milly. "He's too old."

"Strange thing, being a little short mentally, I don't believe he knows he's getting old," said Poole.

Teddy could not be kept off the colt now. He placed his own saddle, with wads of horse-hair sticking from under the seat where mice had found a lying-in ward. Someone had jockeyed him out of the sound article with which he had left Coolooluk six months earlier. He did not discard his flapping overcoat. He put one foot in the stirrup, jumping several times to gain momentum to rise. The noble beast courteously awaited his guest. Teddy mounted, clouted with his old hat; Corroboree, with the sneeze that voices equine goodwill, set off at a dog trot round the yard. Teddy reined in before the ladies and chanted:

> "Me feyther and mother were Irish,
>   And I was Irish too;
>   We bought a tin kettle for ninepence,
>   And knocked up an Irish stoo!"

"He's tired for the day," said Farquharson.

"Phwat did I tell yez about women and thim that's not all there!"

14

"He's all right if you ride about like a girl!" gibed Dan Spires. "Stir him up, Teddy. He's afraid you'll fall off."

Teddy flapped his hat but the charger only mended his pace a little. The gibes began to anger Teddy. Other times, other fashions in the efflorescence of virility. In those days a man would have been considered effeminate to minimize bucking. Teddy yawed on the bit, but the horse was taking no ungentlemanly advantage. Flash Billy reached out with a roping pole and pricked him under the tail. He resented the indignity by gaining his freedom with a smart buck. Old Teddy rolled away unhurt.

Poole spoke aside to Stanton, "Say, Jack, if you like to trust me with that colt for a few weeks, I'll return him fit for Milly to ride, or I'll make a swop for him."

"I don't want to part with him, but if you'll take him on, you can have the pick of the youngsters as I promised."

* * * * *

"Ronnie, do please ride Romp for me," coaxed Milly.

"Is she an outlaw, too?"

"Anyone could stick her bucks," Flash Billy hastened to explain, "but she's a vicious little devil and no two ways about it. She lays down when she finds she can't get red of you, an' when she finds you can lepp back on her as often as she comes down, she'll jump right out of everythink. I'd like you to have a go at her, just to see, but as I'm makin' a lady's hack outer her for Miss Milly I want to keep her mouth from bein' spiled—it's like velvet now," concluded Billy with sweet reasonableness.

"I couldn't risk spoiling your work. You give us an exhibition."

Romp was the daughter of Young Whisker, the famous polo pony that had been purchased for an Indian rajah. Old Whisker, his dad, was as famous a galloway sire as ever put to stud, and, like many other celebrities, the discovery and property of the Potters of Cuppinbingle. His granddaughter, Romp, was a unique beast such as is seen once in ever so seldom in a mob where there is an admixture of pure blood. Her dam, Lady Lochinvar, bred on Curradoobidgee, had been a tall flyer with a swinging stride that could give dust to any amateur racer run for saddles and bridles up the country. Had high jumping attained its present vogue she could have established a record. She had cleared the Curradoobidgee horse-yards, seven feet if they were an inch, and built like a jail. She jumped out of Mazere's orchard in Bool Bool, and no pound could retain her for five minutes. Withal her canter and gallop were pneumatic and her mouth so delicate that a child of four could hold her, and she was never known to shy or even

15

prance in spring. When she was quite old but still a treasure, Milly had received her as a present from Uncle Bert, beloved of children and with pockets full of just the safest nags for them to ride.

Lady Lochinvar's youngest daughter was a blue roan, with black mane and tail. She flashed round the yard in the sparkling day, one of the daintiest fillies that ever tasted the waters of the Murrumbidgee. The small head had fire and symmetry, the chest, shoulders, and well-planted legs promised a weight-carrier and stayer. She was as hard as nails with a grace and strength of action guaranteeing goat-like sure-footedness—the perfect polo pony, with *outré* colouring to make her the darling of a girl's heart. Before two she had been handled and given to Billy to pace. That was fifteen months since. Billy's report was that she was a she-devil and would never be safe as a lady's hack. Milly refuted this with heat. It had grown to a feud between Billy and Milly.

"Wouldn't she be a picture with hogged mane and tail! In a nice light trap with my new breast collar she'd take every prize from here to Melbourne. Will you sell her to me for harness, Milly?" teased Alistair Farquharson.

"If Billy's too much of a softy to train her, I'll do it myself. You can have old Flea Creek for harness!"

The Breaker mounted and the filly went round the yard like an angel. "She's so tricky," said he, "you'd think butter wouldn't melt in her mouth, and then, whew!" He touched her with the spur. Away went the little spitfire, bucking like a demented kitten and rolling viciously on the near side. Billy was out of her way like an acrobat and back into the saddle as she righted without dropping the reins. Cheers from the top rail. Romp went down on the other side.

"She jist doesn't want anyone on her and will never rest till she gits 'em off. I don't mind her now, because I can feel when it's comin', but she'd be a nice safe little picnic for a lady on a side-saddle with skirts," said Billy as he dismounted.

"Let me have a go at her," said Dice. "She ought to be ridden hard for a week and never stirred up till she forgets about bucking."

"Billy is always telling lies about the poor little thing. I don't know why he has such a set on her," said Milly warmly.

"We'll get to the bottom of this, Milly, old chum," said Poole in a comforting aside.

"Let her git her head down an' touch her on the flank same as a lady with skirts couldn't help doin', an' see what the treacherous little tyke will do," said Bowes.

Dice obeyed. Romp was stirred to violent action and by some

16

sleight retreated from every scrap of gear without straining a buckle—a feat possible to perhaps one horse in a million.

"She won't have a skerrick on her, and that's all there is about it," said Billy conclusively.

"You ought to sell her to a circus, Milly," suggested Spires.

"I'll never, never sell her. I'll keep her to look at," said Milly, brushing away indignant tears, "and no one shall ever ride her if I can't."

CHAPTER 2

Cooees summoned the muster to lunch. Near the house Mrs Saunders was met by the cook in wild excitement. Released from muzzles, and led by Teddy O'Mara's champions, the kangaroo dogs had carried out a raid on the beef cask. While the cook rushed to save something there, the big brindle had seized the midday round hot from the dish. The meat supply had been demolished. The cook had a gun and was firing wildly. Canine yelps indicated some of his targets. Teddy rushed to the rescue of his darlings regardless of his own safety. It looked like a dangerous imbroglio till Poole, Stanton, and others applied the brakes.

Mrs Saunders ordered a lunch of eggs, cheese, and tinned fish, and called for volunteers to shoot wild ducks for the evening dinner.

"If Bert hasn't lost his eye he can feed the multitude in a shot or two," said Stanton.

"Long Billy, as soon as you've had dinner, take a pack-horse and ask Mr Milford to let you have a wether to kill. You'll be back before bed-time."

The muster continued cheerfully towards the house. Milly led the saucy blue roan, which rubbed her head against her doting mistress with the assurance of an old hand.

"What's she goin' to do with the blanky filly?" inquired Long Billy.

"Take her to bed with her, p'raps," said Flash Billy disgustedly. "That's allers the way with a lady's hack. Good material spiled, I call 'em." He emitted voluble scares to Stanton about the treacherous filly's heels, but Milly was not to be separated from her, and hitched her to the palings at the bottom of the garden.

*   *   *   *   *

A jovial company sat down to the substituted meal. Mr Blenkinsop, gentleman at large, reviewed A. L. Gordon's poems and Mr Gladstone's latest speech. Others talked of the popularity of roller-skating, the coming pigeon match at Gundagai, or the need of a branch railway line to Bool Bool, and of the new bridge over

18

the Yarrabongo. The bridge was to be officially opened during the coming month. Old Mrs Mazere of Three Rivers—Great-grandma Mazere—was to cut the ribbon.

Milly's mind was on the pony, and, finishing her pudding in a hurry, she stole away from her end of the table. The whole station staff was safe in midday meal or smoko, so she took her gear unobserved and placed the pretty little saddle of black hogskin on the ornate cloth, braided like an officer's, and with horses' heads worked in the corners, and buckled the girths. She had sometimes turned Romp on her back when very tiny to play with her perfect hoofs—impossible that she could be spiteful or dangerous! They had come all the way from Turrill Turrill to Stanton's Plains one season, Milly riding old Lady Lochinvar with Romp following, and neither of the young things the worse for the long trek. "I'll not put any hot old crupper or breastplate on you, darling, and you aren't a villain, are you? It's that awful pig of a Flash Billy."

She kissed and fondled her pet affectionately, and examined the flank, to find it pricked with the spur. "Romp darling, you'll never buck again, will you, except in fun? And I'll not let that Flash Billy touch you again."

She made sure that no one was stirring to frustrate her, and mounted tremulously. Romp walked demurely down the hollow away from the house, without disturbing the heelers and kangaroo dogs snoozing on nefariously full bellies, thence to the open flat along the river and away like the wind, playmates frolicking together.

"Oh, you darling, darling love!" Milly flung down her reins and clasped the filly's neck in adoration, indulged her with a drink from the Slate Pool, from which ducks rose in clouds, and then tried various paces, shouting with glee, and fetched up at a stiff pace in view of the family and guests who had come out on the veranda. Milly was elated to prove the filly a lady. "Look!" she cried. "Look! she doesn't buck or roll or do anything but be an angel like she always has been since she was the teeniest weeniest foal!"

The spectators ejaculated and expostulated. Milly was too engrossed to give ear.

"Look! She's got her head down." The greedy little brute had espied a mouthful of clover. "Look! and while she has her head down I can do what I like with her flank and she doesn't care. Who says she is spiteful and vicious? She hates Billy, and so do I, with his old spurs a mile long. Spurs are loathsome. All you have to do is to have a sort of feeling and horses will race like the wind. No one shall ever ride her now but me!"

"Horses," began Mr Eustace Blenkinsop, who had ridden from Bookaledgeree with Ronald Dice to spend some weeks sitting about or duck-shooting. "Horses," repeated Mr Blenkinsop, to whom everybody listened unless racing to the muster, or hasting to get a beast killed before dark, or otherwise so pressed as to abrogate the polite respect which Mr Blenkinsop's old-world assurance of breeding and superiority commanded, "have a chivalrous affinity with the ladies."

"Get off that filly at once!" commanded Uncle Jack.

"Whatever for? She's as tame as Lady Lochinvar."

"Evidently it is only men to whom she objects," reiterated Mr Blenkinsop.

"What do you say to letting me take Romp home just to set her paces?" said Poole. He had gone down the garden. "It looks as if she has been taught tricks."

"That would be *loverly*! Can I go home with you too?"

    ✲   ✲   ✲   ✲   ✲

"The horses nowadays are a poor lot av dunkeys. Sure, they'd crumple up onder the horses that Poole turrned out up to tin or fifteen years ago, and as for old Poole that died a few years back, sure Oi remimber . . ."

Mick Muldoon stood with his face to the company and his back to the fire, a man of ripe virility as vouched by his hairiness. He had whiskers up to his eyes, they flowed afar on his chest, sprouted from his ears and nostrils and, by contrariness, were scantiest round his mouth, which could be discerned through the ambush, wide and loose, combining an expression of hilarity and ferocity. The dog he had been was discernible in his poise, in the spotted calfskin waistcoat with carved quandong buttons mounted in silver, and in the tilt of his hat, which he rarely doffed.

"Aw, you're allers blowing about the old days," said Flash Billy testily. "It stan's to reason they hadn't the horses we have now, when the breed's bein' improved all the time."

"Oi wouldn't waste me breath on ye," said Mick grandly. "Belting a good beast to pieces and teachin' it vicious thricks!"

"What's the good of listening to an old codger!" snorted Billy, irritable with fatigue and a day that had gone badly.

"Sure, ye're very flash now, Bill Bowes, but the day is soon coming whin my ould coat will fit your behoind, and ye won't be able to spile good beasts with dhirty thricks for y'r own profit, and ye'll have no ch'racter. Moi ch'racter will stand against anny man's."

"What's your 'ch'racter' ever done? You're barmy!"

It was evening in the men's hut. Certain identities like Billy, Teddy O'Mara, and Muldoon had the privilege of eating in the kitchen, but this evening had chosen the hut for its company.

"Hogan's ghost! Billy," exclaimed Long Billy, drifting in from the kitchen, "did you know that young Milly rode the Young Whisker filly up and down the place like hell at dinner-time? Sent her full lick with the reins swingin', an' grabbed up fistfuls of her flank, an' the filly takin' it like ole Flea Creek." Flea Creek, a famous slug, so named for his beginnings, was used to pack salt and pull the water-slide.

"Tell that to the marines!"

"There ain't ever anyone to be let ride her again but young Milly."

"Where did this fish-yarn spring up?" Billy was beginning to be uneasy.

"He's been maggin' to Ellen Humphreys in the kitchen," said Jerry Riddall.

"Ask her, if you don't want to believe me," persisted Long Billy.

"Phwat about yer ch'racter now, an' me being barmy, am Oi? Oi wasn't rared onder a hin, Oi'm tellin' ye," interposed Mick. "They're foindin' out yer thricks . . ."

"That's where you're dead wrong, you —— old billy-goat. Another word out o' you and I'll shy the bread at your ole pumpkin head." Billy got up, kicking a stool over, and left the hut.

"His girl is givin' him the turnip, that's what's up with him, an' he's too fond of thinkin' he's Lord Muck anyhow," said Long Billy.

"Yes," said Jerry Riddall, "an' I reckon young Mr Dice can run rings roun' him stickin' a buck."

"Talkin' o' girls and turnips and such," said Tommy Roper, "there'll be some fun here presently. Did yous twig the play at the yards today atween the boss and Dice?"

"Garn!" said Paddy Leary from Cuppinbingle. "What yer givin' us?"

"Anyone can see Dice and Aily Healey think they was made for each other, and at the same time the boss looks as if he's goin' to hang his hat on three hairs an' make up to her too."

"Fat lot o' chance he'd have, the ole goat. A girl'd be as likely to fall in love with a wombat." This was Tim Porter's idea.

"I dunno! Money makes the mare go," said Jerry.

21

"Aw, that ole pilgarlic! Ain't the Dices got a good place at Bookaledgeree? I'd rayther have it than either Ten Creeks or Jinninjinninbong, stuck up here among the wombats an' dingoes, or Turrill Turrill down there in the droughts," maintained Tim.

"Big share this feller will have with all them young ones comin' on. Besides, Bookaledgeree is mortgaged over the ears and out the other side, an' old Healey would skin his grandmother and sell her hide if he was pushed, an' if ole Skinny Guts puts his money-bags before him it will be a slice of turnip for young Ronald all right."

"Aw, I dunno," repeated Jerry.

"Who do you bet on, Tommy, the ole cove or Ronald Dice?"

"I'll bet anyone my bridle against a new saddle pouch that the ole cove will come out top because ole Healey is as fierce and greedy as hell, I'm tellin' yous; an' the girl will be too weak in the knees to stan' up to him. Ole Healey is like all of them that can't keep money theirselves; he worships the spondulics. He thinks it can do everything."

"Well, so it can," said Jerry eagerly.

"It can do a lot all right, but then again there's a lot of things it can't do."

"Tell us some, Tommy."

"Well, I don't think money would buy the Young Whisker filly from Milly, an' money may make Aily Healey marry old SP-over-J, but I bet you all the money in hell it will never make her love him."

"And ch'racter," added Mick Muldoon. "Money will never buy ch'racter. But phwat do these prisint-day mongrels care about ch'racter? They used to talk about the ould lags, but if you treated the ould lags phroper they was daycint min. Oi've niver seen thim turrn on annyone who treated thim phroper, but these fellers, begor' if ye carried thim on your back for siven years and put thim down for tin minutes to take a spell, sure, they'd take opportunity of that tin minutes to rob ye."

"Here, Mick, never mind about your 'ch'racter' now. If you are such a know-all, why didn't ole Skinny Guts ever marry? Do you know?" It was Red Jimmy, the surveyor's link man, inquiring. His master was working in the district and not averse from a day at the muster or homestead.

"Av coorse Oi know. Oi know iverything about him, and whin Oi tell a thing it's true, not loike these liars wid nawthing in their heads."

"Never min' about that now—p'raps it's like the horses . . . tell us the story."

"Curradoobidgee Poole never married neither," observed Tim Porter.

"He was throwed over by that ole Miss Macorkaran, wasn't he?" said Jerry.

"Sure, a quischin is asked and ye haven't the breedin' to listen to a reply nor the brains to onderstand if ye did."

"I'm the man who knows most about it," piped old Bill Heffernan from Wamgambril Flats, where he engaged in trapping wallabies and dingoes. He had dummied for Larry Healey's uncle on Monaro in '61 when the Free Selection Act came in. He was dummying now for Stanton towards the head of the Wamgambril and had come in for the muster. "The boss here was never after ole Jess Macorkaran. It was she that was after Bert Poole. He was a fine cut of an upstanding man in them days, for all he is a lap-dog now for all the little gurrls that call him uncle."

"And who was Poole after?" The link man had a newcomer's interest in sorting out the identities.

"He used to have eyes for none but Mrs Labosseer, mother of Mrs Harry Milford over the river," said Heffernan.

"Ye're wrong," said Mick. "Bert Poole was engaged to Mrs Labosseer's sister, Emily, daughter of the ould Mazere of Three Rivers, daughter of the same ould Mrs Mazere who is goin' to open the bridge."

"Her that was drownded in the Mungee, and Poole has never looked at no one since," contributed Tommy Roper. "Me ma used to tell me about it."

"Everyone knows about Bert Poole an' the Miss Mazere that was drownded in the Mungee, but Skinny Guts wasn't after her too, was he?"

"Sure, the boss here was hell-for-leather afther Mary Brennan, sister of ould Tim at The Gap, but she wouldn't look at him, and took the veil. That was away back in '57. No, it was '58. Oi'll tell ye how Oi remember."

"We don't care how the hell you remember if you'll only spit it out," said Red Jimmy, who was listening open-mouthed.

"Oi'm the wan to blame for evening me wits to such an assimbly of gissobs," said Mick, retreating in lofty disdain into the ambush of his beard, from which he spat lustily.

"Well, Mick, I didn't insult you or rob you while I got off of your back for a spell or anythink," said Paddy Leary, a cheerful vassal. "Let's have the old stick's love affairs. I wouldn't have thought he'd ever have had enough juice in him to be in love."

"The dried-up ones is sometimes madder after the women than the pot-bellied ones. Look at ole——" began Tim Porter.

"Oh, go and shove your head in a bag and dry up for a bit—Mick has the floor," said Leary.

Mick re-emerged. Racially he was a born conversationalist or monologist: the solitary conditions of the boundaries of the back runs and the taciturnity of the colonials restricted his life. "The master here was woild afther the daughter of ould Tim Brennan that's been in his grave tin years an' more. Oi disremimber whether it was January or February——"

"Never min' wot you disremember, shoot ahead with the love story, for God's sake, an' be done with it."

"He! He!" cackled Jerry. "Tim's gone on Ellen Humphreys and wants the love——"

"I ain't, you —— fool. I want to turn in. We've got to be out before it's light. Why the hell wouldn't she marry him an' be done with it?"

"She niver married annyone. She took the veil an' died in ould Oireland an' was brought home an' buried at The Gap in the flower-garden there. Ye can see the paling fince and the tombstone anny toime ye have the moind."

"Ye're off the track," said Heffernan. "More people has been reared under a hen than knows it, and a duck hen at that. It was Emily Mazere that had 'em all roarin' like town bulls, all but black Poole, him that was sittin' up on the fence today beside young Milly, an' he contrariwise was the only one she wanted. Ole Denny Healey and his brother Larry, the dad of young Aily, was madder than any after her too, and two of the flashest coves that ever dragged a stockwhip in the dust."

"I've often heard mum and the ole man talkin' of it," said Jerry Riddall. "Mum used ter work for ole Mrs Mazere. Mary Brennan was smitten on Mr Poole too, but others reckons it was the boss here, and that neither would give way about religion, and that's why Mary went for a nun and died of consumption when she was only thirty, an' that's what slewed the boss off the skirts and turned him to money-grubbin'."

"What for, when he had no girl to give it to?" inquired Tim Porter.

"Aw, I bet it ain't that what put him on the money-grubbin'. It's in a man, an' nothing won't take it out or put it in."

"You know so —— much you oughter set up as a lawyer."

"Well, I'm not so snotty about it as them that knows less," retorted Leary with a good-tempered grin.

"Seein' as Flash Billy's cake is baked, he can sell that old donkey supper hat of his to the boss. It's used to goin' mashin' an' hanging on by three hairs already," said Tommy Roper.

"Aw, an ole cove like that, he wouldn't be able——"

24

"Don't you believe it! When the spasm takes 'em, the old blokes goes barmier than the young ones."

"I reckon a girl would have to be cross-eyed to take old SP-over-J while Ronnie Dice was in the runnin'," commented Tim Porter. "If I wuz a girl, I'd rather live on the smell of an oiled rag with a feller like Ronnie than take old Ten Creeks with Turrill Turrill throwed in to fatten dingoes."

"But it ain't what you or Aily thinks; it's what ole Larry says that goes, an' he'd rather marry any one of them female daughters of his to a black snake if it had money than to a angel without," maintained Tommy Roper.

"Every dog has his day," observed Heffernan. "Ole Poole had a hell of a fine day, not only all the purty fillies mad after him, but he was the greatest rider and shot, and cleared up the bushrangers, and still goin' strong."

"You're —— well right," agreed Leary.

"My —— oath I'm right. The missus here is workin' herself cross-eyed to collar him now, and Milly would jump at him for a stepfather."

"Fat lot er chance ole Lucy's got if he's never looked at no one since his sweetheart was drownded."

"He might give way when he gets old and silly. He's a good-lookin' bloke yet, an' a nice one too. I'd rather work for him than ole Skinny Guts any day," said Tim Porter.

"For the Old Harry's sake stop yer everlastin' maggin'," complained Long Billy from the inner chamber, where bunks of stringybark stretched in three tiers round the walls. The window was a wooden shutter; wide cracks between the shrunken slabs provided daylight and ventilation. The rouseabout was ready to call it a day after buckjump-riding in the forenoon and a long, hard ride to fetch a sheep in the afternoon. "Come on in, some of you damn' fellers, or the bugs an' fleas will walk away with me. It ain't fair. They're all mustered on me. Come an' take your share. I don't want to be a fattenin' paddick for the whole —— lot."

❋   ❋   ❋   ❋   ❋

The Milfords arrived next morning, bringing with them Kerry, the famous photographer, and the expedition to Bull Creek was deferred in favour of posing before the camera, while the ringing music of horseshoes being shaped on the anvil by a succession of blacksmiths for the forefeet of stock horses never ceased. In a few of the surviving houses of the locality, where there remains an old hand to preserve things of the past, there may still be found stereoscopes and views perpetuating the musters of Ten Creeks

Run and Jinninjinninbong. Through the twin lenses blood horses, long dust, and their daring or dainty riders, now stiff and frail, stand out in seemingly solid relief, so hauntingly still that they touch the heart to tears.

Milly with streaming hair was photographed on Romp, and the Misses Farquharson and Healey on their respective animals showed their hour-glass waists and soft young faces above stifling collars. Teddy O'Mara and Mick Muldoon, SP-over-J, the mad sailor cook, the new surveyor, Flash Billy the Breaker, Paddy Leary, the brazen kangaroo dogs, the blood colts and fillies, Flea Creek, all are preserved for those who can pick them out, as well as a round dozen or more to whom even Larry Healey or Harry Milford cannot put the names today.

There were no moving-picture cameras then to pickle these gladiators in motion in the ordinary day's work, as they performed feats that no rodeo could now excel. The youth of today would deem the old-time commonplaces of that muster impossible, or but senility's drivelling of the glory of days that are gone. In these days there is only one of the Milfords left; for lack of a sympathetic audience, he never talks of his exploits. The young fellows snorting about in motors have no interest for him, and he is nervous in their machines, he who that summer in natural daring rode blood colts down a ridge of black Mount Corroboree, while even the hardened spectators held their breath for the outcome! That spring, too, it was Harry Milford, aided by Larry Healey—the only rider who could keep near him—who put the Bull Flat mob into the trap-yards back of Mount Corroboree after a run lasting from 9 a.m. till 5 p.m.

The stereoscope shows none of this, but only a stillness haunting as the memory of a voice that has lately enchanted and dropped for ever to silence. In the cavern of the lenses all has been stricken to colourless rigidity, granite boulders, flowering trees and shrubs, men and maids, horses and dogs alike, for ever petrified in youth unchanging beside the leaping lacy Coolgarbilli, singing on its way to old Mother of Waters.

Old Blenkinsop—"gentlemanly ole feller"—is shown on Scutty, an imported mare so named for her docked tail, and owing to which she had been early set apart for stud purposes, for the natives would as lief been seen abroad with a donah minus an eye as on a beast so mutilated. Black Harry, the horse-shooter, stood on the top rail. He had shot fifteen hundred horses in those hills for their hides and tails, and by mistake potted one of old Tom Saunders's brood-mares, only old Tom did not take that view of it. Harry had consequently done a term of two years, which did not increase his popularity with the Farquharsons, whose poor relation he was. Poole was taken teaching Corroboree to lead, a part of his education which had been overlooked.

He had put in the morning on the job. "Come, I'll give you a wrinkle," he said to Flash Billy, who obeyed sulkily. "Look out for that trick business—it won't do your reputation any good, unless you think of joining a circus."

Flash Billy made no reply then, but observed to his associates later, "Damned silly ole molly-coddle—you'd think he was trainin' cows. Gone clean barmy in his ole days."

Lucy Saunders joined Milly to watch Poole with the colt.

"Mother, can't I go home with Uncle Bert and Romp? He says I can."

"You are getting too big now to be bothering Uncle Bert."

Milly was no blood relation to Poole. When a toddler she had fought with Marcia Mazere at Three Rivers for the right to sit on his knee. When told that she must give place because Marcia was his real niece Milly had acted so like convulsions that Herbert Poole, J.P., restored her to normality by adopting her as one of his complete nieces and taking her on the right knee; Marcia refused to surrender her hereditary right to the left. Though Milly was long past tantrums, her affection for her Uncle Bert increased rather than diminished. Famous horseman that he was, he took delight in her equestrian promise, while he to the child was a lucky-bag that had yielded such booty as Lady Lochinvar, Romp, and a saddle and bridle.

"She'd be no trouble, Lucy, if you'd like to let her come. Ma will enjoy supervising her lessons, and if she gets tired of her she could go to Ada for a change."

"How would she get home again?"

"Pooh! I could come by myself if I'd only be let. Tell you what. Couldn't Uncle Bert take me down to see Aileen at Neangen and Uncle Jack could bring me home from there? I heard him telling Aileen that he had business that way."

"You could get home easy enough," said SP-over-J, to stop further overhearings.

"Goody! I'll pack my valise. Couldn't I ride Romp?"

"She and the colt are a bit too green. We don't want to dishearten them at the beginning. You better stick to old Ready-money."

CHAPTER 3

QUITE A PARTY left Ten Creeks at sunrise on a glorious morning at the close of the muster. Young Lindsey, Poole's man, had charge of the Curradoobidgee strays, and Teddy O'Mara, accompanied by his redoubtable thieves, was lending him a hand. Poole and Milly rode behind them, Poole leading Corroboree, who followed with the eagerness of a neophyte while Milly had Romp trotting amicably beside Readymoney.

Larry Healey and Ronald Dice joined forces to take their contingent, and, since they had Aily with them but no stockman, SP-over-J remarked, "I'll give you a hand till you get a start."

"You needn't bother, Mr Stanton, unless you like," said Tommy Roper with a wink at Tim Porter. "I'm making their way and can kill two birds with the one stone."

"I want to see what the dingo-trappers are after out by Wamgambril, in any case," said Stanton. Tim returned Tommy's wink.

It worked out that the young men careered round the loose horses, and Stanton rode with Aileen, who was pretty, ever so pretty, and alluringly young. She was also deferential and unfailingly agreeable. It was dawning on her that there was more than banter in what people said of her and Stanton, though she did not take it seriously. Ronald was delightful in his disparagement of an older rival as "gran'pa" and "uncle".

"You be careful," he rode up and whispered to her as they were splashing into the home paddock creek. "It's dangerous to an elderly gosling like that to become lovesick. He might take a fit and you be blamed." The crude wit convulsed the simple Aileen.

The riders kept together till the river crossing where Boundary Creek joined the larger stream. Here Poole branched off to the south and the others continued towards Wamgambril Flats. Milly had the last words:

"You'll come to Neangen for me, won't you, Uncle? You'll have me there, won't you, Aileen? If it's too much trouble for Uncle Jack to go all the way I can easily get down to Stanton's Plains with Ronnie. You're sure to be going to Neangen, aren't you, Ronnie?"

To these suggestions Aileen cordially assented. Ronnie, with a grin at Aileen, also agreed. Uncle Jack intercepted the wink that Tommy Roper threw at Dice and said to Milly, "You get down to Neangen and let me know and I'll collect you from there without troubling anyone."

The Bool Bool contingent remained on the left bank of the Coolgarbilli while the others clattered and splashed among the boulders of the stream transparent as glass rushing onward to the Murrumbidgee. Poole watched them go in a meditative frame of mind. Thirty years ago he and old Jack Stanton had ridden away on similar expeditions with the aunts of Aileen and Milly's generation, and just as gaily as young Dice today, "cut out" rivals and jockeyed for first place. Clearly in the glass of memory stood two girls that were dead—one claimed by cramp in the treacherous Mungee, the other a victim of a confined life in old-world sunless damp—those whom the hands had discussed round the hut fire in the evenings. All the actors in the drama of the previous generation insisted that both these beautiful young women had loved him, Herbert Poole, to the exclusion of all others till the end.

Ah, well, it was all past now, or rather, as he noted the blushes wreathing Aily's delicate cheeks when Ronnie made some remark, it was only the players that changed in the eternal tourney. He enjoyed life as much as ever and found himself more careful to preserve it than he had been thirty or forty years ago, but something had gone out of it. What would he not give to feel again the delight and excitement that once bubbled in his veins! There were plenty of old chaps who still chased the "properties" of youthful joy more greedily than did the young. There was old Jack squinting at little Aily Healey.

"Nonsense, there is nothing in it. I'm getting as bad as the old gossips," he thought. They had been connecting himself and Jack with every eligible and ineligible woman in the district for the last thirty years and would be at the game for the next thirty, by the look of things. If it amused small minds, it did no harm to him and Jack.

As they lost sight of the others among the tall timber and dense shrubs, Poole looked at the bright face of his companion with its button nose and freckles, the hat elasticked under the round childish chin, and the long pigtail aft, and his eyes softened with indulgence. Bless the youngster, a man could never have the mulligrubs while she was about! He reflected with satisfaction that a man was never too old for the affectionate joys provided by the avuncular relationship. There had been a successive crop of such nieces, some of them expanding matrons now, but all retaining their affection for Uncle Bert.

"Do you think goanna fat mixed with wombat grease would take the freckles off your nose, Milly?"

"It might be as good as those recipes they have for making straight hair curly," laughed the little girl. "My freckles go away in the winter, or if I stay inside, but I'd rather be outside."

"Then I suppose we must bear up under the freckles." His eye wandered to Romp, of a beauty to delight Abd-el-Kader, son of Mahi-ed-Din himself, and probably better topped through her thoroughbred English strain than any ewe-necked prodigy that ever carried the great emir. "Think we can make something of the roan mongrel?"

Milly responded with a toothsome grin of understanding: she and Uncle Bert were mates. She was being permitted this as her last tomboy expedition. Upon her return she was to be tutored by Mr Blenkinsop, who had gallantly yielded to importunities to undertake the responsibility for the remainder of the summer at Ten Creeks, and later at Turrill Turrill for the winter, depending on how they progressed.

     ❖   ❖   ❖   ❖   ❖

Dice's company parted from Stanton at the head of the Wamgambril, a sister stream of the Coolgarbilli, which took an opposite course to reach old Mother of Waters.

"We'll put up for the night at The Gap and get Mrs Tim and young Tim to give us some songs," suggested Dice, a sociable fellow.

"I must push on," said Larry.

"You and Tommy can push on with the horses at daybreak. I'll see that Aily gets to Neangen in good condition. What do you say, Aily?"

"Whatever you and Larry do will suit me," said she, with a rosy smile.

As young Celia Brennan could sing like a thrush and was pretty to boot, Larry fell in with this suggestion after hesitation. As Tommy Roper was inordinately curious and had time on his hands he fell in with Larry.

Next morning Larry got away at daybreak. Dice at a more leisurely hour set off with Aileen. He decided to go by Bool Bool and have lunch with old Mrs Mazere at Three Rivers—the old lady was his great-aunt. He enlisted Tommy Roper to deliver the spare nags at Bookaledgeree.

     ❖   ❖   ❖   ❖   ❖

Larry reached home in time for midday dinner, and in response to his father's inquiry said, "I left Aileen at The Gap to come on with Ronald Dice."

"And what the devil did you do that for? If she hasn't any more sense to look after her reputation, what were you there for?"

"Ronnie's not dangerous," ventured Larry, jun., "and if he was, Tommy Roper is there to keep a sharp eye on him."

"If she's not showing by two o'clock, you'll go back after her."

Mrs Healey began to worry as soon as the stipulated hour was reached. Her husband was an unamiable old scrub and she the chopping-block of his displeasures. Three o'clock and five passed without Aileen. Mr Healey waxed ferocious; Mrs Healey was in a stew.

"Her to be capering about the country like a streel and her character gone to the winds," he raged. "I'll turn her out! For two pins she needn't darken my doors again."

"There needn't be such a mighty dust about that," young Larry was game to say. "Ron Dice would be glad to have her darken his."

"Him with not a penny to his name; a waster ridin' about the country after every bit of rag in the world, and the place goin' to the dingoes and briars, and mortgaged up to the neck."

"Well, if he can't put up enough spondulics to suit you, old Jack Stanton wouldn't mind relieving you of her, unless I'm more green than I'm cabbage-looking. You'll have no trouble getting Aileen off your hands; it's Joanna and Norah will be the tussle," said their brother ungallantly.

"What evidence have you of that?"

"Old Skinny Guts was leering at her all the muster like a sick dog at a firestick. He actually danced with her and came all the way to Wamgambril huts—pretended he wanted to look at the dingo-tracks, but he stuck too close to the old chestnut to see any. It will do him good to be jealous of Dice, will bring him up to the scratch."

Larry, sen., ceased to rage. Stanton was rich and a swell. The Stantons of Stanton's Plains were of the earliest pioneers of Bool Bool, and, with the Mazeres, Pooles, Brennans, etc., ranked as first families among the squattocracy.

"Be the hokey-pokey!" Healey exulted to his wife. "If this is true about old Stanton, why there isn't a man from here to Wagga Wagga half so well-fixed as him—a cold-blooded cautious feller as solid as Mount Corroboree. You give Aily a speakin'-to when she comes home. She doesn't want to be compromising herself with young Dice if there is anny hope of Stanton. Dice won't have a stiver to his name when the banks get their share."

"He's such a nice young fellow," said Mrs Healey weakly.

"Nice, nice! You fool! What's the good of *nice*—it's the dough

31

that counts. If a man's as ugly as old King Billy and as nasty—sure, he can be as nasty as he likes if he's only rich enough."

A woman of spirit might have said that some were ugly and nasty without being able to afford it, but Mrs Healey was not a woman of spirit.

Aileen did not reach home till seven o'clock. In addition to Ronald she was accompanied by his sister, Ida, which took the wind out of Healey's grizzle about the proprieties. Ida was a dashing girl with the Dice charm, capable of making herself agreeable even to old Larry, so that he could not erupt while the Dices were present, and he remarked as they went on their way in the moonlight, " 'Tis a pity the Dices have no ability to hold money. She'd make a nice pair with Larry, though he would be better fixed up at The Gap. Old Tim must be a pretty warm man by now with that good property on both sides of the river."

* * * * *

Larry, sen., was neither rich nor nice, nor yet happy nor beautiful. He was the second son of his family, which had gone up in the social scale like a rocket, but the second generation showed no ability to hold or improve what had been gained.

The first Larry and his wife, Aileen, had settled on Monaro among the earliest pioneers. They had tabled themselves as Irish immigrants and were reticent about their past. They were neighbours of the original Poole. By assiduity and disregard of scruples they had secured a good estate. The old days had been enlivened by a rumour that a squatter—some said about Goulburn—had gained his wife by a roistering bet, but none were sure of the man's identity. This story had been fastened on the Healeys in a dramatic manner in the fifties by a bushranger who subsequently died in Berrima jail. On the historic occasion while he held up the whole gallimaufry of first families at a ball at Gowandale he had audaciously claimed Mrs Healey as his wife in full hearing of the company, thus casting the aspersion of illegitimacy upon the whole boiling of young Healeys. The Healeys carried this off as best they could, and it had been taken as wild clash. Nevertheless it had disintegrating results upon the morale of the Healeys. The boys in altercations would be insulted as bastards, and old Healey had had to divulge that it was better for his sons to lie low and take the allegations as lightly as possible rather than stir up the mud of "thrubble".

"Sure, if ye keep quiet it will dhrop, an' there's those that niver want to stir it up. M'Eachern of Gowandale for one, his son bein' married to the bushranger's daughter, an' her yer half-sister, an'

32

there's others. Sure, they're not all married on legitimate daughters of the nobility."

The dearth of maids in that region and generation had made it necessary for the most pretentious to marry a shepherd lass or a *fille de joie* or go unwed. But to be compelled to turn the other cheek because they could not batter the other fellow's nose was as bitter as the milk of seeding lettuce to the belligerent young Healeys. It curbed their dash and crumpled their *amour-propre*.

Dennis, Larry of Neangen's elder brother, had reigned for a time on Eueurunda, which the Healeys had acquired by planting dummies on Simon Labosseer while he was disabled and so that his wife had had to retreat to Coolooluk. The wife of Dennis, a barmaid from Goulburn, was used to wine and spirits, and Dennis, always that way inclined, grew too fond of his drop. As he reached middle age he was a loud, fast man and many women had too many charms for him.

There were rumours of more bastards than his father's. It was the grandfather of one of these who met Dennis one night and nearly finished him. The task failed only because Dennis, like a carpet snake, recovered after being left for dead. He denied that he and old Lindsey, the selector, had met in the dark of the moon where Poole's Creek runs with a velvety Monaro song to join the Eueurunda. It was through old Lindsey that the story got abroad.

The district knew that Jenny Lindsey had gone wrong. The distraught young woman had prevailed upon her destroyer for one more interview. At this, old Lindsey, acting sleuth, had punished the guilty with violence. He then rode madly to Braminderra, a one-pub township where there was also a constable and lock-up, and had given himself in charge. The constable did not know whether to believe him or not, so cursed him and kept him till daylight, when he rode abroad to collect the evidence. Constable Pigeon was of comfortable form and mind and the scene of the murder was twenty-five miles distant.

Lindsey was unable to produce the corpse. "Here's where I waited for him," he insisted. Tracks confirmed this. "Here's where I drug the —— ole scoundrel and swindler and bastard horse-thief from his saddle. When I got through bashing him I flung him down the side there." There was a mark as of a sack dragged across the track and broken sage-bushes, but no sign of Healey.

"You've evidently got 'em," said the constable. "But I'll keep you in custody till I see Mr Healey."

They had gone off towards Eueurunda, calling at Curradoobidgee for refreshments. Here the constable found the vehicle of the doctor from Cooma and Mrs Healey's carriage. Poole on coming home the night before had heard groans from below the level of the road. Search had shown Dennis Healey held on the side of the declivity by the sage-bushes and bracken. Healey was unable to move or speak. Poole returned to the homestead for assistance. Messengers had also gone forthwith for Mrs Healey and the doctor. The state of Healey was that while there is life there is hope, so the constable credited Lindsey's story and took him away with him.

As soon as he was able to make a deposition, Healey asserted that he had been riding a fresh horse, which, startled by a snake, had unseated him. His foot stuck in the stirrup and this accounted for the terrible battering he had received. A thunderstorm late the day following the affray made further reference to the tracks impossible. Lindsey had been released.

Healey never mounted a horse again. His wife met the catastrophe by getting rid of the station and taking a hotel in Goulburn. She was tired of station life. She was no rider, and had not been accepted by the squattocracy as she had hoped. The Pooles and M'Eacherns held aloof because she had not been congenial to them, and also they resented the way Dennis had treated an old friend and neighbour.

Larry, the second brother, transferred to Eueurunda, but ill luck attended him too. His wife died. His eldest son was shot dead cleaning a rifle. The Healeys had paid too much for Eueurunda in the first place, and bad management, bad seasons, and disease in the flocks forced Larry to cut his losses and move to Neangen. Another wife and family had succeeded the first, but life seemed to sour on Larry. He was an ill-tempered failure, feeling that God and man were against him. The old Healeys had seceded from "the wan thrue Church", owing, it was said, to a row with the hierarchy regarding their marriage or lack of it, and the consequence was that the Healeys of the second generation had no religion as a buttress of respectability.

Such were Aileen's antecedents at the time of the muster at Ten Creeks Run. Debts and minor distresses were the family's portion at Neangen. The girls hoped for marriage as a way of mending their fortunes, but the two of the first marriage were as plain as kitchen aprons and without style, while Aileen lacked head to market herself, and the family were alert to prevent their best ewe lamb from throwing herself away.

The news about old Stanton was hopeful. Not only was he rich but he had standing, and most of the higher squattocracy now ignored the Healeys unless they needed a night's lodging when business led them past Neangen.

*   *   *   *   *

Stanton turned back from Wamgambril Flats where the lone selection of his dummy secured the eye of a mountainous horse and cattle run. He retraced his way across creeks and ferny gullies through the cool depths of thousands of square miles of timber broken only by the tiny spring-head flats of the plateaux amid the ranges. There were tucker and tea in his saddle-bags of calf-skin, and a quart pot on the D. He went steadily and mused on the draft of colts and fillies, and what he might net from his wool on Turrill Turrill, but most of all he thought of Aileen Healey and felt young again. A reawakening zest in life was throwing a magic veil over things once more.

Many men older than he took unto themselves wives. It was not as if Aileen were a child. She had come of age this year or two. He could set her off in a way that none of her other admirers could approach. Lucy might think him a fool, though she was not situated to say what she really thought to any devastating extent. Why the deuce couldn't she pull it off with Bert? That would leave him, Jack, free and give him an excuse for marriage which a con-firmed bachelor so well catered for lacked. It would do old Bert a world of good to get married, but SP-over-J did not believe he had the red blood in him these days. SP-over-J chuckled in the elation of the resurgence of his own blood.

A day or two later he announced his intention of running into Bool Bool to sign some papers. Arrived in the little town he rode to the saddler's and gave a satisfactory order for gear including a smart pair of leggings. Next he called at the house adjacent to the bank, the windows of which announced A. A. RANKIN & SON, SOLICITORS. It was the son, a pleasant man in the forties, that received Stanton.

"Well, Jack, what can I do for you today? How's the horse market?"

"Fair to middling. How're yourself and Fannie?"

"Fine, thanks."

"How are things financially—everyone paid up and indepen-dent, or is there a mortgage or two kicking round?"

"As a matter of fact there are a couple going begging, but nothing juicy."

"Do you mind telling me what they are?"

"Old Larry Healey is trying to raise something more on that

dingo-run he has at Neangen, and the Dices want a covering mortgage on Bookaledgeree."

"Who has it now?"

"Tom Saunders."

"Is he foreclosing?"

"No, but the Dices probably want to get out of his clutches."

"Bookaledgeree is a wilderness of briars—cost more than it's worth—tears all the wool off the sheep's backs. Neangen would be better for horses."

"I can get you the bank's valuation."

"I want to work through the bank, if you'll fix it up privately. When I have money going, I like to put it in the old district."

"The right spirit, Jack. If more had it the place would progress more rapidly."

Details of the mortgages on Neangen and Bookaledgeree were followed by gossipy chat about people, no taint of ideas on either side, then Stanton withdrew till next day. Two days later he rode home with a feeling of accomplishment. His next move was to complain to his sister that Milly was running wild. He gave instructions for a letter to Poole stating that if he brought Milly as far as Neangen, he, Stanton, would go there to meet her, since he had to go in that direction to inspect horses that were for sale.

The official opening of the new bridge was not far off, so Poole wrote to Mrs Saunders that he would bring Milly to the festival. Stanton could not be too fussy, but not to be robbed of his excuse for going to Neangen he set out to inspect horses as originally planned. He was spruce as to horse and gear. He was wearing a new hat and had trimmed his beard in the fashionable Prince of Wales clip. He would have liked to shave it off, but for the present lacked the assurance for such an innovation.

By some miscalculation, as he said, he got to Neangen in advance of Milly. "Can you suffer me an extra day?" he inquired of Aileen.

Milly and her Uncle Bert arrived next day, Milly riding Romp, the exquisite galloway, now of perfect manners.

CHAPTER 4

THE MOST interesting public event for a year round Bool Bool was to be the opening of the new bridge. The punt that had carried the main street across the Yarrabongo to join the Great Southern Road from Sydney to Melbourne had in the late sixties been replaced by a wooden erection. This structure in turn had given way to a bridge with ornamental arches painted white, the pride of the inhabitants, and the New Crossing on the edge of Stanton's Plains had been furnished with a punt. It was this punt, which in the course of progress was being superseded by a second bridge, that Lewis Mortimer, the local M.P., had bagged for his electorate. Mortimer had been invited to open it, but the old warrior was more renowned for his tact than his oratory. Old Mrs Mazere, the oldest pioneer and chief of the chief clan of the district, should open the bridge, while he made a speech about the wonders of the valley and the intelligent progressive spirit of the constituents whom he had the honour to represent.

The celebration coincided with Mrs Mazere's seventy-eighth birthday, and the double event was bringing people from a wide radius. The bridge was to be opened in the morning and clinched by a banquet, the evening to be given to a grand subscription ball and supper. The Rev. Archdeacon Fish and the Rev. Father O'Halloran were both patrons of this. Tickets were a guinea each, proceeds to be divided between the local hospital and the Anglican and Roman Catholic churches. Considering the good cause, old Mrs Mazere had consented to open the ball. The subject put the price of wool and maize and cattle and horses in the shade for a day or two and temporarily eclipsed local scandals, only to germinate a fresh crop.

When Milly arrived at Neangen, Julie, her immediate contemporary among the young Healeys, pleaded for her to remain the intervening nights instead of proceeding to Bool Bool. This suited SP-over-J, and Poole, always of placid mind, thought it better not to add to the household of Three Rivers while preparations were raging.

"There's been a great struggle to get Great-grandma Mazere rigged up for the shivoo. Fannie sent to Sydney to get Rhoda to choose a new bonnet, but Great-grandma jibbed at it. It's been picked to pieces two or three times and made look as nearly like the old one as possible, the one she took to when old Mr Mazere died," said Joanna.

"Old Bill Prendergast is coming from Gundagai to drive her over the bridge to open it with his grey four-in-hand, and they've got about an acre of tents put up for the banquet," added Larry, jun.

Uncle Jack felt convicted of family dereliction to be cavorting with the Healeys, and to have Milly and Poole there with him while his sister was away back at Ten Creeks. As a compromise he sent Tommy Roper to fetch her, coupled with the courtesy of announcing that he and Milly and Poole would be coming together.

*   *   *   *   *

Thus when the big day dawned the Healeys had the honour of Poole and Jack Stanton as their escorts. Larry, sen., wife, Joanna, and small fry filled the shabby buggy drawn by a pair of long-tailed horses. Young Larry, Alf Timson, and Norah galloped away from their dust on horseback.

Poole was surprised that Stanton should appear on such an occasion with the Healeys instead of with his own people from the Plains. He knew it would be unpleasant for Lucy Saunders to have Milly in that company, and he felt he owed it to the child to stay with her. "Old Jack must be fairly collared," he mused, looking on. "Old fool, at his time of life! The little girl is sweet and pretty, but weak—the breed is lacking—an old fool with a young wife is as bad a team as a Clydesdale yoked to a sprinter."

Milly and Julie capered round Uncle Bert, but Julie's old Neddy was outclassed by the incomparable Romp, groomed till her hide was like polished granite, richly caparisoned and with smartly hogged mane and tail. The little girls amused themselves counting the snake-tracks in the soft dust, counting the goannas that ran up the trees and looked at them, counting Tommy Roper's dead beasts or Riverina dead sheep, counting anything that made a game.

Aileen, a picture of slender grace in a new habit on her easy old chestnut, Miss Muffet, was attended by Uncle Jack on a showy four-year-old. Movement was to be seen as they turned out of the timber on the Neangen road and came in view of the iron roof of Bookaledgeree among its bower of fruit and ornamental trees, with the cleared mile between the homestead and main road.

Milly looked for her friend Ronald to put the right valuation on Romp's excellencies. Milly was a wholesome young thing still mentally undisturbed by her budding womanhood. Ronald was her chum and admirer; that she might be an intruder had not yet occurred to her. Julie, not of such wholesome mind and absorption, watched for Ronald with an excitement born of words overheard.

As the Bookaledgeree party grew clearer, Aileen's heart fluttered deliciously to recognize Ronald with his sisters Ida and Olive. Mrs Dice and younger members of the family followed in the buggy. Old Dice had been dead some years. Mrs Dice had been Jane Freeborn, daughter of old Mrs Mazere's brother Matthew.

The Dices reached the public road as the Neangen riders neared. Notice of Milly's prodigy could not be omitted. Ronald, while giving this, employed a stratagem to get Aileen, and left Jack Stanton and Poole with Olive and Ida, who made themselves excessively agreeable. Milly was floored by the defection of Ronald, but he was speedily topping the next ridge with Aileen on her silly old chestnut, which everyone was agreed was only fit for dingo baits. Something in the air checked Milly's impulse to overtake them: she had to be content with the admiration won by Romp from every other traveller.

"Look, Ma, Aileen has galloped away from Mr Stanton with Ron Dice," observed Julie, riding close to her parents' shandrydan to whisper sententiously.

"I'm not blind," replied Mrs Healey.

"Hold your tongue, and ride away or you'll get the horse's foot between the spokes," said her father roughly.

The day, one of the hottest of the season, had started auspiciously with a sharp thunder-shower that left the air clear and sparkling and laid the dust, so deep on the rich river flats that if disturbed it could be so dense as to cause collisions. The organizing committee had arranged a procession to approach by way of the right bank and cross the new bridge. Terence M'Haffety, butcher in the old days and later landlord of the Royal Hotel, was Mayor that year, and a fine hearty father of the township he proved, always ready to put colour and dash into his functioning. For the bridge affair he had an energetic coadjutor in his old colleague, Prendergast, another publican from Gundagai, and in the old days "Cornstalk Bill", redoubtable coach-driver. He ran the best hotel in Gundagai, and in the beginning had owned several of the subsidiary lines of coaches later swallowed by the world-wide Cobb & Co.

Prendergast was a coaching authority, and had driven six-in-hand before the Governor in Sydney. He was unhappy away from coaches and horses, and after retiring to be host of the Cornstalk Arms, had returned to the road for his health. In her widowed years old Mrs Mazere made visits to her son Hugh, beyond Cootamundra, and always arranged her journeys for the days when William, as she addressed him, was driving. He was unfailingly delighted to have her. On such occasions the box-seat was sacred to her, and he put extra dash into his driving for her appreciation. There she enjoyed his skill with four or five coachers, which like as not of late years bore the Jinninjinninbong or Ten Creeks brands on their hides. Mrs Bill, or "Squinty Ellen" of earlier years, had been reared in the Three Rivers kitchen, and the pair treated the old lady as a State guest and dined with her in a private sitting-room.

It was now two or three years since she had gone to Cootamundra; time and rheumatics were restricting her activities. The appearance for the bridge was in the family sociable. The coach had had to be abandoned because the box-seat was now too high for the old lady to reach with comfort. Mr and Mrs Prendergast arrived the day before with the four-in-hand of iron-greys, driven at a rattling bat to steady them for the procession.

The ceremony was timed for 11.30. About an hour earlier there was a muster at Three Rivers. The Mayor and Mayoress were to go first, followed by Mortimer, M.P., and his wife, and then Mrs Mazere, decked in new black silk and the adapted Sydney bonnet. Her grandson Philip lifted her up beside Prendergast. The seat held three, so Mrs Prendergast had the honour of sitting beside the great lady. In the back were Mr and Mrs Philip Mazere and Mr and Mrs Jacob Isaacs and Mrs Rachel Labosseer and Emily. After this came Archdeacon Fish and Father O'Halloran, the banker, the lawyers, other business and professional people, and numerous old pioneers.

The procession turned upstream to the new bridge, and those assembled cheered its arrival. Mrs Mazere nodded and smiled under a tricky little parasol in acknowledgment; several rushed to the bit-rings while Bert Poole helped his old friend to alight. It was his arm she leant upon to stand with the Member, the Mayor, and clergy. It was an honour accorded Poole and in sentimental favour since long ago he had been engaged to lovely Emily Mazere, drowned just after her engagement to him had been announced. A little Brennan girl came forward with a bunch of roses. Mrs Mazere took them, kissed the child, and handed the flowers to her eldest great-granddaughter, Marcia, who was lady-in-waiting. The Mayor presented the gold scissors and Mrs Mazere cut the ribbon and smashed the bottle of champagne with a few baptismal, God-fearing words. Poole lifted her back to her seat and the hard-banded hoofs of the coachers made imposing thunder on the decking of the new structure as amid prolonged cheering they crossed it. Then amid handshakings and greetings and congratulations to the banquet in the marquee at which Mrs Mazere sat at the top of the chief table with the Mayor and Member on either side, and an exchange in wives on either side of them, and so on.

There were those who early were not so happy as might have been. One was Flash Billy in his strapped trousers and cabbage-tree forgathering among his kind on the outskirts.

"Did yous see ole Poole ridin' the Corroboree colt, an' him actin' as tame as ole Flea Creek with a couple of hundred of salt on him?" inquired Long Billy, joining him. "It seems he wasn't no outlaw after all."

"Hell!" said Flash Billy. "You know a terrible lot, don't you?"

"What's the matter?"

"Oh, shut your gob, you——. I've bitten me tongue."

"Did yous twig young Aileen and Ronnie with their horses sweatin', an' a long way behind them ole Skinny Guts stuck with Olive and Ider? Ron cut out the old bloke at Bookaledgeree." This from Tim Porter.

"The reel fun," said Tommy Roper, "was the missus when I come an' told her the boss was stayin' with the Healeys and she had to come on her own."

"An' young Milly," contributed Jerry Riddall. "You should er seen her ridin' up on the Young Whisker filly as simple as if it wuz the ole mare. What do yer make o' that, Billy?"

"The —— fillies 'll let women an' lunatics ride 'em every time, that's well known, ain't it? Ain't you heard ole know-all Mick Muldoon skitin' about it, blast you, as well as Mr Eustace Lord Muck the Earl of Blenkinsop?"

"Yes, but Poole an' Corroboree ain't no lunatic nor ole woman neither."

"If you ask me, I think his brain is softenin' an' he is becomin' an ole woman, an' the horse knows it."

"My cripes, I don't know when I've laughed so much," said Tommy Roper. "There was the missus drivin' with ole Dan Spires sittin' up with her like an ole cluckin' hen. Good iron wingey, she was pleased!"

She certainly had been in Roper's ironic sense. Arrived at the bridge she sprang straight over the wheel to express her displeasure to her brother.

41

"I expected you at Stanton's Plains last night to come with me in the procession," she said.

"You can drive as well as I can."

"I can drive better for that matter, but where on earth were you?"

"At Neangen. I sent you word."

"Among that crowd! It is foolish to encourage such people. I won't have Milly getting familiar with them. They ought to be ashamed of themselves to appear on an occasion like this!"

"Great snakes, it's a public function and the bridge will be of more use to them than anyone."

"Yes, but it's a Mazere and Stanton and all our crowd's affair, and considering what old Denny Healey did to the Labosseers about Eueurunda I consider——"

Milly interrupted by rushing up to greet her mother and to announce that the procession was coming. Mrs Saunders turned perforce towards the business of the day. Meeting Aileen Healey on the way to the platform she gave her the curtest of nods, which covered Aileen with confusion since there had been no coolness during the muster. Old Larry she refused to recognize at all, and she recalled Milly sharply from Julie's embrace. Others besides her brother noted these actions.

The banquet was a tedious function with jellies melting and blowflies attacking the meats. Many of the younger fraternity stole away to flirt and gossip in the shade of the big gums along the river-banks, while the Mayor presided flamboyantly and his wife supported him like a sunflower. The more platitudinous, flowery, and distended the speeches the more highly were they esteemed as gems of oratory and wit, and the bridge, officially christened in honour of Mortimer who had secured it, was better known as old Mrs Mazere's.

The old lady was returning to Three Rivers after the banquet to rest for the evening function. Prendergast's greys stood reefing at the bits, with eager volunteers holding the rings. Charlotte, wife of old Mrs Mazere's eldest son, went with her and persuaded her husband to go too, to be out of the way of the drinking. Young Mazeres or Stantons or Labosseers filled up the back for the ride in the chariot of honour, and because one place is as good as and occasionally better than another to the infatuated. Beside her mother went Mrs Rachel Labosseer of Coolooluk, Mrs Mazere's widowed daughter. It was against her husband that the Healeys had employed dummies to obtain Eueurunda, the Monaro station on which the Healeys never throve.

On the contrary, Mrs Labosseer had since prospered and was

42

honoured second only to her mother. Now a handsome woman in the fifties, she was surrounded by sons that were paragons and daughters that were accounted perfect. Her ringing laugh could be heard as Poole assisted her into the sociable and said something about engaging her for a polka at the ball.

"Oh, Uncle Herbert, did mamma ever dance?" exclaimed Emily in surprise. All of the Mazere clan called Poole uncle because of his engagement to their beautiful Aunt Emily.

"Your mamma could dance better than any girl I know when she was your age. She once gave me lessons."

"Mamma, you never let us dance at all! I thought you did not believe in it."

"Because I did certain things when I was young and wicked is no reason I should countenance wickedness now," said mamma, with the finality which distinguished all her pronouncements on matters of conduct for her family.

The volunteers let go, the greys bounded away; no one missed the fine sweep of them up the approach to the bridge and as they lilted round the edge of Stanton's Plains by the way they had come.

"Ah," said Terence M'Haffety, who had a prominent place in the departure. "Sure, they're all roight in their way, but the bist Oi iver saw was ould Poole, the dad of Bert here, swhinging five bays up through the town there, ivery wan of thim on their hoind legs, an' his missus with a baby in her arms sittin' there unconscious as if 'twas a perambulathor! There was a man for ye!"

"You should not have mentioned that," said Isaacs, drawing him aside. "That was the time old Poole came to the twenty-first birthday ball of Emily, and she was drownded just after."

"Maybe Oi shouldn't have, Jacob. Poor ould Mrs Mazere, gettin' very whoite. The last of the rale ould wans left. Not another of the originals left of the first whoites on the Yarrabongo. All the ould Saunderses and Stantons and Brennans with their wives in the cimitery this sivin years or more. Sure, whin the ould lady is gone, Jacob, it's me and you next."

＊　　＊　　＊　　＊　　＊

"This makes me feel young again, William," remarked Mrs Mazere, when the horses had settled down on the level plains. She had enjoyed the outing and reception. "It reminds me of the days I used to go riding over the mountains to Monaro and thought nothing of it."

"You must come with me to Gundagai one of these days. It is too long since you came our way."

"I expect I shall not take many more runs till I go to rest beside

43

Papa in the hollow," she remarked, but not gloomily. "If the Lord spares you to my age, William, you'll know that it is a lonely condition—not one left of my own age for me to talk to about the things we knew."

"I never thought of that before, Mrs Mazere. It will be dashed lonely for some of us to be without you when the time comes. Now ain't those leaders pearls!" he observed to divert her. "I'd like to be driving them for a wedding couple, the next best thing after this here today."

"There will be plenty of weddings about presently, with so many young people. I cannot remember who they all are. . . . I'd like you to drive me at my funeral, William," she added.

"Well, I'll be blowed, Mrs Mazere, for you to think of such a dull thing on this happy day! You're good for another ten or twenty years yet, I'm hanged if you're not! You'll very likely be at my funeral first."

"And I hope everyone will come to my funeral—all the women and girls as well as the men, and say a last good-bye to me. I have known so many of them since they were born, since before they were born, so to speak, and I pray to meet them hereafter."

She had insisted upon attending Emily's funeral long ago against the usual custom for women, and all her women friends had supported her on that tragic occasion. She had continued the practice of seeing all her friends to the grave. In the case of old Tim Brennan of The Gap, and one or two others, Prendergast recalled that she had been the only member of her sex to pay the departed this last courtesy.

On sped the greys, nodding their crested heads in the annoyance of the flies, pulling their burden gaily between the river singing the G minor Ballade over its great boulders and the fields of dark-green maize that stretched away to yellowing grasses that carpeted the foothills of the undenuded mountains where the Gap known as Brennan's let the Wamgambril through.

"If you drive me on my last journey, William," pursued the old lady, "I'd like to be driven like this, and not that dismal creeping pace of funerals."

"Right you are, Mrs Mazere. It shall be as you wish. Mrs Labosseer can be witness. But I hope I'll be too old to handle the ribbons by that time."

*   *   *   *   *

No thought of their end entered the thoughts of others. Poole headed a committee to arrange impromptu sports. Specially enjoyable were these to the rising generation, and the half-crowns

44

they won seemed better prizes and bulked larger than many later honours.

The day was as full of youthful zest and notoriety to Milly as it was of ripe honour and homage to Great-grandma Mazere. Her pony was the wonder of all owing to the tricks taught her by Flash Billy. Mr Mortimer asked for a special exhibition and Milly made Romp kneel while she mounted, and lie down and pretend to be dead, and jump a bush held up in full view of Archdeacon Fish and Father O'Halloran and the assembled squattocracy.

Another notable was Dot Saunders, Milly's cousin, the leading amateur equestrienne of the district and a belle who had more admirers than she could use. Riding at one of the up-country shows last autumn, the Governor, himself a considerable figure *à cheval*, had been so delighted with her horsemanship that he asked her to ride at the Sydney Show. This she had done at Easter, carrying off everything she entered for. She, too, was requested to give an exhibition. Hurdles were placed and she entertained the beholders by her own grace and skill as well as that of her famous horse, the Princess. She was active and efficient, with hands strong and quiet, and was good to see in her tight-fitting habit, and her yellow plaits showing under her billycock hat. She had them all dithering because of her vitality, and above all for the egg-boiler cast of her waist, which in those days was equal to a dowry to a maiden in the marriage arena.

With all the admiration Dot was receiving she saw hardly any-thing of Ronald Dice, the only young man present who attracted her. He and Jack Stanton were increasingly infatuated with Aileen Healey, and making for her the most exciting and successful day she had so far experienced. The Dice girls also had a pleasant day squired intermittently by Poole. There was a sporting chance that he still could be captured, an idea furthered by the comfort of his manner.

Dot was a doer, not a dreamer. When SP-over-J secured Aileen's attention she suggested to Ronald, "What about us riding in the pairs at the next show in Bool Bool, and at Gundagai too?"

"It would have been ripping, Dot," replied Ronald. "Only I have just fixed up with Miss Healey."

"I didn't know she could ride." There was in that locality a gulf between those who could travel on horseback and those who could disport themselves over hurdles.

"She can do well enough for the pairs," said Ronald with that instinct for escaping contention that made him popular. "I didn't dream of looking so high as you, Dot."

"Have you got a horse for Miss Healey?"

"Good enough for the pairs."

"I ought to lend her Susan Nipper, only she takes riding," said Dot to cover her disappointment, and moved away holding her new-fashioned habit smartly round her. So daring an innovation called out observations rooted in admiration and envy. It fitted like a snake-skin to the waist, and as a special feature was destitute of gathers to disguise her back contour, and that was daring for Dot's decade.

She walked straight over to Herbert Poole. "Mr Poole, will you ride in the pairs with me at the show?"

"I should think that grey of Ronald's would pair better with your Princess than anything I've got."

"I've asked him, but he's already fixed up with Aileen Healey." There was a wistful, tired look in the bright sunburnt face, and Poole with his unfailing kindness said, "All right, Dot, if you want me to."

Ronald Dice had a word with Aileen at the earliest opportunity. "I want you to ride with me in the pairs at the show. Don't say no, for I've already said we are going to."

"Oh, Ronnie, how wonderful! However did you think of it! I don't believe I can ride well enough."

"Oh yes you can."

"Perhaps Pa won't let me."

"He'll have to. Dot Saunders is always riding at the shows and she's no end of a swell."

"Yes, but the Governor has praised her, and had her at Government House."

"Well, we'll take it as settled for a start anyhow, and tell anyone who asks you for a dance tonight that you are already engaged."

"Oh, Ronnie, how heavenly!" she breathed, her eyes like stars.

CHAPTER 5

THE BALL was held in the hall at the Agricultural Show grounds, and a number of the oldest settlers, headed by the Mayor and Mayoress, the Member and Memberess, the two clergy and their one spouse, were waiting to welcome old Mrs Mazere when she was driven up in another black silk dress and a shawl from India, and, instead of the day bonnet, an expensive widow's cap of similar origin and modifications. Terence M'Haffety was proud in his office. He was a man of money and consequence in the town, his wife his able partner, and it had been long since forgotten that one had convict beginnings and the other was supposed to have been born in the "Female Factory" at Parramatta.

Mrs Mazere was overcome by the presentation of a long gold chain, and an illuminated address signed by the leading townsmen, setting forth the esteem in which she was held, and wishing her many more happy returns of the day. She had difficulty in controlling her voice but her emotion was drowned in cheers of goodwill. Then followed the opening of the ball by a grand march round the hall to the music of an imported band, the gift of M'Haffety for the occasion. Mrs Mazere walked with the Member, the Mayor walked with the Memberess, the Mayoress walked with Archdeacon Fish, and Father O'Halloran walked with Mrs Fish, and so on down to a tail of beaux and belles for whose delectation balls are really organized. The grand march ended, the old lady returned to her home, whither she was taken by the men who displaced the horses and drew her regardless of dust and perspiration.

The entertainment progressed with a dance or two of honour in which the distinguished visitors and elders joined with cackle and flourish and then retired comfortably to the rooms improvised in the wings of the Hall while youthful enjoyment continued unconfined. The oldsters played cards in their nook, and the real oldsters of all talked intimately of the old days and speculatively of the future. Among those taking part were Jacob and Rebecca Isaacs, the first storekeepers of the town. There were slabs of human drama acutely interesting to Rebecca.

"Sure, Oi saw with me own eyes Mrs Lucy Saunders walk

sniffily past the gurrul, Aileen, and give the cut direct to ould Larry," whispered the Mayor.

"And right, too!" said Browning the carpenter, now of substantial estate, retired, and an alderman. "Think of the dirty trick the Healeys played on the Labosseers."

"But what has that got to do with the Stantons?" remarked Isaacs.

"They bein' all related back and forth, and hangin' together."

"Aw, it can't be that," persisted Isaacs. "Tommy Roper, the little feller with the prize jumpers, was in the store the other day an' tellin' me as how Aileen and her brother was at Ten Creeks for the muster, so why should Lucy Saunders give them the go-by now? If we went about giving the go-by because of what some other family did to our friends some time there'd be no business done at all."

"Sure, Oi'm tellin' ye Oi saw it."

"But Mrs Labosseer herself spoke to old Larry, I seen her, an' asked how old Denny was. I listened, because I was goin' to ask, myself."

"And old Mrs Mazere shook hands with him the same as all the others," testified Browning.

"Och, now ye've said it!" exclaimed the Mayor. "But there niver was annyone to ayqual the rale ould Mazeres of Three Rivers. All these others stickin' on a bit av soide is upstarts. These Saunders is not half the breed of the ould Mazeres, and that Lucy, the widow of Saunders, can act loike a mad dog with stinkin' proide if annyone attimpts to speak to her that she thinks isn't good enough. Sure, hasn't she acted that way to me! But ould Mrs Mazere was niver loike that. Av coorse she'd speak to Healey, or if it was a condimned man she'd speak to him too, just as natural. The rare lady is the rale Christian, you can know it by that."

"The missus says the trouble is that old Jack Stanton is struck on the girl Aileen, and you know my missus can always be depended on for the straight tip."

"My oath, she can that!" said Browning.

"Sure, Lucy Saunders doesn't loike the breed, an' it would put her nose out of jint to boot. The Healey gurrul won't get anny assistance there. Sure, now whin Oi think of it, didn't ould Skinny come with the Healeys, an' Lucy drivin' the four-in-hand herself. Phwat the divul . . . Sure, Jacob, things must have gone pretty far without you havin' the cognizance."

"The cognizance was all right, but things have been as suddent as greased lightning. It's Lucy who hasn't seen it coming, an' now it is too late to stop it, is the opinion of my old woman."

"Begor', ye moight as well try to stop a snowball meltin' in hell whin an ould feller that hasn't been afther the gurruls for years gets it into his head to want wan. Croipes, wouldn't it be a lift to ould Larry!"

"As good as a play," agreed Browning, who had risen to watch the dancers. "Old Skinny is dancing with the Healey piece now this minute, and Ronald Dice is sitting out with Dot Saunders, and Lucy is layin' down the law to Poole. She's had her hooks in there long enough and nothing ever came of it."

"Sure, nothing ever will. He keeps himself natural, being koind to all the little gurruls and the children. Sure, that little wan of Lucy Saunders has more chanct with him than anny of the grown-ups. An' wasn't she a noice little thing with that pony, loike a circus! She's betther than her ma. Sure, a case in pint with what Oi've been sayin', did ye see ould Mrs Mazere with ould Bill Prendergast? For all he's a successful man now, and a pot on him loike a mare in foal, sure, don't we remimber him for iver in ould Mazere's kitchen after Squinty Ellen, his woife. And didn't the ould lady rare her by hand so to speak, in her own thrue religion, an' she frinds now with thim without lowerin' herself or thim, an' none of these airs of excloosiveness like the Saunders and Stantons—thinkin' it roises thimselves to keep others down."

Surely His Worship must have heard that Lucy Saunders said it was a disgrace to Bool Bool to have an ex-ticket-of-leave as Mayor.

"Bert Poole is dancing with the little Saunders girl, and Aileen Healey and Ron Dice have got together at last," reported Isaacs in his turn. "And they look made for each other, I will say that, and she lookin' up at him as if she was swimming in paradise. It's a curious thing, this being in love."

A game ended, the Mayor joined the proprietor of the Royal Drapery Mart. A mass of young people in ball finery were dis-porting themselves to the music of the Mayor's band. The initiated could pick out dozens of the third generation of Mazeres, Stan-tons, Saunderses, and Brennans, the original pioneers. Then there were the later comers and the townspeople proper—the daughters of the banker, lawyer, and clergyman, and also the tradespeople, this being a public hall. There were, too, the Riverina squatters and their families in the district for the summer. Among them were a few notable for their beauty or other public qualities. Con-spicuous was Herbert Poole, J.P., youthful-looking for the late fifties, prosperous, popular, a figure of romance.

"Isn't it a pity," observed Mrs Isaacs to the Mayoress, where these two looked on from another doorway, "that he doesn't

49

marry—him so fond of children. Look at him now with little Milly, laughing and enjoying himself as much as if she was the belle."

"Sure, Rebecca, do you think there's anny thruth in Milly's mother makin' up to him?"

"She'll never catch him. She's too bossy. She ought to take ole Mr Blenkinsop. He'd be one of those chip-in-porridge ole men that would just fit in with her tigrinizing. He'd be a nice figurehead, an' it's awkward for a woman without some sort of a man. Don't the ole bird look nice tonight?"

"Sure, he's loike the Governor! How do ye suppose it is that his woife cannot endure him and sint him out here; he seems as meek as a lamb."

"A man may be a lamb, but there's many things to be considered in a husband that wouldn't matter in a lawyer or a gardener."

Mr Eustace Blenkinsop was the beau of the ball, being the wearer of a perfect dress suit, a uniform rare among the men. To Mr Blenkinsop's mind and education it was indispensable, and he had the art, ingrained through generations, of wearing it without offence in any society. He was a remittance-man, one of those amiable ditherers of whom it is said, "He's no one's enemy but his own." His perfect manners were only equalled by his perfect uselessness, and there was no acute alcoholism to account for it. It was merely his upbringing. As an eldest son in the land of primogeniture he might have been employed as a figurehead in the rule of the cliques over the classes; but a younger son of an indigent branch he was simply one of the unbelievable paradoxes exported by England to the colonies. He was no Gussie—also at that date exported in such numbers as to indicate that the English system of breeding gentlemen must either have had poor material to work upon or be most inefficient to produce so many "culls" patronizing the "beastly colonies" and deploring the life of Australia as bitterly as their families deplored them. Mr Blenkinsop enjoyed Australian life. He was the perfection of kindly content, never guilty of offensive comparisons, and able to meet members of his own sets, did any appear, with the same unembarrassed grace with which he associated with the Stantons and M'Haffetys, the Mazeres, or Mick Muldoon, or Teddy O'Mara. His allowance, regularly remitted and accompanied by affectionate letters, was spent on clothes, courtesies, tobacco, and periodicals. He never needed to pay for board where every door was open to him and where he never doubted his welcome. He was an ornament wherever he appeared—a lily of the field—so enamoured of good manners and a mild disposition is humanity at large.

Many had coveted him as a tutor and Mrs Saunders had scored in having coaxed him to superintend Milly.

He was, as Mrs Isaacs spoke, leading Mrs Lucy Saunders upon the floor. He could dance as agreeably as he could take a hand at cards, or chess, or billiards, or supply a classical quotation.

"In the name of all that's sinsible, can ye suggest either wan of ye whoi ould Mr Blenkinsop is not at home with his family instid of everlastin' phrowlin' about from wan house to another out here, him such a nice ould gent?" demanded the Mayor. "Sure, look at him now, as gintlemanly as a proize rooster with the hins!"

"Who do you think is the belle?" inquired Mrs Isaacs.

"Sure, there's none can hould a candle to Dot Saunders. Look at that yaller hair of her with the pink rose in it, and she's tall, and slim in the middle without too much squazin', an' haughty enough to make people keep their distance without bein' disagreeable."

"Well, now, I was just thinkin' she seems to have her nose a little out of joint tonight. That dress she wore to the Government House ball last Easter is a bit too fine with that great train like a princess, and she's beginning to look old. She must be twenty-seven last birthday." Mrs Isaacs did a computation founded on her own grandchildren and confirmed this. "I was thinkin' Aileen Healey is putting her in the shade. Aileen is a real little beauty, and her dress, for all she made it herself, makes her look girlish and sweet with the flowers round that deep V and the waist straight round instead of peaked, and no train."

"Ah, but the Healeys haven't got the standing of the Saunderses."

"But if a girl has the beauty and the men run after her, the women of standing can't do much against her. Look at Aileen now, doesn't she fit in with old Mr Blenkinsop and his swallow-tail and nice manners?"

It was true that few of the women could equal the girl and none could excel her. There was a slimness, a dainty windblown quality in her prettiness, that gave it the distinction of beauty, and she had the further appeal of gentleness. She was of medium height and her waist had the delicacy of Alexandra's or of the reigning vice-reine's. She had naturally wavy chestnut hair, a little oval face with soft Irish eyes of changing colour under emotion, and her head was set upon her slim flat shoulders with the grace of a flower on its stem. Also flowerlike was her taste in dress, and she had the skill to execute it.

Mr Blenkinsop in requesting the pleasure assured her that she made him feel young again, so like was she to the beautiful Miss Severn of Budleigh Salterton whose beauty afterwards captured

51

young Lord Osgood, heir to the marquisate of Salterton. "Ah me, my dear, I wish I were heir to a marquisate, and young again, and there is no doubt that I should be similarly captured—all over again," he said, the kindly gallantry bringing a blush to Aileen's cheek.

"Aileen Healey is a real beauty," observed Mrs Raymond Poole (*née* Mazere), wife of Bert Poole's young half-brother, who lived in Sydney. Rhoda was home for her mother's birthday and the bridge ceremony.

"It's a cheap sort of prettiness, though," said Lucy Saunders.

"No. I was going to say, that's just what it isn't. She reminds me of Lady Carrington and other English ladies I meet at Government House. It's a pity she's not of better stock. The way Ronnie Dice looks at her it seems as if we might have her in the family. It's a pity when a girl as lovely as that has no family ballast—it leaves her a prey to all the men."

"More likely it leaves our families a prey to her until she catches someone. I wish Ronnie would be successful. After all, he's only a second cousin to you, and it would save me from something nearer."

"Tell me, is it really true about Jack? I didn't give it any credence. They've been marrying him and Bert Poole to every barmaid and widow since the time of poor dear Emily and Mary."

"True! He seems to have gone suddenly off his head. Come till I tell you. It looks like senility to me."

"Oh, he's not old enough for that!"

They moved off to confidences out of hearing.

* * * * *

"Uncle Bert, do you know what I heard someone say?" inquired Milly as Poole was swinging her by the hands in a set.

"Couldn't guess. You tell me."

"Well, it's rather private. I think we shall have to go outside like the grown-ups." Poole suppressed too much of a chuckle and smiled indulgently down upon her as he led her outside in quite the style of amorous pairs.

"I heard Mrs Isaacs saying that Mother is trying to marry you. It isn't true, is it?"

"You might hear a lot that isn't true if you listen to gossip. It's best to let such things go in one ear and out the other."

"Of course I know that, Uncle Bert, about people that don't matter, but you are different. You are not trying to put me off now, are you, because you think I am a child? Mother is not going to marry you, is she?"

"This is the first I have heard of it." As Milly still looked at him questioningly he reassured her, "No, Milly, it is not true."

"I am glad of that," said the little girl with a loud sigh of relief.

"You don't mean to say you'd object to me, do you?" Amusement twinkled in his clear brown eyes.

"Oh no, of course I don't object to you, but I don't think Mother could make you happy." Milly spoke with deep seriousness. She had lately taken to reading romances of the *Ladies' Journal* type.

"Dear me, how's that?"

"I don't think she has the right temperament to make you happy," reiterated Milly out of the store of her imbibings, and added spontaneously, "I don't think she's nice enough."

"Dear me, what a pity for all our sakes."

"Now, Uncle Bert, you are laughing at me, and we had a *compact*"—Milly loved the word—"that we were never to laugh at each other when we were dead-serious."

"All right. I'll apologize and be double dead-serious. What are we to do about it?"

"I had made up my mind to marry you myself when I'm old enough, if you will wait."

"I've waited so long that a little more won't matter one way or the other; but don't you think I'd be rather long in the tooth?"

"Not if you stay just as you are till I am eighteen. I might hurry it on to seventeen if you got impatient."

"The difficulty is that time won't wait for me, and nothing can be done about it." Recollection played round the succession of young things that had tried for his favour, and those other instances in which he had wished to marry and fate or favour had failed him. He remembered also the lamps of invitation lit for him in the eyes of older women. Now here was his little playmate with imitative prattle talking of marrying him. There had been many such, now fecund matrons, delighted when their day had come to receive his generous present and kindly raillery regarding desertion of himself. Milly was a quaint old-fashioned little woman in many ways, but her chatter vouched for her innocence, though it would not be so long before some young chap claimed her too, and only a thunderingly decent chap would be right for Milly.

"Well, Milly, this is great. Just what I have wanted. But I think it had better be a secret engagement, then if you change your mind it won't make such a fool of me."

"Oh yes, it must be a tight secret—a *compact*—between you and me. If that Julie knew she would be jealous, and besides, she's dead in love with Ronald."

"All right, that's settled. I should make a point never to take any notice of what you hear anyone saying. It works out this way. If someone says a foolish thing it is no harm unless it is repeated. It is the repeating person who is dangerous."

"Yes, I see, Uncle Bert."

"Well, now, we had better go in, as another good thing is never to make talk by staying out too long with any partner." Poole laughed gleefully as Milly squeezed his hand and left him inside the doorway.

Meanwhile other lips had said, "Oh, Ronnie, isn't this a divine waltz? I wish I could go on waltzing with you for ever."

"Come out!" glowed Ronald as they approached one of the yawning openings and he whirled the slender yielding form into the dark velvet of the moonless summer night.

Wherever they turned, other couples similarly affected were before them, or else they were in danger of the avid observation of boundary-riders or horse-breakers or hotel slushies. They sped through the long dry summer grasses, full of seeds and burrs, to the far side of the grounds where the roses nodded their heads over the paling fence of what had lately been old Mrs Dr James's domain. Here was refuge for a while, but, disturbed by the murmur of approaching voices, Ronnie tore down some of the palings with his hands and lifted his partner through to seek the track where the Yarrabongo fell round a bend in a song that charmed the night.

Their emotions were beyond words. They overflowed into the fervent caresses of first love, an ecstasy approaching suffering. When breathing necessitated a pause, Ronald could only gasp, "Aileen! Aileen!" and crushing her to him began again, *da capo, da capo*.

"We can't go back after this, darling. You must marry me, now, soon!"

"Oh, I will, Ronnie. I will! Just as soon as you want me to. I'd die at the thought of anyone else after this."

They sat upon a fallen tree. It was rough for the fragile ball drapery, so he gathered her onto his knees. A mosquito stung him and he pulled off his coat and wrapped it round his love.

"Good night, mate!" said some inquisitive strollers. Dice kept still and they passed on with an insulting chuckle and an obscene observation spoiling the beauty of emotion for the two in Eden.

"It's that horrid flash Billy Bowes, isn't it? Oh, Ronnie, do you think they knew who we were?"

"It's none of their business if they did. Flash Billy is going to find his market value going down with a bump, if I'm any prophet."

"But, Ronnie, supposing Pa found out that we had come away out here like this all alone, he'd kill me."

"It doesn't matter what he'd do. You belong to me now. Oh, darling, I love you so, I feel as if I would suffocate."

"I love you, too, but don't you think we'd better go back now?"

"I don't feel like going back to that heat and dust."

"But Ronnie darling, we can't stay out here. Think how it would look. Pa would have a search party after me in no time. We've been away much too long already."

"It will be all right when we tell him we are engaged."

"Pa is so terribly strict with us. I'd rather go back to the hall now."

"Let us run away and get married tomorrow."

"But where would we live? Pa wouldn't let us live at Neangen."

Ronald was only manager for his mother at Bookaledgeree, things were not prosperous and his whole family objected to the Healeys. Ida had ridden up to Neangen with him and Aileen expressly at her mother's command so that Ronald should not be compromised.

Two more strollers passed and asked for a match, trying to discern the identity of the lovers. When they went on Aileen raised herself from Ronald's embrace in panic. "That's Larry. I bet you Pa is raging and Ma sent him to find me."

"I suggest I take you to Great-aunt Mazere. You can stay at Three Rivers without any fear of scandal."

"We couldn't wake the old lady up at this hour, and your cousin Charlotte is here with the girls."

Aily was hastening towards the hall and Ronald had to keep up with her, the bliss of amorous catalepsy dispersed by the imminence of parental opposition.

"Wait! Wait, darling! Don't run like that as if I had been murdering you. Let us go together and brave it out. You are your own mistress."

The girl steadied her fawnlike flight and fears. They regained the neighbourhood of the hall. Ronald lit a buggy-lamp and enabled Aileen to free herself of some of the grass-seeds. She slipped into the toilet-room to rearrange her tresses while Ronald entered the main opening and sought partners. Dot Saunders was just being led out by Larry Healey, jun. She had waited in vain for Ronald and was not enjoying the ball. Ronald looked round for a partner. Milly piped in his ear, "Why don't you ask me?"

The youngster should have been in bed if rightly reared, but Ronald blessed her intervention, looking over her head to see Aileen enter. All evidence of her recent walk removed, she came in with a Brennan girl and carefully steered away from her parents. This took her towards Mr Blenkinsop, who greeted her with a courtly inclination. Aileen chatted with him about the heat and the pity of the floor being so uneven and dusty, as thankful to him as Ronald was to Milly. While this was happening SP-over-J requested the pleasure, and Aileen tripped away on his arm so distrait that she could distinguish no faces in the crush but Ronald and Milly's. The others were unsettled like faces returning to one who has been unconscious.

After one turn of the hall, SP-over-J made some suggestion, which Aileen accepted without knowing what he said, and was presently conscious of being led in the direction from which she had just returned with Ronald. SP-over-J did not tear down palings nor ramp about gathering grass-seeds and risking snake-bite. He helped Aileen to the back seat of the Mazere sociable and climbed in after her.

Larry, jun., a little later reported to his stepmother that he had not been able to find Aily. "It's all right," said that lady. "She's just gone outside with Mr Stanton."

"Aileen," said that gentleman, putting his arm about her, "perhaps you can guess what I want to say. I know there is some disparity in our ages, but your kind words to me from time to time have led me to understand that that makes no difference to you."

Without intentional defection on her part, the last person talking to Aileen would always feel that his words carried greatest weight, and he the happiest favour. It is a characteristic of the world's charmers, male or female, but for success they must also be endowed with the ability to prevent their compliance involving them.

"Oh no," said Aileen helplessly. "Indeed you are not old at all, Mr Stanton."

"You must learn to say *Jack*."

"Of course, Mr Stanton, if you wish it." Aileen's dazed mind was subconsciously taking its hesitant course—anything for peace.

"Well, Aileen, as I was saying," he drew the seductive form closer, unaware of its spontaneous shrinking.

"Oh, if you please, Mr Stanton, it is such a hot night," she murmured. Innate amiability made direct rebuff impossible and disguised her objection to his embrace.

"Yes, it is a hot night—bit muggy, like a thunderstorm. As I was saying—in fact there is no need for me to say anything more; you understand, don't you?"

"Oh yes, please don't say anything. I understand, Mr Stanton."

"Mr Stanton!"

"Pardon me, I mean *Jack*."

"Well, then, I am a bit older, but that I hope will make me all the more sensible. I'll understand better how to make you comfortable than a flighty young fellow. I can give you anything within reason . . ."

Here there was an interruption in the approach of two hereditary occupants of the Mazere vehicle, in the persons of Marcia and Amy, clan cousins in the throes of youthful infatuation. They heard the assurance of Uncle Jack—he was uncle to one of them—about making someone more comfortable than a young fellow would be able to. This was hilarious to the two bright misses. They should not have been "out" either only that it was Great-grandma's big day, and discipline relaxed for the historic occasion. The girls contumaciously went near to the carriage to ascertain the second in this fascinating duet.

"Oh, Mr Stanton, someone is coming," breathed the startled Aileen as the adventuresses scampered away convulsed by the desired information.

Dice was standing outside the entrance pondering which way to go in search of Aileen when the tittering girls ran towards him. "Oh, I say, Cousin Ronnie, such a lark! I'm sure you'll never guess." Communication foundered in gales of adolescent giggles. "We went over to the sociable for something and——"

"I know what you found," interposed Milly. "You needn't make such a fuss."

"Well, smarty, what did we find?"

"Uncle Jack and Aileen. Pooh, that's nothing! Everyone knows all about that. Aileen was on a visit to Ten Creeks, and then I've been up at Neangen with Uncle Bert and Uncle Jack." Her superior tone put the other girls on their mettle.

"You don't know what he was saying," giggled Amy.

"Neither do you. You are only pretending to be smart."

"We're not." They giggled together consumedly. "I never heard anything so funny in my life. I thought we should have died when he said he was ever so much better than a young man, and Aileen said of course he was."

"Oh he is, is he?" said Dice alarmingly. "Where is the sociable? I must go and see or the old Death Adder might sting her."

"Over there behind the sheep-pens," said Amy, alarmed. Ronald strode away like the strong man in melodrama.

"You're nice ones. I'd be ashamed to be you. What anyone says does not matter at all; it's those who go round repeating things who are a menace to society." Milly was pleased with the fine ring

57

of this. Her button of a nose in the air, she continued, "Uncle Bert is the one to deal with this."

"We'd better make ourselves scarce," said Marcia to Amy, the enjoyment of their "scoop" ruined.

"Do you think we had better poke our noses in other people's affairs? It's not a nice thing to do, and generally not wise," said Uncle Bert when the situation was revealed to him.

"Oh, but there was murder in Ronald's eye. You would be full of regrets if anything happened," said Milly in her novelette vocabulary. "Often we must sacrifice ourselves for duty."

Uncle Bert smiled under his moustache. "Suppose we whack the difference? We can go in that direction and keep out of the way unless we are desperately needed."

There was nothing more monumental in Ronald's eye than jealousy and a determination to wreck his rival's plans. He was astounded by Aileen's behaviour. What was she doing in the sociable with the old Death Adder immediately after becoming engaged to himself? She could surely see what had been coming. Tender thoughts intervened. "Poor little Aileen, too gentle and innocent to be a match for old Skinny Stanton!"

The girls had brought Aileen to her senses. "Oh please, Mr Stanton, take me straight back to Ma. I couldn't think of . . ." She balked, unable to utter, "Loving or marrying you." He might say he had not mentioned marriage, and what a fool she would look!

They were out of the vehicle when Dice approached. "Aileen, where are you? This is my dance," he said in an authoritative tone, the conventions operating now that he and Stanton were face to face.

"You will be glad to let Aileen off your dance when I tell you . . ."

"Oh no, no!" said Aileen desperately. "There is a mistake. I must keep my promise to dance."

"Very well, then," said Stanton amicably. "I'll see you after."

The young people went off together but not to dance. Stanton approached Milly and Poole.

"Devilish hot, isn't it?" remarked Poole. "Outside is much the pleasantest place only for the skeets and grass-seeds." Stanton walked towards the hall with Poole. Milly slipped her hand into Uncle Bert's in acknowledgment of the momentous enterprise for the public peace they were engaged upon.

Ronald found Aileen rather scatter-witted. "What were you doing with that old Death Adder in the family coach? What was he trying to stutter for himself?"

"Oh, Ronnie, I don't know. I was so upset. I wish we could go

58

away together and not see anyone." Aileen sounded tearful. She was such an adorable little creature in that state that Ronald was reduced to ditheration and strolled round the outside of the hall holding her comfortingly and kissing her hands and thus affording delectable evidence to the newsmongers.

Stanton shook off Poole and Milly, and went straight to old Larry Healey and drew him aside. This was easy, for Larry had been on the qui vive for a trump call all the evening.

"Ah, ah, ahem!" began the prospective bridegroom. "I wanted to tell you, that is, I didn't want to leave it to Aileen to tell you, but Aileen and I have come to an understanding by which I am a happy man, and I hope Aileen will be happy too. This is no place to say any more, but I'll take a turn up to Neangen tomorrow night or the next day. You'll be home and recovered from the celebrations by then."

"Sure, we will, and pleased to see you. I hope that you and my little Aileen will be very happy. The child is young and there are certain things to be talked over."

"That is so, but no more for the present."

"Who'd have thought this when we used to——"

SP-over-J did not want reminiscences involving their approximation in age. "I'll bid you good night, Larry!" he said, and escaped.

Larry immediately rounded up his flock. Not another dreary moment would he hang round among the revellers. Norah and old Alf Timson could look sheepish together at Neangen as they had been doing for years without sitting up at a ball, and Joanna had been a wallflower except for a dance with Poole and two with Dan Spires, the Ten Creeks overseer, following his introduction to her by Aily. All but Aileen were readily forthcoming.

"Och, I suppose she's with her ould man, and we'll have to give them a few minutes," he observed.

"She's not with Mr Stanton," volunteered the lynx-eyed Julie. "She's round the side there kissing and hugging with Ronald."

"Phwat!" ejaculated Larry ominously.

"I expect she's had to get rid of him. It is sometimes hard," said Mrs Healey, who had not taken Larry as her only opportunity.

"Hold your tongue, you fool woman! Go you, Joanna and Norah, and bring her at wanst."

Guided by Julie they found Aileen with Ronald and told her that Pa was in a state to know where she was, for they were starting for home at once.

"You're making yourself the talk of the town, absent from the ballroom half the night, first with one and then another," said Joanna.

Pa was not long in getting under way in the old buggy, with Julie and Alf Timson as outriders, and Larry, jun., and Joanna instead of Norah left to bring Aileen.

They could not tear her away in disregard of decorum now that she was selected by the richest bachelor in the district to become a member of the tribe of the Mazeres and Stantons, the real geebungs of the community. When she had incoherently prevailed upon Dice to leave her, SP-over-J insisted upon conducting her to the door of the dressing-room.

"Whatever do you mean, have you lost your wits?" demanded Joanna in a heated whisper when she had her half-sister safely in the dressing-room. "You know what Pa is, and to engage yourself to Mr Stanton, and then to be carrying on like a streel with Ronald Dice under the eyes of everyone, why, it's just common indecent!"

"I'm not engaged to Mr Stanton," protested Aileen, and began to cry.

"You can always pipe your eye at every convenient and inconvenient time. Pull yourself together and have a little sense, for the love of God."

An unobserved onlooker was Milly, determined to intervene should it become necessary. She espied Ronald hanging about the dressing-room opening.

"Is Aileen in there?" he demanded in what the student of low-class novelettes of high life considered an appropriately agitated manner.

"Yes, she's dressing to go home."

"Tell her to step to the door to speak to me for a minute."

Milly bounded off full of ambassadorial zeal.

"Oh, tell him, please, I can't see him," wailed Aileen.

"I should think not! Tell him she's dressing," added Joanna. Milly returned to Ronald.

"Is there anyone in there but Joanna and Aily?"

"No."

Ronald strode in. Milly followed wonderingly through such an unprecedented rent in convention.

"Aileen," he demanded, "what the blazes is this about old Jack Stanton giving out that you are engaged to him?"

"It's true, Mr Dice, and can't you see that you are upsetting my sister? Whatever your private feelings are, I think you should control yourself and not make a public scandal, violating modesty," said Joanna, not without dignity.

60

"Scandal be damned! That's on the other foot. Let Aileen speak for herself. Aileen, are you engaged to that old Death Adder?"

"Oh, Ronnie, no, of course not. There is some terrible mis-understanding."

"I thought so, my darling," said he, clasping the girl to him. The excitement and heat of the day had been excessive. Milly's heroine did the right thing. Her eyes closed, her lovely form went limp in her ardent lover's arms. She had been endowed with a weapon potent in the hands of weak femininity.

"She's fainted!" gasped Joanna.

They laid her on a buggy rug. Milly sped to Uncle Bert. She considered the crisis sufficiently mature.

"Uncle Bert"—she placed a heatedly whispering young mouth on his ear—"Ronald rushed into the dressing-room and asked Aileen if she was engaged to the old Death Adder—that means Uncle Jack—and Aileen fell down in a deathly swoon."

Uncle Bert enjoined silence, his arm round his young confederate. He sought his sister Charlotte, Mrs Philip Mazere. A tall, gaunt woman, sparing of speech, her black hair slightly streaked with grey, she was wonderfully like her brother. Her weather-beaten face and work-marred hands betokened a hard life as the wife of the oldest son of Three Rivers, but she was a rock of refuge to all who called upon her. Capable, quiet, she acted where action was needed, observed the golden rule of silence as well as of sisterhood, and was not inquisitive as to motives and causes. Without disturbance she went to the dressing-room. She had seen many accidents, much sickness, and some tragedy in her sixty years.

"She has only fainted," she remarked to Joanna. "You have bathed her face with cold water and loosened her stays, that's all that can be done. Bert, you and Ronald see that no one comes in to take up the air."

Opportunely, Mayor M'Haffety, a little elevated, at that moment burst into an unscheduled gem of oratory and held the people in the hall. It was not so fortunate that Mrs Isaacs, to whom by some faculty all was speedily known, should come to the dressing-room.

"Whatever has happened," she exclaimed. "Can I be of any help?"

"Ronald," said Mrs Philip, "put the horses in the sociable and we'll run Aileen up to Three Rivers and put her to bed, and she'll be all right in the morning."

"That is very kind of you, Mrs Mazere. But we must go on home. Pa will be in a terrible state. He and Ma won't know what has happened."

"You and Larry go on as intended, Aileen can't take that ride now," said Poole.

"I expect it was too far in the heat, and then the dancing on top of it," said Mrs Philip, as calm, as comforting, as pump water.

"Our old phaeton will be better than the sociable, and the horse is in it," said Mrs Isaacs, kind of heart and bursting to be in this promising affair.

"That will be just the thing," agreed Mrs Philip, her mind on the rearrangement of bedding accommodation so that Aileen could have a room to herself. Three Rivers was chock-a-block. Family ramifications were considerable, and it was the custom of everyone coming to town to billet at the old place. Already beds were in the billiard-room and the office. Mrs Philip decided that her grandson's single bed in a box veranda room at the New House, which had been set aside for a young Philip and Matt Dice, would do nicely, and the two dispossessed could take a pillow and rug to the hay-loft.

Mrs Isaacs, returning from showing where her phaeton and old yellow mare were moored, met SP-over-J, and, impelled by her nose for news, told him that Aileen had fainted and that she had arranged for her phaeton to take the girl to Three Rivers. Stanton hastened to the scene and announced that he would take Aileen to Stanton's Plains, and talked of finding Lucy.

"It is more convenient to take her home with me," said Mrs Philip. "She can rest quietly till tomorrow."

"You can be quite at ease," said Poole to Joanna. "She'll be as right as rain with Charlotte. I'll take her home myself tomorrow on the way to Curradoobidgee."

"That is putting everyone to altogether too much trouble," said Joanna, out of whose hands the whole matter was slipping, and who was worried as to her father's idea of what she should do in the circumstances. "I think I had better stay with Aily."

"By all means. We'll find a nook for you," said Mrs Philip.

"You can go home with my sister and we can come in for Aileen in the morning," said SP-over-J.

Joanna thought of Lucy, unable to recognize her that day, and Mrs Ned Stanton, presiding genius at Stanton's Plains, who had been even more gelid, and she faltered. "I think I had better go with Larry, and we can bring the buggy back for Aily tomorrow."

Matters were furthered by Larry from outside asking Milly to find out if the girls were ready and adjuring them to hurry. Milly, hedging against scandal-mongering, gave Larry the bones of the incident. Joanna came out to consult with him.

"The devil!" observed Larry. "At all events you stay by her and see what goes on. It would be just the thing to stay at Three Rivers, as good as going to stay with Queen Victoria herself only for Ron Dice being there. At any rate, I'm the right one to drive the vehicle there and then I'll go on and tell Pa what has happened or he'll be roaring down like a town bull and making a fool of us."

Larry went in with this announcement, but Charlotte Mazere without malice or forethought or hindthought blew him out. "I'd rather have Bert, if you don't mind. He knows the way to the New House in the dark along those lanes, and we don't want a fuss and the whole celebration about our ears."

"The best is for me to drive Joanna and Aileen out to Stanton's Plains at once without any fuss, and Charlotte, you can tell Mrs Ned and Lucy presently so as not to disturb them," said SP-over-J, as his contribution, but Charlotte was confirmed in her plan by Aileen's clasping her arm and whispering, "Dear Mrs Philip, please put me to bed at your house. I have a terrible pain in my head and Stanton's Plains is so far."

"Well, then, Joanna, you can come home with us," said SP-over-J, desirous of keeping something in his own hands, but this decided Joanna to go with Larry.

"You'll promise me, Mr Poole, that you'll bring Aily *yourself*," she said to him. He gave his word and she went away content as people did when Poole promised. This put the affair into neutral hands and eliminated Ron Dice. Joanna and Larry waited to see that he was excluded from the phaeton. Poole performed this office: "Ron, old man, will you quietly tell the others why Charlotte has gone home and I'll bring Mrs Isaacs's trap back without delay." Then he saw the face of his little colleague. "Milly, child, don't you think you ought to come home with me and Aunt Charlotte? You should have been curled up in your possum-rug hours ago."

Milly was suffering indecision. "I'd love to go with you, Uncle Bert, but don't you think it would be well for me to keep my eye on things here till you come back? I don't like Uncle Jack as much as I like you, but still he's not a death adder, is he?"

"Not by any means," replied Poole, again smiling under his moustache. "And that's another thing, these little hard names don't mean much if they are let pass without notice. Well, you keep your eye on things here till I return, and remember that a shut mouth is good for keeping the flies out and the brains in, as our friend Mick Muldoon would say."

"Well, now," said Milly as the vehicle lights made a galanty show of objects in its way, and tucking her arm in Ronald's in grandmotherly style, "you and I must manage this so as not to make a public scandal."

"Aw, hell, I'll punch his blooming old head! I'll break his scraggy old neck!" said Ronald, pulling himself from her grasp, "and you can tell him so if you want something to do, and then jolly well go and mind your own blooming business!"

Milly was temporarily confounded by the suspicion that Ronnie was not so nice as she had thought. She had been investing him with the cloak of the lovely young heirs of the nobility who finally carried off the beautiful Lady Adelines from—from the old—old—*death adders*! This did not seem a bit dashing and romantic like the stories. Perhaps Aileen had not sufficient backbone to be a Lady Adeline, but then again all that the Lady Adelines had to do was to be pretty and weak and faint, and this Aileen was doing very well indeed. The discrepancies intruded doubtlessly because the Lady Adelines and Lord Percys lived in England among castles and ivy with butlers and ladies'-maids, whereas round Bool Bool were only boundary-riders and shearers and common servant-girls, crudely unromantic, and who would have grinned had the missus been incapable of dressing her own hair. Milly decided to seek information from Mr Blenkinsop at the first opportunity. He knew real live lords and ladies, and maintained that Aileen was like the Marchioness of Salterton. Milly was highly looking forward to having Mr Blenkinsop under her own jurisdiction.

She was a little dashed for the moment but still game, and decided to ascertain how Uncle Jack was faring. She found him near the sheep-pens whither Ronald too was walking. They met and Ronald took issue at once. "See here, Stanton, I'll thank you to keep away from Miss Healey in future—the farther away the better. You've nearly thrown her into a fever already, and I don't wonder, an old hide like you after a young girl is enough to turn the milk sour."

"You're mad!" said Stanton. "In future I'll take a gun to you or send for the police if I see you within a mile of my future wife."

"I'd knock your old mug into the middle of next week only it would be manslaughter to lay a finger on such an old crock."

"Now, now!" said Milly in her best manner, stepping courageously between them. "This is not the way for honourable gentlemen to bring a lady's name into discredit. A real gentleman would die of a pent-up heart rather than do such a thing."

"Rats! Go and bag your head!" said Ronald, but amused in spite of himself.

"You want a good sound clip under the ear and feeding on bread and water for a week. Your mother will suffer for the way she lets you run wild, one of these days," snapped Uncle Jack, putting a rough hand on her shoulder.

"Here, don't hurt the child!" said Ronald.

"You're both as silly as a pair of mad old turkey-cocks when they put their wings down and gobble," said Milly, her mettle roused. "What are you roaring at each other like a pair of demented bulls for, and both saying you are engaged to Aileen! Why don't you wait till the morning and ask her? She'll be sure to know, unless she's a Mormon."

"Hip-hooray for you, kiddy! It's a pity the senile members of your family haven't a little of your common sense."

"You get your mother to take you home this instant," snarled Uncle Jack. "I'll take you in hand tomorrow."

"A lady would have a nice time with him, wouldn't she, Milly?" said Ronald, turning away as he saw the inquisitive Mrs Isaacs waddling his way. Milly also thought it good to go while the going was good, and hid herself from her mother to await Uncle Bert.

Larry and Joanna rode away over the new bridge prognosticating what might happen and filled with excitement about what had already occurred. "Pa will belt the stuffing out of Aileen to get herself into such a mix-up," said Larry.

"She's such a weak-minded fool that she deserves it," agreed Joanna.

*   *   *   *   *

When Flash Billy Bowes had prowled past where Aileen and Ronald were seated, he separated from his companions and went towards town. Ronald and Aileen canoodling on a log against the wishes of old Larry or his old Skinny Guts boss was a juicy morsel, but it could be left to Tommy Roper for the present. Something more vital tormented Billy since Milly had put the Young Whisker filly through her tricks before the crowd. Added to this was Poole's exhibition with the Corroboree colt. The renowned outlaw, who got rid of all the cracks in fair fight, tamed in the season, fit for Great-grandma Mazere to ride, and not by the invincible Flash Billy himself, but by old Bert Poole, whom he had decried as going barmy with age! There was that flaming colt as steady as old Flea Creek! Just to show off, that blooming old crawler of a Poole had put the reins over the animal's neck and he followed him about everywhere like a dog till the —— old woman wanted to get on him. No, Flash Billy was not happy.

He took the horse he was pacing—the Wamgambril colt—and led him along the fence of the showgrounds and down under the Stanton Street bridge by the river track till he was opposite Three

Rivers homestead. He had seen Milly riding there from the new bridge with her precious Uncle Bert. Everyone making such a fuss about the brat! Billy thought her too flash for anything and badly in need of being taken down a peg or two. Where would the filly be, and who would be in charge? They never left the old woman alone now. Cripes! she was an age, an' drivin' about in four-in-hands with old Prendergast like a two-year-old. These old birds were a — nuisance. They ought to know when it was time to bag their blooming old heads.

Flash Billy ran through the stables first: there was no sign of the filly there, only Corroboree in a locked stall, and Queen Anne, Poole's big bay mare, the stallion's pregnant lady-in-waiting, in the next stall to ensure his placidity. The filly would be in the orchard. Billy picked his way among the heavily fruited trees and heard her whinny from the river-side. He caught her without difficulty. Ah, the little beauty! Sheer covetous delight in her perfection thrilled him. She would be a fortune to any man. He lit a match, and saw tracks where she had been attempting to clear the high palings. By gum, she had the old mare in her as well as the Whisker strain! She could be learnt to do anything but talk. He wrenched away a couple of palings, led her through, replaced the boards, and went to where his horse was tethered under the trees. He saddled Romp and made her sham dead. Cripes, she did it for him just as obediently as for young Milly; then he mounted and made sure that she remembered other lessons.

"You little queen! You blooming little pearl!" he breathed in adoration. "Remember everythink I ever learnt you!"

There he had her in his hand, and wanted her more than he wanted anything, even the yellow-haired barmaid in Queanbeyan, and he did not know what to do about it. He thought of letting her go free to be lost, but she was too precious. She would make back to Ten Creeks Run for a certainty, but someone might nab her on the way. Lordy, what he would not give to be safe in Victoria or Queensland with that little beauty to do what he liked with! She would be a comfortable living for any man. And that — old Skinny Guts not only had a horse like this but the Corroboree and the Wamgambril and a dozen others. It was not fair, while other fellers just as good, and even better, had not a moke of their own. While he stood there riven by infatuation and covetousness a light turned out of the public lane into the private one beside the orchard.

Curse it! Someone was coming home early. If he dropped the filly she would follow him and he would be found out. The phaeton lights were nearing him in the narrow lane. He took the

66

expedient occurring to his wits, slipped the saddle off and came boldly forward with the filly, leading her by a bridle-rein only. He saw Poole in the light of the lamp as he opened the gate.

"Is that you, Mr Poole?"

"Yes, who's there?"

"Me—Billy Bowes. I found this here little lady down by the bridge. She must have got outer somewhere. Where will I put her?"

"She was in the orchard, but there is no use in putting her there again if she got out."

"Golly, if she got out of the orchard she is a caution—worse than the ole mare!"

"Take her round to the stable."

"All right, Mr Poole. Can I let the horse out for you?"

"No, thank you, Billy. I'm going back to the Hall. Thank you for bringing the filly back. Miss Milly would have been upset to lose her."

"Yes, it'd be terrible to think how Miss Milly would take on if anything happened this here filly."

Poole left his charge at the New House of the old homestead, and as Aileen protested that she was all right, he went straight back with Mrs Isaacs's chariot. He offered Billy a lift.

"No, thanks, Mr Poole. I left me horse down here."

Billy went away towards the river. Why hadn't he brought the filly back to the main entrance, pondered Poole, as the ancient mare jogged along at her unmendable pace. Bowes could not have found the filly unless she was out on the highway. What could he be doing in the river paddocks? However, his thoughts reverted to Aileen. What on earth did old Jack mean, jumping into the young people's hash and acting like—like a death adder. He smiled as he thought of Milly. The little girl was waiting for him when he returned the phaeton to its position. He was amused by her grandmotherly air.

"Well, Milly, old pal, everything all right, I hope."

"Oh yes, Uncle Bert. Ronald and Uncle Jack nearly made a scene. They had a lot of that—I don't know how to pronounce it, but it is spelled c-h-o-l-e-r, and they were very rude to me, but I think I prevented a f-r-a-c-a-s—that's what it is, isn't it?"

"So they were rude to you, were they?" He smiled when she detailed what had taken place.

"Excessively. But I don't mind because of the c-h-o-l-e-r."

"Well, you know, Milly, it's a good thing to keep out of the other fellow's rows, and to have as few of your own as possible. You'll never get any thanks for jumping in, and you might come a cropper, but that was certainly good sense about settling the matter by asking Aileen."

"Yes, you'd hardly believe that grown men could have been so silly as not to think of that, would you?"

"I'm afraid there are more silly people than the other sort knocking about for us to knock up against, and that being so I want to make a bargain with you."

"Oh yes, Uncle Bert. Is it something nice and exciting, can we have it for a *compact*?"

"I should think we could. It is only this: supposing you should ever be in a mess of any sort, a difficulty, it doesn't matter what, and it doesn't matter if it is your own fault, you'll come and tell me all about it, won't you? And no matter how bad it may be, I'll pull you out, if I can, without any croaking. Now do you promise?"

"Oh yes, Uncle Bert. It sounds more solemn than exciting: that will be a real *compact*."

"Yes, a *compact*."

CHAPTER 6

EXHAUSTED BY bodily and emotional activity and aided by a glass of wine, Aileen slept heavily. She awoke a little bewildered to find herself in a tiny white room with a boy's guns and bats on the wall and a pain in her head. Recollection revealed her plight between Dice and Stanton. There was bliss in recalling the passages with Ronald on the log beside the river with its song so sweet and cool —and wild first kisses. She thrilled again and again in remembrance. Then intervened thoughts of that horrid old Stanton, and Joanna and Larry reprimanding her, and Ronald glaring, and now Pa to be faced. If only she could stay in the little room and be ill with brain fever for months and months so that her father would withdraw his objection to Ronald to save her life; or if Ronald would only come and take her away somewhere so that no one would see them again till they had been comfortably married for ages, and had a beautiful home!

"I see you are awake," said old Mrs Philip, entering the room. "You were nice and quiet here. How do you feel?"

"It's my head. It has such a terrible pain in it that I can't lift it from the pillow."

"Lie still, then. I expect you were too much in the sun in your hot riding-habit. It was a very warm day yesterday. I'll send you a nice strong cup of tea."

The tea came with Marcia, Charlotte's granddaughter, a girl about Milly's age.

"I say, Aileen," she began, eager to get ahead of that Milly, who assumed the airs of a grown-up. "Wasn't it exciting last night? It must be wonderful to have men loving you as much as that! They looked murder at each other. Ron Dice stayed here last night and has asked Grandma when he can see you. Uncle Jack Stanton came immediately after breakfast and asked how you were, and said he wanted to see you too. What are you going to do?"

"I don't know. I should love to see Ronnie."

"I'm glad you like him best. If Ronnie proposed to me I could very nearly marry him myself, and he's only a sort of second cousin. Why don't you get dressed and I'll tell Ron to sneak round and see you."

Marcia's mother was a niece of SP-over-J, the daughter of his brother. Marcia's father was Philip Mazere, the third of his name, and Bert Poole's nephew. He was now known as young Philip. Charlotte (Poole) and her husband had become old Mr and Mrs Philip, and the original old Mrs Philip was now Great-grandma to all whether they had the blood-right to the title or not. Old Mr and Mrs Philip lived in the Big House of the conglomerate homestead. Great-grandma had retired to the Old House, the erection that had superseded the pioneer humpy to which she had come from Parramatta in the thirties. Aileen was in a room in the new house built for young Philip when he married. Young Philip had grown up with Great-grandpa Mazere and had managed the place for him when all his sons left him.

Aileen straightway dressed. The thought of seeing Ronnie banished the pain in her head. Marcia, enchanted to be in such an affair, assisted her, talking volubly.

"Everybody said you were the belle last night. Cousin Dot was quite in the shade. They were tired of her dress because they had seen it before. She danced with your brother Larry, and only danced with Ronnie after you disappeared so mysteriously. Everyone was talking about that. They thought all sorts of things when they found that the belle of the ball had disappeared."

When Aileen was ready Marcia told Ronald. Charlotte returned to the Big House. She had been her brother's messenger and he agreed that the best thing for Aileen was to lie still for an hour or two longer.

"Aileen has a splitting headache, Uncle Jack," his niece Maud (young Mrs Mazere, wife of Philip the third) was reporting to him. "Mamma came over and saw her this morning and said she was to have a cup of tea and keep quiet. Mamma thinks she may have been a little too much in the sun yesterday."

"I wanted to drive her home today, but the best place is here with you. You'll take care that she is kept quiet and sees no one."

"Yes, Uncle Jack . . . There is a good deal of talk. Of course I have said nothing, but are you thinking of giving me an aunt?"

SP-over-J, always gauche, looked foolish, nursed his knee, and replied, "Yes, it's true. I think it's about time I settled down, don't you?"

"Well—er, of course, we've often wondered why you didn't, long ago. Only Aileen is rather young, isn't she?"

"Oh, I don't know. It's not as if she were a girl in her teens. I was never more grown up than when I was her age."

"What will Aunt Lucy do?"

"Lucy might marry and leave me alone; besides, she could still look after Ten Creeks when I'm not there, or Turrill Turrill the same way. She likes tigrinizing back and forth."

While this talk extended in the front room Aileen repledged herself among the raspberry canes and lilac-bushes at the foot of the garden whither the lovers had fled, and Marcia and Amy tittered together in a handy retreat.

"Aileen!"

"Ronnie!"

He clasped her to him, renewing the rapture of last night. She was as beautiful in her trim habit as she had been in the frilly ball gown.

"How did the old Death Adder get the notion that you are engaged to him?"

"I don't know. He must have misunderstood in some way. I was anxious to get rid of him, because the girls were coming, and he took too much for granted."

"Just like him! You must give him the straight tip the first moment he says anything to you. You will, won't you?"

"Oh yes."

"I'll announce our engagement at once and that will chuck him out of the field."

"Yes, but, Ronnie, how soon can we be married?"

"Just as soon as I can fix up with Mamma."

"Oh, Ronnie, must you wait for that?"

"I'm afraid I must, but Mamma will soon come round."

"Then I think we had better say nothing about the . . . about us being engaged for the present."

"But if we don't you'll have the old Death Adder dancing round."

"Unless you can marry me and take me away at once. Oh, Ronnie, I'm frightened." Aileen melted into tears.

"Whatever is there to be frightened of, darling?" He was all tenderness. She was irresistible in tears.

"I'm not frightened if I could only stay near you all the time, but I've got to face Pa."

"He can't eat you, and you are over twenty-one."

"That doesn't make any difference. You don't know Pa."

"I'll go up and tell him my plans—face the lion in his den. Do you feel like riding straight off with me now?"

"I couldn't run away from Mrs Mazere like that and get into everybody's black books. Besides, Mr Poole promised Joanna to drive me home himself today. She wouldn't have left me else."

"We don't need to drag good old Bert into it now that you are

71

able to ride. We could make Bookaledgeree for dinner and tell Mamma and the girls and get them on our side from the jump."

"I'm sure Mrs Lucy Saunders and Mrs Ned Stanton don't want me either," said Aileen miserably.

"Don't they! That's fine, then, because they won't be any help to the old Death Adder."

At this moment Marcia kited down the orchard and warned that Mother was coming to see if Aileen was well enough to talk to Uncle Jack. "Run away and hide, Ronald," exhorted Marcia.

"What for? It's your old Uncle Jack who ought to hide his head in shame. I wish I could make myself larger and more prominent," said Ronald, standing forth defiantly where the summer sun shone dazzlingly on the slope and melted away in cool inviting shade among the willows by the singing river where the lazy cattle dozed and the dark-green tobacco grew luxuriantly.

Dice refused to be banished. He escorted Aileen to the veranda. Young Mrs Philip had been reared in the notion that Uncle Jack was not to be trifled with, and the attitude in which nieces are generally disposed towards rich bachelor uncles. To help him to marriage would end the hope of inheriting his property, but to oppose him would not advance her status as a prospective heiress either. The feeling held that Uncle Jack had better not be crossed.

"Dear me, Miss Healey, I thought your head was too bad to lift from the pillow." Mrs Mazere's tone was not sympathetic.

"I thought I'd see how it was, and now I'll have to go and lie down again. It's terrible." The girl was postponing a direct and conclusive issue by edging towards the bedroom.

"Uncle Jack is riding up towards Neangen today and he thought to take you with him."

"Mr Poole promised to drive me up. I hardly feel able to ride."

"I hadn't heard of that arrangement," said Mrs Philip a little stiffly. Aileen seemed a shilly-shallier, and the Mazere clan did not revere that of Healey for the old action about Eureurunda. It was a pity Uncle Jack hadn't sense to pick someone more suitable. However, she'd rather Ronald married Aileen than have her for an aunt. Actuated by this bias she said, "You lie down sensibly and don't be eating hot raspberries on an empty stomach. I'll tell Uncle Jack that probably you won't be going home till tomorrow."

"Oh yes, please, Mrs Mazere, that is very kind of you," said Aileen, straw-clutching. She went to her room. Young Mrs Philip returned to her uncle. Dice disported himself where Stanton could not leave the premises without seeing him.

"Miss Healey really has a terrible head," reported Mrs Philip.

"It's nothing serious, I hope. Does she want a doctor?"

"No. She's a bilious subject, I should think, by the look of her. With a bilious person any little excitement always results in one of these attacks. She needs to lie still and eat nothing."

"Oh well, then, I'll push along, because I have a busy day. You can . . . you can give Aileen my love."

"Very well, Uncle. I suppose I ought to kiss you and congratulate you. You mustn't forget your old niece wants to be loved too, even when you have a new wife," she said, embracing him.

"Oh no, no, of course not," he said awkwardly, but she could see that he was pleased.

As he emerged upon the veranda there was Ronald Dice fooling with Marcia and Amy. Uncle Jack turned back into the passage. "What's he doing here?"

"Every bed in the Big House was full, so they asl ed us to put him up."

"He could easily have ridden home. I don't think you'll find him a fit companion for the girls."

"He doesn't come here much," she said comfortingly.

"The less the better. Don't let him worry Aileen."

The sight of Dice put harsher determination into the day's action for Stanton. He was closeted with the bank manager for a long session in conjunction with Arthur Rankin, the lawyer. Then he had dinner at M'Haffety's Hotel, a rare condescension. Skinny Guts was rarely known to shell out his money for tucker when there were clan members at hand to cosher himself upon.

*　　*　　*　　*　　*

He progressed comfortably towards Neangen on his fine blood horse, paced by Flash Billy, taking note of the land as he went. Soon he was riding the boundary of Bookaledgeree, a fine property when Tim Brennan had sold it to the Dices, but mismanaged ever since. There had been foot-rot in the flocks—it was to be seen from the main road—and would be again as soon as the drought broke. The old cockatoo fences, perfunctorily topped, wouldn't stop a milking cow, and there were fields of briars dragging the fleeces off the flocks. There must have been hundredweights of wool tufted about the paddocks.

Stanton's mind went back about thirty-five years to when they used to admire the sweet briar-bush in old Mrs Mazere's garden, which old Mazere prized so much because it was English, and which had been a rare plant to the native-born . . . By Jove! old Mrs Mazere had little dreamt then what a bad thing she was doing for the country.

Beyond the homestead the Yarrabongo showed in cool beauty

between its drapery of shrubs, and ahead was the Bookaledgeree Creek, another fine stream. It was one of the best-watered places in the colony and had a good deal of open grazing land. It needed pulling together, though, and instead of doing that Ronald Dice was always dressed up in knee-breeches and long spurs riding about on a flash horse and fooling with the girls. Well, there was one girl he wouldn't be able to fool with much longer. Stanton had satisfaction in the scope and power of his mortgages.

The reports from all over the country were of an old-man drought. The weather could break even now, though Stanton had never known a spring drought to break before autumn. This meteorological experience was corroborated by every old hand he knew, both those of the Plains and the green grass country. Turrill Turrill was suffering, but he could shift surplus stock to the mountains. Bool Bool and all that country from Ten Creeks to the Upper Murru noidgee and right back to Coolooluk and Mungee via Monaro was a world of its own, the value of which could not yet be computed. Future generations would awake to it. A native of the green grass country, the love of these wonderful ranges, streams, and valleys held first place in Stanton's affections.

He reached Neangen as Larry, jun., was penning the calves for the night. Old Larry gave warning to the women and went to receive him.

"We've been expecting Aileen and Bert Poole all the afternoon. Aileen is all right, I hope."

"All but a bilious headache. Young Mrs Philip is in charge of her and they talk of driving up tomorrow. Aileen is all right there."

"She couldn't be righter anywhere except with her own mother," responded Larry, satisfied for Aileen to be in the famous Mazere headquarters under the direct guardianship of Stanton's niece. "Come in! Come in! Leave your horse. Larry will put him away for the night."

"I was thinking of riding back in the cool."

"What's your hurry? 'Twill be cool enough in the morning."

"I'm rather pushed for time. This drought—though we don't feel it much here—terrible in Riverina. I want to get away without delay and see the state of the stock and grass, but I wanted to leave this matter about Aileen fixed up."

"Sure, we can talk that over this evening when the family has gone to bed. There's no hurry, and you or the girl might want to change your mind. There's others in the field." Old Larry laughed and showed his long tobacco-stained fangs. He had had time to collect himself and to decide upon the most profitable hand to play. Old Jack was biting hard and greedily.

The prospective bridegroom went inside to be greeted by the women, to have a wash in the spare-room, and to sit on the veranda in the cool among the roses till summoned to the evening meal. Afterwards the family engaged in singing round the piano.

"Sure, it's a pity Aileen isn't home. She's our musician," said old Larry. "She can play anything at all and she sings like a canary."

SP-over-J decided to get a new piano for Turrill Turrill and to send the old one up to Ten Creeks Run.

While the evening was still young Mrs Healey ordered the children to bed, and said she would go herself because she had not yet recovered from the bridge celebrations. Joanna and Norah murmured something about a batch of bread. Larry, jun., went to look at the horses and did not come back.

SP-over-J was not a word-waster and never bilked a vital issue.

"Well, since I'm in a hurry to get away and likely shan't be back till after Christmas, I thought I'd just ride up to confirm what I put forward about Aileen last night."

"That's all right, Jack. There's no hurry."

"As a matter of fact there is, rather. I want to get back to Riverina early this autumn. I'll just come up for the wedding, and I'm ready for that in January, as soon as Aileen can get ready."

"Oh my, oh me! a man in love! What a hurry we're in! You must remember I haven't had time to hear what my little Aily thinks yet."

"She has accepted, and you are agreeable. We don't have to consider anyone else as I can see."

"That is very fine as far as it goes, but a young girl in love doesn't look much ahead, and though I've had rather hard luck of late years, and Neangen is not to be compared with Eueurunda, where Aily was born, nor yet with Little River, where my father started, but still an' all we're a very affectionate family and our little Aily is welcome to stay with us for ever unless we could be sure that she was bettering herself."

"I'm well able to provide for a wife and family and to give Aileen as much as she's had with you, and a great deal more."

"Oh, sure. I know that, Jack. Your whole family were always thrifty, enterprising fellows, but it's this way: when I married Aily's mother, the old woman, my mother-in-law, would not let me have her till I settled a nice little nest-egg upon her, and she always said it was such a blessing that she will expect the same for her daughters."

SP-over-J marvelled that this piece of business had never leaked out, though what every other husband in the district got with or gave his bride was popular gossip. However, he expected to have to weight his scales against the love in Dice's balance. "I think you'll find me satisfactory there. I mean to provide for her in my will, and as a wedding present, do you think she would be satisfied that I shouldn't press the mortgage I hold on Neangen—for sentimental reasons she might like it though it's not very valuable; or she might prefer Bookaledgeree . . ." Stanton smiled slyly in his beard and watched the effect of this.

It winded old Larry, but he was a good poker-player and took some long puffs on his pipe before replying. Then he knocked out the ashes and chose a stalk of the lovely trembling grass nodding its beads by the veranda-post and cleared the stem and puffed and blew and spat before trusting himself to speak, but he didn't deceive SP-over-J.

"Well, now, that's rather handsome of you, Jack, but there's time—there's plenty of time. We must ask Aily herself. Sure, I've been keeping you up. Meself I had a snooze this afternoon, but probably you've been up all day, and not so young as we used to be, riding after the girls thirty years ago—or getting on forty years, isn't it?—an' the girls not as willing to jump at us as we could have wished." Old Larry got in his dig. SP-over-J did not relish it, but said nothing. Larry warbled on, "An' the girls getting more independent every generation. There's no telling them what or who they should marry these times."

"Oh well, suppose we call it a day," said Stanton. "You can let me know in a week's time what you think."

*   *   *   *   *

From Dice's end the drama proceeded gaily. By noon on the day following the ball all the township discussed it. The notoriety of the happenings at the ball and the attentions of Stanton had established pretty little Aileen as an exciting beauty. Ronald had youth, the popularity of personal charm, and a crushing mortgage on his family's property: SP-over-J was never a favourite with men or maids from his youth, and now age was against him, but he owned much property. Their handicaps and assets made the men's rivalry lively entertainment for the onlookers.

As Stanton was riding back to Bool Bool he saw Poole, true to promise, conducting Aileen to Neangen. With him in the Three Rivers buggy were his sister Charlotte, Aileen, and Marcia. Behind them rode a boy to take the buggy back from Bookaledgeree. The boy was leading Miss Muffet, and Poole's big bay ran tractably on the off-side of the fat Three Rivers pair. They met where the main road bounds Bookaledgeree, sloping away to the Yarrabongo on one side and facing the cool peaks of the Bogongs up the valley of Bookaledgeree Creek on the other.

"Aileen, are you quite well?" inquired SP-over-J, drawing to the back seat, where she was sitting.

"Oh yes, thank you, Mr Stanton. It was only a bilious headache. I am going to ride home from Bookaledgeree."

"I left your colt in charge of young Philip at Three Rivers. I never handled a better-tempered animal. Anything else was on account of bad handling, whether intentional or otherwise I don't wish to say without complete evidence, but I advise you to keep your eyes open," said Poole.

"What do you mean?"

"I'll have more time to explain when we meet again."

"I'm off to Turrill Turrill at once," replied SP-over-J, watching the effect on Aileen, but she tilted her parasol, and it was Marcia who was delighted by the radiant relief that lit the lovely little face.

"Oh well, it can go for the present. We must be getting on or we'll keep Mrs Dice late for dinner."

SP-over-J did not approve of this descent upon Bookaledgeree, but in view of family entrenchments did not know what to say. He thought for a moment of turning in with the buggy, but lacked the dash, and let the moment pass. He said nothing, deciding to allow his mortgages to do the talking with old Healey. He dismounted to shake hands with old Mrs Philip so that he could also shake hands with Aileen. She was careful to reach across Marcia for that, and SP-over-J had to be content with, "Well, good-bye for the present, little girl. Take care of yourself!"

Aileen looked back after him and waved her hand, relief in all her being. Uncle Jack's words had such delicious significance for Marcia that she kept digging Aileen in the ribs and repeating "Little girl, take care of yourself!" in heated whispers. Aileen accepted this without protest, in the spirit in which it was tendered. She was a gentle soul.

Her satisfaction in being rid of Stanton was diminished by her reception by the Dices. Ronald came to meet the buggy as it approached where he was loading hay from a late crop. He could not leave his work for longer than a greeting, and when the buggy went on, Marcia's repetition of "Good-bye, little girl!" increased in facetious intensity.

"Dear, oh dear!" murmured Bert to his sister in the front seat, "were we ever as gigglesome as that over nothing when we were young?"

"You and I weren't, for we had so much trouble and responsibility that it made us a pair of old sober-sides, but remember how

Grandpa Mazere was always snorting about the silly 'skitting' of the young people."

The watch-dogs of Bookaledgeree announced the visitors, and the family streamed forth to the stableyard to meet them.

"Well, Charlotte, this is a surprise and honour," said Mrs Dice. "It's not often you pay us a call. You've only been here once before, haven't you, when I was ill?" She kissed Marcia and shook hands with "Miss Healey".

Ida and Olive shook hands with her laughingly. "We have to congratulate you, haven't we?" said Ida. "When is the wedding to be?"

Aileen was drowned in blushes, her pulses bounded. Olive's contribution caused a drop in her temperature. "You must give us the receipt for turning such a confirmed old bachelor into a gay young lover, dancing at balls."

Marcia spluttered uncontrollably.

"That's what it is to be the belle of the bridge-opening ball. Your dress was lovely. No wonder Mr Stanton was finished," added Ida.

Poole was seeing to the horses. His sister maintained her habitual non-committal calm.

"Well, Miss Healey, it's not fair to pounce on you like that," said Mrs Dice. "But it is such a surprise. Jack Stanton has had the reputation of a woman-hater for so long, but you can never trust any man where a pretty girl is concerned. I expect your brother will be the next to collapse and startle us," she turned to Charlotte.

"I wish he would," said she quietly. "If only he got some nice woman of a sensible age to take care of him."

"But there'd be no romance in that, would there, Miss Healey?" cried Ida.

"Come inside into the cool. Isn't it a dreadful drought we're having? I've never seen the garden so dried up." Mrs Dice went ahead with Charlotte.

Aileen was bewildered. Hadn't Ronald informed his family, or had they refused to accept the announcement and were battening down the engagement with SP-over-J to get rid of her? What was she to do? "You're all making some mistake or only funning," she said, so near tears that the murmur was scarcely audible.

She did not see Ronald till they assembled in the dining-room. Marcia was curious beyond articulation. Aileen looked towards Ronald appealingly. His face reassured her.

"Aileen, you must sit beside me," he said, but Mrs Dice, who wielded the carving-knife, thought otherwise.

"No. Charlotte will sit on my left and Bert on my right. You will go next to Charlotte . . ."

"All right, and Aileen on the other side."

"Couldn't think of it," cried Ida gaily. "We'd make an enemy of SP-over-J for life."

"We're not going to care about him. He's only a last year's stack of hay." Ronald was gayer than Ida.

"Even that won't be sneezed at if this drought doesn't break," said Mrs Dice.

"You had better keep me company, Aileen," said Poole kindly, to succour the girl in her evident distress, and exercising the privilege he enjoyed in all the houses of the clan.

"That will be lovely," she responded gratefully, slipping into the seat which Ida had designed for herself, and from which she could not remove Aileen as Poole laid his hand protectingly on the back of the chair.

After dinner Aileen felt that the whole household was bent on preventing her from seeing Ronald alone. She insisted on riding to Neangen, an arrangement that was accepted because it permitted Charlotte and Marcia to return to town that afternoon. Ronald put her on her horse, and while placing his hand for her toe managed to say, "Aileen, I'm coming up to see your father the day after tomorrow at latest. I must get this bit of hay in first. We are short-handed."

"Oh, Ronnie, then it is all right."

"Of course, you silly little chicken, what did you take me for?"

"I'm so tired of hearing about old SP-over-J. They all act as if I was engaged to him."

"Let them have all the fun they want. Our turn is coming."

"But you don't know Pa: and what was SP-over-J doing up this way? He must have been at Neangen."

"Well, he is off to Turrill Turrill without waiting to say his prayers. That looks as if he jolly well knew his cake is dough."

"Sssh!"

A touch to Aileen's toe and she was safely in her saddle and took the reins, which Ronald placed in her fingers with an enveloping hand-clasp that spoke volumes of reassurance. Good-byes were repeated, and Aileen rode away in comfort with Curradoo-bidgee Poole.

"A pretty little thing," said his sister, who never said unkind words of any.

"Pretty enough, but dear me, a weak-looking little creature—doesn't seem as if there was much ballast there. I don't like the breed. I'm surprised at Jack Stanton at his time of life." Mrs Dice had raised her voice so that Ronald should not miss a word. He was waving his straw hat to Aileen, looking handsome and appropriate to the weather in white ducks, hastily donned for dinner. He went away to change again for his haymaking, pretending not to hear his mother.

❖   ❖   ❖   ❖   ❖

Poole and Aileen journeyed peacefully through the blazing summer afternoon, delightful beside the singing streams in deep, cool, fern-clad gullies. Giants of the untouched forests shaded the winding bush road round the spurs of the Bogongs whence they could see for miles along the Yarrabongo, now become the Mungee. Its course was marked by the river gums and draped in blossoming shrubs away beyond the fish-hole where the *Ornithorhyncus paradoxus* romped like dolphins near sunset and reared their young in the banks.

"I think there can be nothing better than that in the world in natural scenery, as far as I have seen on the stereoscope," remarked Poole.

"Yes, it is pretty, but very lonely," replied Aileen. "So many hills always seem to smother me, till I am frightened, and the river sounds like a great sad wind. I like Monaro much better."

"Oh, of course, Monaro beats everything else in the world, I am sure."

Conversation between them was scrappy. Poole was no talker. Neither was Aileen. She charmed in being softly responsive to the emanations of others. Not only men of all ages, but old women found her delightful for this quality alone. Poole wished to help the little girl, surrounded completely, as he judged, by persons neither sympathetic nor helpful, but Aileen gave him no opening. If young Ronald and she really wanted each other, he reflected, and their attraction was more than a flash in the pan, they were adults and surely could take care of themselves. Jack was a fool at his time of life to come between young people, and deserved to have his whiskers singed. To be off out of the district in such a hurry was a good sign, but what had he been doing in the direction of Neangen? Old Jack was a deep one in a business deal; not many could outwit him. Perhaps old Larry would let something drop on the matter.

However, Larry could be as close as SP-over-J when it suited him, and Poole learnt nothing. Aileen arriving with Poole after a couple of days with Stanton's niece put Larry in good humour.

"Well, my girl, too much excitement and dissipation," he said affectionately. "Sure, you'll only be young once, so you do well to make the best of it." Aileen was relieved but not deceived by the family affection poured out before Poole. She retired to her little skillion bedroom. Julie, who shared it with her, went too, carrying her sister's valise.

"How have things been—any ructions with Pa?"

"My, yes! When Larry and Joanna left you behind with Ronald Dice mooching round we thought the roof would come off, but it's been all seganio since old Skinny Guts came up yesterday and fixed everything up about marrying you."

"Was he here?"

"Yes. He stayed till this morning."

"Fixed up everything—whatever do you mean?" Aileen felt it would be heavenly if she could faint till everything was satisfactory for her and Ronald.

"I listened. I sat inside the door of the drorin'-room in the dark while SP-over-J and Pa was on the veranda. You'll be awful rich. I'm going to live with you. Joanna and Norah will be as jealous as old cats, but I'd rather have Ronald Dice."

Aileen felt as if a steel net were suspended above her.

"Let me have room to dress now, there's a good girl." Julie departed, desirous of improving her chances with Mr Poole. She hoped he would give her a pony like the one he had given Milly Saunders.

Aileen flung herself on the wallaby-skin beside her bed, but comfort would not come. She did not know how to pray except to repeat something by rote night and morning. What with the original Larry's terrific row with the Church, which had resulted in excommunication, and the second generation having married heretics, but without adopting a new faith, religion in Larry's family had degenerated into remnant superstitions more hampering than helpful.

Catching at present straws, Aileen was thankful for the presence of Poole for the night and the consequent postponement of her troubles. All was geniality with old Larry showing off the affection of his elder daughters and bidding them sing, though it were better artistically that they first had died. If one daughter had captured old SP-over-J, the toughest matrimonial nut to crack in the whole district, another might secure Poole. Neither Joanna nor Norah had Aileen's looks, but Poole was not so austere as Stanton, and one match often helped another.

Aileen said good-bye to Poole next morning with a sinking heart, and he had no sooner been lost from sight than her affectionate father called her to an interview. He began all right. "Well, Aily child, you've done very well for yourself. It will be a great lift to us all, and you'll be rollin' in silks and luxury ahead of the whole crew that out of jealousy has tried to snub us."

"What do you mean, Pa?" inquired Aileen faintly, wishing the floor would hide her.

"You want to be a little coy about it, do you, but, sure, Mr Stanton hasn't let any grass grow under his feet. He wants ye to name the first day after the New Year. But, sure, ye needn't be too hurried for a week or two, or maybe a month—ye've got him in the palm of your hand, and now's the time to extract the best turrums." Larry showed the least result of the good governesses that his mother had secured, and in moments of stress relapsed into the bog-trotter brogue of his parents.

"But, Pa, I never said I'd marry Mr Stanton. I h—— I don't like him." Aileen's voice was faint.

"Well, thin, he's so eager that all ye have to do is sit quiet while I get the most elegant turrums an old man ever laid out for his darling."

"But, Pa, I don't want any terms from Mr Stanton. He must be crazy."

"Sure, he's crazy with love, and that's a fine thing in a lover, especially if he's old and rich."

"But, Pa, he's a horrid, skinny old man, as old as you are."

"Och, that counts nothing in love's young dream."

"But, Pa . . ." Aileen felt impelled to insist upon love's young dream, but faltered and left it to Ronald. One day more now and he would be at Neangen. She must stave off talk of Stanton till then.

"Pa, I don't like Mr Stanton. Please don't plague me about the horrid old creature." Aileen was rescued by tears. They had more effect than anything even with old Larry when he was not at bay, and brought the temporary relief so ardently desired.

"Well, well, now. A little soft excitement is natural. We don't have to make up our minds about the day in a hurry." He let her go to her room and commanded the others, "Sure, leave the child be for a day or two. She's a bit startled about it all for the present."

"Pooh!" said Julie, as the old man left the sisters together in the kitchen—they had dispensed with a servant owing to hard times. "Aileen won't have old Skinny while Ronnie is about, and I don't blame her. I wouldn't either, would you, Norah?"

"It would depend on whether I loved him."

"Would you, Joanna?"

"You bet I'd love anyone as rich as old SP-over-J, even if it was Teddy O'Mara. Aileen would be a fool not to jump at such a chance. She could cover the floor with sovereigns if she liked."

"You mean if old Skinny liked," said the astute Julie. "I wish Ronnie had the money. Why is it that nice people have no money and the rich ones are always nasty?"

"I know lots who are both poor and nasty," said Joanna, "and I prefer the rich variety."

❀   ❀   ❀   ❀   ❀

Aileen restlessly awaited Saturday. She expected Ronald about sundown, but the sun was still high when she began to peer down the road that showed for half a mile before it disappeared in the stately timber to reappear as a white gash rounding a spur where the trees had been cut down beside the telegraph line. Her father, enjoying his Saturday-afternoon laze on the veranda, was facetious. "Sure, the mailman will assume great importance, though belike an old man will talk more through his cheque-book and leave the sentimental twaddle to them that has nothing else."

Aileen was relieved to accept the mailman as cover. The hoary old rascal on his ambling brumby followed by his piebald screw with the packs did raise the dust round the spur an hour before Ronald, and brought Aileen a letter in an unfamiliar hand.

"Sure," said old Larry, "is that what you've been lookin' for, and ye tryin' to persuade me against me senses?"

Aileen went to her bedroom with the letter, but the curious and indelicate Julie also had right of entry there and plumped herself on her bed, staring and unabashed. "Aren't you going to open it? Is it from Ronnie or old Skinny? Show me the writing."

"Do run away and leave me alone."

"I will if you will show me the letter."

Aileen popped it down the front of her gown and ran up the orchard. Julie pursued, piping shrilly, "Aileen has put her letter down her front and won't open it."

"You come here or I'll give you a lift under the ear," said Pa, and Aileen escaped. She got out of the orchard by climbing a quince-tree, thence to the hay-shed on the hill. Hidden in the sweet new hay she felt safer and opened the letter, every minute raising her eyes to that streak on the spur for a delivering horseman.

STANTON'S PLAINS,
BOOL BOOL
Thursday Night.

My Little Darling,

I hardly know how to begin my first letter to you. There is so much I should like to say to you and tell you but I will make it short as I must be away at daybreak to Riverina. This is not the season for a man to neglect his business and I must attend to business more than ever now so that I can give you everything that your little heart desires. After you said the wonderful words which made me such a lucky man on Tuesday night, I went home hardly believing it could be true and that I a somewhat older man could have such a prize ahead of young fellows full of poetry and sentimentality.

I was sorry I could not see you next morning but I wasted no time but rode straight up to see your father, which I think was the right thing to do. I was on my way back when I met you with the Pooles today and was glad to see that you had quite recovered. Well, as you will know before this reaches you, I had a nice talk with your father and you will be happy to know that he offers no objections at all and was most welcoming to me and willing to trust his little girl to me. The only thing now is for you to name the day that will make me an even happier man than I am now, and I want it to be as soon after New Year as possible. I am eager to have my little darling in a position where I can give her all that her little heart desires. . . .

There were pages and pages. SP-over-J, like many silent people, babbled like a brook on paper, those uninteresting weedy brooks in flat country. Aileen, looking up for the fifteenth time, saw the desired figure, and slipped behind bushes safe from observation across the cow paddock to the highway. The approaching horseman flung off his shying beast with extravagant athleticism when he was yet some yards distant.

"Oh, Ronnie, I thought you'd never come! I never want to part from you again," she exclaimed, her cheek against his, her arms tight round his neck.

"Tell me, darling."

"It has been terrible. You heard them all at Bookaledgeree, and it has been the same ever since. Everyone has it settled that I am engaged to old SP-over-J, and the mailman has brought me a letter from him yards long. Oh, Ronnie, you'd think I was married to him already to read it. What am I to do?"

"Put his old screed in the fire and tell him to go and bag his old head. If he can't take a hint he'll have to be given a good bump."

"I've been careful not to stir up things, but I'm afraid of trouble with Pa, and your mother did not seem to want me."

"We can't let fathers or mothers stand in our way. We aren't children."

"I'll slip back through the horse paddock now."

"No fear! You aren't ashamed of me, are you?"

"Oh no, but there will be such ructions."

"The more the merrier if only things are settled. Come on, let's gamely open the ball." He tucked her arm in his, but the dogs, accepting Aileen's introduction, failed to make a noise and no one witnessed their approach. They had to go right inside to be seen. Old Healey said "Good evening" cordially. He was never inhospitable. Young Larry inquired, "Did you put your horse in the stable?"

"No, I hung him up."

"You're not making home tonight?"

"No. I came specially to see Aileen and your father."

"Good! I'll let your horse out." People liked young Larry. He was genial and obliging.

Supper was an uneasy meal to Aileen with delight and fear intermingled. Joanna and Norah looked on enviously. The "ructions" element of having a lover one loved would not have weighed so heavily on them as did the lack of all but dud eligibles. One such arrived a few minutes later than Dice. He had been teetering round for ages. The family could not decide whether it was Norah or Joanna he favoured, but Norah had the more patience so to her he was credited. Old Larry said he only wanted a place whereat to spend Saturday night in the summer. This was Alf Timson, son of old Timson of Wombat Hill, Monaro, a bachelor ten years younger than Larry *père*, who managed a summer station at Billy-go-Billy twenty miles up the Jenningningahama. He was of the early pioneer families and better than nothing. He followed all the motions of other men, but lacked style. He was useful now to preserve normality, and in the drawing-room after dinner kept his end up by singing "Juanita" in a reedy drawl with his eyes closed. He stuck to his host after the singing for a good-night pipe. Ronald did likewise. Old Healey talked politics.

"Damn old sleepy sawney Alf! Why the deuce can't he make himself scarce?" thought Dice, but at last was forced to retire, and to the same room as Alfred, without having put his case.

He rose early, but Alf also forwent beauty sleep, while old Healey took a treble share. Ronald saw that opportunity had to be made. They rode out during the morning to see some travelling sheep pass to a station farther up the Jenningningahama and Dice said, "Mr Healey, I came up to have a few words with you about an important matter. Will you come on ahead, now?"

"Sure, you're free to say anything to me you like."

"Well, Mr Healey, Aileen and I have made up our minds to get married and I thought I'd like a talk with you about it."

"You've made up your minds, you say, you don't mean Aileen has?"

85

"Oh yes, I do. Aileen has made me very happy by returning my affection. I have her promise and we want your goodwill so that we can publish the engagement."

"Hold on, now, not so fast. What has Aileen said that makes you think this?"

"Everything that is necessary, Mr Healey."

"This is rather complicated. Stanton of Turrill Turrill has been before you with a very open-handed offer to make handsome provision for my daughter. What provision do you propose to make? How much of Bookaledgeree can you settle on your wife?"

"I haven't had time to accumulate old SP-over-J's money-bags yet, but Aileen prefers love in a cottage to begin, and long before I'm old Skinny's age we'll have more than we need."

"You'll soon find that this love in a cottage is no match for the bailiff. Sure, this love they talk about doesn't last over the honeymoon, but a good solid property and money in the bank is the greatest comfort there is to the young and the old all their lives. The longer they're married the more firmly they'll find out the truth of that."

"Money is a handy thing to have about the house, all right, but it's not the chief thing at this stage of the game. It is much more that Aileen and I are cut out for each other and don't mind how much hard work is ahead of us."

"That sounds very fine, but, me lad, have ye anything to call your own at all?" Larry's own financial plight enabled him to put his finger unerringly on Dice's. Foot by foot he exposed the young man's prospects as having nothing more solid than hope behind them, hope founded more on optimism than business acumen. Everything was Mrs Dice's, mortgaged over the limit, and in bad repair. Even the horse Ronald rode could not have been separated from the estate in the event of foreclosure. The case of Bookaledgeree was that of Neangen only that Mrs Dice's was the more valuable property. It was nearer to town and had more detimbered acreage, though where the scrub had been extirpated, briars high as houses and denser than a wall with tearing thorns had taken its place.

Driven in a corner, Ronald said, "At any rate, Aileen and I think a tremendous lot of each other. It would be a sin and a shame for either of us to think of anyone else, feeling as we do. Aileen is nearly twenty-three and I am going on for twenty-four, so we hope, even though you think we are foolish, that we shall have your consent and good wishes."

"No child of mine would have my consent to sacrifice herself to poverty while every luxury was waiting for her. It is my duty as a father to see to that. This talk about love is not worth that," said Healey, snapping his fingers. "People ought to be held down for such lunacy while common sense is left to those surrounding them, so I'd thank you to say no more of this to Aileen."

"You surely wouldn't want Aileen to marry without the proper affection, no matter how much money the man had?"

"In this case Aileen will be thankin' me a year from now. She is an innocent little gurrl and doesn't know her own mind. There are plenty others, you go pick one of them now like a sensible fellow. Why not one of those young Saunderses or Stantons with a nice little nest-egg behind them belike, and leave Aily be. 'Tis the chance of her life. Sure, she doesn't know her own mind. She's a trifle bemoidered with all the fuss and attention, a modestly reared little gurrl like she is!"

"She's a grown woman. Let us have her tell us herself what she wishes when we go back to the house."

"Sure, 'tis no good of askin' them that's got the fever. 'Tis those lookin' on knows their foolish state."

He did not forbid Dice the house nor adopt an unfriendly attitude towards him. On the contrary Dice now found it as difficult to escape from his host as before it had been to take him aside. The presence of Timson was also unremitting. Curses upon the gawky booby!

He managed a few words with Aileen at parting. "Send that silly letter back to the old Death Adder and tell him he is barking up the wrong stump. Your father doesn't believe you care for me and thinks you would be happier with the money-bags. You must convince him."

"Oh, Ronnie, Pa is only pretending. I'd rather live in a salt-shed or a tent with you than at Government House with that horrid skinny old thing."

"Then you must be firm. Take no notice of the Death Adder's letters after you let him know that he is making a fool of himself. Just wait patiently, no matter what anyone says. I could put up a little two-roomed humpy on the other side of the river for us to begin."

"Oh, Ronnie, that would be divine!"

"All right, then, you go and write a letter making that as plain as the old strawberry bull and give it to me so we can be sure it is posted."

She did as bidden. She returned SP-over-J's effusion with many thanks and stated her regret that anything she had said in the embarrassment of being disturbed by Marcia and Amy had made him think what he expressed.

CHAPTER 7

AILEEN'S MISSIVE, gently worded, caused SP-over-J to write short incisive business letters to the bank and old Larry. Woe to young love when old love puts on golden spurs.

Stanton stated his inability to understand so inconsistent and heart-breaking an attitude—many sheets. He detailed his luxurious plans for Aileen—promises and offers that left all other lovers at the starting post.

Aileen wrote to Ronald. Her father intercepted the letter. There was in that locality no pillar-box with the Government as accomplice. Aileen had to depend upon others, and learnt how undependable others could be from her point of view, how careless of the axiom about a shut mouth and the flies. Her father forbade her to write to Stanton unless the letter met his ideas. He took her to Monaro and put her in charge of his sister Joanna.

This change was better for Aileen and she got a letter posted. Ronald was making a desperate effort to pull Bookaledgeree together. The season favoured him. Even Bookaledgeree was dry, the creeks lower than they had been for years, but stock can hold out indefinitely in hot weather with plenty of water, and the wicked briars proved a stand-by. The brassy unyielding skies were spreading an old-man drought on Old Man Plain, and all the plains north and west of Riverina to Bourke and Broken Hill and the great nor'-west. This meant profits from agistment to those who held runs in the mountain country, and the Dices benefited, though only slightly compared with their liabilities.

The place being stocked to the limit, the young men were full-handed. Ronald slogged all the week. The dilapidated dog-leg fences, which had not been replaced by split rail nor even stud fences, while the progressive had taken to posts and wire, entailed vigilant boundary-riding to keep sojourning stock from invading neighbouring runs. But on Saturday afternoon arrived the weekly razor hour and dressing-up prior to gallivanting, and there was nothing to prevent a hardy energetic young man in love from taking the track beaten years before when other Monaro or Bool Bool lovers had come and gone by the channel of the Jenning-ningahama.

By starting immediately after dinner on the Saturday following Aileen's removal, Ronald arrived under Poole's window by daylight.

"How's Aileen?" he inquired after waking his host.

"Asleep, I reckon, unless she's listening for you."

"Great Scott! is she here? That's luck."

Aileen had insisted upon paying her respects to old Mrs Poole, now nearly eighty-six, since Mr Poole had been so kind as to wait in Bool Bool and bring her home after the ball. She found her cousin Sheila amenable to her purpose, for she had a fancy for one of the young Pooles. Both girls revelled in their luck in being allowed to spend the week-end at Curradoobidgee.

"Have you knocked SP-over-J out of the running?"

"He's never been in as far as I am concerned. Aileen can't abide the old Death Adder. Old Larry is after the money-bags, of course. Let him go and marry 'em himself, if he wants 'em."

"Yes," said Poole equably. "You and Aileen are both of age, and if you care for each other in the right way you need not let anything block you."

"We don't mean to."

"More power to you! Old Jack, I reckon, will recover. There are plenty candidates for the job of missus of Turrill Turrill, much nearer his own age. I reckon an old man takes no end of a jump in the dark to marry a young girl. Don't you want some grub? And turn in till breakfast. There's a spare bed in the next room."

"Thanks! I put the horses in the orchard. I'm awfully glad you are on my side. Would you mind not mentioning my visit or Aileen's to anyone who would take it back to Neangen or the old Death Adder."

"I shan't spread the news. There will be plenty others to spare me the trouble. So long! See you at breakfast."

The young folks had a merry Sunday and in the evening Dice had the felicity of riding part of the way with Aileen towards her aunt Joanna. Sheila did not mention Dice's presence at Curradoobidgee. The lovers were safe for the moment.

The following Saturday Ronald followed the same procedure. Aileen was not at Curradoobidgee this time, so after breakfast Ronald rode over to Aunt Joanna's. Joanna Healey had married one of the Gilberts, and the pair had settled on the outward flanges of Gowandale, which adjoined Poole's. Aileen had had a letter asking her to meet Ronald without the family's cognizance, but the exigencies of bush homes were such that she could not wander forth for hours without being missed and arousing microscopic

89

curiosity. Ronald had to ride boldly up to the selection and call upon the family.

He was received cordially enough. Aileen appeared without any fuss among her cousins and with her Aunt Joanna—particularly with her Aunt Joanna, who had received instructions. Aileen was chaperoned to look at the flower garden and perambulate the orchard. Ronald lacked the training to carry on an impassioned yet private declaration in the teeth of a duenna as Latin beaux can do. He had to be content with whispering over a rose-bush, "You'll have to write to me."

"I'm afraid Pa has got on to us and there is no hope. Aunt Joanna is on his side."

Alf Timson had recognized the tracks of Dice's horse up past Billy-go-Billy, and, sheepish though he was, found it amusing to mention at Neangen. Young Larry, too, was yet unscathed so had neither sentimentality nor sympathy concerning young love. The money-bags were more attractive to him and he did not enjoin silence upon Alf, so when for the third time Ronald tested his horse with that stiff journey he did not find Aileen.

*   *   *   *   *

It was not so simple as Poole suggested. The bridge was opened in the middle of November, and by Christmas Ronald and Aileen's love affair had become succulent news from Monaro to Bool Bool. The male wits had bets on it; the women took sides, and most of them were for Ronald and against SP-over-J for interfering with young love's dream. The Stantons objected to the Healeys. The Dices were also firmly against having Aileen in the family. Aileen's mother, the second Mrs Larry, was only a boundary-rider's daughter. Worse, her father had been demented in his later days, and his wife had had to take a stock-whip to him to get him out of bed. He grew violent and there were gruesome stories of the numbers of men it had taken to hold him towards the end. His madness was attributed to the effects of drink on a head badly damaged by sun-stroke, and he was safely dead, but there were partisans to point out now that Mrs Healey's brother, a drover down the Bland, was a weird specimen too, as mad as a meat-axe though he had never been sun-struck. Some said Mrs Healey herself was a poor weak sort of a creature, others maintained that that was all anyone could be with old Larry. Some detractors said that Aileen was lacking in get-up-and-go, but these were all over thirty, and women at that. Aileen had merely to appear in one of the fairy dresses she made so cleverly and her unarmed gentleness set men and younger maids a-raving.

There was little unknown to those two high priestesses of family history in Bool Bool, the Mayoress and Mrs Isaacs, their penchant for news being aided by their respective callings. What one did not hear by way of gossip at the bar when whisky let discretion out, the other discovered or had corroborated in friendly confidence in the back room where accounts were settled over wine and cake—Mrs Isaacs always kept this part of the business in her own hands. Thus everything came to light as authentically as possible with mutable human affairs. There was also a great deal of gossip among the Mayor and Corporation.

"Sure, they've been tellin' me that ould Larry has sint Aileen off to Sydney to his brother Dinny," observed Mrs M'Haffety to Mrs Isaacs. "Young Ronald was trapesing up to Monaro wan Saturday night afther the other."

"Aileen will be able to write to Ronald from Sydney, unless they keep her under lock and key."

"That's thrue. I wonder will the young people win."

"Not they. They'd make a nice pair if they had everything laid out for them, but they lack the backbone. I was told for a fact that SP-over-J has the mortgages on both Neangen and Booka-ledgeree, and that puts old Larry against Ronald."

"You don't mean to say the ould jew lizard is quoite as mean as that!"

"You don't know as much as I do about people when it's a matter of money. Old Healey would sell his mother, and the Dices are not going to be turned out of house and home for a girl they are dead against in any case. Old Jack has both families properly bailed up."

"What a pity for the young people. Poor darlints!"

"They could run away if they liked. Look at me and Jacob. We hadn't a penny and had to help keep our parents and the younger ones. Jacob started out with a pound's worth of goods on his back in a box, and look at us today!"

"But thim days has gone. Sure, Aileen and Ronald couldn't start on a pound hawking a few rags."

"Well then, let them put up with the other circumstances," said Rebecca firmly. "If people are above making their own fortune they will have to do as they are told by those with money."

Aileen found alleviation in her banishment to Sydney. Aunt Dennis was not averse from having her: she was a dainty bait in the hotel trade. She spoke to her niece solidly. "If the old Death Adder, as you call him, makes you sick in spite of his money, and the young one hasn't a penny, and seems to be a thriftless sort who will never put much together, now is your chance to forget him and escape the old lizard, or whatever he is, by choosing a young one that you can marry with pleasure, as well as him having the spondulics."

"Oh, I couldn't forget Ronnie!"

"That's what all the girls think at first, but looking back after a few years I bet the half of them wonder why; and all this fuss about old Stanton's money—has he got so much when all is said and done? I suppose your father thinks anything big above a spring-cart and those wombat holes about Little River, and I believe Neangen is much worse. Some of those old squatters, who are such big potatoes in the bush, are only very mangy cockatoos in Sydney or Melbourne. When I was in business in Goulburn"—she had been barmaid at the Commercial, the smart hotel of its day—"I thought the Healeys were somebody, especially when they bought Eueurunda, the talk of the day. God save me, I was never in such a forlorn hole in my life. As for those old frumps at Gowandale and Curradoobidgee, horrors preserve me from them! My Ellie and Aileen have both made fine town matches, and I advise you to do the same. Two of my barmaids also married real rich fellows—one of them living in a mansion at Potts Point, and neither of those girls, nor my own either, had half your good looks. Wake up! You don't want to be a bushwhacker all your life."

Mrs Healey was an independent mind. She had earned her own living before she married, and supported her family after her husband's crash (old Denny was a pitiable wreck, with a male attendant), not in a noble way of life it is true, but she had a good name in a legitimized business, one of few open to her sex at that date.

"Marry if you get the chance," she continued. "I shouldn't worry about saving the family. They're all big and strong enough to look after themselves, and if SP-over-J is like a lot of old shell-backs I've seen in my time, the family may not get anything out of him in any case."

Aileen said little in response to this plain wisdom. In spite of numerous admirers of her beauty and the excitement of her first experience of city life in lively surroundings, she was heartsick for Ronald. He wrote her impassioned screeds and she replied in similar key, but he could not leave the stock in the present season to visit her.

From this point of vantage, and adjured by Ronald, she also wrote something to SP-over-J. He instantly put the screw on old Larry, who wrote fiercely to Mrs Dennis for allowing Aileen to carry on a correspondence, but she had the truculent independence of sisters-in-law who feel their marriage has not been the bargain they fancied, and told Larry she was not a jailer, and if he was not satisfied with Aileen's behaviour he was free to superintend it himself.

Aileen returned to Neangen after a matter of days; she had not the backbone to accept her aunt's offer to remain in the hotel and defy her parents, and craved only to be in the neighbourhood of Ronald.

*   *   *   *   *

Ronald found it impossible to see her or communicate with her at Neangen. Gossip grew to a storm. Tommy Roper, horse-fancier and raconteur, returned to Ten Creeks from Riverina, whither he had gone to remove stock for Stanton, and had a good yarn with Flash Billy, who was minding his bits and training tackle carefully these days to the end that certain things might blow over now that the boss was away at Turrill Turrill and had his mind otherwise occupied.

Billy hoped for his part that the old man pulled it off with the Healey jam-puff. "She wouldn't be so —— interfering as that long-nosed old hag of a Lucy."

"It won't help you the littlest bit," said Tommy. "Might be outer the fryin' pan into the —— fire. Ole Lucy has raised such —— hell with old Skinny Guts about the Healey filly—'fraid she would lose her nosebag and roof—that I heerd ole Skinny got her to call her dogs off of him by swearin' that she shall allers be left to poke her nose inter things on Ten Creeks while the happy married couple is at Turrill Turrill, and vizzy-versa, as the cove said. Old Skinny had to butter her up about bein' a great manager—as good as Mrs Labosseer at Coolooluk by his make-out—an' she is to save him from the thieves and robbers by which he is surrounded, them bein' you and Long Billy. It stan's to reason that ole Skinny will want to cart his new missus down to Riverina to be outer reach of Ron Dice—the dandy bloke—an' you'll have ole Lucy summer an' winter to make your miserable little life happy."

"Blind him! I hope he can't git her. I hope she elopes with young Ron the night afore the weddin'."

"The night after would be more fun to them lookin' on."

"I think it's pretty stinkin' of a man to git a girl by holdin' his mortgages over the head of her family and the family of her lover, straight wire, I do. Serve him right if he fell off his horse an' broke his neck."

"No —— fear of him doin' that. It's the sort of thing that happens to innercent little blokes like you an' me."

"I heard that everyone has tried to call ole Skinny off. They even tol' ole Great-gran'ma Mazere, an' they don't worry her about much these days, an' she's a reel ole daisy, offered to help Ron with one of her farms or somethink, but his ma is the old lady's niece and put her off, as they don't want Ron tied up with the Healeys and old mother Healey's lunatic taint."

"Good iron wingey! for the ole woman. I wonder if she'd help me if I pitched a pitiful skyte. But it's ole Larry is the pill to swaller. It would take thousan's to pull him outer the hole an' keep him above water."

"My cripes, I wonder why Ronald doesn't carry Aileen off. I heerd the ole man keeps her locked up an' beat her, an' that she's got a fever. He might send her off her chump. Ron's been ridin' up to Neangen every night, an' old Larry comes out with a gun to him. Things is pretty hot, all right."

"My cripes! You're right! I heerd as I come through Bool Bool that Ron took no notice er the old goanna, thought he wouldn't pull the trigger, but he shot the horse from under him, an' threatened he would shoot him just as quick if he come again."

"My cripes, you don't mean it!"

"It's a fact. My —— Continental, it is."

"When did this happen?"

"The night afore last."

"What horse was it?"

"Spondulix."

"Spondulix! My cripes, what a loss. What did young Ron do about it?"

"He couldn't do nothink. Had to leave him there."

"He was reel dead?"

"Dead as mutton when it's in the cask a week. Ron picked up his saddle an' walked away. The old goanna didn't shoot while he was walkin' away."

"Did he hoof it all the way to Bookaledgeree?"

"I don't know about that, but the other come through ole Alf Timson. He was down in Bool Bool to meet some sheep."

"Sly ole sawney, Alf; is he still after Joanna?"

"Norah, ain't it?"

"How the devil do I know? He don't know himself. What is ole Skinny doin' to keep his end up?"

"Sendin' fat letters every week to the girl an' thin little ones to the ole man. The mailman let it out to ole Billy Prendergast."

"I'll betcher there's more business in one of them little letters to ole Larry than in all the fat ones put together."

"We ain't got any way of provin' it."

"What'll be the end, do you think?"

"If Ron can't git some way of takin' the girl by force, like a feller

I onct saw in a play-actin' piece in Sydney, when I took them Cuppinbingle horses down to Kiss's Bazaar, ole Skinny an' Larry between them has the weddin' arranged to take place under the nose of everyone in Bool Bool at New Year."

"Go on! You don't mean it! It'd be a lark if the two ole blokes could only marry each other, as they're so shook on it. My cripes, that would be fun! If there could only be some way of palmin' ole Larry off on ole Skinny instead of the filly, an' when they got to their room . . . Good iron wingey! Ha! Ha! Ha! Ha! Haw! Haw! Haw! Haw! He! He! He! He! He! He! He! Ho! Ho! I could bust me sides thinkin' er that!"

"What's the good er thinkin' er what won't never happen. After all, ole Skinny deserves to win in a way: he's made up his mine."

"My cripes, you're right! If I wanted a girl that bad, I'd have her anyway. I can't understand anyone gettin' so worked up over ole Joanna or Norah, can you?"

"No. Women an' horses is jes' the same. It's this way . . ." Their confidences of equine amours grew unfit to chronicle and beyond the immediate action of this narrative.

CHAPTER 8

THE ROMANCE of Bool Bool had ripened richly in the short time between Aileen's return from Sydney and the afternoon that Tommy Roper and Flash Billy discussed it on the meat blocks near Ten Creeks stables. It was true that Ronald had put his case before old Mrs Mazere, and that his mother had checkmated him there. She withheld mercy on account of the impecuniosity of the Healeys and because the breed was in bad odour with the clan. She worked upon Great-grandma with regard to the alleged mental taint on Aileen's maternal side. Jane Dice was not so sympathetic to young love that she would risk being turned out of Bookaledgeree by crossing the mortgagor and being left with a distasteful daughter-in-law in addition to her other worries.

The drought in Riverina was not so urgent to SP-over-J as his personal affairs, so he returned to Bool Bool. Old Mrs Mazere summoned him to her. She was a fearless old mother of her tribe and servant of the Lord, according to her lights, and spoke plainly about the danger of perpetuating a bad mental strain.

"I am afraid you have been listening to spiteful gossip," said Stanton calmly and respectfully. It was not the custom round Bool Bool to resent old Mrs Mazere's advice. "I have investigated the matter, and it seems plain to me that Mrs Healey's father went off his head only because of delirium tremens and a sun-stroke. That sort of thing can't be inherited. Even so, it might skip Aileen. She would have more chance with me than dragging along in poverty and worry . . ."

"It's the children. Parents take on a heavy responsibility before God."

"I come from a hardy practical strain, and it would take a lot to send old Larry Healey off his head, I should judge."

"The Healeys have sometimes failed in moral principle and are irreligious—they are neither fish nor herrings. Yoke not yourself with the ungodly, my boy."

"I should never think of calling Aileen ungodly. I'm sure she will make a great little churchgoer as soon as we are married."

"Marriage, my boy, is for better or worse."

"If it should be worse instead of better I am better placed than a thriftless fellow to face things."

"But you surely wouldn't force a girl to marry you against her will?"

"I am sorry you have been told malicious tales. Aileen accepted me before there was any thought of Ronald. He had every chance, and there was never a squeak out of him till I had fixed it all up both with the girl and her father. I watched them together at Ten Creeks during the muster and they took no interest in each other, but as soon as I honourably announce my intentions, he goes off his onion like a dog with a bait. You notice his mother doesn't take him seriously!"

"I'm sure, John, I only know what I've been told. You must excuse an old woman for meddling, but I have seen you grow up, and we are nearly all gone now—your mother and father . . ."

"I am glad you have spoken to me, because I am able to tell you about the facts. You've been told fish-yarns. I mean to do everything for the little girl."

The old lady, her face criss-crossed by sun-cut wrinkles deepened by nearly fourscore years, looked at him out of honest eyes that had never issued a furtive glance, and placed her frail knotted hand, brown as a mummy's, on his sleeve. "Ronald came to me in distress, so I sent for you, and you have been good enough to come too: there is only one thing more. I should like the girl to come and stay with me here, and tell me the truth, so that I could judge if this thing is seemly or not. I should like her to be with me in the presence of both you and Ronald. Will you bring her to me and leave her with me for a few days?"

"I should like to, but it depends upon the girl herself and her parents. At any rate, thank you, Mrs Mazere."

"Good-bye, John. The Lord bless you and keep you always, and guide you and yours in His way."

SP-over-J backed out. He mounted his fine horse and rode out of town, not towards Stanton's Plains. He wanted a longer, harder ride, and felt too ruffled to go to Neangen. He decided to ride straight through to Ten Creeks though the day was already far gone. It would suit his mood to surprise that lot of crawlers and sharks, sponging on him and eating their mutton heads off.

Old Mrs Mazere was too genuine, too kind for anything but respect. It was that crawling, whining, squealing mongrel Dice that incensed him. Stanton's awakened blood seethed with the fury of senile passion after protracted quiescence. Mrs Mazere's intercession hardened his determination to anger. Aileen he would have, alive or dead, willing or protesting.

He reviewed his sex loves. Adolescent fancy had first been awakened by Rachel Mazere of Three Rivers, her of Coolooluk these days, Simon Labosseer's widow. Losing her to Simon left no scar. Deeper emotions had speedily been stirred by Mary Brennan of The Gap, sister of old Tim, who reigned there now.

Ah, that was a different affair! He could still picture Mary, regal, glowing, altogether lovely with her crown of hair like new copper tinged with red, and generous disposition to match her splendid proportions; and oh, the kindness of her soft Irish heart that warmed and melted him like the sun! There never was another like Mary. She could turn a man into a saint.

Yet she would not be kind to him. It was Bert Poole of Curradoobidgee that she had loved. With all her generous warm nature she *would not* be kind to him, Jack Stanton, no, not even after all hope in Bert's direction had been killed by his engagement to Emily Mazere. No, rather than take him, Jack, she became a nun, forsook the world and died young, the legend for all to read on her headstone at The Gap.

After that there had been episodes with other women, sordid episodes out of which he never came with credit or satisfaction, being too cautious and lacking in generosity, so he had given the king of indoor sports a rest this good ten years till a sudden conflagration was started by Aileen Healey. This tormenting madness had not racked him for years, and honour, friendship, mercy—it mattered not what—could go into the discard so long as he could satisfy desire.

Recalling his past defeats he felt savage. He would not in his old days again be among the ruck and a laughing stock, no matter what it cost in mercy and money. Of the old folks who had seen him go a-courting nearly forty years before, only old Mrs Mazere and the M'Haffetys, the Isaacs, and a few tradespeople survived. There remained his immediate contemporaries, who had ridden with him where welcome lights of tallow candles and great log fires and bright eyes shone from the old homesteads at the full or dark of the moon, in the heat of summer or the nipping frosts of winter. Foremost of these had been Poole. He too was still unwed, but it was much more romantic that one's bride should have been drowned just after the engagement was announced, than for one's love to take the veil rather than accept him; and Poole seemed obtuse to matrimonial opportunity or sensual urge, and content to fool about as uncle-in-general to the younger generation.

He laughed aloud, scaring a drove of wallabies from Wamgambril Flats, and whistled once more to his muzzled dogs that persisted in calling attention to the endless possums in endless trees till they were hoarse and footsore. Curlews and plovers wailed about the bridle-tracks, and away up the deep cleft that let Corroboree Creek through from Mount Corroboree, black and forbidding, he could hear the dingoes howling. The night was cool and crisp, heaven after the heat of Riverina, purified by the aroma of hundreds of miles of undespoiled eucalyptus forests with a rippling creek every mile or two—his native habitat, no other country to compare with it! Drought could not reach here. In years to come this would be the choicest part of Australia. All the night voices suited his mood, from the wind-like music of the streams to the howl of the dingoes and the clack of his horse's hoofs striking fire on the flinty ledges.

He thought of Aileen, and what old Mrs Mazere suggested about taking her to Three Rivers for observation. Hang it all, they acted as if he were an ogre, while all the time he was giving the girl the opportunity of a generation. A dozen other women would leap at it. Not for any money would he risk inviting either Joanna or Norah Healey, nor yet Ida or Olive Dice, or half a dozen others about Bool Bool to be his wife; and there was a widow adjoining Turrill Turrill who had done everything but ask him point-blank to marry her. Rose and Flora Farquharson, too, of Keba, were always riding up the Coolgarbilli to see their friend, Mrs Bob Milford, because her girlhood's home adjoined theirs, but SP-over-J slyly noted that they invariably came via Ten Creeks Run, though over the river there was a better track direct to Jinnin-jinninbong. Nevertheless, behind this full field of possibilities again rose Mary Brennan's ghost. Mary would not have him on any terms when he was *young*, and Rachel Mazere, pretty as a fairy in those days, had laughed at him too, and taken Simon Labosseer, the Dutchman, who had been considered inconceivably ancient at thirty. He had thought of Mrs Labosseer again during her early widowhood when she was still in the thirties, but instinct had warned him that she would be no more amenable than she had been in her teens, and he had persuaded himself that the barrier was the children. He was not the kind of softy to sweat his eyeballs out for another man's brats!

He was often swept by rage against Aileen. In his sane moments he estimated that all the blame could not be laid on Dice's cater-waulings. He and the public must have some fuel for their fire in Aileen's attitude. Mary Brennan would not take him when young, Aileen was considered a martyr to be taken by him though he was not yet sixty, as active as anyone, and *rich*. His heart hardened. He would not allow her to escape and fool him now as he had been fooled when callow. To do his better side justice, he would then be overcome by senile fondness. He would make such a pet of the little thing, dress her like a doll, make a queen of her, so that she could not help being happy, and the envy of the country.

Ten Creeks homestead spread before him in the dawn. The season's foals and their dams were waking on the river flats, and perfumed blue smoke was curling from the kitchen chimney of rough logs. Long Billy was saving his reputation by disturbing the milking cows from their beauty sleep on the clover patches. The sun kissed the peaks over the river and threw back the reflection onto Mount Corroboree as he descended a little stiffly from the saddle, flung the reins to the waiting rouseabout and went inside to see if Lucy and Milly were up.

*   *   *   *   *

Ronald put his case before Poole and appealed for his influence in saving Aileen. Poole had also seen Aileen's tears. He knew the Healey side of the case intimately, and had the temperament to make a more just and moderate estimate of it than anyone, and he so little liked the attitude of his youth's companion, that despite principles against meddling he felt impelled to say something to him. Hearing that Stanton was back in the district he found business to bring him to Bool Bool and then thought it would be nice to see how Milly was getting on at Ten Creeks, and rode round that way. He was alone with his host in the evening when Milly had been banished to bed and Mr Blenkinsop was setting her a literary exercise in the schoolroom.

"Don't you think, Jack, that you and I have left it so long that we had better leave marriage alone altogether now? Aileen's a taking little thing, but rather a child."

"What the devil have my affairs to do with you?"

"Nothing at all to do with me, Jack, merely an interested bystander. I've known you for a good many years, and, of course, I can't shut my ears to all the talk. Some of it isn't nice."

"If you are going soft, and like to make a billy-goat of yourself listening to the old women."

"It's not only the old women, it's the generation that has grown up since our day. They have a right to their point of view about those of their own age. If the girl was willing, I should not say anything about the difference in age."

"That mongrel has been squealing to you. If I offered him a few quid I bet you'd hear no more about his love affairs—not with Aileen. He needn't think he's dealing with an old woman with softening of the brain."

"You are only possuming, Jack. Can you tell me honestly that you're not putting the screw on old Larry, and letting Jane Dice know that you could put the screw on there too if you liked?"

"Go to hell and mind your own business," said SP-over-J with the snap of a dingo trap.

"Sorry to have put you out, Jack. It is none of my business of course, only I hope you will be able to keep your noddle later if things don't turn out exactly paradise. Chickens have a way of going home to roost. It is sometimes better to squabash things in the egg stage."

"Keep your advice for yourself. You may want it."

"I may. Well, old man, it's not worth quarrelling about. I'll say no more."

SP-over-J recovering himself said, "If you're anxious for a job in the affair, why don't you come and lend me a hand as best man at the wedding?"

"I should be glad to under different circumstances."

"What's the matter—jealous?"

"Perhaps I am. If you could assure me that the girl is willing I'd gladly stand up with you." With that they called it a day.

❀   ❀   ❀   ❀   ❀

Poole, nevertheless, was not at all satisfied that Stanton was not putting the screw on. Ronald's tale could not all be the result of overheated imagination. The coming marriage was the scandal of Monaro as well as Bool Bool. Miss Jessie M'Eachern asked her old friend for the facts, as he believed them, next time he rode over. Miss M'Eachern was famous in those days as the first native spinster of the districts, and earned further notoriety by reigning alone on Gowandale, the original pioneer holding, and making of it one of the most thriftily managed properties in the Southern District. She was a spry dame in the early fifties and by her ability as a grazier and her disregard of the conventions was accounted eccentric.

Only Miss M'Eachern knew why she was not Mrs Herbert Poole. It was a long-standing puzzle to Poole upon which he cogitated even now. Her name had been unfailingly coupled with his in their young days and there were still some who betted that they would end their days as man and wife.

"What is going to happen?" she inquired of the Stanton-Dice-Healey entanglement.

"The wedding is coming off after the New Year unless some miracle intervenes."

"Why don't the young people elope and have done with it? They could get a berth as man and wife.

101

"Aileen is no match for her family, and Dice's folks have the whip-end of him too. SP-over-J is capable of foreclosing on both places if he doesn't get his way, and Larry has shut the girl up and beaten her, unless the talk is all lies."

"Most talk is. The girl is over twenty-one. She can do what she likes."

"But you don't know old Larry's methods."

"I think I can estimate them. You must remember he tried to marry half a dozen of us before poor Sissy Gilbert was simple enough to take him, so he must have shown some of his qualities."

"But you didn't accept any of us, Jessie. You refused Hugh Mazere after being engaged to him for months, and you refused me twice. Did you put me in the same box as Larry?"

"Surely you heard the common talk of why I broke with Hugh. It was nearly as noisy as the clash about Aileen and young Dice today."

"Well, the talk was, the talk was . . ."

"Why do you hesitate?"

"Well, they used to chaff me, and when I was fool enough to believe I had a chance I found you were only pulling my leg, so you see how far from the bull's-eye talk can be. Now that I've the pluck to tell you the truth, why don't you tell me why you gave me, as well as Larry, a slice of turnip?"

"Well, the first time, I could see you didn't want me very much. If you had wanted me a little more, I should have taken you then."

"By Jove, Jessie M'Eachern, do you mean that I have missed all these years just because I was awkward! I've never been much at laying on the soft soap."

Miss M'Eachern rose and went down the narrow old drawing-room where they had danced together long ago, and where the bullet hole put in the wall by the bushrangers to warn the men was plainly visible. She stepped out on the veranda where the roses still clung—yellow, white, pink, and deepest purple-red—where she had taken him one Leap Year night to exercise her pre-rogative and had met humiliation. In the height of summer glory the perfume of the roses filled the hot afternoon. A zephyr from Cootapatamba softly swept the grasses, girth-high in the home-stead enclosures, and rippled the tussocks on the undulating plains towards Curradoobidgee. Poole rose too and stood with her on the edge of the old veranda where he remembered sitting with her one night under the stars while the dancers whirled past the windows to the skirl of old Rab M'Intosh's bagpipes.

Rab, the Eueurunda shepherd, had gone with Mrs Labosseer over the ranges but had always pined for Monaro and had come back there—to the M'Eacherns—to die. He had requested to be buried near his old hut, but it had been in inimical ownership at that date so the good M'Eacherns had compromised by putting him on a dainty ridge at the side of the orchard with a fine view of the sweeping plains where mile upon mile of gowans waved in summer beauty, and to which he had transferred his Scottish affections. The ripening grasses were high on the mound with its carved wooden head-board; the palings grey with years of blazing sun and whipping winter sleet and winds. The old man had been wont to muse that the long-legged black callant from Curradoobidgee was seeking Miss Jessie for the other side of his hearth against the time that Stepmother Poole should be gone to the land of the leal. But old Mrs Poole was still very much mistress of the Curradoobidgee fireside and Miss Jessie and the long-legged callant—still a bachelor—were talking on the exact spot where they had talked a generation past.

The old shepherd with all his second sight could never puzzle out what had gone wrong between them. Neither could Poole, and he was still curious. That was a braw run stretching round for miles, and in spite of the parching season, provided plenty of picking for the dots representing plentiful flocks and herds, mud fat. All these years those miles might have marched with his portion of Curradoobidgee, but he had missed through being a little too slow. He could hardly accept that.

He looked at Jessie critically. She seemed unnecessarily shrivelled. She had lost some of her teeth and her longish nose was too near her chin: he had not remembered her eyes being so small in the old days, and she had a tendency to whiskers, but Gowandale was a beautiful property. Nearly all the original run was Jessie's now. She had retained it intact by paying off the family shares year after year.

Yes, Gowandale was a beautiful property and Jessie a smart business woman.

"Jessie, you say I failed the first time because I didn't seem to care enough. I suppose I was just as stupid the second time in expressing what I felt, but surely the fact that I came up to scratch a second time was evidence that I cared all right. What was wrong with me the second time?"

"There was nothing wrong with you, laddie; it was simply that you didn't care for me, and I could see it."

"You saw wrong, Jessie. What made you think I didn't care?"

"You only came asking me because Rachel Labosseer said no."

"What made you think I had asked her?"

103

"I knew by a word here and there while you were putting the matter before me."

Poole reflected that women were the devil to find things out. Keep the mouth shut tight, yet from a grunt or an ahem they would know everything.

"I don't see why you would have nothing to do with me because of that. I told you honestly about poor Emily Mazere."

"I didn't mind about Emily, but you only came to me because Mrs Labosseer wouldn't have you."

"That doesn't hold water. There must have been something up with me as none of you would have me, only poor Emily. Perhaps I'm as bad as Larry Healey, and Emily had a lucky escape to be drowned."

"Now you are havering, laddie." He did not know how near to sobs was the little old-looking woman, her withered face as brown as leather by half a century's suns. It was a slap to his vanity to learn that he had made such a hash of proposals, he, supposedly such a killer among the girls in his heyday. He had not done as well as the obnoxious Larry, who had a second wife and might have a third the way things were going.

"Well, Jessie, it's not too late yet, and you can't accuse me of caring for anyone else now. My record for the last thirty years ought to convince you. We are very good friends and could keep each other from being lonely old willies in our last days."

She was silent. He was apprehensive, but the plains were more than beautiful to him. There was a long stretch ahead of him yet, unless he broke his neck or a tree fell on him. It would still take a good horse to get rid of him, only he had long since learnt better horse-taming methods than to submit his osseous parts to unwarrantable strain. Good old Ma could not last much longer. Even now she was a bit off, though her presence made the retention of younger women as maids or visitors convenable. When she was gone he would be in a fix. A man, if he had not a mother or sister, needed a wife. Old Jack had a sister, but was not satisfied. It was not a housekeeper however that old Jack was after, but that fever that had seized them all years ago. He suppressed a smile to realize how far it was from that towards Jessie; but those plains were wonderful and Jessie had made them pay like hell.

"It's not too late yet," he reiterated. "We've wasted a lot of time. There is no sense in wasting any more . . ."

By a gesture she stopped him. Her weatherbeaten features did not convey her suppressed emotion. "Yes, it is too late, Bert," she said in a low voice. "Just about twenty or thirty years too late.

I'm too set in my ways now. I could never settle down to domestic work completely. The station and the stock and buying and selling are my life now." She was the acutest person on Monaro in a horse or cattle deal, and even made money out of fowls and pigs and fruit.

"You needn't give that up, Jessie," he said, relieved by her refusal. She did look old, and no bridal figure. She saw his relief and it hurt again as of yore. He had always been relieved by her refusals, and pride now, as in days gone by, stood between her and a union of calm friendship.

"Well, then, Jessie," he said with his old winning smile, now ambushed by the squatter's beard, well kept, with very little grey amid the black. "As you won't have me at any price, young or old, and we have both for one reason or another got nothing from the marriage basket, what do you say to helping along the love affair of the young people who don't seem able to pull themselves out of the lickhole?"

"Have you a plan?"

"I thought if you were ripe for another investment you might do something to turn the screws off Dice or old Larry. That part must increase in value as relief stations as the country gets stocked up."

Jessie M'Eachern was happy accumulating and then investing. She asked searching and technical questions that only the bank or lawyer could answer.

"I have put myself into a corner with both old Larry and Jack and can say no more, but you were always kind to the Healeys and might begin afresh and see if you have any influence."

❋ ❋ ❋ ❋ ❋

The gossip of the hotel verandas was that old Jess M'Eachern of Gowandale was in Bool Bool on a special visit of respect to Great-grandma Mazere because she had been unable to attend the bridge opening owing to wool-washing and shearing. She had ridden down with one of her nephews and stayed the night with Alf Timson at Billy-go-Billy on a Friday. During Saturday morning she pointed out how the place could be made to pay twice as well as it did, Alf with meek stubbornness seeming to agree, then he saddled-up and arrived with her at Neangen about sundown.

The three were made welcome and Miss Jessie devoted particular attention to Aileen on the strength of the girl's recent visit to Monaro and a night she had spent at Gowandale. Aileen was looking wonderful. The brilliance of excitement enhanced her delicate beauty. Miss Jessie kept her talking in her room whither Aileen had been the one to pilot her.

"So, Aily lass," she said. "You're going to be married soon after the New Year, I understand."

"Yes, Miss Jessie," said Aileen with no self-conscious radiance of a bride, but a startled furtive air.

"Now, what would ye like me to gie ye as a present?"

"Thank you, Miss Jessie. You are too kind." There was an absence of normal enthusiasm.

"Well, well! Here's every lassie in the world going to be married but mysel'. I'm the only lonely one. Can ye tell me the rights o' that?"

"They all say, Miss Jessie, that when you were a girl you had ever so many more beaux than any girl has now; didn't you like any of them?" said Aily, always kindly.

"But, lassie, love's a game in which there must be two to do the likin' and lovin', and baith must be awfu' sure, or it's a bad estate. Are you sure now that you love with all your heart that auld man, auld enough to be your grandfather almost; is there not some nice young laddie ridin' aboot the country keekin' at your bonny wee face? Ah, but lassie, it's good to be young and bonny and have some braw young laddie worshippin' the ground you walk on. It wouldn't matter gin you had your hand in his, if you had only the stars above you for roof and the bracken for a pillow, that would be heaven, and everything else would come."

"That's what I think too," said the girl, and halted upon realizing her admission.

"Then, lassie, why not hold fast to the right and let the Lord take care of the rest. You don't know who may be on your side."

"Oh, but it's not myself, Miss Jessie. I have to think of——" Aileen halted apprehensively. She detected movement in the room adjoining. The wall was of slabs and some of the wide cracks were closed only with strips of unbleached calico, papered over. Every whisper could be heard by an ear on the other side. Aileen began to do something unnecessary for Miss Jessie. She was obviously terrified of being overheard.

"Well," said Miss Jessie in a low murmur, making a noise to cover it, "only be sure, lassie, that you love your laddie—anything else is wicked and will bring no happiness because it can have no blessing."

They were not permitted to be alone together during the remainder of the evening, so Miss M'Eachern forsook romance and talked business with her host. She let Larry gather that she was seeking investments as well as paying a state call on old Mrs Mazere.

"By cripes, old Jessie is a real jew—she'd make a bargain of her grandmother's grave. She must be bursting with spondulics—chance for you, Alf, riding about with you and staying the night with you."

"Perhaps she'd no more think of takin' me than she did you when you asked her," drawled Alf. Larry scrutinized his visitor's profile against the night where they were smoking a final pipe on the veranda, but could not detect intentional malice.

"Remember what I tell you, lassie," said Miss Jessie as she kissed Aileen in departing on Sunday afternoon to spend the night at Bookaledgeree.

She progressed in the high and brilliant sun, the air irradiating like an electric river along the track, which to practised eyes showed that many a wallaby brush, lyre-bird, goanna, or snake had written the tale of its passage in the soft grey dust.

"Poor country and full of dingoes," remarked Miss Jessie to her nephew. "It's a stand-by in droughts. Otherwise it would take a terrible-sized run to make a living, and too many horses and men to boundary-ride."

All was delightful amid the great trees but for the stench of the dead cattle—Tommy Roper's mob—that marked the Route like milestones as they had succumbed to thirst and starvation on the way to the land of refuge from the drought-smitten western slopes. Boundary-riders had taken advantage of the carcasses, and in the area from which the brands had been cut had deposited staggering doses of strychnine. All dogs went tightly muzzled.

Miss Jessie reprimanded her corpulent old mare for shying at a bovine corpse, and broke into a canter on a level stretch above the river that she remembered from the days of her youth, when the world had had a different complexion. It recalled to her that she had had to wrestle with a situation more difficult than Aileen's. Loving Poole deathlessly without response, she had weakly given in to Hugh Mazere, and then, after the engagement had held for months with satisfaction to both families, had had to find courage to break it. Aileen needed a similar spirit and her problem would soon be solved, Miss Jessie reflected as she rode along over thirty years later among the tormenting flies and the palpitant drumming of cicadas, and, reaching the valley of the Bookaledgeree, turned into the Dice homestead.

The Dice family had come to Bookaledgeree fifteen years before, and the only members of it to whom Miss M'Eachern was known personally were Ronald and Matt, but this did not detract from

107

her welcome. She spoke of riding on later to Three Rivers, but Mrs Dice said, "It would never do to let Aunt Rachel Mazere see you desecrating the Sabbath by unnecessary travel." So Miss Jessie consented to stay the night.

Ronald took her to look at the yearlings in a paddock below the orchard, and there they set to the topic of the hour.

"I'm surprised to hear you have let old Jack Stanton take little Aily Healey away from you, laddie. When I saw you at Gowandale a few weeks ago I thought . . ."

"Well, you see, Miss Jessie, he has a wagon-load of money-bags and all I have is a double mortgage on my mother's property, and old SP-over-J has got in here too."

"But laddie, you're strong and young and handsome and have your intellect; the world's big financial men often started from less."

"It's not me, Miss Jessie, it's poor little Aileen."

"She's a grown woman of legal age—it may sound bitter to say so and too bad to bear at the time—I've been young and in love, so believe me, laddie, I know—but a lassie who does not think more of love than the bawbees is not worth greeting for." As she got on in years Miss Jessie forsook the locutions of her governesses for her parents' vocabulary.

"Little Aily doesn't care for the bawbees, Miss Jessie. Old Larry shuts her up and wallops her. He shot my best horse dead under me, so you see it's more of a siege than you think. My family too are against Aily, and dying to get her away from me by marrying the old Death Adder, so I couldn't bring her here."

"I'll give you a job for a beginning on Gowandale. I'm losing my brother Bruce's boy at Christmas. I'll want an overseer, and you know the work. I could put you in the old wing where my brothers used to sleep—one room could be turned into a kitchen."

"Miss Jessie! Do you mean it! Is this a fair and square offer?"

"It is the offer of a sentimental old maid who wants to help young love, and it is good business too for both of us. Your brother Matt is old enough to take on the management here."

"When does that offer start?"

"From the day you set foot on Gowandale, and I'll give you a month's wages for your honeymoon—that means I'll hold the place for you till the beginning of February."

Ronald threw his hat in the air and was about to whirl Miss Jessie in his arms when interrupted by other members of the family announcing the evening meal. He whispered, "I'm off up after tea to try to see Aily, and you won't start for Bool Bool in the morning till I can tell you my luck."

Miss Jessie laughed. "That's right laddie, a man that isn't enthusiastic about his love affairs is only half a man. Give Aily my love and tell her to be brave."

"Ronnie seems in a terrible hurry all of a sudden," observed Ida, as her brother vaulted the orchard fence of stout split rails and disappeared.

"A young man is generally in a hurry except to say good night to his dawtie."

"Ronald doesn't get any chance of seeing his lassie these days. I suppose you heard about his infatuation for Aileen Healey?"

"Yes. She's a bonny wee thing."

"She's pretty in a way, but there's not much in her. We'll all be glad when SP-over-J marries her and takes her away to Turrill Turrill so that Ronald can forget her."

"There's many a slip 'twixt the cup and the lip in love affairs. Ronald may . . ."

"Oh, but Miss Jessie, we don't want him to. We wish he would marry someone nicer."

Miss Jessie diverted attention to acreage and briars and clips and staples and drought, and her hosts said she talked just like a man and did not care for anything but business and money.

Meanwhile the lover sped along the way Miss Jessie had come. He could not risk another horse; besides, a bullet that could drop his horse under him was a cogent warning, so he tethered Spondulix's successor about half a mile from the house and approached on foot. The Neangen dogs were notably efficient, and a man on foot an object to arouse suspicion in dogs of whatever standing. They made a great racket but none was off chain, thanks to the liberal bait-laying, and Ronald put them off his purpose by fully passing the house and featly returning. He had a juicy bait prepared for the fat old bitch who always lay about the house because she was of a famous line of children's guardians. No lights showed in the windows and Ronald arrived safely outside Aileen's skillion. He knew this was shared by the gimlet-eyed Julie, but he rested on her being of an age to sleep like a lost opportunity. Here he found the old nurse dog chained but he was a favourite with her and by fondling cut short her welcoming yelp and withheld the bait. The window was closed, so he stood back in the shadows and waited. Soon a snore or two through the flimsy walls announced that some of the four females were asleep. Some were not accounted for. Awful should Aileen be among the snorers and those awake, the enemy! There was a wide crack in Aileen's wall beside her bed with a piece of tin tacked over. A stout penknife soon made an opening. Ronald paused again. The moon was high enough above the feathery peaks of the ranges to illuminate the little room. With the aid of a switch he could have placed his missive on Aileen's chest, but fearing it might come first to Julie's eye, he called softly "Aily! Aily! It is Ronnie."

She sat up as from a dream. "It's Ronnie. Be careful." He was now encouraged by Julie's whole-hearted and vocal slumber.

"Where are you? Are you hurt?"

"No. Don't move or say a word. Here is a letter." The girl clasped his fingers through the aperture and rained kisses upon them till a movement in the night startled them. They halted petrified for a moment, but it was not an inmate.

"Good night, darling!" he whispered presently. "Read your letter. Nail up this crack in the morning."

She listened, breathless while he moved away softly. A willy-wagtail chirped, "Sweet pretty creature! Sweet pretty creature!" Old Bessy gave a sleepy yelp and some thuds as she disturbed the tormenting fleas. A mopoke called. A plover clicked by the creek. All was quiet.

Aileen quietly applied a match to the candle and read of Miss M'Eachern's offer and the instructions for placing her reply in a mortice hole in an old post down where the road wound round the spur.

> Meet me, darling, some night. Send me word what night and where I shall meet you. I shall have a couple of horses waiting and we can ride straight through to Gowandale without stopping. Miss Mac will take care of you and stick to us about getting married, and we'll have a good home right from scratch. Be brave, my own love, and we soon shall be all in all to each other. I'll ride up every night for your answer.

Here was deliverance! If Ronald had reached the house in spite of the watch-dogs it would be much easier for her to get away from it. Her family followed no way of life nor mind to breed insomnia. The weight of the mortgages might have kept old Larry awake but he had found a royal road away from them. Aileen's silly clamour about Dice never gave him a qualm, and so long as Pa was not venting his undisciplined disposition directly upon her, Mrs Healey's somnolent soul found ready unconsciousness.

Aileen lay awake thinking over her reply to that wonderful letter and how she could privily deposit it in the old post. In the morning it seemed less easy than during the night.

Ronald reported his progress to Miss M'Eachern before she left next morning. "You want to be sure that you love each other better than anything else in the world and then go ahead," she said.

110

"You've only to tap on my window some night and I'll take the lassie in till we can all away to the minister."

A few days later she detailed her offer to her friend of Curra-doobidgee, who had ridden over to spend Saturday night and hear the news.

"I could see that the girl is being forced to marry Stanton against her heart, but there is little that outsiders can do by meddling if the main parties can't settle their own affairs."

"Talk about doing nothing, Jessie, you have pulled the whole thing out of the fire. We have only to wait the next move."

"We'll see! We'll see! If the girl hasn't the strength of will to help herself now, she must take the consequences. These are not old days when girls can be locked in a keep. She could slip out any night and take a horse and away to her laddie."

"But poor little Aily, she's such a gentle little creature. She's like a bird in a net."

"That sort of woman can often work a great deal of sorrow for herself and others by her lack of stamina," persisted Miss Jessie, in what Poole thought an unsympathetic tone. Miss Jessie was thinking of days gone by and the courage she had needed both one Leap Year night and later to free herself from a big mistake.

On Monday night Ronald rode to the old post, but there was no message in it. On the second night he retired ostentatiously and when Matt was snoring crept to the stable for his horse and rode quietly away in the moonlight. The third day he had to go for cattle up Bookaledgeree Creek, and by a bit of stiff riding included his pilgrimage in the day's work. The next day he packed salt in the same direction and again made the detour. The fifth day he rested his horse and worked near the homestead. On Saturday night he took French leave of Matt's horse, and on Sunday—play-day—being free of his time, in the afternoon he rode towards Bool Bool and when safe doubled on his tracks and once more sought a message.

He went in broad daylight, but could find no trace of anyone but himself in the bracken at the base of the post. A beautiful bush of "old man" almost hid it and the aromatic putty-grey flowers and viscid leaves rested without a disarranged twig. There was no shred of paper anywhere.

Each day, on finding no message, Ronald grew more disappointed, but hoped valiantly. It would be awkward for Aileen to escape the vigilance of her family, and she was not of the mould to slip out in the night and go so far alone. He wished he had asked her to ride away to Bookaledgeree without a message and then he

111

could have taken her with him to Gowandale. He was worried lest he should miss a message about an appointed tryst.

He was correct about the difficulties besetting Aileen. She got away near the end of the week on the pretext of special broom-stuff that grew near the spur. Julie was detailed to accompany her, but Aileen galloped ahead while Julie was wrestling with her old neddy, and so reached the post with time to spare.

She left Miss Muffet on the road and went on foot. As she was about to insert her missive in the deep mortice hole she caught the glitter of a black snake coiled in the recess. It almost brushed her face in making its exit and was joined by a second. They disappeared in a hole at the base of the post. Aileen with a scream of terror fled to her horse and was riding along the road by the time Julie overtook her. Aileen had the abnormal terror of poison-ous snakes inculcated in bush children. She was too frightened to approach the horrible spot again. The prospect of marriage with SP-over-J grew less repellent by comparison. Larry's ceaseless exordiums about the duty she bore her mother and sisters were working, and, imbued with the superstitions of her forebears, and nervously overwrought, she took this as a powerful omen against what she contemplated. The whole family were unfeelingly against her, even Norah was not so kind as usual. No luck could ever attend her, Larry maintained, if she forsook the saving of her family and for her own selfish pleasure allied herself with thrift-lessness. This the burden of every aspersion day after day.

She had prayed to God for guidance by some sign or happening, and to her fear-burdened soul the deadly black snakes were the response. She longed wildly to meet Ronald somewhere and tell him this mental and spiritual angle of her ordeal, but this wish remained unanswered. There were only the serpents, which multi-plied in her dreams. She was continually springing from bed tor-mented by a nightmare in which she was pursued by reptiles, and there was no one to help the distraught little soul.

It seemed at length to her fevered imagination that the way to absolution was by sacrificing herself for her family's good.

CHAPTER 9

GOSSIP RECEIVED fresh life from the invitations. It was to be a full-sized wedding. People said that SP-over-J must be paying for everything, and grinned to think that whatever the rights of the romance, old Larry was selling dear.

"There ain't no flies on old Larry!" commented Tommy Roper.

Aileen pleaded for a quiet wedding from her Aunt Denny's in Sydney, but Stanton was not to be fobbed off like that. The hardness and cruelty in him, the outcome of sensibilities perished in youth, demanded full triumph. His own set and circle, subscribing to the legend that his early love preferred a nunnery to him, should publicly witness his success with the prettiest girl of the district.

Some still pitied the girl, but these were mostly young and sentimental and of no business promise. Now that the wedding was announced general opinion was that the girl had done "thundering well for herself". "When she gets past the first fever of spooniness," said Ida Dice, "she will be very glad to find herself in the lap of luxury instead of in a stringybark bed in some boundary-rider's hut."

Everyone of any standing, and many without, known either to the bride or bridegroom's family, was invited. Miss M'Eachern of Gowandale was one of the few who refused. She could not be absent from home so soon again. She wrote to Dice to know the rights of the case. He replied with bitter words about Aileen. The cynicism of his associates had tarnished his faith in her.

"All this fuss about old Larry and Stanton is ridiculous," said Ida. "If Aileen had wanted you she could easily escape. I think myself she is a weak-minded, selfish creature. She would have liked you best if you had money. Any girl would prefer a young man to an old scrag if things were equal; but she hasn't got the courage to take you without anything."

"Yes," agreed his sister Olive, "and if she felt one-tenth what you imagine about marrying old Stanton she would not want all this big wedding waved in your face."

"That isn't Aileen's wish, I'm sure."

"I don't know: she is very fond of pretty clothes. Old Larry

113

wouldn't risk a rumpus or breakdown if they were marrying her by force, neither would old Jack. The show wedding must be to please Aileen because she is a young girl and wants it. Old Jack wouldn't spend an extra penny if only he was concerned; he's never for society fuss and feathers.

Ronald saw that he would make a fool of himself to lie down under his defeat. He took it recklessly with more drinks than he should have had, with everyone and anyone, from Tommy Roper to Mr Eustace Blenkinsop, to whom he muttered misanthropic platitudes about women.

The Dices received a full and formal invitation. This smote Ronald as brazen insolence, which he did not know whether to attribute to SP-over-J or old Larry. His sisters asserted that it showed Aileen was not so unwilling as her weak amiability led him to suppose.

"You go," advised Ida, "and show that you don't care any more than she does; plenty better girls than she is, ready to go with you."

"I'll march right up to the altar and denounce old Skinny Guts. When they ask about the impediment I'll say that any fool could see he was one, and that they locked the girl up and walloped her and shot my horse under me; and she can speak the truth then."

"If you think she would have the pluck to stick to you then, you would make an unholy fool of yourself," said Ida.

"Yes, she'd faint or cry, and you'd be looked upon as a brute, and then she'd be hustled away and married quietly out of sight."

"I'll give her the chance anyhow, and then I shan't have anything to be sorry for afterwards."

"You'd have a great deal more to be sorry for if you made a fool of yourself like that."

The wedding was to be in the new church of St Matthew, but lately dedicated by the bishop. It was largely due to old Mrs Mazere that the church had gone ahead so vigorously in the district. The new structure was to have a spire in memory of Philip and Rachel Mazere, for which purpose the original Philip had apportioned £300 in the famous will, which he had changed every time a family member crossed him. The early church of the sixties, now known as the Church Hall, was to contain the wedding breakfast, and M'Haffety's Hotel and Isaacs's Royal Drapery Mart between them were the providers. Mrs Isaacs was enchanted to be where the news was made, and gave personal attention to the bunting and such dry eatables as the mart could supply, while the M'Haffety end of the outbreak was effulgent as effulgence was in the surroundings.

Each fresh detail was more exciting than the last.

"I hear that Milly Saunders is to be bridesmaid with Julie," remarked Rebecca to Norah.

"Is that so? Sure, then, Lucy Saunders must have given in."

"There's more than that: Bert Poole is to be best man."

"Who would believe that, whin I heard he did iverything he could to call ould Stanton off. Sure, if he comes round, it shows that the gurrul Aileen must be quite happy to marry, and all this fuss of Ronald Dice's, phwat do ye make of that?"

"Aw, young men in love can make an awful noise one week and forget all about it the next. They say he drinks more than he ought now, and that would account for his capers."

"But sure, he might have been dhruv to it by disappointment."

"My opinion is that people aren't drove to things unless they have a mind that way."

"That's thrue, too, Rebecca. At anny rate, ould Jack will be glad to have Poole standin' up with him. They went coortin' together often enough long ago. I wonder now who will Poole be takin'? He might be the next."

"I hear that Ronald is going to denounce old Stanton in church."

"Och, that would be pot-valiant. Whisky talks like that."

"I expect old Larry and old Jack will be glad when it's safely over."

※　　　※　　　※　　　※　　　※

The day arrived. It was a droughty summer even for Bool Bool, that valley of the blest. The Yarrabongo had never been so low in the memory of the generation in possession. The dust was deep on every road and lane, upon every roof and ornamental tree that stood by the wayside. The January Wednesday dawned in brazen splendour. By nine o'clock the hydrangea bushes and pumpkin vines were drooping in the heat and the fowls had their wings spread for air in the shade of the drays and blacksmiths' sheds. People converged upon the church from every side. Buggy-load after buggy-load of women in voluminous silk dust-coats and almost opaque gossamers were escorted by men also in dust-coats and with fly-veils on their panama hats. Not only the church and vicarage grounds, but lanes adjoining, were peopled by harness horses stamping and switching against the tormenting flies. The early arrivals eagerly watched the appearance of certain persons and families. It was not only the largest but the most exciting wedding the new edifice had known.

"There's Lucy Saunders. She hates it like poison, too, but we all had to come round," whispered Mrs Ned Saunders.

"There are the Labosseers!"

The widow and Emily, two of the sons and a married daughter

followed the lady of Coolooluk to a pew. Anything she did created interest in the little town where the family had high standing.

"I didn't think she'd come, did you? I'm sure she doesn't think the Healeys much chop," said Rebecca.

"No, but they are all rolling up to stick to ould SP-over-J. Sure, they're as clannish as cockatoos."

"Dot Saunders can have Ron Dice now that Aileen will be salted down. Not much of a match for her, but she has eyes for no one else."

"There's herself! Sure, I didn't think she would come. I heard the ould lady told SP-over-J . . ." This was swamped by a more interesting murmur.

"The Dices!"

"As large as life! Don't look round."

All eyes turned upon these arrivals. Being near town, they had their regular pew. Mrs Dice leant on the arm of her eldest son, who was walking straight and defiant, handsome and young in a smart new suit. He settled the others and took the end seat on the aisle. The bridegroom appeared shortly afterwards accompanied by Poole. Stanton was expensively tailored but looked nervous and tired. Poole looked splendid and unruffled.

"Do you think Ronnie will really make a howl?" whispered Marcia Mazere to her cousin, Dot Saunders, in the choir. Dot hardly knew one air from another, but it was the correct thing for the young women of the clans to sing in the choir of St Matthew's.

"No! That's all nonsense. He found out long ago that Aileen didn't really want him. Look at Bert Poole standing up there with Uncle Jack; he wouldn't be there if it wasn't all ship-shape."

The church was profusely decorated and the flowers were wilting in the heat. The scent of roses and honeysuckle and a dozen other perfumes intermingled, and the air was made heavier by orange blossom from the shelter of the broad chimneys at Three Rivers.

Stanton took one glance round the congregation to find Dice glaring balefully at him, and did not dare look up again. The assemblage fell throbbingly quiet awaiting the bride. Dozens of young women in elaborate summer gowns with bustles and panniers and flounces almost held their breath with excitement. In the charged and drowsy air the song of the Yarrabongo as it fell over a cliff beyond the Glebe filled all the day with the suggestion of cool sweet peace.

The bridegroom suffered an agony of nerves. The quiet following his entry grew into restlessness again. People fidgeted and whispered and turned their heads to look for the bride.

116

"Perhaps she's not coming at all," whispered Marcia to Dot.

"Don't be silly. Her mother is here."

"Won't it be awful if Ronnie makes a fuss?" persisted Marcia.

"He won't do any such thing. He wasn't as much in love as all that."

People could no longer surmise that Aileen had eloped with Dice, as they had been predicting to within an hour of the ceremony, when here he was for all to see, and though SP-over-J would not have glanced towards him again for the price of the Corroboree and Wamgambril colts combined, it was worth double that to know that Ronald was inside the building. He had sent Poole to the hotel early in the morning to ascertain that Aileen was well.

The ordeal of waiting wore away to relief. Mrs Arthur Rankin (Fanny Mazere) started her organ. Welcome sound! Aileen had not eloped; she had not fallen sick of brain fever; she had not even fainted; she was only ten minutes late. She approached along the aisle on her father's arm, a fairy apparition in intricate bridal finery of satin duchesse or marchioness, or whatever it was called in that decade, and tulle and lace and orange blossoms.

"The prettiest bride I ever did see," whispered Mrs Isaacs to Mrs M'Haffety.

"Not as pretty as Rachel Mazere that was."

"She was darker and smaller."

"And *she* couldn't hould a candle to poor Emily that was drownded."

"But we never saw Emily as a bride."

"She was just like a bride that night of her birthday ball." Faithfulness to the past showed that Norah and Rebecca were growing old. "Ah, look! Did ye see the look the poor pet cast on Ronnie Dice, like a frightened angel!"

As Aileen came up the aisle Ronald turned of deliberation and glared at her. She was clutching her father's arm gazing at her feet, but as though mesmerized she lifted her head as she came near Ronald. That look was salted away in sentimentality by Bool Bool, and is a legend today with outsiders, when the principals have forgotten the emotions from which it sprang. There are old folks thereaway, when the cynical say there is no true love, to contend that they saw it naked in the eyes of Aileen Healey that sweltering day, and matched in the eyes of Ronald Dice, careless of onlookers; but people imagine what pleases them of amorous romance, unconvinced by evidence that sexual love *per se* is a transient emotion.

117

As that may be. Aileen's foot in its white satin slipper tripped in the coconut matting, but the alert Larry lifted her safely along. She was closely followed by her two half-sisters as bridesmaids, who closed up the space behind her, and next came Milly and Julie, Milly delicious in self-importance, with the whole weight of the ceremony as a public concern on her shoulders, and a model faithfully copied by Julie. It was Stanton who paid for the elaborate costumes of the two little girls and the bracelets they wore with orgulous air becoming the Garter.

It was no light thing for Milly to be upholding her uncle as bridesmaid. Her sympathies at first were with Ronald, but such aspersions as Death Adder and Skinny had put her on her relative's side. By insisting that Aileen resembled the beautiful Miss Severn, later the Marchioness of Salterton, Mr Blenkinsop had made her a figure of romance to Milly, whereas Ronald had failed in not carrying off the lady by force, and when her Uncle Bert was tabled as best man, Milly was eager to be a bridesmaid.

SP-over-J was immensely encouraged by the child's support and became so indulgent that her mother was unable to enforce discipline. Lucy Saunders had strenuously objected to Milly's taking part, but when she found the tide against her, adopted a more neutral manner. The Stantons were clannish, and if Aileen could not be kept out of the family she should be accepted and made the best of. Poole being best man further reconciled the widow to Milly's participation.

Mrs Dice put her hand on her son's arm as old Healey lifted his daughter along. That gesture also became history.

"Aily is like Cinderella and the ugly sisters," whispered Mrs Raymond Poole (Rhoda Mazere).

The bride and her father reached the altar rail. The brides-maids fidgeted with their finery and flowers and jewellery. A hush fell upon the congregation. Inside, the flies buzzed in the per-fumed heat; outside, the cicadas' hirrient filled the heavens; horses could be heard stamping in torment; a vehicle rumbled over the bridge and clattered up the stony main street; a dog barked; the song of the Yarrabongo floated in as cool and clear as a sigh from paradise. Poole, observing the ethereal loveliness of the bride—old Jack's young bride—was carried by that song of the river back to the funeral of his own bride-to-be, nearly thirty-two years gone. He remembered that river song for ever. All this crowd and heat and perfume and undercurrent of strain brought a sense of unreality, only the faint cool music of the river remained.

Dearly beloved, we are gathered together . . .
First, it was ordained for the procreation of children . . .
Secondly, it was ordained for a remedy against sin, and to avoid
*   fornication . . .*

The pronouncement was squeezed affectedly in the Oxford brogue from the throat of the clergyman, and many, in the circumstances of the old man and the young woman, reputedly unwilling, were shocked by its grossness.

Thirdly . . . . Therefore, if any man can show any just cause why,
*   etc., etc., let him now speak, or else hereafter for ever hold*
*   his peace.*

The clergyman paused. Tension tightened. Stanton felt beads of perspiration coursing down his forehead and wilting his high stiff collar. Aileen was not conscious of the service. Everyone looked at Ronald Dice, but the mesmerism of the mob, more powerful than any police force, had him in its grip.

Dot Saunders watched the drama spellbound from the choir. If one could be loved, even hopelessly, by the right man, it would be happier than not to be loved at all by him!

Tension relaxed. The clergyman was proceeding: *I require and charge you both, as ye will answer at the dreadful day of judgment when the secrets of all hearts shall be disclosed . . .*

There being no impediment, the betrothal words were murmured and then: *Who giveth this woman to be married to this man?*

Larry's voice, confident and loud, rang out, "I do."

People almost smiled. It became a normal wedding, abnormal only in size and showiness.

Soon all was chatter and laughter. There was a rush to congratulate and kiss the bride and to strew roses in her pathway. On the arm of her husband she looked more lovely than ever. Excitement lent colour to her delicate cheeks and starriness to her translucent Irish eyes. Aileen was not a thinker. Her own volition was in abeyance: she moved in accordance with the plan forced upon her, her overwrought emotions blurred.

Ronald was quite normal. There was nothing else he could be, without making a sorry show of himself, and any normal young man would rather cut himself off from heaven than make a fool of himself before a crowd of his associates.

It fell out conveniently for him to offer his arm to Dot and proceed to the wedding breakfast. That was altogether recovering from foolishness as he was the envy of half a dozen eligibles who pursued that popular beauty.

"Old Larry looks as pleased as a cat licking his whiskers after a feed of Christmas turkey," he remarked, "and *Uncle* Skinny as if he had been to the dentist and got it over; isn't it dead funny?"

"Too funny for words," said Dot. "Aren't you coming over with me to kiss my new aunt?" She was singularly deficient in a sense of humour, but Ronald amused her.

"I'll leave the kissing to you. I'm afraid Uncle Death Adder might kiss me by mistake."

He was in a gay and reckless mood. "Look at Ronald Dice," they whispered. "He came to the wedding after all. He's with Dot Saunders—a much better match for him."

"All that talk about him and the bride must have been yarns."

"Yes, you never can believe a word you hear."

Others, who said that they never took their eyes off him, recorded that he did not speak to the bride or bridegroom nor to any of the Healey family.

Stanton was so nervous that had old Larry palmed Norah or Joanna off on him he could not have detected it until afterwards, but with Aileen's hand on his arm, with all the clatter and joyous excitement of the young people and the orthodox behaviour of their elders, relief and gratification were his. He had not been fooled by Aileen's non-appearance, as his strained imagination had feared, and was glad now that he had insisted upon a show wedding.

Triumph and satisfaction were equally old Larry's. He had the elation of the gambler when chance has favoured him, and was more than genial. SP-over-J was almost genial too. Life had never been better. Ghosts of the past were banished by this summer festival, by this rebirth of passion in Indian summer.

The wedding breakfast burst. The bride and groom were in the centre seats, the bride's parents conventionally placed. The bridegroom's parents being in the cemetery, his sister Lucy and other near relatives closed up the ranks to support him. Milly and Julie were seated on either side of Poole, who accorded them the deference due their exalted state. There were older bridesmaids as well as lay maids and widows who would fain have had the little girls' places.

The toasts were long and florid and in execrable taste in some instances, and in others singularly short but adequate. The bridegroom mumbled for the bride; the bride's father and the clergyman did their duty; the field was thrown open. Mr Blenkinsop, always a pattern and an ornament upon such occasions, repeated his reference to the Marchioness of Salterton. Souls less felicitous said it was to be hoped that others would now follow the example of SP-over-J and take themselves off the shelf. Poole of Curradoo-bidgee was broadly mentioned. He was unperturbed. He had had thirty years of it.

Milly, feeling for him, whispered in his ear, "Uncle Bert, if you feel embarrassed, you can mention that I'm waiting for you. What do you think?"

Poole seriously and graciously whispered in reply, "Thank you, Milly, that's fine. I'm counting on it. But perhaps we had better not make ourselves conspicuous now, just a hint will save my bacon." He had already officiated for the bridesmaids, he rose again to respond to the toast of the bachelors and to explain why he remained one. He was greeted by hearty applause and said little, but he was sure of appreciation in that audience. He deplored that he was not a favourite with the ladies except when they were too young to marry, and liked him as an uncle. (Laughter and cries of denial.) He had now fixed his hopes on the grand-niece class, and if several young ladies he had promised to wait for did not all disappoint him and run off with younger cavaliers, as several had already done, he still lived in hopes! (Laughter.) SP-over-J and he had been boys together. They had gone possuming many a night. (A voice: "Was that all you did?")

"Well, we may have ridden a buckjumper or two by daylight and had a polka or two by night." (Hearty laughter.) "SP-over-J, I have known so long that if he has any serious faults I have forgotten them, and as for the bride, one of the loveliest I have seen in a long and wide experience as an uncle, I've carried her on my shoulder when she was not so tall as she is today, and now wish her and her husband all luck and prosperity on behalf of the envious bachelors. I call upon Mr Alistair Farquharson and some of the others to respond on behalf of bachelors who are not so long in the horn as myself."

Those who kept an eye on Dice said that never a toast did he drink, but threw wine or champagne out of the window beside him. At any rate, Dot Saunders, now that Aileen was out of the way, secured him as a partner to ride at Gundagai and other agricultural shows.

Everything went without a hitch. In the afternoon the bride and groom left for Gundagai, thence to Cootamundra to catch the Southern Mail for Melbourne. Old Larry kissed his daughter in overflowing mood. "Sure, what you've done is so right and full of common sense that I can see good luck shinin' ahead of ye like a great white road."

Aileen wept becomingly—the best of good form for a bride. She could not confide in her elder half-sisters, nor her careless half-brother, Larry, nor in her silly mother, puffed like a frog with pride and satisfaction. The Healeys were well pleased with their attainment financially and socially.

Not only the Bool Bool *Courier* recorded every jam-spoon and antimacassar presented to the happy couple, but the *Town and Country Journal* had nearly a column.

Old Bill Prendergast had been commissioned to do his best and responded with a newly painted carriage and his peerless greys in heavily plated harness. Very fine the turnout looked clipping down Stanton Street and across the bridge and the flats in the direction of Saunders Plains, to rise on a farther eminence and disappear in the glittering day on the grey ribbon of road towards the Nanda ranges.

Bool Bool returned to its stewed fruit and junket—popular summer fare. Its bridge opening and ball, the spree of rumours preceding its grand wedding, the wedding itself, had been peaks of interest in the prosaic flats of everyday existence.

Ronald's love affair faded. Many of his elders had had an equal or greater reverse and now as ageing patresfamilias or expanding grandmammas were none the worse. Old Larry Healey himself had had several, and two wives. Tim Brennan of The Gap had had a whopper, so had Ned Stanton, brother of the latest bride-groom, and Hugh Mazere, son of Great-grandma, had been thrown over, after public engagement, by old Miss M'Eachern; and goodness me, to look at her now she did not seem much to miss. Old Mrs Bill Prendergast, now a shapeless waddling mass, for all she was upholstered in wonderful silks and hung with jewellery, and always with such a squint that it rendered her almost non-human, had nevertheless on a lower stratum once wrought desolation among stockmen and bullockies from Mungee to Gundagai.

Ronald did not expose his heart. He would have found no sympathy at home and did not want to be a butt abroad. He was too busy and too much under his family's eye to take to drink, though in spite of drinking no toasts he had been very drunk the night of the wedding, but so were Dan Spires and Tommy Roper and Cross-eyed Prendergast and Billings and a few more. Mr Eustace Blenkinsop, English gentleman at large, and Teddy O'Mara, untamed horse-breaker, sat down and wept together on the front veranda of M'Haffety's Hotel, regardless of social codes or witnesses, for the simple reason that they could not stand up either singly or arm-in-arm, but it was all of trivial rather than tragic import, and ludicrous in the consequences to Mr Blenkinsop.

That was the start of a spree upon which he spent the last of his quarterly remittance on whisky, a tin of boiled lollies, and a bag of onions. The sweets were to propitiate society, the onions to comfort a tongue debauched. His delirium was sustained till he spilt the sweets along the aisle at Sunday service and solemnly offered the onions at various drawing-rooms including the vicarage, the bank, and Three Rivers, to the delight of the wags that abound in bush townships. However, in a circle inured to similar family skeletons, and in view of the occasion, it was minimized as his first outbreak of such magnitude, and opportunely he was retiring to Ten Creeks, removed from temptation. "Such a gentlemanly old feller even when he's drunk that it's impossible to help liking him!"

The drought continued. The bodies of sheep falling as they reached the promised land punctuated the Route even as the earlier beeves, whose hides were now dry and empty. The crows and dingoes had a good season, the drovers and their employers a hard one. The employers had shattering losses. The drovers had plenty of work with all the world of shifting stock but it was in a world of shifting sand and stinging flies, and disheartening to crawl all day long tortured by sandy blight behind weak suffering animals on a route already littered with stinking carcasses, to the accompaniment of a devil's chorus of crows, to deliver half the flock with which they started.

Owing to the severity of the drought, SP-over-J did not extend his honeymoon to Tasmania. Aileen did not seem to care whether she travelled or not. She acquiesced in every suggestion in a way that was paradisiacal to the shah that is in all men, even in old SP-over-J. It was a novelty after his experience of the Stanton-Saunders-Mazere clans, who were mostly stiff-necked and spirited females and mule-stubborn males. After a while it bewildered him. There seemed nothing to catch hold of. He recalled with relief the early opposition of his sisters. There was something natural in that. He was glad to hear from Lucy that she was preparing the house at Ten Creeks for the bride. The heat was so intense that he intended to return there.

He bought Aileen extravagant clothes compiled by fashionable dressmakers and was proud of the sensation caused by her beauty, but it contained the sting that elderly bridegrooms with purchased wives unfailingly suffer. Even the most tactful shop and hotel attendants would mistake him for Pa, while dashing fellows were deliberate with the thrust. SP-over-J was relieved that Bool Boolians did not witness his discomfiture, and the apathetic Aileen did not seem to be aware of it. He wished it had been practical politics to have Milly with them. The youngster must have changed, he reflected, under the influence of old Blenkinsop. Not long since he felt she had merited summary correction, but she was surprisingly nice about his wedding. She had been at the carriage door at the departure. "You know, Uncle Jack and Aunt Aileen, you can count on me when you come home if you want me to keep you company at Ten Creeks Run, or anything."

"Would you like Milly to keep you company when we go home?" Stanton inquired one day as he and his bride were strolling in the Botanic Gardens.

"It would be nice, but just as you like."

"Well, we'll have her, then." It would be refreshing to hear Milly declaring as flatly as a smoothing-iron whether she did or did not like a proposal.

CHAPTER 10

I**T** **WAS** the second day of the Bool Bool Show.

The hall where the ball had been held was full of fruit and grain and vegetables, samples of women's needlework and cooking and children's school exercises. Table decorations that had won prizes the day before were wilted now. The draught-horses and bulls and rams had won their blue ribbons, as had also the farm produce, the cockadoodles and ducks and canaries, and old Mrs Mazere's pot plants and honey and preserves. The merry-go-round was doing a stirring business. Many hundreds of watermelons had been consumed in great pink slices on Watermelon Hill and elsewhere.

Old Tom Saunders's prize dairy cow had been milked in the morning, and Diamond, son of Nanko, one of the aboriginal old hands, had requested a drink. He had been ordered to hold his hat. There was more than he could swallow; he passed some to his friend, Teddy O'Mara. It was also too much for him and the silly creatures put on their hats, milk and all, with the result that their beards when dry were as if dipped in cold starch, and pursued by the flies like honey.

The wits had not recovered from this side-splitting fun when they were enlivened by a shindy between old Parsons and Porter, farmers on the Three River flats. For several years Porter had won first prize for the best bag and sheaf wheat with the same specimens. Celebrating at the Show the previous year, Parsons, carrying his liquor better, had treated the prizewinner till he was dead drunk and then purchased from him the prize specimens. This year, when grain was pinched with drought, Parsons took both prizes with Porter's ancient exhibit. Ferocious language ensued in the hall. Porter with a stout stick threshed the prize sheaf forthwith before the company. He then gathered up the straw and striding across the ring to the judges' box strewed it upon the gentlemen, local and imported, complacently smoking there, with his opinion of them as fools and duffers and liars and hypocrites, etc., who would not know oats from barley.

Pillaloo!

Porter next fed the prize bag wheat to the prize hens and turkeys of the Riddalls and Browns, and from their pens extracted eggs to paint his perfidious rival's hat and beard till he was more distinguished than Teddy and Diamond.

A most diverting forenoon!

Mr Blenkinsop, English aristocrat and kindly soul to boot, sought to aid peace by inviting the belligerents to a cool drink with him. Porter and Parsons were flattered, but one of them spoke contemptuously of shandygaff, and Mr Blenkinsop felt constrained to take them to the Woolpack where real spirits could be procured. They set off in Parsons's old buggy unnoticed except by the rabble about the gates.

All seats were occupied regardless of the sun to watch the "lady jumpers", first on the afternoon programme.

"Dot Saunders is the best lady jumper in the colony," said Mrs Isaacs, in her front seat in the grandstand.

"Sure, I wonder annyone bothers to compete against her annywhere after what the Governor himself said about her last year," said Mrs M'Haffety.

"Mostly it's the smallest waist, not the best rider, takes the prize," said Isaacs.

"That's thrue! Ould Richard Mazere, whin he is judging, has a weak oi for the woman rayther than the horse."

"There's more like him," observed the Mayoress.

"But Dot is the best jumper as well as having the smallest waist," contended Mrs Isaacs.

Dot was taking her turn in the ladies' hunters, on one of Poole's personally gentled thoroughbreds. He took his hurdles with economy of action, and never clouted the rails, a perfectly mannered beast, but ahead of his day. More popular with the crowd was the chestnut of Miss Polly M'Ginty of Mungee Crossing Hotel, who stood on her hind legs and pawed the air at the entrance and backed and bucked away from the leap. It took a couple of men to lead her into the ring. Polly was of lower social stratum and vociferously barracked for by all the boundary-riders and drovers and breakers and dealers and spielers that the meeting attracted. She was a heavier woman than Dot and laced to the last inch in a skin-tight habit. From her bosom, harnessed to the contour of a stuffed Christmas turkey, protruded her gold watch-chain, and a horseshoe brooch fastened her choking collar. A jockey's cap let the sun burn her face crimson, and was not nearly so becoming as Dot's bell-topper with its floating white veil.

At last Polly's Lottery went at her hurdle with such fury that the sleeve of her rider's habit was torn from the armhole, and there extruded something white like a calico shirt—wonderful how women lived and breathed and rode terrific horses in the stays and layers of rags that the mentality of that day conceived as God-imposed on womanly females!

Miss M'Ginty was applauded as properly modest that a white petticoat, much befrilled, could be discerned inside her skirt. Dot the practical, it could be detected, wore quite mannish breeks beneath her taut skirt, and wantonly exhibited her shape. It was such an attractive contour that "nuff said", as the wags of her prime expressed it. There was certainly enough said at the time by the judges of virtue and convention.

Lottery, in her excitement, struck the rails, jarring her rider's back and knocking many points off her chances. Dot, cool and slim, was coming round a second time on Princess, her own celebrated mare. She popped over so neatly that it was impossible without carefully calculated points to tell whether this or Poole's Oedipus was the better. Poole's horse had been named by his old stepmother, and many of the squattocracy thought the name referred to a species of frog.

Another rider had a treasure in Larry Healey's mare The Bird, and yet another in Beeswing, belonging to Ronald Dice. There were a dozen others as well, and while the judges were walking the horses round and walking round the horses and measuring and estimating, Milly, instigated by youthful admirers, slipped into the ring and ran Romp at the stiff four-railed jump set for the men's hunters. The little roan cleared it with inches to spare, licking her chops to be at it again. Amid cheers there were cries of, "Give all the prizes for the ladies to the youngster: she's won 'em by long chalks." "Give her a special prize, one for herself and another for the filly!" "Send round the hat!"

"That settles it!" said Milly's mother to her sister. "She is getting quite out of hand. She must go to a good stiff school for a couple of years to take the nonsense out of her. She does what she likes with poor old Mr Blenkinsop."

"Has he been on the spree since?"

"He hasn't had the chance, but I think it punctured his poise a little."

By order of her mother in the grandstand and her great-uncle in the judges' box, further exhibitions by Milly were stopped, but two pairs of eyes were directed. one towards the filly and the other towards her rider, with intense admiration as they left the ring. The first was Jack Bowes, the second young Larry Healey.

A column of dust like a smoke barrage announced the approach of a vehicle from the flats across the bridge and soon it was whispered that SP-over-J and his new wife had returned from the honeymoon. They proceeded directly to the grandstand, the stir of their passage for a time eclipsing the drama in the ring. Dot relaxed interest in the points of the ladies' hunters to note if Aileen's arrival disturbed Ronald, but she could detect no sign. Milly summoned the nearest vassal to take charge of Romp. It was Billy Bowes, but they were at loggerheads, and Larry sprang forward, so to him Milly entrusted her adored.

She reached the space before the grandstand and kissed her uncle and aunt, all eyes upon them, some for the smart Melbourne bonnet the size of a cup with a sash tied under the bride's chin, and others to see how the wearer looked, and if there were indications of a broken heart or approaching motherhood, and how old Jack might be weathering it. Aileen was amiable as ever, and quite animated for her.

"What is on?" she asked, taking her seat.

"Gentlemen's hunters, just starting," said Norah.

"There goes Tommy Roper on old Albatross, see him soaring over the sticks like a bird."

"There's young Larry on Abracadabra, a devil of a horse, but Larry could ride a steam engine."

"Is Dice entering Spondulix this year?" inquired someone in a voice purposely loud.

"Ssssh! He was shot under him: didn't you hear?"

"Here comes Dice now on a horse of Poole's."

Some of the curious saw, or thought they saw, Aileen's face pale as though she were going to faint, and said that her heart was in her eyes as she looked towards the best of riders on the best of beasts, all natural grace and unstudied efficiency, but others said that some people were so weak-minded and sentimental that they could see anything in any face that they wanted to. None could detect that Ronald glanced in the direction of Aileen, and he was in the ring longer than any other rider. He won in the pairs with Dot, and following that they seemed to enjoy each other tremendously. They rode on the merry-go-round, they ate watermelon together, and all was as it should have been—a young man who had caterwauled after one beauty removed from him by a wealthier suitor, was seemingly just as taken with another, a sight and incident far commoner than a prize bull at an agricultural show.

"Sure, look at Ronald and Dot," observed Mrs M'Haffety. "'Tis plain to be seen he's forgotten Aileen entirely."

"He couldn't have thought much of her, then," said Rebecca.

"Ah, 'tis Aileen will be glad now that she did not listen to his

128

noise. Sure, anny gurrul who depinds on a man's affections is not knowing much of thim."

"They're all right if they're everlasting looked after, but you cannot afford to let them slip."

"Lord save us, what's this!"

This had reference to the two farmers with Mr Blenkinsop, Diamond, and Teddy O'Mara, who had returned from the hotel in a state of complete equality—no, not exactly complete; Parsons and Porter still had the sanity to hoe their own furrow, however unsteadily, but the two naturals were as a single thought under Mr Blenkinsop's baton.

Uncle Jack was taking Milly and her new aunt, his sister and several other clan members for refreshments when they were confronted by a changed mortal. Gone was the exquisitely conventional surface. Mr Blenkinsop's clothes were covered with dust, his hat over his ear, his face flaring red as he reeled precariously from side to side, a bag of onions under one arm and a tin of boiled lollies under the other.

He swayed up to Aileen, with one hand on Diamond and the other on Teddy O'Mara, his merchandise escaping him. He tried to pick it up, so did his aides-de-camp, and all three rolled together. Teddy sat up and laughed, his stiff white beard now encrusted with dust like a statue, and chanted:

"Me feyther and mother were Irish,
And I was Irish, too;
We bought a tin kettle for ninepence,
And knocked up an Irish stoo!"

Diamond wiggled on his belly after the onions, boys grabbed fistfuls of the sweets, cheering and calling, "Go it, Diamond!" "Go it, Teddy O'Mara!" "Three cheers for Eusty Blenkinsop, esquire, two ends of a rogue and a liar!"

Porter and Parsons, carrying themselves better, helped their comrade to his feet and he addressed Aileen, "Ah, Marchioness, I'll see you tonight in the conservatory when we can get away from this rabble. You needn't pretend you don't want to—you had a different tale till your clod of a husband came along with his money and title."

Stanton drew his wife aside. "You are not yourself, Blenkinsop, you'd better go to bed."

"Yes, leave the young lady alone," said Parsons, "she's married the old feller now and there's no use in playing up about it."

The lamb had become a lion. "How dare you address me! Serfs,

129

clods, descendants of criminals and menials, fellows with neither education nor breeding—and I, Eustace Blenkinsop Osgood—to think that this is my lot year after year, to associate year after year with inferiors—people more ignorant than my father's bailiff and tradesmen . . . Stand up, Diamond and Teddy O'Mara, I am associating with you to show what I think of the society to which I am reduced. I shall take you both to call on all the first families round Bool Bool—you are just as worthy to enjoy my society as these other grooms and galoots. To think that I must spend my days in such a milieu! I, Eustace. Up, Diamond! Come on, O'Mara, I of ancient lineage will . . ."

Such a crowd had collected that Stanton took his wife out of it while the wits enjoyed the association of Diamond and Teddy with the blooming English swell. A constable came to restore order. Parsons and Porter were claimed by their embarrassed families. The constable would have locked the other two up but for the intervention of Mrs Labosseer.

"Teddy O'Mara, get up at once! Go and sit in the shade of my buggy till you are able to sit on your horse and then ride straight home to Coolooluk. You hear what I say!" Teddy recognized the voice of authority and staggered off obediently. "Diamond, you ought to be whipped. You go straight back to camp at once." The constable escorted one of the last of a vanishing tribe outside the gates and let him lie down under a tree to be eaten by the flies till he should be able to travel, and warned the boys not to touch them.

"Those poor creatures haven't sense, but what are we to think of those who sell liquor to them or those who laugh at their state," said Mrs Labosseer. "I hope I shall live to see the day that those who sell liquor to the simple and those who jeer at them are horsewhipped." Such was her rectitude and personality that the wags slunk away, bottling their delight in the incident for reminiscence.

The downfall of Mr Blenkinsop was a sensation. There was no one but himself to whom it mattered, so Mrs Labosseer, with a sense of Christian responsibility, again came to the rescue. She got her son Eric to take him to Three Rivers. "Poor old man has no one to take care of him. Ask Charlotte to take him in, and as soon as he is fit to travel I'll take him to Coolooluk till he recovers, unless, of course, Jack Stanton is prepared to take him to Ten Creeks, though he is no fit tutor for Milly after this."

"Glory be! Who'd have thought it!" said Mrs M'Haffety. "Sure, perhaps 'tis to be seen whoi his family unloaded him on the colonies."

"Didn't I tell you! Men may seem lambs, but it's wives who know their own sorrer with them."

"This beloike is the ind of his career as a fine gentleman among us. The ould scut! Who'd have thought he could be so insultin'!"

*   *   *   *   *

Milly went home to Ten Creeks with her new aunt, much against her mother's wish, but she was in such favour with her uncle that Mrs Saunders's wishes were outweighed. Milly's older relatives considered she was getting out of hand, and would become an oddity if steps were not taken to tame her. In face of the collapse of Mr Blenkinsop she was the subject of family discussion.

In a different circle she might have been hailed as a prodigy, but in hers any outstanding character or intelligence was disparaged as eccentricity. She might find scope for unusual energy in prodigies of household operations that jeopardized the peace of her associates, or she could be the horsewoman and whip of the age; though her cousin Dot did not escape aspersions of horsiness, and the opinion that what she needed to settle her was a husband and half a dozen children.

As the months passed, Mrs Saunders liked less and less Milly's association with the Healey boys, one of whom was always at Ten Creeks, while Milly herself did not care for Joanna, who also took up her residence there to keep Aileen company. Aileen, in sooth, needed a companion for herself and to relieve SP-over-J. Approaching motherhood made her a suffering and impossible sleeping companion. Towards the end of the year she was for ever waking up screaming because of snakes that pursued her in all guises, and the marriage bed in the last century was a pen from which a spouse could not lightly desert. Stanton, in whom habits of solitude and singleness were deeply ingrained, was glad to abdicate to a sister-in-law. Even he agreed that Milly was growing too old-fashioned, and at New Year helped with the wherewithal to send her to Miss Lisset's most select establishment for young ladies at Edgecliff, Woollahra, where none but the daughters of pure merinos were catered for. Milly was eligible because there was no unpunctuality in her fees and she belonged to one of the oldest and most respected pioneer clans in the Southern Districts.

When her departure was settled she asked Uncle Bert to take care of Romp during her absence. Poole rode from Curradoobidgee to say good-bye to Milly and to take charge of the pony personally. Milly laid upon him a firm injunction, "Don't let that awful Flash Billy touch a hair of her head or tail or he would be sure to spoil her in some way."

131

CHAPTER 11

MILLY WAS absent nearly two years. Her mother, to keep her from the Healeys, went to Sydney during some of her vacations, and Milly had spent others with school friends.

Life from Bool Bool to Monaro and Ten Creeks Run and there-abouts pottered along. The drought had been followed by such wet years that bottle and fluke and all the ills of too much rain were prevalent. Norah and Joanna Healey were both ranged. Propinquity with Joanna had done for Dan Spires, the overseer. Dan had selected towards Wamgambril Springs and they were dragging to make a home. Norah's disappearances from Neangen, to stay at Ten Creeks with Aily, seeing what had come to Joanna, had stirred Alf Timson at last, and he and Norah were estab-lished comfortably enough at Billy-go-Billy. Old Mrs Poole, Bert's stepmother, had died high in her eighties, and Bert was without a permanent housekeeper. Aileen's baby was in his second year, a fine child, but his mother did not recover from his advent. She was listless and backachy, and the child seemed too much for her even with the aid of the best nurse girls procurable. She could not endure the heat of Riverina and so Ten Creeks saw more of the family than usual. SP-over-J was secretly mortified to have made a wreck of his bride, and for pride's sake spared no expense for attempted medical reconstruction.

Poole's state had been discussed by the oracles of Bool Bool. "He'll be sure to marry now. While the old lady was there she was a great boss, they say, but now we'll see what will happen. There may be a chance for old Miss M'Eachern yet, and there's the two Farquharsons at Keba and the Dice girls at Booka-ledgeree."

"He'll be dhruv to marry now, but it will take a lot of dhriving to get him towards Lucy Saunders or anny of thim others. He'll surprise us by bringing home some flibbertigibbet from the town. Whin they get ould in the horn they are niver contint with wan of their own age. Look at ould Jack Stanton."

Milly arrived in Bool Bool one morning unwarrantedly, but preceded by lengthy telegraphic communications from Miss Lisset. The reason of this appearance was the news received from

Uncle Bert that Romp was lost, though she had been stabled every night or kept in the orchard with a six-foot paling fence, as she had already shown the tendencies of her high-flying dam. It was an appalling catastrophe to Milly. Without permission she left immediately for Bool Bool. Poole met her at Goulburn, so deeply did he feel this end to the guardianship of the sacred filly. When morning came and Milly disinterred herself from her rug and stepped out on the platform, he was startled to find her no longer a child.

"Uncle Bert," she said, after the sleepiness had vanished, "I do so appreciate your thoughtfulness in coming to meet me like this. I know it has been an unavoidable accident. I am inclined to think there is something underneath. Where is Flash Billy?"

"Droving down the Bland the last I heard of him. He and Tommy Roper had a contract to go to Queensland."

"How did he come to leave Ten Creeks?"

"He and your Uncle Jack fell out over Billy's methods with young 'uns. I warned Billy the time of the muster when he taught Corroboree and the filly bad tricks."

"I bet he has done something with Romp for spite."

"That would be rather roundabout, wouldn't it? Romp never meant anything to your Uncle Jack."

"Yes but it was through Romp and me that Billy got found out. I was the one who always said straight out what I thought of him."

"You must be careful never to let prejudice make you unfair, Milly old girl. Billy, I reckon, behaved as well as he knew how; he never had much of a bringing up."

"I shan't say a word to anyone but you."

"That reminds me, the night of the bridge opening, Billy brought Romp back to Three Rivers. She had broken out of the orchard and would have got away only for Billy."

"You never told me."

"Forgot it till this brought it up."

"I'm sorry if I've had wrongful thoughts of Billy. If Romp hasn't been stolen she would make back to Ten Creeks."

Poole could not keep his glances from his young friend, and her general appearance and composed vivacity of manner attracted admiration from strangers. She was assuredly a young woman, though her hair was still in a plait and her skirts short. Her velvet hat was tipped away from her face and had a smart bow dangling at the back; her dress was to the tops of her neat buttoned boots and made with the prevailing bustle at the back; the sleeves outlined her round young arms snugly, and were met with gloves half-way to the elbow; the materials were quiet but good, the ensemble decidedly fashionable. She had a "figure", with the slim waist and other rounded lines, indispensable to beauty in her day, already plainly indicated. Miss Lisset's was renowned for deportment, and all Milly's actions were instinct with energy and grace. Her features were irregular, but her eyes and mouth were frank, expressive, and winning; her complexion, rooted in radiant health, and now rid of freckles, was rosy, and her sincerity and freedom from affectation or unreasonableness made her a favourite. Poole noted that her collar was fastened with a childish brooch he had given her, and decided to present her with another befitting her budding womanhood.

She insisted upon going straight to Ten Creeks though only men were there, it being August and the worst winter weather still to run. Poole felt this awkward now that Milly seemed so grown up, but to break this to her was not possible inside delicacy. Aileen and SP-over-J were at Turrill Turrill. Lucy Saunders was at Stanton's Plains, and as a married caretaker was on the Run, she volunteered with such willingness to go up with Milly, that Poole sensed here a fresh, or rather an old danger. This he obviated by suggesting that the headquarters of the hunt should be Jinnin-jinninbong over the river. This held. The Mesdames Milford were glad of visitors to enliven the isolation of their winter season when often weeks passed without a fresh face appearing, while the Milford brothers, in Poole's idea, were worth half a dozen of the rouseabouts or boundary-riders that operated on Ten Creeks Run.

Poole had offered a reward of £50, but Romp had not yet been traced. The night of her disappearance had been marked by heavy snow, wiping out all possibility of tracking her. The suspicion was that she had been stolen by someone who had awaited such weather. If not, it was argued that she would make back to where she had been bred.

A tremendous search began. Bushmen thought nothing of a few score miles to serve an old crone or a bearded and blasphemous brother, and youth and beauty in feminine form was enough to send them riding a thousand miles in their dreams. Several blades were there because they had caught a glimpse of the new Milly in process of being turned out by Miss Lisset. Foremost was Larry Healey, who had seen her arrive at Bool Bool, where he hung about Dot Saunders, which he assumed the right to do since his sister had entered the clan. Another was Cross-eyed Prendergast, who saw Milly take the coach at Gundagai, and his crony Billings to whom he had imparted the news. Someone going for the mail had told the Farquharsons and Cuppinbingle, and, things being slack, old Mick Muldoon thought he might as well take a turn up, so did his master, who was always interested in a promising filly, equine or human, especially human, and the whisper of Milly's points had reached him. He and Alistair Farquharson travelled together. Hearing that Poole and Cuppinbingle Potter were to be members of the search, Rose Farquharson said she would accompany her brother and pay a call on Mrs Milford.

When the hunt had been out a number of days Long Billy, the senior Ten Creeks rouseabout, announced that he had picked up the tracks of a shod horse among the brumbies out by Gyang Gyang Creek at the back of Mount Corroboree, where the black-fellows' borah rings faintly exist to this day. He persisted in this story though he could not find the tracks again for others to examine.

"Sure, he couldn't thrack a fowl!" said Mick Muldoon. "He couldn't tell the difference betune the thrack of the filly and a bull in spring tearin' up the scrub with his horns and pawin' dhrains all round."

But as there was no other trail, the seekers proceeded in that direction, and Long Billy and Teddy O'Mara were led by crows to the remains of Romp. She lay near the Corroboree rings under a cliff of granite, the fissures of which had of old harboured tons of bogongs for the feasts of the aborigines in their ceremonial retreats. Crows and dingoes had done their work, but it was a shod horse with a hogged black mane and tail, and enough of the hide remaining to establish that it was blue roan, and blue roans were scarcer than red roans or piebalds or black-dappled greys.

It was a depressed party that mustered at Jinninjinninbong that disagreeable sleeting evening. To Teddy O'Mara was left the breaking of the news. Milly refused to be satisfied. She wanted the hide for tanning, but the scavengers of the bush had spoiled that. "She was in a flinty gully, missy, under a great wall, and must have lost her footing and broke her neck," said Teddy.

"Someone must have pushed her over," sobbed Milly. "She'd never be so clumsy as to lose her footing. She was bred there."

"Ah, but the horse that doesn't lose his footing sometimes hasn't been foaled yet," said Alistair Farquharson.

"Yes, but Romp wouldn't fall over that precipice, she knew the place. Horses don't make mistakes like that. I want to go out and see her myself. If she had been some old screw that didn't know the mountains it would be different. Did you leave her there, just as she was? Poor little thing, to be torn to pieces by dingoes and those vile old crows!"

Milly was all child again before this bereavement. The men

felt convicted of barbarity to have left the remains unburnt or unburied. Alistair volunteered to carry out this duty, while Milly had to go back to school immediately. This she consented to, meekly, also to contrite apologies to Miss Lisset for her high-handed action in leaving her establishment. Miss Lisset, however, understood Milly and was a friend in this crisis. Milly never gave the trouble generated by some of the meek specimens who were all and more than convention demanded.

Thus Milly was banished again till the following Christmas twelve-months, when she was to return home to take up life on the plane of an adult of seventeen.

CHAPTER 12

Ronald Dice had not seemed to be aware of Aileen at the Bool Bool Show the day she returned from her honeymoon, and no word or message of any sort passed between the young people thereafter. Shortly afterwards Dice left the district. He naturally desired a change. He went to the Macfarlanes of Junee, who had summered their stock on Bookaledgeree and who gave him a post as manager of one of their stations down the river.

It was during the winter that Romp was lost that SP-over-J sent Aileen to Melbourne to a specialist renowned in such cases. Norah took charge of the baby at Turrill Turrill, and Aileen was quite well enough to travel alone after being put carefully into her carriage at Wagga Wagga, with the guard aware that it would be to his interest to see her through the customs and intransigent change of trains at Albury.

Aileen, with a cup of horrible tea and her own breakfast, was comfortably seated when an agile young man dashed into her compartment and banged the door after him. Aileen looked up startled. It was Ronald Dice.

How handsome and young he looked belting into the moving train in the reckless way he swung on and off a horse; so different from SP-over-J, riding blood horses too spirited for his years and hop-hop-hopping with one leg and clinging to the pommel till at last he clambered up.

"Oh, Ronnie!" she breathed, her pale face flooding with unusual colour.

"Great Scott! It's you! How the deuce . . . Well, it can't be helped! I never dreamt of finding you here. I'll get out at the first stop. Don't be frightened. I shan't eat you."

"Oh, Ronnie, I'm not frightened. How could I be, of *you*!" she breathed, joy lighting her frail face, irresistibly appealing. She had nothing else to say. She was not a talker, nor was she embarrassed thereby. She just looked at her *vis-à-vis* and smiled.

"Have some of my breakfast."

"No, thanks . . . Say, Aileen, just tell me one thing, and then I'll never bother you again."

"What is it?" She was so gentle, so defenceless, that stricture eased in him. He was casting off something that had constantly pricked for more than two years.

"Why didn't you answer the letter I left with you that night? You might have had the decency to do that. You led me on to think you cared as much as I did. I was dead in earnest, and that was a good square offer, and you were twenty-one and had the right to defy your parents if you wanted to. You might have known how serious it was to me. Why did you let me go on till Spondulix was shot under me, risking my life and making a fool of myself before the whole country? Just one word that you had changed your mind would have been enough."

"Oh, but I never changed my mind. I did care just like you did," said Aileen, earnestly, spontaneously candid. Then she paled with dismay, to realize the irregularity of this confession now that she was a wife and mother.

"That's what you led me to believe! Well, you might have left a little note, not let me ride the tails off all the horses night after night for nothing till I was sick at heart."

"Oh, but Ronnie, I did—I tried, I mean. I got away at last and wrote a letter to say I would meet you, and when I got to the old post"—she recoiled in horror in the recollection—"I was just putting my hand into the big mortice hole when a monster black snake whizzed past. I thought it had bitten me at first, and I jumped back nearly on to another. Oh, Ronnie, it was terrible! It seemed like an omen. I never could try again, and they all took fine care I had no chance of sending you a letter. It seemed as if luck was against me." She was weeping now, hopelessly, uncontrolledly, relievedly. They had the world to themselves—a world of bushland with queenly trees, their silver-green foliage glinting in the morning sun. They were sealed in their own company for hours unless some accident stopped the train. Fate was giving them the opportunity that the snakes had frustrated, thought Dice; he had not Aileen's hesitancies.

"Is that true?"

"Yes. I've dreamt of those snakes ever since. Snakes come after me when I try to sleep till they are driving me mad. The doctors, I know, think I am mental, and talk about hallucinations and curing me of my 'obsession'."

"You needn't worry about the bally snakes any more. I'm sure they will be killed. I'm glad you have told me, but if you felt like that, why didn't you just slip out and come to me? The day you got as far as the old post, were you riding?"

"Yes."

"Oh dear, dear! Why didn't you gallop straight on to me? All we had to do was clear out to Miss Mac. She was waiting to stand by us."

"Oh, Ronnie, I couldn't do such a thing! I had Julie with me. She would have gone back and told Pa and they would have given chase and perhaps have shot us both."

"No damn' fear! Julie would have followed you most of the way and by the time she got back to tell them we would have had a good start."

"But supposing you had been away from home. Oh, Ronnie, you don't blame me, do you?"

"No, I don't blame you, but you've made a hell of a mess of everything by not playing up to me ever so little." He could not be cruel now. He knew that the action he outlined had been beyond Aileen's timorous nature. His gorge rose against the ogres who had surrounded her. He would gladly have strangled both Larrys, and as for old Skinny Guts—cowardly old death adder to trap a girl—he deserved to be thrown in a pit full of tiger snakes and adders. There was no hope of his dying yet. He was not much past sixty and like all useless old crawlers took superb care of himself.

Aileen continued to weep so pitifully that Dice feared she would be ill on his hands. He had heard tales of her hysteria and delicacy, from home, not without comments on her tainted heredity and what he had luckily missed. He saw now that there was nothing wrong with the poor little girl, as gentle as an angel and unfitted to cope with the sharks among which fate had pitched her.

"Cheer up!" he said, wrenching himself from fierce regret and wiping her eyes on his handkerchief, hers being inadequate. "I'm glad you have told me this. It has lifted a hundred thousand tons off me to know you weren't pulling my leg."

"I never thought of doing such a terrible thing," she sobbed.

"Well then, there's no need to cry. I feel like throwing up my hat."

"But it's all too late now. I might as well be dead," she wailed.

"Don't you believe it. A live dog is better any day than an ark full of dead lions. Cheer up, we can still see each other. There is no law in the world to prevent that."

"Yes, we can see each other, that will be nice." She cheered perceptibly immediately.

"You bet your bottom dollar it will be nice." The young man was reflecting savagely that he owed no loyalty to any person around Aileen. They brought on themselves anything that might happen. As for the old Death Adder, he was a symbol of the snakes that had worked on his side, and relentless determination over-came young Dice, so gay and good-natured that he was a byword.

Aileen's head rested on Ronald's shoulder as he soothed her. Soon he had her smiling at his observations. Later they had a jolly picnic meal together. Dice got tea at a station and bribed the guard to keep people away from their compartment. Aileen, rapt in the bliss of the passing hour, felt the despair of years disperse. Just to have Ronald near once more was balm to her frazzled nerves. The past fell away, the future was unshaped. She had no thought of impropriety. With Ronald it was a different matter. His purpose was devoid of qualms, but lack of illicit experience would restrain him more than he could estimate.

The heavenly hours vanished and the outskirts of Melbourne were outside the windows.

"We're nearly there. Oh, Ronnie, when shall I see you again? There can be no harm in us just *seeing* each other?" Her words were a quivering plea.

"No harm at all! Of course we'll see each other all we jolly well want to. I reckon I had better not disturb you in Melbourne. You hang on to that old specialist johnny and get strong. I'm only down with a few special fats that have gone on ahead in trucks and shan't have more than a night or perhaps two in Melbourne. Are you going up to Ten Creeks this spring?"

"Yes. The heat at Turrill Turrill knocks me out completely."

"All right, I'll see you up there. Macfarlane has Goraig Flats for the summer and gave me the offer of managing. I'll be right on your way to Stanton's Plains, you can stay and have midday grub with me. I might have one of the girls to housekeep."

"That will be heaven!"

"You bet it will! I'll drop over some Saturday nights. Now, remember, no more snakes or any tommy-rot like that."

Aileen was smiling radiantly. Dice stooped and kissed her. "There, I had a right to kiss the bride on the wedding day, so I'll do it now. Better late than never."

He picked up his valise and had gone before Aileen was met and taken away in a carriage. She went like one in a dream, a comfortable glowing dream free from snakes and death adders.

Melbourne was a lovely city.

CHAPTER 13

THE YEAR of the loss of the Young Whisker filly, a new scandal entertained the curious about Bool Bool.

The Saunderses were a narrow-minded conventional family. In early days there had been rumours that the original Saunders need not have been condescending to ticket-of-leave men, but never more than rumours. Old James Saunders had founded a family of great rectitude, especially as concerned the strait-laced virtue of its women. Against any of the daughters or daughters' daughters there had never been a suggestion of irregularity till now there were whispers about Dot. These were not long in reaching the two arch-priestesses of the local news service.

"Haven't you noticed?" Mrs Isaacs bent forward and whispered portentously, though they were quite alone in the private parlour of the hotel.

"Mother of God prayserve us!" exclaimed Norah M'Haffety. "Is there anny thruth in what ye're sayin'?"

"Jacob said to me, 'Where are the eyes of all you old married women that you couldn't notice? Are you all asleep?' "

"But how could the like of that be thrue, and her with eyes for none but Ronnie Dice, an' sure they'd have made a nice pair, but what under the hivens has Larry but his ould hat?"

"Jacob says that old Larry done so well holdin' up old Jack Stanton that young Larry thought there might be money in the same sort of capers. Isn't it terrible, and Dot could have married anyone."

"Now, who could be thinkin' out the wickedness of people. God hilp us all with families of our own."

"We can be thankful we have them all reared and married."

"Our grandchildren aren't rared or all married yet—an' wan of the Saunders! Afther that it would seem we were niver to be safe till we're all in our graves buried and the tombstones rared upon us and Masses bein' said for us, Rebecca!"

"It will be a terrible blow to them all, they so stuck-up. It will bring them down a peg or two."

"Sure, wan gineration builds up and the other pulls down with both hands; doesn't it seem as if that is what it was to be with the ould families about here?"

"Don't say a thing to anyone or we might get into trouble."

"We can keep our mouths shut, we in public positions in the town, but it's not sayin' we have to do the same with our ears and eyes."

There was a tragedy ripe in the family of Tom Saunders, sen., eldest son of the old original. To certain families it does not seem that certain classes of disgrace can appertain till one sad morning there it is, in the same way that it might happen to the most obvious sinner.

When Dot's fall became known to her family, old Tom horse-whipped her and flung her out the door one night. Only her mother's intervention saved her from being kicked while she was down, with perhaps intensification of tragedy. Following that there had been difficulty in preventing Dot, the gay and fearless rider, the darling of many hearts, from doing away with herself. Her brother and sister guarded her through the night. Mrs Saunders, wearing and persistent, pointed out to her raging spouse that it was no help to blare their disgrace to the whole district by casting the girl out. Things were not yet beyond mending. Dot did not deny her paramour. He could be made to marry her and if they set up out of the district dates could be cloaked and matters patched.

Old Tom sent a letter to Larry Healey, jun., demanding his appearance. This also was Mrs Saunders's counsel. Young Tom had been for putting a bullet in Larry.

Contrary to expectations, Larry appeared at Saunders Plains without delay. Old Saunders conducted him to the drawing-room for the interview. Mrs Saunders and Tom were close at hand in case of need, another brother guarded Dot and a sister saw that the one maid who was in for the day was kept deep in blanket-washing and spreading-out far up the orchard.

Neangen had gone up in the stirrups since the profitable disposal of Aileen, and Larry was spruce and well turned out. He had the address and fine features of his Uncle Dennis, the once debonair and engaging. He could hardly believe what had resulted from his intrepidity, but under the surface was quaking as he came before old Tom, lean and austere. When old Tom looked at him, he so boiled with rage that he could scarcely breathe, and had to clench his hands to keep from lifting a heavy chair with murderous intent. He could in that hour like a Spartan father have killed his daughter for having brought this upon him.

"You know what I have brought you here for," he gulped.

"I can't say that I do," said Larry, off-handedly.

"By God, if you deny it, you bastard son of a lag . . ."

"I didn't come here to be insulted," said Larry, getting to his feet. "You're the son of a lag yourself, if all was known. I'll stand no such aspersions against my mother who was as good a woman as ever lived and of as good family, and it is for all to know." This was true. His mother had been Sissy Gilbert of Maryville, Monaro, and the Gilberts had the same standing in pioneer sets as the Saunderses and Stantons.

"Yes, Pa, we have nothing to do with his mother," said young Tom.

"If you will state your business civilly," said Larry.

"My daughter Dorothy," stammered the old man, the humiliation more bitter than death. Larry said nothing. "There is no need for me to say any more. You must do the straight thing at once."

"And what have I to do with your daughter Dorothy?" Larry had felt exhilarated, riding along, to think of himself on one occasion with Dot, when the Saunderses were so hoity-toity and snubbed his sisters and himself.

"God, if you deny it, I'll leave you to my son, and you don't go out of here alive."

Young Tom took up a loaded gun.

"So! You've trapped me like bushrangers in a lair and would force me to make a decent woman of your —— of a daughter to save my life. If I had known I was coming to such a den I could have come armed too." Larry was well within the conventions in the fine contempt he felt for Dot to have "lowered" herself.

"Have a care," said Tom, jun.

"Give him a chance," said the old man. "My daughter says you are the man; do you admit it?"

"I admit I may have been one of them."

"Take that back, you swine, or you die," roared Tom, jun., levelling his piece. The younger man's ire had the effect of control on his father.

"Now, this mud-slinging will help neither side. I think it will be generally admitted that my daughter was not in any other man's company."

"What about Ronald Dice? She made herself the talk of the country with him, and he came bothering my sister to such an extent that my father was compelled to shoot the horse under him as a warning."

"You've been warned once," growled young Tom.

"Dice has left the district this two years and more. You'll stay here under guard till matters are arranged," said old Tom.

"You needn't try to come the Tsar to such an extent," said Larry, who was quite startled inwardly. "If I had any hand in it— if Dot thinks I'm the principal one, I'm willing to marry her for a consideration, but I have no means these hard times, and don't want a woman and youngsters tied round my neck in poverty."

They swallowed the insult and turned to terms. No thought of what the girl was suffering occurred to them. An adult, she deserved her punishment. All was proceeding without reference to a wilful young woman whose suffering and shame were beyond endurance. She could hear through the wooden walls all that was passing and could not be restrained. Thrusting past her mother and brother she appeared behind young Tom and seized his fowling-piece. Direct at her betrayer she pointed, and pulled the trigger. Her brother had the presence of mind to strike up her arm. Only an atrocious family group above the mantelpiece was damaged. Larry, seeing the volcanic determination in his fellow fallen-one's eyes, leapt to escape, but old Tom got between him and the door. Young Tom was wrestling with his sister against the discharge of the second barrel. His mother came to his aid. Dot relinquished the gun and confronted Larry.

"You'd marry me, would you—for a consideration. You would, would you! You'll never have the chance. I wouldn't marry you, not if I was paid a thousand pounds a minute for the first year. You were *one* of the men, were you, *one* of them! My God! It serves me right! A thing like that, a miserable crawler that I wouldn't have wiped my boots on. It's no use of croaking and groaning to a miserable nincompoop like you to patch things up. The thing is to wipe them out so there is nothing left. I'll follow you, Larry Healey, till I pot you. It doesn't matter where you run, I'll wait if necessary—one bullet for you and another for me. That will settle the score. I don't want judge or jury. I know the justice of it. Another man!" she cried with bitter abandon. "Do you think if there had been another man that I cared for that I would have . . . oh, what is the good of talking! Marry me! I'd like to see you get the chance. You can go. I'll wait my time—a bullet for you, no argument about the rights of it with me."

Overcome with vertigo, Dot was taken away and laid upon her bed by Mrs Saunders and Tom, jun. Mrs Saunders presently returned seeking some medicament. "It is her condition," she took opportunity of remarking to Larry. "It is to be expected. She will be more reasonable later."

Larry was not comforted. He was inexperienced in the hysteria of Dot's special condition. She had always been the upper spirit both from natural characteristics and because of her more assured social position. Her determined glare convinced Larry of her purpose, and she was a capable athletic girl who could reach any retreat possible to him. Threats from his own sex might be discounted as fifty per cent bluster, but the cold reality of female deadliness struck new terror to Larry so that he would have abjectly apologized to old Saunders and married Dot that afternoon had she been willing.

"If Dot feels so badly about it, I couldn't see her suffer so terribly. I'm sorry for what's happened and what I said. I leave it to you and her, but I warn you I haven't a stiver in the world," he said with natural humanity and manliness.

Mrs Saunders reported later that Dot had gone into one faint after another.

"It will most likely kill her," remarked old Saunders, hoping it would.

"We'd better send for the doctor, or we may be in worse trouble," said Tom, jun.

"No, we'll wait a while." Mrs Saunders wished to keep the affair secret, and had had much experience of pregnancy in herself, her daughters, and her neighbours.

Larry said he would wait too. "As soon as she is able, tell her I don't want to distress her. I was always ready to do the right thing by her, but having a gun held to my head without warning raised my dander."

Old Saunders was a harder man than young Healey yet had time to be or would ever be. He saw that Larry meant what he said. He accepted his apology and sat with him on the veranda. Tom, jun., put Larry's horse in the stable. Mrs Healey let the serving girl hear her explain that there had nearly been a terrible accident through the gun going off accidentally and that it had given Miss Dot such a turn that she was prostrated.

Midday dinner was a difficult meal for all. Mrs Saunders did not appear, being in attendance upon Dot, and her other daughter disappeared at intervals to reinforce her. In the afternoon Mrs Saunders reported that Dot was much better. Larry's request for an interview was granted. He found it particularly undermining to see Dot pale and in bed—Dot always so tireless and vital.

"Dot, I'm sorry," he began. "But they held a gun to my head and of course I wasn't going to sit down under that without giving better than they sent. Why didn't you let me know, yourself?"

Dot merely raised her head and spoke in a low voice that should not carry to the household, but there was more cold fury in it than in her earlier ultimatum, of which it was a reiteration.

"You'd marry me, would you? You'll never get the chance. The taste I've had of disgrace is enough for me."

"There needn't be any disgrace. We could clear out to some place where we're not known."

"You're *one* of the men, are you! You can't wipe that out, you cur! No, I have given you fair warning. I don't care if it takes till I'm eighty, I'll wipe the whole thing out."

"But Dot . . ." Mrs Saunders, hearing Dot's tones rising deliriously, beckoned Larry to her.

"You must not excite her now. It's not safe. You must wait till she is herself," she said soothingly. To have Larry eager to mend the breach was such a relief that the trouble seemed almost over. Dot was beside herself for the present, but she would simmer down. Mrs Saunders felt herself in command of the situation.

"We'll send you word as soon as she is herself."

"Only let me know," said the contrite Larry, further brought to his proper proportions by the rage in Dot's final glance as she fixed it on him as he left her. The Saunderses had to let him depart.

"Don't try to get out of the district," warned Tom, jun., "or I shan't save you from a second shot. I'll tell the police to keep an eye on you if you try any gerrymandering with me."

Larry, feeling as limp as chewed string, averred that no such intention was his. The fury breathed by Dot, of whom he had thought swaggeringly as his mere donah, was disintegrating.

*　　*　　*　　*　　*

As the days passed and he received no summons he grew more and more uneasy. He feared Dot behind every tree and heard her horse's pursuing hoofs in each turn of the road. He was no seasoned villain, but merely a bumptious yokel overwhelmed by a con-flagration he had by some hazard started. Another week passed and he began to fear Dot would shoot him in his bed on a moonlit night. He took to sleeping in odd places where he could not be found, and as Saturday came said he would spend Sunday with Norah and old Alf and take a couple of days' spell, for he was feeling so off he believed he had a touch of the sun.

He found Alf and Norah in a depressed state of mind. They too had had a disappointment in the premature birth of a child some little time before. Norah had been to Monaro for a rest with the Timsons and Healeys and had consulted the famous Dr Brady of Cooma, an oracle among the women. His opinion was that Mrs Alfred Timson would never have another chance of motherhood. This was calamity to the pair. Their breathless expectation of a child had been touching. They were not beautiful, nor young, nor particularly capable, nor ambitious, the simplest of folk, a child to them would have been the apex of romance and fulfilment.

So real was their disappointment that Norah braved convention and confided in Larry. As his catastrophe resulted from the situation reversed, he blurted out, "Hell! Did you ever hear of anything like that! I wish to God some others couldn't have a child!"

Norah was so kind, Larry's distress so pressing, that he confessed the mess he was in, how he was in terror of Dot being on his tracks and that he really had come to Billy-go-Billy to hide himself.

"A beautiful child to be born in sin and not wanted—the misery of it, and my poor darling born dead!" breathed Norah. "Glory be! Why should things happen so topsy-turvy? It would seem that the Lord has made a mistake in this. Larry boy, tell me more about it. Surely to God you would jump at the chance to marry a fine young woman like Dot Saunders, the belle of the whole district, and so much above us all. How did such a thing happen at all? How could it be true?"

"God knows! I hardly could tell myself till it happened, and then it couldn't be undone."

"But you could marry her at once and not wait a day."

"Damn it, ain't I telling you she won't have me at any price and is going to shoot me. You bet she means it, too."

"The poor girl is distraught with the disgrace. Oh, Larry, if only I could have had that baby. A little baby all my darling own, how happy I should be—a blessing to me and a curse to that other poor girl."

Norah's none too brilliant mind took hold of this idea, and later she put forward a plan to Larry that shone like sunlight on her large ungainly features. "Larry, I could help with that baby. Couldn't Dot come here and I could pretend it was mine? She could pretend she came to take care of me."

"Dot Saunders take care of you! Too thin! Some of these old scandalmongers would see that sort of thing through a ten-inch board, and how could Dot disguise herself," but he was touched by the kindness.

Norah reapplied her mind. She took Alf into her confidence, and laid their combined wisdom before Larry, the light of noble purpose illuminating her. "Larry, I want you to take me to Bool Bool with you at once to see Dot Saunders and her mother. Alf

147

and I have thought it all out. I'm not resting on Dr Brady's opinion, and I want to consult Dr Byng."

"You can't do anything with Dot, I'm sure."

"You leave that to me. You never know where the blessing of God may rest. He never shuts one door without opening another." Norah had such confidence that Larry took hope and bent to her will. Alf had already done so, and when morning came trembled like a child as he saddled up; this, to the shyness bred of solitary sequestered years, was a dangerous conspiracy, but Norah was shining with faith and purpose.

"Not one word even to the folks at Neangen," she counselled. "Do they know of your trouble, Larry?"

"It hasn't leaked out yet, but it soon will, if Dot stays mad." Dot, by her wild intransigence, had put the big boot on her own foot with a hardiness becoming the Baron Sir Robert Shurland, of *Ingoldsby Legends*.

"Then God be praised for that! Not one word to anyone!"

Norah's stepmother was entirely deceived by the pilgrimage. "Once you start going to doctors, you'll never stop," she observed. "They'll take all your money and do no good. I'm sure I'd never worry about not having children. The other way about is worse."

Larry said that he was feeling so "cronk" that he would consult Dr Byng, too, so the three rode away from Neangen together to Saunders Plains, Alf and Larry both dependent for courage upon Norah. Mrs Saunders received her civilly enough and she unfolded her simple proposal. Mrs Saunders stated that it had been necessary to guard Dot night and day and they were at their wits' end. Dot would not consent to see Norah, so Norah dispensed with consent and went bravely to Dot, while certain family members stood to in case of necessity. None arose.

They at times detected the sound of sobs and then murmuring voices, and waited with mounting curiosity. Dot at first was hard and bitter and not to be reached by any sister of Larry's, certainly not by poor unbeautiful old Norah, whose love affair had been a target of ribaldry for years, and whose failure in motherhood also had been treated with less sympathy than ridicule. But the warm sympathy, the first Dot had experienced since her fall, melted the despair and hate in the distracted young woman, and soon Norah had her in her arms.

"You must think of that beautiful little baby that is coming; for its sake you must pray to keep calm and have a tranquil mind. Larry is wild to marry you any moment."

At this Dot stiffened to vengefulness again.

"Well, then, never mind. He must take his punishment and

148

be left out of his share of the lovely little baby. I want you to give it to me. You could trust it to me, couldn't you, dearie, and then if it ever happened that you wanted it back . . ."

Dot was now near to sobs.

"You could trust it to me, couldn't you, dearie?" wheedled Norah with wisdom generated in love.

Dot was shamed to recall how she had mimicked Norah on horseback, sitting askew with the reins untidy as she gee-upped her stumbling old mare with a quince switch. The lowly Norah had hitherto received little notice except as a butt for sharper wits, yet came now to show a way from the suffering of weeks. Dot relaxed into tears, as saving as rain on a drought-scorched plain.

"I could pad myself to deceive people," said Norah, fertile in detail. "You can go away somewhere for a rest. This accident that nearly happened with the gun has shaken your nerves. You could hide at Billy-go-Billy. Winter is coming and Alf and I often don't see a soul for weeks, and you'd be beautiful company for us."

When Norah rejoined the others, Dot was sleeping. It was a case of any port to the family. After the last week or two with Dot they were in no mind to cavil at the callow simplicity of the proposal. Father and son were for brushing it aside, being suspicious of a deep-laid plot to blackmail later on. Old Saunders was a conventionally religious man as far as attendance at and support of the church was concerned, but without any Christian charity. He was all for marrying Dot to her betrayer by force, but Dot's violence had crumpled him. Dot bashing herself to pieces as she threatened, and as even her father did not doubt her capable of doing because of his attitude, was a scandal he could not contemplate with equanimity. He quailed before her frenzy, for his fear of having a mad daughter was as terrible to him as the shame of an unvirtuous one.

Mrs Saunders had no misgivings in risking blackmail, and immediately embraced Norah's plan. Parting with money hurt old Saunders second only to shame, but Mrs Saunders rose here too. Norah was to be helped in every way if only she could bring Dot to reason so that she would hush up the affair.

Dot would not consider Larry on any terms. Mention of him drove her to phobia, so he was banished with a salutary sense of defeat that cured his previous tendency to self-complacency in his accidental conquest.

It was finally announced that Norah was going to Sydney to consult a great man there about her case because Dr Byng had reawakened her hopes. Her plan was to seek help of a convent of

149

which she had knowledge. She was sustained by Christian faith and longed to be a church member again, but had been restrained so far by the unrelenting enmity of her father.

Old Saunders raised his bristles upon the intrusion of creed, but Mrs Saunders would not have balked at Voodooism, Mormonism, or even cannibalism if thereby she could avert the overhanging disgrace. The family were solidly behind her, so all that Tom, sen., could do was to shut his mouth and open his purse.

Norah left amid the guffaws of the wits. She had a queer taste to make such a fuss when the result might be another old Alf, like a sleepy lizard. Norah, however, kissed him, and he was worth it. He had entered upon the adventure with the enthusiasm of a child and the fortitude in preserving the secret worthy of those who keep their first big confidence as a shining trust.

Those that saw Alf putting Norah in the coach saw Dot Saunders leaving too. Mrs Saunders told people she was going to have a change in Sydney.

"Sure, Tommy Roper says she looked wretched," said Mrs M'Haffety. "And she was takin' mighty little luggage with her, and the last time whin she wint to ride before Lord Carrington there was no ind of a fuss and airs with her own horse and saddle and all."

"We'll wait a while and see," said Mrs Isaacs. "It will all come out in the wash. There is something funny about that gun accident that made Dot so sick. One person will hear something and another see something and after a while the pieces will all fit together."

❖   ❖   ❖   ❖   ❖

Norah's machinations progressed. Whatever had been the original Healey's quarrel with the Church, and however bitterly the Church had failed him, it did not fail Norah. The nuns were not intransigent about her story of Dot's being so afraid of the sea that she had to remain in Sydney while her husband was called to England to see his dying mother. Norah provided a wedding ring and settled Dot in lodgings recommended by the sisters. What these good women thought of discrepancies in the story never transpired, they were too charitable to scrutinize that side of the affair. Dot's family were stated to be in New Zealand with the exception of her Aunt Norah. The sisters regularly visited the young woman and during indisposition nursed her. The absent husband was by inference of the Catholic faith. Mrs Saunders saw that funds were forthcoming. Norah's demands were moderate.

After two months Norah returned to Billy-go-Billy, radiant, and the knowing whispered that the Sydney doctor had been efficacious. Jokes about Alf Timson's approaching fatherhood were popular. The kinder smothered Norah with advice about being careful this time, and for the remainder, it was winter and few people visited Billy-go-Billy.

Dot Saunders was a long time absent and people threw out leading questions about possible attractions. Mrs Saunders was hazy. She said that she was anxious about Dot's health; all that riding over hurdles was not good for a girl. Later, people heard that Dot had been ordered to Brisbane for the sea trip. The subject slept.

One piece of news as the year drew to a close was that Mrs Alf Timson had gone to Sydney again to be near her wonder-working specialist for the great event. People wondered where old Alf got all the money for this.

"He's had a good nest-egg salted down somewhere," observed Tommy Roper over M'Haffety's bar. "He's always been one of those safe sawney old chaps; never has a spree or goes in for any money-wasting antics."

In time Mrs Alf returned, and went direct to Billy-go-Billy without delay in town. The few who saw the baby said it was very big for its age. It was a great success. Alf was for some time afraid to touch it. He could only gaze amazedly.

"She's so lovely," breathed the worshipful Norah. "I'm afraid they'll be wanting her from us."

Kind as ever, she had wanted the name to be Dorothy, but feared this might be a pointer. Dot, however, with a spark of the right spirit, said the child's sole and only name should be Norah, after the only person in all the world who had wanted her and welcomed her.

"And Alfred," said Norah. "He wants her as much as I do, and he dotes on children. If ever there was a dear, good, kind husband, it is my Alfred."

"Then her name is Norah Alfreda," amended Dot.

CHAPTER 14

THE YEAR that Milly returned from school Lucy Saunders came up from Turrill Turrill some weeks before Christmas with the intention of putting in her time about Bool Bool. She could not endure the heat at Turrill Turrill and did not enjoy Ten Creeks now that she was no longer mistress there.

"I cannot stomach that Healey crowd," she complained to her sister-in-law, Maud. "I don't care how much we are connected with them, it doesn't make them any more palatable to me."

Neither Norah nor Joanna was seen much at Ten Creeks now, but Julie in her eighteenth year, a gossiping deceitful girl with whom no secrets were safe, was much more offensive.

SP-over-J, happening to be in Bool Bool, went to meet his niece as she got out of Prendergast's coach, and said, "Well, Milly, are you coming to Ten Creeks? You can come straight up with me now if you like. Your Aunt Aileen hasn't anyone to keep her company, only the servants. I think I'll be able to find you a horse or two worth riding." Stanton was cordial. Milly had retained his goodwill since the marriage.

"How is Auntie now?"

"Couldn't be better. That Melbourne doctor did wonders. A couple of weeks under him was worth all those other quacks put together."

"I'm dying to see the baby."

"He's a great chatterbox."

"I must teach him to ride before he is too old. I'll go up with you now if Mother will let me."

Mother proved amenable because Julie was kept at Neangen to attend her mother, who was ailing. Milly then said, "Say, Uncle Jack, let's telegraph for Uncle Bert to spend Christmas with us. He need not stay at Curradoobidgee for it now that his stepmother is dead." This was also agreed, and Milly sent a long telegram before leaving Bool Bool next morning. They travelled by buggy-and-four to take Milly's portmanteaux, and halted for the midday meal with Dan Spires and Joanna at Wamgambril Springs.

"Who's in Goraig Flats now?" asked Milly. "I saw fowls about and a woman's washing on the line."

"Ronald Dice is managing there this summer for the Macfarlanes of Quondong."

"Is he married?"

"Not yet. One of the girls is with him."

"Then you be sure to tell him to come and see me," said Milly in her old frank way. "I haven't seen him since Uncle Jack's wedding." She was unconscious that this might be delicate ground.

"I expect you'll have droves of spoons after you now that you've grown into such a swell young lady," said the amiable Dan.

"I'll get old Bill Heffernan to lay baits for them," said Uncle Jack. He was almost genial with this niece.

Milly found her aunt's careworn listless look replaced by full cheeks and well-being. The baby was now two years off, as the Ten Creeks people put it, a merry toddler named Lawrence John after his father and grandfather, and a pet with all. He was guarded by a grey mongrel called Towser, one of the progeny of old Bessie, the ancient nurse dog at Neangen. There was no danger of Lawrence's straying into the bush while Towser was about. He had wondrous patience with all small things. Strangers and adults bored him, but the baby could fall all over him, take his bone from him and poke things in his mouth and ears to Towser's fatuous content. Larry had carried him over as a puppy just after Aileen's return from the honeymoon. Mrs Healey insisted upon this guardian, because but for one of Towser's forebears she would have lost Aileen when a baby, and Mrs Bob Milford, over the river, likewise would never be without a canine guardian, for her eldest brother had been lost at the age of three, and never a trace of him again from that day to this.

Milly reached Ten Creeks on a Wednesday, and owing to the telepathic way news spread, there was by Saturday night a full house in her honour. There were Cross-eyed Prendergast and Billings from Gundagai, who had seen the coach come in and suddenly bethought it a good spec to pick up a few colts. There were a young Mazere and Alistair Farquharson. Milly would have attributed Alistair's visit to chance but that he brought a special present. He confessed that he had run into Cuppinbingle Potter in Yass on Thursday. Potter had mentioned travelling from Goulburn with the little girl from Ten Creeks and that she was the likeliest filly he had seen for years. Trust old Cuppinbingle's interest in every mare or maid of promise or performance!

Years before at the muster Alistair had been sufficiently attracted to tease Milly, and later had been the one to take charge of the cremation of Romp's remains. He had been so touched by her owner's grief that he saved one of the hoofs and had it mounted as an ink-pot with silver finish and shoe.

The person who seemed to find most patent pleasure in reunion was Ronald Dice, who came over with his sister in response to the message delivered by Dan Spires, and was so firmly pressed by Milly to stay the night that Aileen added her formal invitation. SP-over-J was compelled to murmur his too because Milly was the centre of attraction and hanging on his arm affectionately. She was the only niece of the liberal broods who would have thought of swinging on SP-over-J's arm. It clinched her popularity. She clearly had never looked upon him as an ogre, who had taken Aileen from her young lover by unparliamentary measures, an attitude grateful to him. In the glow of it, and as victor, he could manage to be outwardly civil to Dice though he did not forget being called to his face a death adder, a dried-up old hide, etc. Stanton was at ease since the Melbourne physician had restored Aileen. It was a pleasure to look at her these days with health and colour glowing in her cheeks after two years of exasperation because she looked like a wilting martyr.

After dinner when the lamps were alight and dancing on the veranda was started, Alistair Farquharson produced his offering and presented it to Milly in the shadow of the raspberry canes at the bottom of the garden. Her eyes filled as she exclaimed in her wholehearted, unaffected manner, "That is so kind of you, Mr Farquharson. Will you please not mind if I don't open it at once. I want to keep it till I am quite alone."

"Certainly, Milly, and I hope you will like it well enough not to call me 'mister' in that stiff way. You make me feel as old as Mr Potter."

"I'd like to call you Alistair; it is such a pretty name," she responded, flitting away to deposit her parcel, unconscious of the thrill she left with its donor. Returning, she rewarded him with a long dance, a creature to enthral a man in her rosebud maidenhood, polished by Miss Lisset and decked in a fashionable dancing frock of accordion pleats with a sash outlining her dainty waist, and wide frills of fairy lace at neck and elbows. But then she went to Dice's arms with noticeable alacrity and Alistair stood in the shade of a rose-bush and watched their every movement. Ronald was exercising all the old charm that Milly had found in him when she was in knee skirts and had championed his cause with Aileen, only later returning clannishly to her uncle because he had been called reptilian names. She was much enjoying being grown up—almost—and back on Ten Creeks Run with the horses.

*　　　*　　　*　　　*　　　*

Potter of Cuppinbingle and his neighbour of Keba shared a room that night, and since it was on the veranda outside the drawing-room they were safe to converse.

"The little jam-puff will have 'em all left at the post before another year is past, I'll make you a bet on it."

"Do you think so," responded Farquharson, so interested that he was self-conscious.

"I'm flaming well sure. A pity she has eyes only for that Dice, and he's running strong with the Missus."

"Oh, that was all over long ago."

"Not a bit of it! She's not the sort to close a thing—no ballast there. She fixes her eyes on Dice like a hungry dog on a bone and never takes 'em off. I wonder what old SP-over-J thinks of it. If I'd cornered a young woman with me money and she looked at the fellow I ousted like that, I'd want a padlock and chain on her."

"Perhaps Milly will take his mind off."

"Not a bit of it! He's only using the girl as a cavalry screen."

Farquharson was encouraged to hear this, but at the same time longed to punch Dice's head. "Someone ought to give old Skinny a hint."

"Nice job that would be! If a man can't look after that sort of affair himself, he deserves all he gets." Rumour was that husbands more than one had what they may not have deserved via the audacity and fascinations of Cuppinbingle Potter.

"Now, if I were your age, Alistair, I'd give Dice a run for his money. There's that Larry Healey got an evil eye on her too. Larry's a taking obliging devil, mind you; he's never a sour-guts, and if he got out a little would make a topping fellow, but in connection with the filly I wouldn't use him for dingo baits. If Tommy Roper is correct he carried on over the odds with Dot Saunders."

"Dot Saunders is not that sort. She's a high flyer and has been away out of the district for ages. Tommy Roper often knows more than really happens."

"I've generally found there's a good deal of fire under his smoke."

"I haven't been talking to Tommy since he started off to Queensland on that droving expedition with Flash Billy."

155

"That soon blew out. They had the devil of a shindy according to old Mick Muldoon."

"What became of Billy?"

"According to Tommy, he got in with a circus and does trick training with horses. That was Billy's downfall here, taught the best colts tricks in hopes they would be sold as outlaws. Poole blew out his little game there with Corroboree." Ensued talk of Corroboree and his form at Randwick and Flemington, for which he had been prepared by the Cuppinbingle trainers.

Other chat proceeded in other apartments. Stanton had to dismiss Towser from the cot of Lawrence John. The dog was forbidden the house because of fleas, but was so faithful that it was difficult to exclude him, and excluded he had excavated like a wombat to lie under the flooring beneath his charge.

"Poor old chappie, I hate to see him turned out," said Aileen. "We'll never lose the baby while Towser is on guard."

Milly had to share her room with Ida Dice. They conversed volubly as they undressed, but in cautious whispers. The slab walls afforded no protection against eavesdroppers, and there were popular ribaldries abroad of what women had heard from men's rooms and vice versa. Milly wanted to talk of Ronald, a dull subject to his sister; Ida to hear of Cuppinbingle, who by his address and assurance in well-worn innuendoes could banish dullness from the ladies. Milly was eager to look at her present, and as soon as Ida was settled, stole out to the sitting-room. When the article was free from its wrappings, the tears at first blinded her, but when they were wiped away she was startled.

This was not Romp's hoof. It was too big.

Milly had a natural gift for the points of a horse—points that can neither be taught nor expressed, but which have to be felt by a kind of sixth sense. A wild hope came to her. Then doubts. In the fitting and curing the hoof might have been enlarged or squeezed out of shape: or the hoofs might have been destroyed and Alistair, meaning well, have substituted.

She spoke with him next morning. "You were most kind to go to so much trouble about that lovely ink-pot . . . The hoof looks so big and different, I should not have known it. Are you sure the jeweller gave you back the right one?"

"There could be no doubt about that."

"You are sure it is Romp's hoof?"

"Quite sure. I went out to the Corroboree rings myself the very next day and attended to things as I promised."

"Perhaps it looks different from what I expected done up that way. You won't mind if I don't let anyone see it for a while."

156

"Not at all." Alistair liked to think of her treasuring it secretly. While breakfast was impending Milly wrote a letter.

Darling Uncle Bert,

Alistair Farquharson has brought me one of Romp's hoofs set as an inkstand, and it is not Romp's hoof at all. Alistair is certain, he says, that it is the hoof of the blue roan that broke its neck over the precipice. If this is so, the horse that was found dead is not Romp at all, and she is still alive somewhere. I am so excited. I could not be deceived in Romp's off-front hoof. It was small and double-banded and wide at the heel and smooth as a bottle. This bulges a bit like a cask that is going to burst the hoops. I am writing to you at once as you said if ever I wanted you to let you know. Even if you weren't coming for Christmas you will come and see as soon as possible about this, won't you? I don't think we should delay, do you?

This was entrusted to Farquharson to post when he left on Sunday night.

So important did Poole consider the missive because of Milly's acumen that he demolished the rough miles between Curradoo-bidgee and Ten Creeks several days before he had intended to set out for Christmas.

Milly had been sure of his response. She was enjoying the ascendancy known to an attractive maid where pioneering left men so natural that she had only to say to one man go, and to another come, and off they went tantivy with knightly willingness, being so placed that they had the horse-flesh and could make the time. Milly accepted all such service as unselfconsciously as the numbers of spirited horses and her skill in backing them, her knowledge of the ranges with the glorious sunlight and air above, the hundreds of square miles of streams and trees gay with gyang-gyangs and cockatoos, parrots and magpies, satin-birds (bower-birds), lyre-birds, blue tits, and a hundred other species; and down below, the wallabies, wombats, kangaroos, goannas, lizards, and the occasional excitement of a snake.

The tall quiet man who had just reached the sixties was pleased by the prospect of seeing something of his young friend. Still strong, lithe, lean, and full of experience, but retaining simplicity of heart, he could hold his own with many that were only half his age. His hair showed but little grey, he had escaped baldness and a broken mouth, and his clear brown eyes still looked serenely and gallantly on life and found it good.

The men were out on the run when Poole arrived, but Milly had stayed in expecting him. Towser being assured that Poole

157

had no evil design on the heir, and other preliminaries past, Milly brought out the hoof. One look satisfied Poole that it was not Romp's. It had carried more shoes than Romp at the date of her supposed passing had had time to do; it had suffered from an unskilled smithy, whereas Poole had shod Romp himself as a very special beast.

"That never carried the Young Whisker filly or any other beast bred between Cuppinbingle and Curradoobidgee," was his pronouncement.

"Then Romp is still alive! That was another horse fell over the ledge." Milly was all excitement.

"If we could be sure that this is the hoof of the Gyang Gyang corpse we could establish the first fact. Blue roans are not common. I have never seen another of Romp's size in the Southern District."

"Didn't you look at the dead horse when it was found?"

"You've caught me napping. The beast was in such an unholy mess in the mud and slush that her hoofs were out of sight. I was deceived by her general size and the mane and tail, and the pieces of hide remaining were blue roan, and I was working on the theory that she would probably make back to Mount Corroboree."

"Didn't you look at the hoofs?"

"Stupid of me! I looked for the brand, but the near-side shoulder was bare to the bone."

"Alistair Farquharson swore on his honour that this hoof came from that beast and that the jeweller could not substitute it. I knew all along that Romp was never fool enough to fall over a precipice. How did she get away from Curradoobidgee? She never tried when I had her up there."

"You'll remember I told you she was trying to get away from Three Rivers the night of the bridge opening."

"So Flash Billy said. I bet he has taken her away and done something with her."

"Now, you mustn't go on a theory without facts, that's what I did trying to find the filly at Mount Corroboree, and you see how I got fooled."

"We must start somewhere. Find out where Billy is and watch him to see if he still has Romp. I don't think he could bear to part with her. It can't do him any harm so long as we say nothing till we are sure. We'll have it as a secret like we did when we ran things when I was little. It makes me feel scrumptiously young again."

It suddenly made Poole feel abominably old—old! He would

need to watch himself lest he decline into senile folly worse than old Jack's.

"I could get the police to find the whereabouts of Billy, could pretend I wanted him for his advantage, so that it would not arouse unjust suspicions about him." This was agreed upon, and Poole turned to other topics.

"You must come and keep me company at Curradoobidgee as soon as Aunt Aileen can spare you," he said at dinner. "I could get some of the nieces over when you come."

"Oh, that is not necessary. I'll come and housekeep for you now that dear old Mrs Poole is dead."

Poole wondered was Milly still a child in innocence, or had she put him in the complete uncle class.

Mrs Lucy Saunders, hearing that Poole was at Ten Creeks, arrived there for a visit on Boxing Day, but though she suggested it, she got no invitation to Curradoobidgee, and Poole returned there a day or two earlier than he would otherwise have done. When Milly turned her face up in the old childish way for a kiss, he affected not to see and attained his horse before saying good-bye, feeling depressed to be so obviously an uncle.

❊   ❊   ❊   ❊   ❊

At that date on Monaro, operating from Braminderra, was a smart young trooper in whose hands Poole placed the matter of tracing Billy Bowes. Shortly after New Year he was informed that when last heard of Bowes had joined Sparr and Leamington's Circus, which travelled all over Australia, in full strength in the cities and divided for the small towns. Bowes was in the division that operated in Victoria. Further information was a roster of the horses employed in the ring by Sparr and Leamington, with brands and ages as far as practicable. Asked confidently what class of horse was sought, Poole narrowed it to galloways, red or blue roans.

In due time Constable Purkis reported that the only horses of such a description were a red roan in the New South Wales branch, and a blue roan five years off with a blotched brand, white hind foot, and star, in the Victorian branch.

The star and white hind foot were misleading, for Romp had no white spot. Constable Purkis supplied a country paper in which was a story of the clever circus pony that could buck herself out of every piece of tackle without breaking or straining a buckle.

"I knew," said Milly.

"Still, it is only circumstantial evidence," said Uncle Bert. "Billy trained your filly to that trick, he could train another."

"He could train any donkey mongrel to buck, but he could not find another so clever as to get out of everything like a conjuror. Will you take me to that circus to look at that pony?"

"But it's away in Victoria and they might hear of us coming."

"We needn't let anyone know we were going. We could just slip off together quietly."

"Then we should be in the soup! People would think I had . . ." He was going to say "unlawfully abducted you," but on the brink he substituted "that we were murdered, and all the papers would advertise it. Instead of secrecy we should have the whole bally country buzzing."

"I suppose we might have to tell Mother and Uncle Jack what we were off to do, and then it would be all right."

Poole took refuge in the need for secrecy and agreed to think out a plan.

CHAPTER 15

IT WAS a lively year for Ten Creeks Run. Aileen, well and happy, and the baby at a most interesting age, were staple attractions where men outnumbered women, and there were occasional visits from Milly's school friends. Above all there was Milly, and there was not a foot-loose man of any age who would have thought forty or fifty miles on Saturday afternoon and again on Sunday night, or the prevailing financial stringency an insuperable barrier to spending a few hours within sight and sound of her. The Mesdames Milford, too, over the river, enjoyed visits from one station to the other a-horseback.

Among the men that swarmed in Milly's direction certain persons stood out as of definite intention. These were Alistair Farquharson, Potter, a young Stanton from Mungee, Matt Dice as well as Ronald, and Oliver Brennan from The Gap. There was also Beverley Dash, a surveyor new to the district, and the hopeless slave Ted Billings, now overseer in place of Dan Spires. Some of these brought women with them occasionally.

Of the crowd, Ronald Dice was the most envied, for it was plain that he was Milly's favourite; but hope would die in none of them until Milly should be disposed of. To keep an eye on Milly, ostensibly, her mother was frequently at Ten Creeks that summer. Aileen let her manage to her heart's content. If any woman could not agree with Aileen, the fault would not be Aileen's bossiness, and Lucy wanted to be at Ten Creeks, so made herself more agreeable than when she had been missus-in-chief.

Poole began to find the distance between Monaro and the lower Coolgarbilli so insignificant that he, too, thought nothing of dropping in to spend Sunday, and, since he was not pressed for time, often arrived on Friday and did not depart till Tuesday.

"There's fresh talk of a match between Mrs Lucy Saunders and Curradoobidgee," said Mrs Isaacs in her back parlour.

"He'll be dhruv to marry someone now that he's on his lone."

"Yes, an' Lucy bein' put out of her nest, will be more desperate in her attacks."

" 'Twould be very suitable. He's a quiet man an' used to a managing woman raging about, an' well able to affoord a wife,

161

an' it's better dacincy to the dead—meanin' poor Emily Mazere who was drownded—than for him to be runnin' round afther some young thing like ould Stanton did."

"But that's turned out very happily now. Aileen is looking bonny and her boy is a beauty. That last doctor in Melbourne fixed her up completely."

"Marriages for property are jinrilly always more sinsible in the end. There could have been no thruth in half the talk. Ronald Dice, I hear now, is just wild afther Milly, an' she is favourin' him."

"She's only a girl yet. Her mother I hear means to take her to Sydney for a season when she is eighteen."

"She's comin' on, an' she'll have to marry. They haven't more than a penny without, an' if her mother doesn't look out she'll be takin' up with some of these scrubbers before she comes out in Sydney. Ida and Olive is always over there too thryin' to pick up something in the crowd."

"Well, if old Joanna and Norah got off, the Dice girls should stand a better chance; they're good-looking."

"Ah, but they're waitin' for something more profitable than they'll catch in the ind."

Lucy Saunders had a similar idea one pleasant Saturday afternoon at Ten Creeks. "I think some raspberries would be nice for supper," she suggested to Poole, who had arrived while Milly, Aileen, Ida Dice, and Flora Farquharson had gone for a bogey.

"I hope they are in a safe place," Poole had observed. Lucy recalled that his uneasiness was reminiscent of the fatal Saturday afternoon long ago when his bride-to-be had been drowned. She did not allow his thoughts to linger in such a channel.

"They've gone to that place where the water is drawn from, more danger of getting bruised on the boulders than being drowned there. Some of the men have gone to the Slate Hole to shoot ducks. Our only hope of distinguishing ourselves is with the raspberries. If you'll hold the billy, I'll pick."

Soon they were busy among the canes. "I see Potter and Alistair just dropping in," observed Mrs Saunders.

"Farquharson has it awful bad. You'll soon be losing Milly if you don't look out."

"Oh, she's only a tomboy yet. Now is the time I miss her father. I do need someone to help me guide her, someone who would understand her."

"Milly is a ripping youngster. She has lots of solid ballast in that head of hers."

"Yes, but I do feel the need of a man to guide her."

"There's not much in the present crowd to pick from." He

looked away at the hills over the Coolgarbilli, glorious under the sinking sun, wondering where was the man good enough for Milly. "Reckon he's never been foaled," he chunnered.

"She seems taken up with Ron Dice for the present."

"That's not half good enough. A fellow that was making such a noise about Aileen two or three years ago is not steady enough for Milly. Matt is steadier, but as poor as a church-mouse, and not much head for getting on."

"Oliver Brennan has joined the throng lately."

"He is the best of the boiling, but the religion is the trouble there."

"Yes . . . Larry seemed infatuated at the start, but he's never here now, thank goodness. I don't want any more of the Healeys."

"Larry, mind you, is a taking fellow in his way—good-looking, and a great rider. If only he had a chance he would make a fine man, but in connection with Milly, he's not to be considered. He and Dot were for ever together till she went away, but she's well able to look out for herself."

"I should hope so. It's to be hoped she picks up something better than Larry while she is away."

"Girls like Dot often pick the crooked stick."

"She used to be all eyes for Ron Dice, but he did not seem to respond."

"Perhaps that's why she turned to Larry."

"Financially and socially, of course, Donald Potter has a position that none of the others can touch, and he's foolishly infatuated."

"But good heavens, Lucy! You wouldn't mention him in the same breath with Milly! He's old enough to be her father, and apart from that no fit associate for an innocent girl."

It relieved Mrs Saunders to hear Poole condemning as fatherly, in connection with Milly, one who was nearly twenty years his own junior.

"Perhaps it is fatherly ideas he has."

"You should encourage him, then," said Poole, with his serene smile. "Cuppinbingle is a topping place, he has heaps of money, is a jolly fellow and no end of a nob—just right for a woman of experience."

"Too jolly for my taste. Money doesn't attract me like good qualities. I should like a congenial companion. If Milly marries I shall be desperately lonely. Don't you feel lonely too, especially since your dear old stepmother died?"

"Sometimes, but I'll have to put up with it. The women all gave me the go-by for someone else."

"You can't have asked the right one. You should try again." She looked at him with an encouraging laugh, but he said the billy was full and he had better go for another vessel, and turned away noting that Jerry Riddall was penning the fat calves, and Long Billy hitching old Flea Creek to the water-slide to go down where Milly was swimming, so she must soon appear now. He was·shot with delight by the thought of plunging with Milly in the cool of the evening, while the rocks were still warm, in the river pools banked with maidenhair, mint, and mimulus, and heavenly with the scent of tea-tree and heath, with the agile water goannas lifting their tails like an old lady her skirts and scampering away—but that he could never do in this world. Men and women did not dip together unless indecent, or man and wife, and Milly was decent as the dawn, and he was over sixty and she only seventeen.

There was Saturday night discussion in the hut. Old Heffernan had come in from Wamgambril and he had an instinct for news rivalling Mrs Isaacs's, with the added tang of malice.

"Ole Lucy got the Curradoobidgee blackfellow copped yet?" he inquired.

"Nope," said Long Billy Riddall. "If you ask me, the ole cove is as dead shook on young Milly as any of the young 'uns."

"An' he's jist as likely to be in the runnin'."

"Not he. She's dead shook on Ron Dice. Allers was, when she was in pigtails, an' before he got sloppy about the Missus."

"Sloppier than ever now, ain't he?"

"Garn! I don't think so."

"Don't be a —— mopoke. That's what cured her. They went to Melbourne together that time they reckoned the new doctor done miracles. Tommy Roper had it from a feller—you know, Jerry Porter, Tim's brother. He was workin' on Turrill Turrill, an' left—got a job truckin' some fats that Dice was in charge of, to Melbourne; an' you oughter know, Billy Riddall, your own brother, is guard on that train, an' he told Jerry Porter, an' he told Tim and Tommy. He reckons if ole Skinny Guts knew . . . well . . ."

"Garn! You're makin' it up," said Jerry Riddall. "He never told me."

"Musta forgot. You don't know you're born yet."

" 'Rared onder a hin'," contributed Long Billy.

"Yes, Dice is only makin' a blind of the young 'un. Ask Jane Humphreys, she's seen 'em kissin' an' muggin' like a house on fire."

"Seen who kissin' and muggin'?"

"Dice and the Missus, of course."

"Garn! You're makin' it up."

"All right! How much will you bet me? Did I make it up about ole Skinny? Who seen him goin' off the hooks first?"

Heffernan, prevented by environment from indulgence in illicit life beyond getting the better of his fellows in petty ways or an occasional alcoholic debauch, found peculiar zest in contemplating all likely deviations from virtue or honesty.

"Well, if that's true, I'll —— well eat me hat!" said Long Billy, meaning to keep his eyes open in future. Old Heffernan was a knowing old cockatoo, take him all in all.

Family scandals were then eclipsed by the tales of Red Joe, the surveyor's link man, who had arrived with his master in time for the evening meal. These were all of shooting blacks in Queensland, and of the virility in handling the gins afterwards, splendid red-blooded tales to tickle the ears of real men of the mettle which makes mighty soldiers or lovers.

*　　*　　*　　*　　*

The summer slipped past, perfumed and cool by the singing Coolgarbilli and its creeks, draped in ferns and foliage where the gyang-gyangs and other parrots decorated the tree-tops. As March shortened the days and brought a nip to the nights, the movement of stock down the Murrumbidgee should have begun, but there was no profit in shifting livestock about for their health that season. It was a dreadful year of strikes and soup-kitchens. Abundant seasons and over-production coupled with the maldistribution inseparable from the civilized world's system of economics had that spring culminated in one of the recurrent financial panics of the generation. It was impossible to realize more than a shilling or eighteenpence per head for fat wethers, and it cost more to truck them to Homebush than was procurable for them. Inferior stock could not be given away. Boiling-down came into fashion again. Money was scarce. Breaking banks and bankruptcies were common, and people had other preoccupations than moving from place to place for the climate.

The Isaacses, for example, had their hands full in standing to the district with liberal credit till money should circulate again, and dispensed it with a friendly generosity that gave them first place with the old inhabitants till the end of their days.

In the circumstances Stanton decided to leave a good deal of stock to take their chance in the mountains, and suggested remaining there himself with his family to see that dingo-hunting was not neglected. Aileen assented willingly. Ten Creeks was no lonelier or colder than Jinninjinninbong, where the Milford women stayed winter and summer, having no other holdings to shift to, also Aileen had been informed by Dice that the Macfarlanes were to leave some sheep at Goraig with himself in charge.

The days were short and bleak in the valley of the Coolgarbilli, from which the sun departed early over the high wild ranges back of Corroboree, and on many a southerly sideling the frost and upstanding icicles rarely melted. The station-hands shot a heavy harvest of possums and wallaroos for their winter pelts from which to make the great rugs in which they curled o' nights and slept like the blest. Visitors disappeared from Ten Creeks and Jinninjinninbong. SP-over-J was called to Turrill Turrill, for there was disease in the Riverina flocks. Lucy was there to housekeep; Milly kept Aileen company at Ten Creeks. Milly preferred Ten Creeks and Bool Bool to Riverina, and that winter Ronald was an additional magnet. None to her had his charm.

A dozen men could appear armed with valentines or packets of bull's-eyes, or jujubes or sugared almonds or Scottish mixtures, or gorgeous work-boxes, or scrap-books, or a riding whip, or a saddle cloth, or a carved quandong, or any other current bait, and Milly might be gracious or indifferent, but Ronald's voice penetrated and thrilled immediately among a score of others. The turn of his head lent romance to the day; a banal joke from his lips was convulsing. Why? Milly could not have said.

This was plain to Ronald, though for a time he thought of her only as one of the little girl sweethearts that have sweetened the way of all kindly, cleanly young men of virile charm in the bush. It was Aileen who became aware of Milly's more adult emotions, and was uneasy lest she should lose her own kingdom till she recognized in Milly the requisite subterfuge.

Ronald greeted Milly with whole-hearted cordiality when he came and was guarded with Aileen, and for further example he was so unrestive and agreeable in the company of Lucy Saunders that she could not suspect there might be another at hand for whom he pined. Even Jane Humphreys felt while Mr Dice talked to her that she was a charming wench and had as good a chance as the ladies of being in the running.

When Ronald appeared on Saturday evenings to spend Sundays, it was Milly who met him and who could be heard laughing with him and arranging to try his horse, whereas Aileen sometimes did not appear till the evening meal. He always brought two offerings, whether of sweets or ornamental scraps, which pleased Milly, for the "gooseberry" in her day shared in such spoils equally with the rose herself. For the same reason Aileen did not begrudge Milly her perquisites.

Ronald came one afternoon in June with the depressing news that his employers had decided to take the stock out of the mountains.

"My goodness, Aunt Aileen, Ronald says he has only come to say good-bye. Isn't he mean to desert us? Won't it be dull?" Milly was frankly downcast at the prospect of his departure, but immediately thought of letters as the next and more progressive stage. She was not looking at Aileen or she would have seen her face paling. Ronald, looking over Milly's head, was touched to tenderness and complacency.

SP-over-J was at Turrill Turrill. Ronald and the overseer were the only men among the inside family that week-end. There had been snow on the hills. Mount Corroboree had a white cap and the Jinninjinninbong ranges, reflecting the setting sun, looked like iced Christmas cakes, which made it cosy beside the music and heat of the great log fires. Aileen wished to be rid of Milly, but the attraction for her was too great, also for the overseer. Release came through Lawrence John, who was wrestling with a cold. Milly, with a young girl's joy in a baby, in her abounding energy gave more attention to her little cousin than did his mother. It was her delight to smuggle him to her bed these cold nights.

"I hear Lawrence John," said his mother, "and, ah ha! he's away from my room."

"I'll go to him. I want him," exclaimed Milly, forgetting Ronald in the plaint of her animated doll. Aileen did not gainsay. As Milly left the room the draught from the door caused the flame of the lamp to lick its chimney to blackness. The overseer sprang up to shut the door and went out with Milly and away to his own room; he too was suffering a cold.

"Oh, Ronnie! Are you really going away, when?" broke from Aileen.

"I have to be back at the Flats ready to start operations early on Monday morning."

Aileen looked at him tremulously. "How can I bear it?"

"You have Milly and the nipper."

"Yes, but SP-over-J. Oh, you don't understand; the very thought of him makes me feel limp and tired like I used to before I found you again."

"Cheer up! Let's hope he breaks his neck one of these days."

"Oh, but he won't. I'm afraid you'll break yours."

"Say it is too cold for the nipper and go down to Turrill Turrill. I could easily pop across from Macfarlanes."

"Oh, I couldn't! They'd see through that. I was so anxious to stay up here; besides, Lucy is settled there now."

"But you're the boss, when all is said and done."

Aileen shook her head tearfully. "Will you write?"

"Rather risky, don't you think; everyone knows every letter and who it is from."

"You could write to Milly and I could read between the lines."

"Poor old Milly. She might read between the lines, too."

"She's only a sentimental little girl. Besides, I want Larry to marry her when she is old enough."

"It looks as if Larry and Dot would be more likely."

"Do you think they will make a go of it?"

"It seems to have blown over, and she is away, but if what they said was true they ought to have married a year ago."

"What did they say?"

"I don't want to throw any stones or I might get my own glass shivered, but Dot went the pace for a while. That's generally the end of horsey women."

"Perhaps it's only horsiness, and they make the rest up."

"Very likely."

He was not going to traduce Dot. She had too plainly favoured him. He felt rather guilty, having found her a grateful refuge in the days of his despair, and having sheered off callously only after a certain trip to Melbourne. The look in Dot's eyes had sometimes shamed him in light of what he himself had been through. Now here was young Milly, so straight and sincere, more affectionate and generous than Dot. He did not want to hurt her himself, and he did not think Larry good enough for her. At any rate Milly did not consider Larry at all, and Larry, if Ronald knew anything, had reaped a harvest from Dot's reckless disappointment.

Otherwise there were his own affairs, and a virile young man still enamoured of his one-time love, now the wife of the hated old conqueror by wrongful pressure, does not live by platonic bread alone. Lawrence John took a lot of comforting that night. Milly could not leave him.

Jane Humphreys, successor to her sisters, when she knew the Missus and Mr Dice to be alone, suffered overweening curiosity to observe them. She was not always able to hear what they were saying, but the amateur construction of the house afforded opportunity for the eye. Before retiring she entertained Long Billy with the result of her observations. Billy came in for more familiar treatment when most of the kitchen courtiers were dispersed by winter.

"Golly! If you want a circus, you oughter sneak inter the back passage and see the Missus and Ron Dice kissin' an' muggin' like . . ." She doubled in giggles.

"Garn! You're makin' it up! Where's young Milly? She's supposed to be the gooseberry."

"The kid is squawkin' an' she's lookin' after him."

"The next one'll have to be called Ronald," said Long Billy with loud delight in his own wit.

"You shut up! You shouldn't say such flash bold things to a girl."

"Better by a long shove than doin' them. A pity young Milly doesn't come upon 'em suddent. It'd cure her. I wonder what she would do."

"Oh, she's too simple. She wouldn't understand. They'd smoodge her over with some yarn. I heard some of what they was sayin' too. It was real rich . . . these swells if you ask me . . ."

"Fat lot of swell about old Healey and his wallaby-run at Neangen!"

"But they used ter own some reel swell place on Monaro."

"Got it in a swell way too, if what you hear is gospel."

"Well, the Stantons and Saunderses and Mazeres are real swells."

"Some of the old coves is, but some of them others will be lucky to have as good a job as I have, if I know anything. Tell me what you heard."

"You tell me something first."

"I know so much I don't know where to begin. Suppose I tell you that the horse killed out at Corroboree rings wasn't Romp at all."

"Well, I never! What was it, then?"

"An' what's more it was chucked over there, just to lead 'em astray."

"Did you know at the time?"

"Er course I did. What do you take me for?"

"Smarty!"

"I wuz smarter than the others, even ole Poole who's supposed to be such a crack—better'n a black tracker—he didn't know no better neither."

"Why didn't you tell him?"

"Sometimes it pays not to tell all a cove knows."

"Pooh, I suppose they knew all the time and just didn't want to upset Milly."

Jane had a masterly way of discrediting Long Billy's most important announcements. He made a further effort.

"But the Young Whisker filly ain't dead at all!"

"Well, I never! Tell me about it."

"Only if you tell me what you heard 'em say first."

There followed an unsavoury account of Dot Saunders and Larry Healey as touched upon by Dice and Aileen. Only great Sodoms afford safe cover for irregularities, and even the greatest cities sometimes unexpectedly belch their secrets.

CHAPTER 16

It was a cold wet winter and the dingoes hungry and bold. Foals and calves that came out of season were not safe from them and kept the rouseabouts and boundary-riders busy setting traps and laying baits and trying to get a tough old enemy or two with the rifle.

Aileen was terrified of dingoes and had a notion that they would carry off Lawrence John, but he was safe with the faithful Towser, who never let his charge out of his sight during the day and kept within scent of him by night. His mother slept with her head under the blankets and wept with fright when the howl of the pack was borne down the deep lone gullies of Ten Creeks and Jinninjinninbong by the spifflicating winds from the source of the Snowy. She could have gone to Riverina but SP-over-J was there, and to remain at Ten Creeks relieved her of his company. Milly stoutly stuck to her post, though trekking to Turrill Turrill would have taken her nearer to Ronald.

Her fibre was different from Aileen's. The lonelier and louder the howl of the dogs on the wild winds the more she enjoyed it, and when it was augmented by the wail of curlews and plovers as well as the clamour of the chained station dogs, she listened enchanted. It seemed like a tocsin of something more intrepid than pottering about the house, gardening when the ground permitted, playing with Lawrence John, and occasionally going out on the Run in the hunts for the shy rock-wallabies, whose skins made luxurious bed- and buggy-rugs. It was her delight when night had fallen to walk on the ridge beside the Coolgarbilli and imitate the moan of the dingoes. There was a deep gully on the other side of the river walled by precipitous cliffs through which Mountain Creek in musical hurry joined the larger stream, and which was a congenial highway for the canine depredators. It was sport for Milly to decoy them to the river's edge. Her mimicry was so good that they would come in force. The men set traps and baits there and a dozen brushes, as well as a few paws left in the traps, were credited to Milly, who was cherished by the station-hands for her courage and high spirits. The overseer was her avowed slave, as were several of the hands, who could not express their feelings. They could, however, discuss her among themselves.

"Wonder who'll carry her off?"

"Alistair Farquharson has the runnin' to himself these days."

"Aw, she looks on him like a brother an' seems sweetest on Ron Dice."

"Too much of a kid to know her own mind."

"Wait till she does and there'll be some fun."

"I reckon she knows her own mind now. I'd like to see them tryin' to marry her off to some old hide like was done with the Missus . . ."

"Oh, the Missus, she's a ——, one of them faggots that lays down under things an' lets everyone do what they like with her."

"I reckon there'll be a big bust-up there one of these days."

"There ought to be if ole Skinny Guts ain't blind."

"Perhaps he's tired of her now an' don't care."

"All the same, he wouldn't be wantin' another bloke to make a mug of him. You jist wait a bit!"

"Do you think young Milly knows?"

"Not she! Too innercent. Doesn't know how them things is worked. Golly, wouldn't I jist like . . ."

"Like what?"

"Aw, nothing. I was just thinkin' how some fellers has hell's own luck."

"How do you mean?"

"Aw, to git a nice innercent young girl."

"But what about the girl's luck?"

"That's different. Their luck is to git a lot of spondulics for theirselves without sweating their eyeballs out for it, an' a nice little treasure like ole Skinny throwed in."

There followed guffaws and unprintable obscenities about procreative functions and existence in general, and in particular as applied to Mr and Mrs Stanton of Ten Creeks Run and Turrill Turrill.

*   *   *   *   *

While Aileen found life an intolerable ache of inaction till Dice should return to her neighbourhood, Milly was considerably if not worthily employed. Mr Blenkinsop had done her good service during his reign, for the conventions of his education at least directed him towards the classics and he had supplied Milly with a pile of these. She read every other romance procurable, from Miss Braddon's to Rhoda Broughton's, and one or two of her admirers were astute enough to discover her preference for books before sweets. The pity was the absence of anyone to introduce her to the best literary pabulum for her vigorous ripening intelligence.

Lack of engagement of her mental energy in such an environment resulted in entertainment through her many admirers—neither consciously nor maliciously as a coquette, but inevitably. She had been strictly reared in the convention that a man must make all the sexual advances. In her code a girl should not lower herself by pursuing her predilection, but must stifle emotions till they were wooed into life. It was a useful inhibition in Milly's case. Her adolescent fancy clothed Dice in romance and the correspondence with which he favoured her became engrossing. Her letters were so frank and open that neither her mother as guardian, nor Aileen as rival, could find in them cause for alarm. Ronald's were in the same style, with not a line of capital for a breach-of-promise action. Occasionally there was a message on which Aileen could feed her heart, though it was to "Aunt Aileen".

Nevertheless, Milly's imagination was engaged. She hungered for the tone in Ronald's letters that she felt must develop. This made her sometimes play up the faithful Alistair, whom the winter had not deterred from riding up every now and again. Aileen's loneliness too induced her to coax her brother, Larry, to visit her. He had to come across snowy ranges, and had not been at Ten Creeks for two years, but being in a chastened mood after his danger and kind rescue by good old Norah, felt a sudden family affection and decided one Saturday to ride over and visit Aileen.

He was too ashamed to go near Norah those days, so happy was she in the success of her hoax. There was something imbecile, almost indecent, in this ratty old pair's obsession with parentage, even vicariously. Larry had not seen the child and lived in mortal terror of it. Dot's name was never mentioned to him. He kept sedulously out of the Saunderses' path and they never by line or word took any notice of him. He could not marry Dot when she so truculently repudiated him and was not even in the district, and thus in an unexpected way he had escaped the consequences of their fall.

He arrived at Ten Creeks one August evening. He saw Milly. He was dumbfounded by the change in her. He had liked her and been friendly with her in her hobbledehoy stage, and the new Milly in winter association threw him headlong into a torrent of passion. A gun could not have kept him away thereafter. Aileen's loneliness was an excuse for his presence and in bad weather he could break his journey with Dan and Joanna at Wamgambril Springs.

His entanglement with Dot had started with the bad influence

173

of what had transpired with Aileen. Times were hard, he had been looking round for a girl from a propertied family. Their interest in horses and Aileen's marriage into the family had thrown him and Dot together. The combination of boredom, disappointment, waywardness, and lack of self-discipline, had been responsible for what followed, and Larry was as put to it as Dot to comprehend why. It had done something to generate in Larry what in his day was called a soul. He felt real shame in light of the swift clean flood that overtook him concerning Milly. A decent record would have given him more courage.

Soon the intensity of his passion smothered all scruples of unworthiness, leaving only determination to possess at any cost and all hazards. Sophistry upheld him. In the first place no one knew of the disaster with Dot but those whose interest it was to bury the secret. Norah and Alf could not divulge it without making of themselves a laughing-stock from Bool Bool to Monaro and back to Queanbeyan and Yass. The Saunderses were unlikely to deflect Milly from him at the sacrifice of Dot and their own shame. The Stantons and Saunderses though a clannish family had internecine rivalries and would rather have let outsiders know their disgrace than for one arm of the family to confess inferiority to the other.

Larry blessed Dot now for her fierce repudiation of him which left him without public scathe. He hoped she would collar some other fellow and all would be safe. Thus in the beginning there was no obstacle but Milly's attitude. She laughed at him. There had been no change in him from chrysalis to butterfly. He was the same old Larry and her fancy otherwise engaged. Larry, however, in his first real surrender was so whole-hearted and engaging that he did not alienate her.

*　　*　　*　　*　　*

Spring broke at length. The Macfarlanes, upon the advice of their mountain manager, were to remove their sheep to Goraig Flats early that season. Dice came up well ahead to see to fences, etc., and was the real inauguration of the season on Ten Creeks Run. SP-over-J arrived shortly after to be ready for the horse muster. He was glad to be with Lawrence John, for he was not wanting in parental affection, and the boy, now a little over three, was full of allure.

Aileen began to live again.

Another who found a renewal of life was Cuppinbingle Potter. He was described as a man of the world and fitted the description in all that the term implies of the sexual activities of a lusty, open-air man entering the forties. He had such a sparkling reputation for cicisbeism that SP-over-J, imperilled by a young and very pretty wife, was uneasy by his established visits to the Run. His fears were groundless. Aileen was much too insipid. A man who handles thoroughbred horses applies the same standard to women, and it is a high one. Since clapping his eyes on the blood filly, as Cuppinbingle thought of Milly—far from disrespect—all other women had grown stale. She was very young, and often he halted with the unhappy reckoning that when a girl rising eighteen would be thirty-six, a man of forty-two, alas, would be sixty, and the world simply alive with men ready to act with Mrs Donald Galliard Potter as Mr Donald Galliard Potter had earned renown by acting with a good half-dozen ladies, whose husbands, he flattered himself, had been entirely fooled. His own tactics would make him for ever suspicious if in possession of an attractive wife. Then Milly would banish melancholy. He would be at the top of his form and appetite for ten or fifteen years yet, and ten, even five or two years with Milly was a heaven of reward for a subsequent eternity of cuckolding or discontent. The girl was a thoroughbred. It was in her carriage and her mellow little waist, plump yet supple, and achieved with a minimum of the lacing necessary to other women. And oh, the peach and roses of her skin, her luxuriant shining hair, her soft and saucy chin, round and comfortable, denoting stability! He had noted that the little heart-shaped faces like Aileen's had no strength back of them. When he betrayed husbands it was likely to be with one of those enchanting little baggages without the backbone to stand firm to either side. But Milly had mettle. It was in the play of her lips, in the flash of her clear, brave, grey eyes. She was sure to have a paddy, and there was nothing in the whole gamut of passion so thrilling as a thoroughbred with her monkey up. Milly in a corner would fight gamely, life or death, not survive by compliance. And the fragrant youth of her!

The thought of Milly clothed only in her own luxuriant tresses lured him on to accept the noose of matrimony, that being the only noose that could be spread for Milly. Once married of her own choice he felt sure she would stand firm as any woman under heaven had ever been known to stand. It gave the hardened philanderer the best thrill in years to dream of teaching Milly her first thrills, of breaking her to matrimony. Appetite had him in full cry the year in question and he was confident enough to appear at Ten Creeks without subterfuge. He was specially affable to his hostess: his technique embraced all women more or less, but never missed the young and beautiful.

"He's using Milly as a blind," cogitated Stanton, his suspicions alert towards Cuppinbingle while they had gone dormant in regard to Bookaledgeree.

Potter knew to a nicety how the competitors were placed. The child, he calculated, was taken with Dice, but nothing serious— a girl's day-dream of love rather than the mastering passion itself, and a glance exposed Dice's tactics. Milly, the peerless, unbacked filly used as a blind for that other piece of mere rag! Cuppinbingle snorted at the lack of judgment of some fellows, consequent upon being "rared onder a hin", as his retainer put it. He chuckled to estimate how Milly would take being used as a screen. Make that obvious to her—himself careful not to be the bearer of bad news, and Dice's pot would go on with a whack. Then what remained but the tail of a poor field. Lucky for him that Milly was hidden in the scrubs at Ten Creeks instead of in her rightful stall among the débutantes, where she would soon begin to feel her oats. Financial stringency had postponed the society year projected. He could dispose of Dice easily enough, though it was not his man-of-the-world philosophy to spoil sport where he owed no allegiance. He must pull strings and make others do the work. A string unexpectedly pulled on him caused him to pull one almost unintentionally in return.

One Saturday night in September several were sitting round the fire at Ten Creeks, a frost still crisping the bridle-tracks without and making it cosy within. Stanton, Dash, the surveyor, and Potter were left in the dining-room while the others drifted to the sitting-room, from which sounds of gaiety streamed. Stanton's jokes were frequently ill-placed and rarely merry.

"I was thinking of going to Bool Bool tomorrow," he observed, "but I'll have to leave Mr Dash to chaperone my wife—not safe to leave her with a lady-killer like Potter."

To be thus marooned with his ancient host, who was hood-winked by Dice and to watch Milly's eyes brightening for the fellow, to hear her laugh ringing out for him as she played his accompaniments while he mushed love songs, which even the dummies knew were for that short-weight, Aileen, put Cuppinbingle off his form, or he would never have rapped out, "Lot of chance I have with the field in full possession of a gay young flipper like Dice."

"We'd better get Miss Milly to give us a song," said Dash, also somewhat a man of the world. Stanton rose abruptly to watch the tableau in the next room, himself unseen in the doorway. Milly was at the piano. Larry was hanging round her turning the leaves, Ronald was singing a saccharine atrocity with a chorus about,

"Right into the arms of my truly love,
Singing tooralai, ooralai, aye."

He had a true ear and a sweet lilt in his voice. He was looking towards Aileen. Her gaze was towards him in the light of the fire, her heart exposed. SP-over-J let his guests enter his drawing-room alone. He walked out bareheaded into the uninhabited universe under the blazing, frosty stars, and circled the premises hot with a fire perhaps as old as the sun's rays, for all that can be proven to the contrary. Possession of a pretty young wife had long since lost its novelty. A sense of triumph had shaken down to the prosaic salt beef and damper of married existence, but was there danger of him being fooled before the world? This would be worse than defeat before marriage. But very likely old Cuppinbingle was trying to put him off the scent, he would be cunning enough for that. Aileen was rendered mushy by any sentimental song no matter who sang it. SP-over-J went inside with his eyes open.

Ronald was now scuffling among the music head to head with Milly, and Potter sitting near Aileen paying her meaty compliments, by the look of her. Larry was agitating for a game of forfeits, a device highly popular among the amorous to procure a kiss. Stanton watched the game critically and was entirely deceived by appearances. Ronald not once but several times passed by Aileen in favour of Miss Farquharson and Milly's school friend or Milly herself, while Cuppinbingle with great flourish approached his hostess. All was normal as far as Dice was concerned. There were always a lot of idle remarks flying about, and if a man went about with a chip on his shoulder because of them he would be safe only in an asylum, reflected the boss.

✿   ✿   ✿   ✿   ✿

Larry's fervent wish was to hear of Dot picking up some decent fellow and settling out of the district. Her family wished likewise. They heard something far less satisfactory. When the trouble had been averted, old Tom objected to the continued expense of keeping Dot in Sydney, and ordered her home. She again proved refractory. She did not want to see Bool Bool again where her shame would be everlastingly thrown in her face. The family were alarmed. How was Dot to support herself? The second scandal promised to be worse than the first.

"She can go to blazes so long as she keeps out of my sight," said her father.

"But people don't keep out of knowledge even if they are out of sight," said Mrs Saunders. "Look at what we know about the skeletons in other people's cupboards though they think we know nothing."

"That's mostly true," Tom, jun., had agreed. "But it is a great help to keep a thing as private as you can. If it is public it is the first thing told to a newcomer to the district, while if it's pretty well squashed it can only be told as a rumour and not given so much credence by the fair-minded. People may suspect something cronk about Dot, but they couldn't be sure if only she would behave now. She must come home and go straight."

"It's no good of trying to drive her," said Maud. "She'll go mad again and that will be worse, as people will say it is in the family."

They inquired what Dot proposed to do to support herself. She replied that she had taken a situation as housemaid at a first-class hotel. She was a strong, capable young woman, and like all squatters' daughters worth the name, able to do anything from baking a batch of bread to ironing a stiff white-bosomed shirt, driving four-in-hand and shooting, or making her own frocks. The work of a housemaid was no hardship physically.

"Housemaid at the Wynyard, where people from here and Monaro stay!"

"I don't care!" said Pa. "I wash my hands of her. She has gone mad. It didn't come from my side of the family, anyone can see that, and I don't care what people think. Hardly a family but has a lunatic of some sort in it, and they have to put up with it. Look at the O'Maras, respectable people as ever breathed, and in a good position, yet there is old Teddy running about the country."

Pa overlooked Ma. Stupid of him considering he had had a generation of her perfectly feminine conventional persistence in getting her own meek way in face of the most truculent male decrees, flapping of wings, or loud bellowings. Ma's health became precarious forthwith. Her heart played up. Pa had to be up at all hours of the night warming irons to put in the bed and to administer teaspoonfuls of brandy. Worse than all, he could never talk on any subject, whether the price of wool, the curse of fluke, the scoundrelly bumptiousness of the working men in relation to the great strikes, the breaking of the banks, or the deterioration in horse-flesh and youths since his young days, because Ma had to detail her symptoms with abounding garrulity; and the married daughters could not be absent from their own families to nurse Ma, and people incessantly inquired if Dot realized her mother's break-up, and commented upon her continued absence in Sydney, enjoying herself, while her mother needed her so sorely.

Pa became as rabid to have Dot home as he had formerly been to get rid of her, and wrote a letter. The missive wrung his withers, but parenthood is full of similar shoals and tribulations. He ordered and pleaded in turn. He execrated Dot for her lack of filial affection to let her mother die in cold blood, and stated his willingness to let bygones be bygones if Dot would settle down at home and take care of Ma. The price of a first-class fare was enclosed.

Dot was not sufficiently iconoclastic to desert a dying mother. She returned to Saunders Plains. She became retiring in her manner and was seen abroad only at church, and that rarely. She put her retirement on the state of her mother's health, but people surmised that something must have happened in Sydney.

"Must have been trying for some smart city chap and got left," said Lucy Saunders. "And she's getting on now. If she doesn't soon catch someone, she'll be an old maid."

"She always was a bit high and mighty, and being in Sydney, I suppose she doesn't think anyone is good enough for her now," responded her brother Jack.

Only Mrs Isaacs was sure of the cause. "It came off all right," she said to the Mayoress. "I wonder what they did with the child?"

"Now, do ye really believe it was thrue, Rebecca?"

"True as that we sit here."

"Some of thim Sydney doctors is terrible smart now, they might have taken methods. Sure, it's a wicked thing to think of!"

"It wouldn't do to whisper a word about it, us in business."

"Sure, ivery heart knows its own sorrer."

"I hear Larry is now wild after Milly at Ten Creeks. If they don't look out something will be happening there, too."

"Milly's a noice choild—not that sort."

"It's the most unlikely that seem to go off the rails. Look at Dot—who'd have thought it, and with Larry Healey, who they've always turned their noses up at."

"Sure, Milly ought to be sthopped from marryin' a feller like that, if it's thrue."

"It's true as eggs are not fish. You couldn't deceive Jacob."

"Still an' all ye can't prove it, Rebecca."

"It will all come out in the wash."

Fortunately they had heard nothing to throw suspicion on the parenthood of Mr and Mrs Alfred Timson at Billy-go-Billy, and the little Norah Alfreda throve in love and indulgence.

Larry, hearing of Dot's return, had a fresh access of fear. Conscience-smitten, he scraped up a five-pound note, not without personal sacrifice, seeing the times and the strain put upon his exchequer by the Ten Creeks adventure, and sent it to Norah.

179

She wrote in return a kindly letter, heavily sealed and ambiguously worded, begging that he should not act so again, as it was not necessary. Larry was much relieved that Norah did not ask him to go to Billy-go-Billy, for the thought of his daughter filled him with terror. Norah wished to minimize Larry's ownership of her treasure. As a certain young lady did not care for him, she prayed that she as well as Larry would soon be happy with someone else. This, Alf and Norah calculated, would be safer for their foster-parenthood than if the two parents were to marry.

Mrs Saunders was equally relieved that Norah begged her too never to send another five-pound note.

"God bless old Norah and Alf," thought Larry. Norah's hope that he would be happy with someone else seemed to free him officially from obligation to Dot, and he turned more assuredly to Milly. Dot and her family entirely ignored him and this released him from blame in the episode unmentionable. He felt sure it had not been divulged even to Milly's mother, though she was a sister-in-law of Saunders Plains.

He was familiar with every gully and spur and sideling, wombat-holed or lyre-bird decorated, where the gyang-gyangs screeched or the eagles nested on the way from Neangen to Ten Creeks homestead. He had reached that degree of obsession when he would have bartered his soul for a kiss from Milly, and his un-disciplined desire led him to day-dream of situations to give him possession of her, as he despaired of winning her conventionally. He was too engrossed to observe the aftermath developing under his elbow, and the miraculous way he had escaped, without scathe or responsibility for his dishonourable conduct with Dot, was dangerous to his mood.

"Milly, don't you think you could care some day?" he pleaded one week-end when he had her alone, decorating the vases for Sunday.

"Now, Larry, you're always squeaking like that. Let's look at it from practical real life. I don't think I ever shall, but supposing I did, what then?"

"We could marry and settle down like other people, couldn't we?"

"Goodness gracious, how terrible! Just look at all the old married women, so dragged-out looking and like a bundle of hay or a clucking hen if they try to ride again. Just that old dull life, on and on; oh, dear me, no!"

"But it would be duller if you never got married and were an old maid. Now, *that* would be terrible."

"Why?"

"You'd soon be sick of being in some other woman's home and bossed about."

"But I could have a home of my own like Miss M'Eachern."

"Nice dried-up looking piece of old leather she is!"

"Then I'd like something entirely different."

"How do you mean, different?"

"Well, I'm reading a story about a girl now. A lovely young man loved her so much that he broke into her father's house and carried her off one night."

"By Jove, if that's all you want, I'd break into Goulburn jail and carry you off by force—this very night. I'd think it no end of a lark."

"But I don't want you to. If you did . . . oh, well, it's no use. I can't explain."

"Is there anyone else you'd like to break into your room and carry you off? What about old potty Potter?"

"Wouldn't he be a card!" Milly laughed merrily. Larry was reassured.

"Or Alistair Farquharson?"

"You mustn't make fun of Alistair. He is too good for me really, only that I just don't want to marry him."

"It's not Ronald . . ."

"This talk is getting very silly," said Milly, going to place two glass slippers filled with violets on the mantel and keeping her back turned. From there she escaped under the excuse of seeing what Lawrence John was doing, but the faithful Towser was on the job, moving his long-suffering head aside each time his master tried to poke a stick in his eye.

Larry walked about the ridge where the music of the Coolgarbilli was like an urging wind and all the world wild and untrammelled as his thoughts, which ran dangerously on some way of compromising Milly so that her family would welcome the disposal of her to himself.

CHAPTER 17

SP-OVER-J PASSED quietly by the veranda of the men's hut where Long Billy, Tim Porter, Mick Muldoon, and a Keba rouseabout were patching pack-saddles to take rock-salt to the back of Mount Corroboree to trap wild horses, which had lured away several of the station yearlings. The time of the muster was at hand again and the usual crowd gathering at Ten Creeks. The boss paused to give an order, and incautious voices reached his ears.

"What do you think of ole Bill Heffernan's bet now?"

"Aw, I dunno. Wait till old Skinny Guts gits on to it, there'll be a shindy worth watchin'."

"He must know it now or else he's a bigger mopoke than ole Teddy O'Mara."

"Perhaps it ain't any good of him knowin'. What could an ole whistle —— like him do about it?"

It suddenly came to Stanton that these references were to himself. Any boss of men must be of foolishness out-fooling the Teddy O'Maras to imagine that he is generally mentioned in any more flattering terms by his vassals in a free country, but there was more in this than that to SP-over-J. Old Skinny Guts was bad enough, but that other epithet contained an aspersion to make any he-man take his gun, if offered direct. To overhear it bandied about among rouseabouts—a doubt upon his virility, the parentage of his child! Hell! His wife's child.

Had he plucked himself together at that moment he could have put two and two together concerning his heir's immediate lineage, and nothing under heaven could have dickered with the sum total, but an old man does not retain sanity and sweet reasonableness when he hears his employed hands obscenely discussing him, especially when a neighbour of Potter's proclivities has already flung a suggestion in his teeth. The rage of hell racked Stanton's thin bosom. He would fling the brat in the Coolgarbilli and its —— of a mother after it. A shot would do for Dice and a couple more in the backsides for the rouseabouts who dared to describe him thus.

Never in his life had such stinging humiliation been his. It blackened the sun and poisoned the air, the divine air in that region of eucalypts and singing streams. He turned to the stables cat-footed, and took out his horse—the Wamgambril colt—to the sheltering gully back of the stables that carried Breakfast Creek, along which he escaped unseen to ride he cared not whither so long as he could ease his rage. On he went, on and on, past Gyang Gyang Creek and Corroboree Creek, taking no note of the time he was consuming or the sweat he was drawing from his horse, or the circling eagles and crows, the fluttering gyang-gyangs, or the willy-wagtails tweetering, "Sweet pretty creature! Sweet pretty creature!" or the scattering kangaroos, or the horse and cattle tracks which might have been valuable data to the musterers. After a time he was right at the side of Mount Corroboree where he had not been since the search for the Young Whisker filly.

His horse was a trifle blown through being driven up pinch after pinch without mercy. Stanton got off to give him a spell. Then he rode by the old Corroboree rings, where the tall daisies were budding, to the edge of the precipice over which Romp had fallen, and for a wild moment felt like riding off it too, but the Wamgambril, mountain bred, would not be urged within danger. Stanton dismounted again, and while giving his beast a chance to recover set in motion a loose rock. Down it went, breaking through half-grown trees and the unfurling tree-ferns with the thunder of a cannon to crash into the stream below. Rock after rock followed with reverberating echoes in the far-reaching quiet, which Stanton had all to himself. The startled bird citizens whirred up and away in flocks, chattering about the phenomenon as they flew.

The aching immutable stillness had its influence. One might beat with rage against that for an eternity with no effect but to demonstrate human impotence, human insignificance. Nothing came from his outbreak but the refreshing perfume of broken tea-tree, heath, or bracken. The rocks crashed without injury to any-one or anything under the deep blue bowl but a pinprick or two to the stately scrub.

The exercise relieved rage. The quiet restored reason. Stanton reflected that probably the rocks had echoed no such racket since the black men had come a generation back to celebrate and feast on the bogongs. As a boy he remembered them trooping from Mungee and Coolooluk. Now only Diamond, son of Nanko, and a few pathetic specimens remained. They had vanished, leaving no trace but the indistinct circus rings where the immortelles blossomed, but never a tree invaded to this day. Not long and he too would have vanished, and what the sense of his agitation?

His horse, now sweat dry and recovered his wind, provided the final touch of healing by snatching at the sweet heads of kangaroo grass, his good appetite unperturbed by the cannonade, which he had accepted after a preliminary jerk and toss of his imperial head. Mother birds returned to their labours; the silence was filled with the endearing clamour of ever-hungry nestlings. Stanton turned towards home feeling a little sick from foolishness. After all, what had he to go upon? Nothing. He laughed when the term, which had maddened him, was applied by some wag to one of his associates, and thought none the less of the butt of the pleasantry.

He was thankful he had said nothing. No one but his horse suspected what a fool he had been, and he was dumb. Far down the gully from whence the music of a creek ascended could be seen leafy bowers of tree-ferns, sassafras, and tea-tree, and spear-pointed trees of matchless grace indicating young timber. Above rose Mount Corroboree, black and forbidding, silent and still for ever, a dignified sentinel above the tree-tops—mile on mile, ridge on ridge of greens melting into hazy blues with distance.

He rode homeward steadily where to the west the white clouds were massing in mountains fringed with molten gold, of magnificent beauty, and presaging a thunderstorm.

❄   ❄   ❄   ❄   ❄

The household awaited the boss in vain for the midday meal. A rouseabout testified that he was coming towards the house from the garden when he last saw him. Investigation showed his horse was not in the stable and the boy was regarded as an unreliable witness. When Stanton was four hours late there was speculation as to where he could be.

"I'd go and look for him only I don't know which way he went," said Ronald.

"I'll go with you," said Larry.

Milly put on her habit and Larry saddled her horse, a beautiful creature named Merrylegs, lent by Uncle Bert to compensate for the loss of Romp. Larry tossed her to her saddle saying they would go down the Coolgarbilli. Milly looked back for Ronald, but he said, "I'll go the other way," and Milly could not desert Larry without confusion. Ronald stood with Aileen on the veranda watching Milly's spirited and skilled departure on a mare plunging and reefing with spring rejuvenation.

"I must to horse too," said Ronald jocularly, "and, fair madam, a kiss if I bring your good man safely home, and three or as many as I like if I find him with his neck broken."

"Oh, Ronnie, how wicked you are! Ssh! the servants will see you, and you are claiming your payment in advance."

Milly came out on the clearing and looked back. "Whatever are Ronald and Aunt Aileen doing," she cried gaily and innocently. "You'd think he was kissing her like anything."

"I wish I looked as nearly like kissing you," responded Larry.

"Don't be silly!" admonished Milly, dashing away at full gallop.

"Do you think anything could have happened to Jack?" said Aileen after a while.

"Not a bit of it. He's mooching about the run somewhere. Very likely had a bit of tucker with him. It's silly to go looking for him. Nothing ever happens to an old codger married to a beautiful young wife against her will. He'll be thriving when we are both eighty and toothless."

"Lawrence John is very quiet," said Aileen a little later. "I expect he has fallen asleep on Towser." She went to the dining-room where they had left the child with his faithful friend. He was not there. Aileen went through the other rooms, then out on the back veranda. "They must have gone for a walk," she remarked going towards the kitchen. Here she found Jane reproducing her own drama but without the complexity of a deceived husband.

"Have you got the baby and Towser here?"

"No, Mrs Stanton. He was in the dining-room when Miss Milly and Mr Larry went off riding."

"See has he gone down to the hut." He had been known to do that.

Long Billy presently returned without the child. "Old Towser must have him asleep somewhere," said the rouseabout, and set up a whistling.

Everybody whistled. A dozen loose dogs responded, but not Towser.

Fear clutched Aileen's heart. Had the child toddled into the Coolgarbilli, and was Towser guarding him there? She rushed along the bank while others made for the stables, creek, or searched among the raspberry canes and gooseberry bushes in the orchard and garden.

Long Billy called Mick Muldoon to him behind the stables. Towser was there stretched in his death sleep, the foam of his passing agony fresh upon his muzzle.

"Sure to hell, some dog has brought him a bait an' now 'tis beginning to look loike as if the choild is lost entoirely. If it's this way Towser got the bait, beloike the young wan has wandered into wan of the little holes beyant the cow-yard. Sure, 'twould take no

185

more than a billy of water to drown a choild of that age whin he tumbled into it."

Milly returned at that moment and Long Billy told her the news. Milly immediately took charge. She went to her aunt. "Old Towser has had a bait," she said. "That is why Lawrence John has popped out of sight. When did you last see him? He was in the dining-room when I left."

"That's when I last saw him, too," panted the terrified mother. "Ronald and I stood a while watching you and Larry and when I looked round baby was gone, and we couldn't see him anywhere, and we couldn't find Towser."

"Ronald hadn't set out when you missed the baby," said Larry, astutely. "How long have you been looking for him?"

"Not fifteen minutes."

"Then you and Ronald were over an hour on the veranda. Towser and Lawrence John must have roamed towards the stables together, for Towser would never have left the child, and it would be out there towards the kennels that the dog would bring a bait. We must scour round that way. It will soon be dark and there is a thunderstorm brewing."

"If Towser had a bait, baby is sure to have sucked some of it too. I can't bear to think of it," said Milly.

"Bear up, little woman," said Larry, kindly. "We must keep our heads for Aileen's sake. If the poor little nipper got any strychnine he won't be far."

They ran out together searching again under every bush, beside every log, in the cow-bails and calf-pen and kennels. Mick followed the creek at the back. "Sure 'tis as clear, 'tis loike a lookin'-glass. He couldn't be there in his little whoite frock widout Oi'd see him. But sure, Oi'm afraid 'tis the river he's wandered to, and that's a horse of a different colour."

"It's a judgment on me," gasped Aileen, running hither and yon, desperately. "Jack will kill me. I don't care if he does. I deserve it. Oh, God, what am I to do?"

Dice tried in vain to calm her. Here was not only a lost child but a distracted woman advertising illicit love.

* * * * *

SP-over-J did not hurry. Watching the sky, he estimated that he had plenty of time to reach the house before dark and to escape the storm which seemed to be passing round by Jinninjinninbong. He had rubbed his horse down a little with his saddle-cloth and a brush of tea-tree, not wishing to look too much as though he had been riding for a doctor. As he came in sight of the homestead clearing he detected unusual movement afoot. Skirts—his wife's and Jane's—fluttered on the ridge by the stockyards; men and dogs could be seen and heard in several directions. He first encountered Milly, down near the home slip-rails, for she thought the baby might be in the drain there under the long grasses.

"Oh, Uncle Jack! Lawrence John is lost and we can't find him anywhere. Poor old Towser took a bait and that's how he strayed away."

"What's this? Tell me again! Where was he last seen?"

"Larry and I started to look for you about an hour or two ago and left the baby in the dining-room then, and when we came back he could not be found."

"Where was your Aunt Aileen?"

"She was just on the front veranda with Ronald. It doesn't seem possible that he could get right away out of sight so quickly." Milly's words uttered in innocence were a bomb. Stanton could not trust himself in the presence of his wife or Dice. The demon that had erupted earlier burst out again with redoubled fury.

He shouted for Larry and the men and they set off in circles round the house, so that no possible nook might hide the child. Night was falling without a moon. Jane and Milly and the cook were ordered to have a meal ready with all expedition. One man was dispatched on a speedy colt for the Milfords, the most expert bushmen of the region. Another went to summon the black trackers by telegraph from Cootamundra.

Dice was frantically active among the searchers, but it was presently pointed out by the curious that he kept far away from SP-over-J.

It was feared that the child was in the Coolgarbilli, but it was impossible to see into its recesses till daylight. If he was still alive there was danger of the other creeks with which the area was veined, and there were dingoes. To guard against them the place was dotted with groups, each group lighting fires and keeping up a hullabaloo.

Milly was out among the hardiest. There was none to gainsay her. Larry was delighted to have her company and constituted himself her special cavalier in a thoughtful way that was comforting to Milly. About ten o'clock the threatened thunderstorm burst. The heavy downpour filled the creeks and created a dozen rivulets of sufficient strength to sweep away a toddler were he still abroad, and damped the hopes of the seekers. Nothing could be done in the dark and rain, but the men remained abroad owing to dingoes, and because it did not seem human to go to rest with the pet of the station lost in the bush.

Milly called her little cousin till she was hoarse and weary. She was among the party that was dispersing the dingoes towards Mountain Creek. Larry made her a shelter from the wet in the burnt-out bowl of a great tree. The men built fires to dry themselves and boiled the billy and ate the snacks with which each saddle-bag had been provisioned. The night progressed. Larry persuaded Milly to lie down on his coat and saddle-cloth in her shelter, for nothing could be done but keep the fires going. Milly consented in preference to going back to the station, and soon dozed off. Waking after a time she crept near to the fire, wondering had there been any news.

The party had been joined by others from Stanton's posse and were talking, not expecting to be overheard by Miss Milly. Larry was absent taking his turn in keeping up the ring of dingo-chasing fires along the precipice.

"I don't reckon we'll ever see the pore little kid again," said Long Billy. "He's in the river. That's where he is."

"Sure, ye niver can tell. Mr Potter himself was lost whin he was a nipper. He was out near a week, an' him none the worse for it, but he was nearer five."

"A year or two makes a great difference in the strength of little blokes, and there wasn't no thunderstorm and creeks perhaps."

"A terrible thing for his mother," said Tim Porter.

"She'll feel it a judgment on her," said Jerry Riddall. It was at this point that Milly was sufficiently awake to grasp what they were saying.

"Yes, carryin' on there in open daylight with Dice and her youngster bein' lost. It oughter cure 'em both."

"Anyone with eyes in his head that sore 'er that day she was married when she looked at Dice would know how it would turn out. Old Skinny Guts could force old Healey to sell her but he couldn't stop her bein' sweet on Dice. You remember I told you that the first time she ever come to the Run," said Tommy Roper.

"Do you think Dice is as sweet on her as she is on him?" This from Tim Porter, always alert for romance.

"My bloomin' oath, he is! Ain't he allers here takin' the place of old Skinny completely?" said Long Billy. "If I told yous half of what I know, it would raise whiskers on a duck egg."

"Do you reckon ole Skinny knows?"

"Must be blind as a dead goanna if he doesn't. What do you reckon, Mick?"

"That a shut mouth is good for keepin' the flies out and the brains in."

"Supposin' you hadn't any brains to keep in, what'd you do?" asked Paddy Leary of Cuppinbingle.

" 'Tis yourself that should know that without askin' annywan else whatever. Sure, ye've had a power of practice." The guffaw was against Paddy.

"You haven't been rared onder a turkey hin, eh, Mick? But tell us, isn't it young Milly that Dice is cocking his eye after?"

"He that has eyes to see, let him see," said Mick.

"Anyone can see without eyes or brains that Larry comes to see her."

"An' a daisy he is too, to come an' see anyone! What about him an' Dot Saunders? Tommy, you seen her goin' away an' comin' back, too, an' you reckon . . ."

"Tommy has done enough reckonin' to run a store," said Paddy Leary facetiously.

"He generally reckons right, too," said Roper himself. "I say that Larry was the man all right."

"If so, whoi didn't he marry her? It would have been too good a match for him to miss," said Mick Muldoon.

"Old Saunders took a gun to him, that's why. There was near murder done."

"If things were as Tommy reckons, ole Saunders would er been glad to pay Larry to marry her," asserted Tim Porter.

"Do you reckon ole Skinny would do anything if he knew about his missus an' Dice?" inquired Jerry Riddall.

Milly retired, to reappear breaking a twig and coughing. "Where is Mr Healey?" she demanded briskly. Larry was heard coming from his rounds with Dash, the surveyor.

"Larry, I shall go home and see how Aunt Aileen is. There is no need for you to come." But he insisted upon accompanying her.

She did not speak on the way. The night to her had turned much darker than it is possible for a starless night to be. Larry attributed her silence to her distress and the discomfort of the search and held his tongue.

Milly found her aunt alone with Jane Humphreys, sister and successor of Sarah and Ellen, departed in matrimony. Jane could do nothing but weep in face of her mistress's distraught manner. Stanton had not come to her nor sent her any message before joining in the search. She could neither pray, weep, nor rest. It was a terrible night for her, wandering in and out of the silent rooms, stopping to listen where nothing came back out of the silence of the bush but cooees and whip-cracks, or when there was a lull in these, the lorn wail of curlew or plover. The night-birds and dingoes had always frightened and depressed her.

189

"Have you found him?" she asked Milly and Larry, seeing the answer in their empty hands.

"Not yet, Aunt Aileen. We must wait till morning. You must bear up." Larry was touched to see the havoc of the night's events in Milly. She looked white and ill and there was a stricken look in her eyes almost like Aileen's.

"It's no use! It's no use!" wailed Aileen. "It is a judgment on me. Where am I to go? What am I to do?"

"I'm afraid she'll go dotty," Jane confided. "She seems to be wandering, and talks about snakes—unless, of course, she's got the D.Ts."

"Don't be silly! How would Aunt Aileen have D.Ts.?" said Milly reprovingly. "They only come to old boozers."

"Well, it was only that my dad allus talks of snakes when he has 'em, an' I thought the missus might have had a nip to make her bear up."

"What she needs is a little spirits now," said Larry.

Mrs Stanton was persuaded to swallow a nobbler, but it produced only a temporary doze. Milly was also persuaded to take her first dram, and, by its potency on an empty stomach, forced to accept Larry's help to a couch, where under a warm rug she slept soundly till dawn. She awoke to see her uncle meet his wife.

"Have you found him, Jack?" she wailed, running towards him.

"No," he snapped, without seeing Milly, or it might have restrained him. "What does it matter to you whether he is found or not? A nice mother you are! A —— with your —— while your child is lost. I don't see that it should matter much to me either, since I don't know whether he is mine or not. Dice is . . ."

"Oh, Jack, I swear . . ."

"What does it matter what you swear? You haven't got mind enough to tell the truth. Get out of my sight and my house! I've had enough of you." He pushed her as he passed, not a rough push, but she fell under his hand. He walked through the house and out, never looking behind.

His thrust was deeper in the heart of Milly than of Aileen. Where was Ronald now? Would he step in before the world gallantly to stand by his love? It is to be doubted if that aspect of it disturbed Aileen. She was too stricken. Remorse and a sense of retribution justly fallen was so crushing that neither loyalty nor desertion on Ronald's part had now power to affect her. It was Milly who was still normal enough to suffer. On the way home with Larry, trying to operate on the high code laid down by Uncle Bert years before, she had been persuading herself that what she heard was but ignorance and evil-mindedness from the lowest of station-hands, when lo, following it was this scene between her uncle and his wife!

She wilted under the blow and longed to steal away and be lost for ever like little Lawrence John. But actuality and common sense called for action. She rushed to her smitten aunt, who had sustained no injury from the fall but was in a state of nervous collapse. She just lay still and moaned, unresponsive to entreaties that she should get up and lie on the bed.

Milly put a pillow under her head and went for Larry. He lifted his sister onto the couch in the sitting-room. Together they settled her in comfort.

"Come, Sis, you must not give up hope yet," said Larry kindly. "You stay with her, Milly, and I'll fetch Jack."

Milly stepped out the door with him, a hand on his arm. "No, Larry, don't fetch Uncle. He was very angry. He gave Auntie a little push, that is why she fell down."

"He mustn't carry on like that. Aileen didn't know the dog was poisoned. Even if it had been her fault, it doesn't make it any easier for her."

"It wasn't that exactly. You and I must take care of Aunt Aileen ourselves and not let anyone notice. Uncle said terrible things."

"What things?" he demanded sharply.

Milly was too inexperienced to keep her counsel under such a blow. Her face was so set and white that it startled Larry. "Terrible things! I can't bear to go on living if they are true."

"Tell me."

"About Aunt Aileen and Ronald and little Lawrence John. Poor darling little Lawrence John; if only I could find him I'd take him right away and I'd keep him and work for him myself. I'd go to Uncle Bert and ask him to have us and let no one ever see us again."

Larry thought of the embrace on the veranda when he and Milly looked back; how much would it be safe to deny? "Your uncle is driven loony by the loss of the nipper, you mustn't take any notice of him or of anyone else till things settle down again."

"But, Larry, I've heard the men laughing about Uncle for a fool—oh, it was too horrible and nasty!" Virtue and decency, all the ground at the base of ordered existence, seemed to be slipping away.

"None of it's true. Surely you know better than to give any weight to the filthy talk of that kind of scum. Come on, little chum, you and I must stand together and pull this thing through for the little chap's sake."

The appeal to her courage and indispensability was a lucky one.

She was not in love with Larry. It was easy to dismiss the observations she had overheard about him. They were foolish in any case, as no one would ever think such things of Dot.

"I wish we could get Uncle Bert here. He would tell us what to do."

"That's a rattling idea. He's a good one in any scrum. Let's send him a telegram. The mail goes from Keba to Yass today and we could send Long Billy or Jerry."

The necessity of filling the breach saved Milly from the worst effects of her wound for the time. With Jane and the cook and Larry she planned for the impending siege and then cared tenderly for her aunt, forcing a little tea between her lips as a duty; Aileen had become an unclean thing to her.

SP-over-J remained abroad with the men. Dice followed the same tactics and kept away from SP-over-J. He would have given something to know what Stanton suspected of him. A word or two overheard was a revelation. He had felt rather smart and satisfied of just revenge on Stanton till now the sordidness of his position was revealed by the loss of the child. He was puzzled how to act. If the cat was not out of the bag he did not want to be rash.

*   *   *   *   *

The Milfords arrived at sunrise and leadership immediately was theirs. They brought with them the station muster of men and Mrs Bob Milford, wife of the elder brother, to be with Mrs Stanton. Also with them was Ignez Milford, a bright little girl who could ride like a cossack and sing like a thrush. They were all on horseback and cantered up with imposing clatter of pack-horses with provisions, dogs, whips, etc. Mrs Harry Milford had a young infant, so Mrs Bob had sent her children to her to be safe while she herself came abroad.

Harry Milford took charge. He said dingo danger could be dismissed considering the numbers abroad, also poisoning by strychnine by Towser's bait, or the body would have been near about. If the child had not gone direct to the river, one of the creeks must have accounted for him, and it was for the body that the search recommenced. The company was divided into squads within a horseshoe circle, the open end being the Coolgarbilli.

A long bright day wore away barren of result.

Mrs Milford, resourceful and kind, did her best for Aileen, but could not induce her to sleep or rest. She wandered about in pitiful fashion, evidently beyond reach of blame, sympathy, or hope.

"I'm afraid for the poor little soul's reason," Mrs Bob reported.

"The suspense on her is dreadful. She seems so afraid of snakes and hasn't thought of drowning at all. I keep persuading her that it is too early for snakes, but it doesn't seem to reach her."

"There is more in it than shows," said her husband, privately. "Cuppinbingle Potter has been telling Harry the baby got away while she and Dice were carrying on together, and there was a terrible shindy between old SP-over-J and her."

"All a bottle of smoke most likely."

"At any rate, keep your mouth shut and your eyes open. They say old Jack hasn't come near her since it happened."

"He blames her most likely for negligence, and the rest is made up by evil minds. Poor little soul; it is enough to send her mad."

The same sort of watch was kept the second night as the first. The following day was given to exploring the river, clear as glass and showing every stone in its bed. The deeper holes were dragged. It was surmised that the body had been washed into the Slate Hole, so called for the ridge of slate rising on one side of it. It was deep and full of snags. A swamp near by was full of tea-tree springs and a wondrous refuge for wild ducks. A man there in spring could fill his pockets with the ducklings, irresistibly engaging, but they could never be tamed, and the swift Coolgarbilli was always at hand to bear them back to their wild comrades.

A telegram from Poole stated he had been laid up for some time through having cut his foot with an adze. It had been a near go and he was quite helpless. The black trackers were helpless because of the rain.

On the fourth day Harry Milford said, "No man go today where he has been before. Going over the same ground we are likely to get in a rut."

But they sought all day again without result.

On the fifth day he said, "He could be hidden in some little hole covered by a bush. There's no telling where he may be."

"Sure, he's in the Slate Hole, an' 'tis a judgment on ould SP-over-J for takin' the gurrul against her will. It niver pays to have thruck wid the Divil. What comes in over the ould gintleman's back runs away onder his belly."

"Not onder a hin?" inquired Paddy Leary.

"I reckon it's old Larry's things oughter run away under his belly, not only the poor little Missus's," said Tim Porter. "It was him made her marry ole Skinny when she didn't want to."

"Yes, an' both him an' Dice dayserting her now. Sure, that's loife all the time."

Mrs Bob's brother had been lost. Mrs Milford did not remember the occurrence, for she was the nurseling at the time. She did not refer to the incident in Aileen's hearing.

"Mother missed him all her life, still does," she said to Potter and a few more. "The body was never found, and my mother always thought he might have been stolen. I believe she has not given up hope of seeing him yet, but how could she know him?"

"Look at me," said Potter. "I survived after a week."

Mick Muldoon as a lad had been in both hunts, for Potter and Sammy Argyll. He told an unbowdlerized version in the hut.

"It's not thrue that niver a thrace of little Sammy Argyll was seen. That was made up to comfort the mother."

"It hasn't comforted her much."

"Sure, I know what I know."

"Old fool," muttered someone safely out of hearing. "If he happens to be moochin' round where he can't help knowing a thing, he thinks it's cleverness and gets so big in the head he busts his hat-band."

"I heerd all about that story too," said Tommy Roper. "Everyone knows it down the river."

"Spit it out, then."

"Let Mick tell it if he reckons he holds the patent on it. Down the Murrumbidgee there near Broken Dray Crossing on Cuppinbingle, the bullockies won't camp there, they reckon the baby cries there at night."

"Och, you're thinkin' of ould Bowes and his woife, that was drownded whin he was drunk and buried there, they say their ghost can be seen there."

"Pooh, what would they have a ghost for? They never had anything terrible done to them."

"They say the ole man walloped the ole woman something cruel, an' she pushed him in the water when he was three sheets in the wind."

"Bunkum! Mick, tell us about Sammy."

"Sure, he was eaten by the blacks."

"Eaten by the blacks!"

"Sure. It was a terrible dry year and ould Bowes saw wan of the gins wid a whoite choild's arrum in her dillybag. Sure, all the men knows it, but it was kept secret for fear it moight drive the mother mad."

"I don't believe that. The blacks are not cannibals, and they're tame."

"They weren't so damn' tame thirty or forty years ago."

194

"That's true; if you had seen them gathering up where them rings is behoind Corroboree ye'd have seen how tame they were. There must have been goings-on up there to turn the stomach of a man if they could only be known."

Horror at the fate of little Sammy Argyll trailed off into a computation of droughts and floods as milestones to fix the year.

"Sure, the ould pioneers knew what loife was," said Mick. "No sittin' round on your behoinds loike a lot of ould hins like ye do today."

Sympathy was flooding towards Aileen, looking always before her with a strained, lost look, asking no pity, seeking no comfort. Out of decency the search was continued for a week. By that time Mrs Bob felt she must return to her brood. The men also dispersed. They had been there over a hundred strong, and from fifty miles distant. As the news spread, neighbourliness dictated that men should ride over to hear if the child had been found, and, finding the search still on, they joined in.

A brake of boughs was thrown across the river at the exit from the Slate Hole should the body rise after the seventh day. Some of the leaders like the Milfords, Potters, and Farquharsons were awaiting this. The lesser lights had gone. Teddy O'Mara, wearying of the concentration, set out alone for Curradoobidgee to the assistance of his old liege Poole, knowing that he was disabled. He took a bridle-track seldom used, branching off from the Bool Bool road, where his horse shied so violently that he was nearly thrown, while his dogs rushed upon the startling object. Fortunately, they were securely muzzled.

Teddy saw the child lying under a tea-tree shrub. He was the victim of flies to a terrible degree, dirty and tattered, but alive. He moved and raised a feeble cry. Teddy's brain helped him sufficiently to wash the little fellow's face. He then rolled him in his shirt and coat, and, mounting, went off hell-for-leather to Mrs Harry Milford with the child in his arms. It did not occur to him to return to Ten Creeks Run, seven miles behind him. Mrs Milford had been a Miss Labosseer of Coolooluk, to Teddy a sacred breed. He would trust the child to no one else. This was all to the good, for from where he was, Jinninjinninbong was a mile or two nearer than Ten Creeks and an easier track.

Mrs Harry rendered prompt first aid, and when the little body was laid in comfort she wrote a note to Dr Rickart in Queanbeyan, and to save time dispatched Teddy on the best horse left on the place. She sent little Tommy Milford, a child of ten, on the next best nag to take the news to the parents.

* * * * *

While this had been happening at Jinninjinninbong the final stages were reached at Ten Creeks.

Milly had felt it her duty to question Ronald. "What are you going to do about Aunt Aileen?" Her severity was not alone for her aunt's lapse, she was suffering the shattering of a girl's first sexual ideal. A revelation, as yet but dimly realized, but transcendental and exalting, had been desecrated. Her wholesome innocence had left her open to an ugly shock.

"What have I got to do specially with your Aunt Aileen?"

"Don't pretend! Don't be a hypocrite! I looked back that day and saw you on the veranda—the day when Lawrence John was lost."

Ronald gnawed his moustache and spoke warily. How much had she seen? He could not recall what his actions had been at that hour. "I don't know what on earth you could have seen."

"I saw you . . ." She balked. "You have no right to kiss Aunt Aileen," she finished.

"Great Scott! haven't I!" thought Ronald, but he controlled himself and said, "You must have seen double."

"It's not only then. Others have seen at other times and talk about it."

"People will always talk; that's what they think their yapping tongues are made for." Milly was silent and so white and withdrawn that he could not feel his way. He blundered like a man coming on horse pickets in the dark. "Great Scott, Milly! I thought you would be more grown-up than to make a mountain out of a mole-hill. Supposing we take notice of the tittle-tats; supposing I did kiss your aunt, hang it all, I've kissed you too, and was there any harm in it? The blooming world would be depopulated if a fellow wasn't enough of a man to take a kiss from a pretty girl now and again."

"But *I'm* not married," she stammered, "and it can't be such a little thing when it made Uncle Jack act so terribly, and Aunt Aileen is out of her senses and talking about everything being her just punishment."

Milly could endure no more. Her face growing whiter as though she were about to faint, she turned from him. She felt need for counteracting action and went to the kitchen to see that things were in hand for the next meal. Red Jimmy, the surveyor's link man, was there, gossiping with Jane and peeling potatoes. His words arrested Milly as she approached.

"I dunno so much about that. What about my boss? He's no milksop. When we wuz in Queensland we went shootin' the blacks. When we potted the most of them, some of the gins was

196

left and there was a piccaninny, and the grass in Queensland is high like reeds and we hid, an' we soon sore a gin come creepin' back, and piff, she went! Much better fun than shootin' a few ole kangaroos," said the man, with a swagger.

Milly felt sick. This concerned a man who had spoken of love to her on the veranda among the roses, yet he could trap a poor black woman with her baby and shoot her: and Ronald—and Potter too—could say those vulgar things about population, and then want her to marry him. She had imagined wonderful things about passion, yet passion was men, and men were this! She shut herself in her room and threw herself on her bed in the pain of disillusionment.

"I've kissed you too, and was there any harm in it?" Ronald had said, little realizing the delicate inner gossamers of maidenliness he was rending. His one kiss had disturbed her considerably. Her first kiss from a lover. To her it almost meant betrothal. Into betrothal she felt sure their friendship must progress after that electric kiss, yet he dismissed it as a promiscuous scattering of favours, she and her unclean aunt lumped together. And that ready phrase about depopulation!

When Cuppinbingle had been feeling his way with her, playfully, jocularly, as an experienced philanderer alert to retreat or advance as propitious, she had told him he was a wicked, bad man. He asked why. She näively mentioned what respectable echoes she knew of his gallantries. He laughed indulgently till his middle-aged spread had jazzed. He smothered her in blushes and confusion, making her feel she was an innocent baby. Inculcating the lesson of the double standard in all its assurance of the early nineties, he had used the identical phrase about the world being depopulated unless, etc.

Milly thought that depopulation was no great matter but could not express such heresies to a circle doing duty with a few rigid primitive conventions in place of mutable ideas. Such notions would earn a girl derision as being "strong-minded" and make her much more unpopular in the marriage market than flightiness. Potter had been an artist, laughing her out of her notions but indicating that she was lovely nevertheless and because of them. She had turned from him as a rake, to Ronald as a spotless white knight. And now Ronald disclosed himself as of the same quality as Donald, whereas Milly had kept herself unspotted—but Ronald! Who can estimate the anguish of a high-spirited maiden when awakening to the electrifying passion of first love to find the reptile lust confronting her?

She would go to Uncle Bert and live for ever with him and never let any man speak of marriage to her again.

She made Ronald uneasy as to Stanton's attitude, and what would be the safest procedure. How the devil had the old Death Adder acted in the sight of Milly?

Mrs Bob felt it cruel to leave the distraught Aileen with a woman as young as Milly. She sought Stanton. "Mr Stanton, as soon as possible I wish you would bring your wife to me for a week or two. It will be necessary to give her change and company. I fear for her reason. It will be better when it is all over . . . If she would cry it would help."

Stanton mumbled a few words of thanks and seemed unable to express himself, which Mrs Milford took as natural. Going from her, he encountered his brother-in-law and rapped out, "Mrs Milford is talking about taking Aileen to Jinninjinninbong. You can do what you like about it, or Dice can make arrangements. I'm done with her. I don't want any other man's — about me."

Larry was thunderstruck. He had heard a word or two and was aware that Aileen and Dice had fooled about a bit—but this! He did not know whether to attribute it to the state of Stanton's nerves over the loss of the boy or to take it seriously. He emitted a soft whistle and stood on the veranda pondering, and wishing he could see Milly, a chronic state with him. Golly, didn't he wish old Bert Poole had not taken this time to put himself out of things by an accident befitting a new-chum. He would have been a steadying influence on the whole mad caboose, and the man to deal with old Jack. Why the blazes hadn't Dice and Aileen a little more sense—getting into a silly mess like this!

SP-over-J was mowing a wide swath. He encountered Dice after leaving Larry. "You can make arrangements for removing your property," he snapped. "I don't want her on my premises any longer."

Dice did not affect to misunderstand. It was too serious for that. He walked into the house and found Mrs Milford and asked could he see Mrs Stanton. "I can't leave without saying a word to her about the little chap and how sorry I am."

"Yes. Poor little soul seems dazed. It would do her good if you could make her break up. She was down the orchard a few minutes ago."

Ronald found her there. "Aileen," he said, going direct to the point. "Stanton seems to be upset about you and me. God knows we were harmless enough, but I want to say that if he doesn't return to his senses, and cuts up rough, I'm ready to do whatever you wish. I'm sorry for what you have been through and if I have

198

made things worse for you I'll do the decent thing as far as I can. You understand, don't you? You only have to let me know."

"Oh, but I can't," she wailed. "The snakes are there."

He saw that she was for the present beyond comfort—or further disaster. He shook her hand and withdrew, running into Larry, who was hanging about aimlessly wondering where Milly could be hidden. Everybody was tired and aimless.

"What the deuce have you and Aileen been up to? Old SP-over-J has been raising a pretty dust to me. He talks of turning Aileen out."

"Let him bag his head! He can't do that."

"He can go away and leave her here, though."

"See here, Larry, the old Death Adder has got some bee in his bonnet without any foundation, but if he is going to turn dog about Aileen, I'm ready to do all I can. I suppose Milly will stand by her—she's a game good girl that, all right—and you might, as Aileen's brother, take a hand by letting me know. You were all damn' strong on tying her up to the old mongrel."

"It's not as serious as that, is it?"

"I don't know what it is with a loony old piker like that. Aileen is so upset that she doesn't seem to understand what I am saying to her, but you can let her know when she comes round."

"When all is said and done, you can't expect Jack to let you run about with his wife under his nose."

"What could you expect? You locked the poor little thing up and forced the old Death Adder on her—shot my horse under me when I made a good straightforward offer. Serves you jolly well right now!"

Larry saw that Dice was in no mood to be reasoned with, or to climb down, and remembered his own skeleton too vividly to preach. His present state, too, had awakened him to an understanding of what Dice and Aileen must have gone through, without any sympathy from him, and he said nothing to increase disharmony. "Keep cool!" he advised. "Ten to one it will all end in a bit of a squiff."

They walked out the back way towards the stables together and rode to the Slate Hole to see if the brake had detained anything. They disturbed clouds of ducks and engaged in a scudding competition on the still water of the Hole with flat waterworn stones. Larry was the champion. Harry Milford was there too, and after a while they returned to the homestead. As they neared, little Tommy Milford came from the other direction at full gallop. They cooeed to stop him. "My God, don't let him go to the women! It looks as if something has happened at home," said Milford.

The little boy, his face wreathed in smiles, shouted his good news and held out a note. His excitement and the men's incredulity rendered him unintelligible, but when they were sure of the news they broke into a cheer and turned to tell everyone about the place. Mrs Bob was commissioned to tell the mother, but it was Milly who broke the good news, "Oh, Aunt Aileen, little Lawrence John is alive! Teddy O'Mara found him and took him to Jinninjinninbong to Mrs Harry Milford. Come, we are all going over at once."

Aileen looked at them uncomprehendingly and broke into tears and sobs that unnerved the men.

"It will save her reason," said Mrs Bob. "You just leave her to us and get the horses saddled, and, Jane, put the meal on the table immediately."

Aileen was silent and passive in the hands of her niece and neighbour.

The company snatched a snack and set off as soon as Aileen was sufficiently composed. A spirit of joy was general. A miracle had relieved all strain and suffering.

All from Ten Creeks except a couple of caretakers were riding over to Jinninjinninbong to see how the little chap was. Jane was permitted to go too. Milly said Mrs Harry must have her hands full with two families, two infants—one an invalid—and would need help. In face of the miracle SP-over-J so returned to sanity that he dispatched a messenger on the Wamgambril to bring Dr Byng from Bool Bool to reinforce Dr Rickart. He did not ride beside his wife. Milly did that, and since Larry rode next to her, the decencies were preserved. Stanton rode with the Milfords. Dice chatted pleasantly with Mrs Milford and the little Ignez.

The reversal of what had gloomed for days as a tragedy elated everyone. Tongues wagged in all sorts of surmises.

"He must have walked straight away through the two large creeks before the rain when there was only an inch or two of water at the crossings made for Mrs Saunders's four-in-hand," said Harry Milford.

"Sure, he's a strong choild and well set on his feet. If ye just keep peggin' along at a snail's pace ye can go moiles in a day. 'Tis to be seen by crawlin' sheep that have to be lifted on to their feet."

"He stuck to the track, that is how he got so far and kept out of mischief."

None of the seekers had ridden far enough along the way the

child had gone, thinking it beyond range in view of the storm, and none had come by it. Some never could credit that the child had been so far as the spot that Teddy O'Mara later pointed out. Whatever, the glad fact remained that he was alive, and it lent high spirits to the travellers, catastrophic to the birds along the way. The pomegranate crests of many gyang-gyangs and the tails of half a dozen lyre-birds were offered up to Milly and Ignez. Lesser birds like magpies, rosellas and lories, satin-birds and black cockatoos and button-birds, were popped off in exuberance of spirit, leaving clamorous orphans.

On arrival at Jinninjinninbong they found the child had had a teaspoonful of wine drop by drop and was asleep. But for the blowflies in ears and eyes he would have been all right. Mrs Milford was a capable nurse, and for the remainder, the doctor was awaited.

Aileen was taken to the child. She had not spoken and was quiet now. She took one look at the little tortured face and fell on her knees, burying her head in the bed, whether praying or not none knew. When Milly persuaded her to rise, she looked so wan that bed was suggested. Aileen acquiesced. The spare bedroom had been prepared for Mr and Mrs Stanton. Larry stepped in here so appearances were preserved. "Milly, you take care of Aileen, there's a brick, and I'll hang on to your uncle. They have both been through it."

Beds sprang up everywhere like mushrooms and half of the visitors went to Mrs Bob, a mile distant, helping to remove her family.

Dr Rickart arrived next day, followed by Dr Byng a day later. Mrs Milford was highly commended for her first aid. The child was progressing, moderation was what was needed. Great care must be exercised with the ears and eyes, but even there the doctors hoped for complete recovery.

Dr Byng remained some days, enjoying the good shooting and the rest from professional duties in the famous valley and in the wonderful gardens of the two women. There was stimulating rivalry between them. Mrs Bob had a bed of Prince of Wales feather as tall as maize with streamers feet long, and borders of double English daisies and anemones, others of wallflowers, stocks, and foxgloves, bordered with violets. Mrs Harry had beds of pinks and carnations that smelt like heaven, and wide borders of sweet-william that the bushmen rode miles out of their way to see and smell, and all who ever saw those borders of sweet-william were unanimous that they never saw any to equal them. She had also a laburnum-tree like a rain of gold, and purple lilacs, and honeysuckle over an arch at the entrance, and a hedge of pink roses all round the enclosure, and two strips of fleur-de-lis, purple and white, and bushes of rosemary, and daffodils growing in a lawn of rye-grass, which Mr Blenkinsop said always reminded him of England.

Aileen was too listless to speak, which was considered normal by the medical men after the shock she had undergone. Milly was a source of strength and a pleasure to all, more particularly to Mrs Harry, who, with nothing but scrub help and her augmented household, had her hands full. Milly was constantly thrown with Larry, who laid himself out to be a comfort to her. Dice had wounded her irretrievably, her Uncle Jack was out of it, and Uncle Bert unable to come to her assistance for the first time in her young life. Larry filled the breach with unflagging zeal.

Dice was one of the first to leave. He prepared for departure the morning that Dr Rickart said there was no doubt about the child's recovery. When his horse was saddled and his valise strapped on, he sought Milly. "I'm going, Milly; ask your aunt if I may see her."

Milly returned in a few minutes. "Aunt Aileen says to thank you, but it doesn't matter."

"What does she mean by that?"

"I don't know. She is still very worn out."

"No wonder! Well, I'll not disturb her, but I want you to understand and to let me know, if it is necessary, that I am ready to help her in any way I can."

Milly regarded him so fixedly that he blushed.

"You're too young to understand some things, Milly, though you're a brick, and you will let me know if Aileen needs me."

"I expect she will let you know herself if she wants you for anything. I promise to give your message correctly."

"Thank you for that. Good-bye."

"Good-bye." Milly turned away without extending her hand.

Dice went to Stanton. "A word with you, Stanton, privately."

"I don't want private or any other sort of words with you."

"You can please yourself, if you prefer others to hear. It was you I was considering. I have nothing to be ashamed of and nothing to hide." Thereupon Stanton consented to move towards the cow-yard, at that hour untenanted.

"I wanted to say, that if you think you have anything serious against your wife in connection with me, you are making a flaming fool of yourself. After she was married I never saw her till the child was nearly two years old. If you don't treat her properly, and want to get rid of her, I'm just as ready to take on the job now as I was when you cornered old Healey like a dingo in a trap to keep her a prisoner and shoot my horse under me when I made a fair and square offer of marriage that the girl wanted to accept. All the world knows that, and that an old dried-up Death Adder like you couldn't get a young woman to love you for your own pretty old hide."

"Is that all you have to say?"

"All, except that I hope your horse rolls on you and breaks your neck—*soon!* Have you anything to say to me?"

"Only that if I catch you within twenty miles of any of my boundaries I'll blow your brains out."

"All right, then, see that you treat Aileen properly. There are plenty who will let me know if you don't."

"You go to hell and mind your own business."

Thus they separated. Dice was in high spirits, feeling himself on top of the situation as he returned to the house to say good-bye to his hostess.

"I wonder if there is any truth in the things they say about him and Mrs Stanton," remarked Mrs Harry to Mrs Bob as they watched him depart.

"The difference in attraction is so great, one could not wonder, and if people have no foundation for gossip, they'll gossip without," replied Mrs Bob.

"Yes. I'm sometimes afraid they'll concoct an affair between old Mr Blenkinsop and me, when he stays so long."

"I don't want much more of Mr Blenkinsop's company after what I heard over the river. I must tell you the unexpurgated story of his antics at the Bool Bool Show that time, as soon as we have a chance."

This, till the intervals of the search, had not reached Mrs Milford. Mrs Labosseer had not considered it Christian to tell her daughter when home for her confinement anything beyond that Mr Blenkinsop was inclined to drink and had to be kept out of town. The old man was not such an ornament as of yore. His prestige was gone and he was increasingly dependent upon the Christian charity and hospitality of Mrs Labosseer and her daughter.

* * * *

Lawrence John progressed in the competent hands of Mrs Harry Milford (*née* Labosseer) and none so proud of his judgment nor so justified in his faith as Teddy O'Mara. The Yass *Tribune*, the Queanbeyan *Age*, the Bool Bool *Courier*, and the Goulburn *Herald* all carried the story in full, and it was the crown of Teddy's career to know that he was prominently mentioned as Mr Edward O'Mara.

Aileen lost somewhat her distraught expression with the days and could reply normally when addressed, but she never spoke unless addressed. Milly's mother was ill content to be out of such a big event, so came up from Turrill Turrill to take charge.

SP-over-J was relieved to let Lucy have her way. She superintended—rather dictated—the return of Aileen to Ten Creeks, and with the aid of Milly ran everything. Aileen was like a child, which was attributed to the strain she had undergone. SP-over-J was not unkind to her, merely indifferent, but that no one specially noted. It was the most comfortable state of affairs for Aileen. She had never been assertive. Stanton's notion of throwing her out of doors evaporated. He knew the truth of what Dice had said. Dice might have fooled a little with Aileen, but to make a bobbery about it would expose and advertise his own failure as an elderly husband as well as a young lover. His contracting arteries left him less and less insurgently virile. The easiest policy was to keep quiet and allow matters to drift.

Lucy Saunders advised a stay in Sydney for Lawrence John under some eminent specialist for eyes and ears. To this Stanton agreed if Lucy would go too and take charge, which she was more than ready to do. Milly firmly announced her intention of remaining at Ten Creeks with her uncle, and he was delighted to have her. Her mother suggested several guardian-companions. To these Milly scornfully objected.

"You can take care of me, can't you, Uncle, better than anyone else?" she said, swinging on his arm, which to him was the one bright spontaneously affectionate oasis in an arid stretch.

"I'll try, Milly, if it takes a gun and baits," he said, almost jocularly.

"You be sure that she behaves," said her mother.

CHAPTER 18

NORAH ALFREDA was developing into a wonderful child whose fond parents had no doubt of her genius. The thought of her remained terrifying to Larry. Norah attributed her brother's failure to visit her to his devotion to Ten Creeks Run—and Milly. Norah pleasured in this, for she was fond of Milly and felt that possession of Norah Alfreda would be more secure if Larry married someone other than Dot.

To Dot, likewise, the thought of the child was objectionable. Her family never mentioned it, and should some outsider talk of the prodigy produced by the funny old pair at Billy-go-Billy, Dot would slip from the room. She was doing her duty invincibly as housekeeper and nurse to her mother, who was increasingly devoted to the cultivation of rheumatism, bunions, indigestion, and such respectable afflictions. Advancing age was curtailing Mrs Saunders's perpetual preoccupation with the petty mechanics of physical existence, and having nothing mental or spiritual to take its place, her ailments, real and anticipated, were her hobby.

Dot became no less aloof. The spirited young woman had grown silent and retiring. For a time all the family had been eager to dispose of her matrimonially, but her rigidity erected a barrier against amorous advances. The family accepted this after a time. "We can afford one old maid," they said. She would be indispensable as a caretaker for Pa and Ma as they became troublesome. The old people also foundered in this attitude. Only Dot articulated no opinion about her past, present, or future.

There were still admirers. Her smart comeliness of shoulder and waist and fair face made her desirable. Dice found the wistfulness that had crept across her features like a veil, appealing. Gentleness rather than courage or wilfulness always attracted him. He was curious how so strangely different a Dot could have developed and cock-of-the-walkily inclined to attribute it to her failure with himself. They met at church, to which he sometimes drove his mother, and Dot's indifference reawakened his interest. Attributing her demeanour to pique did not fit with the difficulty in recapturing her favour. Soon it was Dot's face instead of Aileen's that filled his dreams and he became a frequent visitor at Saunders Plains.

SP-over-J heard this with relief. Any sure disposal of Dice was preferable to his being a devourer in the neighbourhoods of Ten Creeks or Turrill Turrill, and since Dot had not known enough to take her good chances, let her make Dice safe.

No recall reached Dice from Aileen, Milly, or anyone else, so he flattered himself that he had retired from the field in full possession of his spurs. "Things all right between Aileen and the old Death Adder?" he inquired casually of Larry one day in Bool Bool.

"Of course, and likely to remain so, if you don't go acting the goat again."

"No danger of that. You'll never see me within twenty miles of that zoo again unless by accident."

* * * * *

"Ronald Dice is running after Dot Saunders now fit to break his neck," said Mrs Isaacs in M'Haffety's private parlour.

"Sure, thin, there wasn't anny truth about him getting into trouble with ould SP-over-J."

"It was true enough, but men run round from one to the other. A girl that sets too much store on a man is laying up sorrer for herself."

" 'Twould be a good way of settlin' Dot an' clearin' up the trouble with ould SP-over-J. It's curious, if there was anny truth in what you said of Dot, that it niver leaked out."

"Must have come off before its time and that's how it was so easy hushed up. It must have given old Saunders the pip, though, paying up for it. A thing like that is not managed without a good sum of money. I hear Aily's little boy's eyes are likely to recover."

"Sure, people was sayin' it was a judgment on her, and thin by a miracle she's got her choild aloive."

"Maybe she's taken the warning and that's why she sent Dice about his business."

"Oi'm surprised at Lucy Saunders not havin' more sinse than to leave Milly up there among all those men like wolves. Sure, some women niver learn. That's the next trouble we'll be hearin' of, beloike."

Something of such babble reached Milly's ears. Her only companion of her own sex for days at a time was Jane Humphreys, whose notorious stepmother was not married to her father, her real husband being occupied with "doing time" for sheep-stealing from Brennan's Gap. The Humphreys family had a hut on a selection in the scrub between Wamgambril and Goraig swamps, reputedly a sink of iniquity at those seasons when Riverina shore, and old Humphreys went down the River as slushy or odd man about the sheds. Jane was all ears to the gossip that poured through Ten Creeks kitchen, and Milly not sufficiently experienced or other-worldly not at times to be interested in Jane's divulgences.

"They say, Miss Milly, that Mr Ron Dice is now kitin' off every Saturday night to stay at Saunders Plains. Ain't he just a proper lady-killer! He's such a flirt he can't help himself. He'd throw sheep's eyes at me if there was no one else about. He is a limb!" Giggles testified to Jane's unqualified admiration.

She could not understand that she was cutting Milly's heart with the jagged edges of a broken ideal. It was one of Milly's tragedies that no one understood. She had to work her way alone through this crash of something vital from heaven to the mud. No one knew how she was suffering nor was capable of understanding why. The men would only laugh and make coarse variations of the depopulation theme used by Potter and Dice; the women would treat it as something in regard to men not to be cured and therefore to be endured without vulgarity. She ached to tell it all to Uncle Bert, feeling that his understanding would include sympathy, though even he had failed her by absence at this crisis.

She kept away from Bool Bool because of the stories of Ronald's pursuit of Dot. Flora or Rose Farquharson sometimes kept her company at Ten Creeks, visits pleasant to both of these, who found Cuppinbingle there too, and they were willing to overlook his premarital gallantries so long as he would settle down afterwards. Milly's favourites were the Milfords and she often went over the river for a night or longer. Mrs Harry's baby was an attraction, and Ignez, who played the piano by ear to the wonder of the district, worshipped Milly in a way that was particularly heartening to her just then. She adopted the little girl as her sister and they swore eternal fealty. In imitation of herself and Uncle Bert, Milly made a compact that should Ignez ever be in difficulties Milly would rescue her, and the little girl sealed the promise in a precocious and hypersensitive memory.

*   *   *   *   *

At that date Uncle Bert wrote that Sparr and Leamington's circus in its entirety was coming to Goulburn. Constable Purkis informed him that the man who performed with the blue roan under the name of Broncho Bill was in reality William Bowes. Poole wanted to know what Milly thought about seeing the circus in Goulburn, for it was hardly likely that Flash Billy would venture to Yass or Queanbeyan.

Milly replied that it would not do for him to risk travelling at present, that she might get Uncle Jack to take her to Goulburn to see the pony herself. This letter was written to cover Milly's definite plans. Since Poole was not available, she turned to the eager Larry as her instrument. He was on hand like the hardy sunflower each Sunday. She had found him the most sympathetic companion available for weeks. He was the happiest of all by Dice's deflection towards Dot. Such a union would take Dot clean off his conscience and settle the fascinating Ronald.

Milly spoke to him one Saturday night. "Larry, I want you to do something very important for me. I must have someone I can depend on."

"You know I would do anything in the world for you if you would only do one little thing for me."

"Yes, but I need a true friend like Uncle Bert who would do anything for me out of friendship and not want this silliness in return."

"You can trust me. Test me in any way you like. I can't pretend that I want to be your uncle, but you'll find me Johnny-on-the-spot."

"And you won't want something in return?"

"No. I'll be dead square, and if you don't want me I shan't squeal about it after."

Under pledges of secrecy Milly explained all she suspected about the blue roan. Her determination was to go to Goulburn, slip into the circus, and, if she recognized Romp, deliberately abduct her and make home without legalities.

Larry could scarcely believe his ears. In his day-dreams Milly was constantly in some discreditable situation from which she could be redeemed only by becoming his wife. Here without his own scheming was a congenial adventure, for which he was eminently fitted, and which would throw Milly into his company for two or three days—unchaperoned.

He dissimulated his exultation. Milly not wanting to be engaged to him! Whew! She might as well be married to him at once as this! To all appearances it was an elopement: all that was un-planned was the parson to tie the knot at the finish. He must be careful not to alarm Milly at the beginning. He took up the enter-prise with a surety that commended him to her, and planned with care. He also provided the money necessary, which might have been beyond Milly. They were to ride to Queanbeyan, thence to Goulburn by train.

The circus was to be in Goulburn three nights—Thursday, Friday, and Saturday. Milly, having laid her plans, told her uncle she was going over to Jinninjinninbong to stay with Ignez.

"All right, you can stay over there for the rest of the week if you like, or you can come with me to Stanton's Plains, for I have business in Bool Bool this Saturday. But what about Jane? You had better take her too, and she can help Mrs Milford."

"She was crying about being homesick the other day. You could drop her at the selection as you go and pick her up as you come back. She might get a bit forward at Jinninjinninbong."

"Oh, very well. To be safe you had better stay with Mrs Milford till I send for you. I'm expecting a wire that might take me to Riverina."

"All right. To make sure, supposing I come back a week from Friday?"

"All right. Your aunt and your mother might be home by then too."

The way seemed miraculously cleared. Milly rode away to Jinninjinninbong with a rouseabout, as far as the boundary, to let down the heavy slip-panel.

Ignez was enraptured to see her, and Mrs Milford warmly pressed her to stay a week. Milly, however, explained that she was on the way to Keba to stay with the Farquharsons while her uncle went to Riverina, and she had come by Jinninjinninbong for the better track.

"Someone must go with you," said Bob Milford. Protest was unavailing. "I couldn't let you go over that crossing alone. It's a steep, slippery bank."

"If you'd just see me over the river that would do."

After supper they were surprised by the arrival of Larry Healey, who said that two of his mares had been seen making towards Boundary Creek. One of them had been foaled out towards Mount Corroboree.

"Looks like a put-up job to me," said Milford to his wife. "But I suppose it's none of our business. The girl is too good for Larry, but if her mother doesn't keep a better eye on her, I can't."

Larry spoke to put the Milfords off the track. "Are you going my way in the morning?"

"I'm not going back to Ten Creeks," Milly replied. "Are you?"

"Not till tomorrow night. I'm going towards Corroboree first."

"Then you can see me on the way to Keba and Mr Milford need not be troubled."

"Ah, Milly, you can't deceive me like that. I believe you and Larry are eloping."

"No such luck," said Larry.

"Don't take any notice," said Mrs Milford, noticing Milly's confusion. "The men always think we are dying to elope with them."

"You can't deny it. That's what happens all the time."

"Yes, when we go silly, and you don't know how many are sorry afterwards," retorted Mrs Milford good-humouredly.

Larry escorted Milly next morning, but Milford went too. He was satisfied when he saw Milly past Dingo Sideling and Larry gone towards the back of Corroboree. Milly was permitted to go the last ten miles to Keba alone. Behind a pinnacle she reined in and was, after waiting, rejoined by Larry, who said he had watched Milford genuinely turning back across the Coolgarbilli.

"I'm afraid he was suspicious all the same," said Milly, but so long as he did not frustrate their plans, Milford's suspicions were what Larry desired, who cared little about rescuing the blue roan and immensely about compromising Milly.

They reached Queanbeyan and caught the train. In Goulburn Larry proposed to call Milly his sister and put up at the Commercial, but Milly's horse sense stood to her. She had the address of a most exemplary boarding-house where her mother had stayed when visiting a dentist. As her mother's daughter she was welcomed. Her story that she had come to meet her mother was also readily accepted by Mrs Wilson. The story of the lost Lawrence John was known to her and she was interested to hear of him. Milly said she would visit a friend, whom she hoped would take her to the circus. This also was plausible. Milly was a girl who won the trust of older ladies.

Larry, as a disguise, had a three-days' beard, which was effectual and almost more than he could bear in contact with Milly, but her approval was sustaining. With a slouch hat well turned down and a dark handkerchief round his neck it would have taken a searching glance in the shade of the tents to detect the usually spruce Larry. He secured seats in a nook where they could hunch behind their neighbours.

There was no difficulty in recognizing Flash Billy in Broncho Bill, with his wonderful mustang from the plains of Arizona, where on the biggest ranch in the world he had lassoed more steers in a day than had ever been seen on the tin-pot cattle-runs of New South Wales. So said the barker.

Milly was so excited when the mustang Prairie Nell appeared that she thrilled Larry by grasping his arm. Milly had no doubts about it being her own lost friend from the moment she entered the ring, the carriage and contour were unmistakable to one who knew horses. Larry was similarly convinced but desired proofs before taking action. He did not relish the possibility of being arrested for horse-stealing, a charge that would fall on him rather than on Milly. It was three years now since the Young Whisker filly had disappeared—time for her to have had a two-year-old the spit of herself. This beast had Romp's crest and croup, her gait, and every other point, but she had a big star on her forehead, two white hind-hoofs, and a curious white patch on the hind-quarter.

"That's whitewash," said Milly. "It's too white to be real. I once made a piebald of Lady Lochinvar for fun, so I know."

The pony performed with mettle and precision and won the hearts of an up-country gathering by her pluck at the high jump and through the blazing hoops in artificial light, by the way she sat down and lay down, and finished by divesting herself of Broncho Bill and every shred of tackle without breaking a buckle.

"Aw," muttered Larry to the man in front of him, taking care to keep out of sight, "I bet if I saddled her she wouldn't get out of the girths so easily."

"No, nor me," replied the man, who happened to be Paddy Leary, the trainer from Cuppinbingle, with just enough alcohol under his waistcoat to render him mellow.

"Why don't you challenge him?" said Larry. This was all that Leary needed. He shouted to Broncho Bill. That gentleman was most accommodating. He made an announcement in an assumed nasal twang.

"I guess an' calkerlate any gent that likes can come an' girth this little mustang of the prairies and the result will be just the same."

"All right, sonny, let me have a go at her." Leary went into the ring, and as he passed, Larry whispered, "There's a young lady here thinks the white spots are only put on; just find out."

"Right you are," said Leary, pleased by a commission from a girl. He buckled the mare cruelly tight and wiped his coat-sleeve on her quarter and scraped his boot on her hoof, Milly instantly noting the white on Leary's coat and boot. It is hard to deceive the ingrained bushman about a horse that is a personal friend. He can usually be depended upon to recognize after two years or so a horse he has seen only once or twice. As the points of an old master to a connoisseur of pictures, so are the brand, age, sex, breed—all the points of a horse—to a man reared among them. It is also instinctive. Might as well tell a man he wouldn't recognize his wife.

The right prick to her flank and Romp jumped out of her tackle as before, and was led away amid great enthusiasm. Leary returned to his seat and was thanked by Larry from the rear, who to explain his curiosity said, "Those marks are put on to make her look like a mustang."

"She looks damn' like the Young Whisker breed to me," said Leary.

"You're right. You wait going out and have a nip with me."

Broncho Bill now gave place to the marvellous equestrienne, Mademoiselle Yvonne. Prairie Nell was out of this act, and in her place half a dozen snow-white cart- or plough-horses of wide spread convenient for the tableaux of hoops, tights, etc. Larry and Milly noted that it was a big act engaging numerous hands as well as performers, and departed to take their bearings. Larry raced Milly to Mrs Wilson's in a cab and was back again to keep his appointment.

Leary was enthusiastic about Larry's plan and eager to earn a quid or two, because he was "broke", and put to it to get back to Cuppinbingle without walking. Larry had to make sure that Leary kept reasonably sober and held his tongue for the next thirty hours or so. He was calculating that Flash Billy would hardly make a fight for the pony and lay himself open to a sentence for horse-stealing.

Larry arranged for a horse-box on the Queanbeyan branch of the train for Friday night. The squatters on that line found no trouble in being accommodated, and Larry and Leary acted for Potter of Cuppinbingle with convincing assurance.

They were to seize Prairie Nell next night while the main act was employing most of the circus-hands. In this Mademoiselle Yvonne acted with her greys, the clowns with their blacks, the trapeze artists hung like monkeys from their knees above, and the spectators were engrossed.

Milly left Mrs Wilson happily, that good lady never doubting that she was to meet her mother. The night trains passed Goulburn at such an hour that no one except of necessity met them. Milly stole into the first half of the circus again to pass the time, and from there was to go to the waiting-room at the railway station.

Leary was again to the fore. Tonight he bet that he could ride Prairie Nell without being thrown. The crowd took it up with a whoop. Flash Billy had immediately recognized his fellow trainer of earlier years, and was happy that Paddy was taking him seriously as Broncho Bill. He was, however, uneasy, and thankful that after Goulburn his division of the circus was to go to the northern towns. His possession of the pony was secure in a general way. He held a receipt showing that she had been purchased out of Tumbarumba Pound. He had seen to that as early as practicable. A Pound receipt for a horse was as good as a Torrens Title for land. This information had been supplied to Poole by the police. The only way to regain possession of the horse lawfully would be to open the case through the police—a very tricky case, but likely to go hard with Bowes in the end, for Milly had a hoof of the horse that had been killed as a blind, and the circumstances of Bowes's dismissal could be adduced. Larry agreed with Milly that possession of Romp would most likely settle matters without further trouble. He might as well have whistled up wind as tried to show Milly any importance in constitutional methods.

With a woman's facility in leaping fusty entanglements of law and its roundabout reasoning she had tried the case and settled it on its merits—justly, too. There was her very own darling. She had known from the beginning that Flash Billy had taken her. He had played a cruel, mean trick with another horse of similar hide to put them off the track, but Milly had not been deceived. Nearly three years had her precious pet been in the hands of the enemy, doing tricks for idiots to laugh at. As for Billy's silly old Pound receipt, a wombat with a blind eye could see that that didn't count. The impudence of that insufferable Billy!

Larry chortled: if Milly stood charged there wasn't a juryman in the Southern District who would go against her.

Paddy Leary was thrown, to the joy of the crowd, and stood up scratching his head and clowning rather well. His drunkenness this time was feigned. He followed the pony out, muttering and blaming the Mexican saddle. Most of the hands were now in the big tent. Leary reappeared with a racing pad and his own bridle— he did not want to render himself liable for the theft of such articles. He insisted upon resaddling. The boy in charge thought it was all part of the performance and watched him mount with a grin, but Paddy was not the smartest trainer on Cuppinbingle without something in his coconut, if it was only cunning. While the boy stood back to let him enter in the wake of the blacks and greys, Paddy drove the pony round the wagons and guy-ropes, and was gone like a streak. The boy, bewildered for the moment, thought the man drunk and the pony bolting. Broncho and the boss, all the people of authority, were engaged. The frightened lout ran first to cooks and understrappers; before he could get anyone to take him seriously Romp was being led into her box on the train where a dainty supper and cool drink awaited her, and Milly began kissing her and crying over her like a long-lost sister.

When it came to the attention of Broncho Bill he said, "I know that bloke though he don't know me, an' it won't be hard to get hold of the pony again." The Pound receipt held good against Paddy and his ilk.

*   *   *   *   *

Larry and Milly were both in an excitedly happy state, though for different reasons.

"I say, Milly, don't you think I deserve a kiss too. I'm as good as a horse, surely?"

"Not so good as Romp. No man is as good as she is except Uncle Bert, and he gave her to me."

Larry sighed prodigiously. Milly relented. "I really am so happy that I might give you a kiss when we get safely home, but we mustn't do anything silly now; I'll go back to the waiting-room so that I shan't attract attention. I'm going to write a letter to Billy." Larry joined her later to share a packet of refreshments.

Broncho Bill's work was done and he took on the pursuit of the thief himself. He followed the Yass road nearly out to Breadalbane, but no one was abroad at that hour to inform him if such a beast and rider had been seen. He had not noticed Milly or Larry, and while he puzzled for a clue or track never guessed that Romp was in her box at the station.

Paddy was hidden in the box with Romp. As the train started Larry handed him his reward and the letter that he was to deliver. Paddy lay low till next morning when he gave a boy sixpence to act postman, while he popped on a "goods" and unostentatiously departed for good old Cuppinbingle, where Miss Milly's adventure lost nothing in the telling.

Milly's letter ran:

> To William Bowes,
>
>   I knew you took Romp from the start and killed another horse to deceive me. I have taken her home with me tonight. I shall tell the police in Queanbeyan and Yass.
>
> Mildred Saunders.

When Flash Billy read that, he knew his partnership with Prairie Nell was ended, and firstly cursed his stupidity to have ventured into the region, and secondly was filled with splintering regret that he had not secured a foal. Such a prodigy could not escape from the circus without regret from all, from slushies to stars. Young Sparr was for enlisting the police from Goulburn to Albury, but Flash Billy said, "No go! The Pound receipt might do for the police, but not for that —— of a girl. Damn her for a ——. Her people are the toffs of Bool Bool—there ain't no flies on her. The mare and her dam was gave to her by Curradoobidgee Poole, another geebung, him that shickered up all the bushrangers on his own in his day, and is still run after by all the girls because his sweetheart, the beautiful Emily Mazere, was drownded. Milly has only to let a squawk outer her an' the whole flaming country would be agin us buzzing like mad blowflies. I'll make meself scarce droving in Queensland till it blows over. I wish I knew if they'll reely set the police on me or not."

"If that's the case, a walking ticket is the best thing for you, I reckon, but any time it's safe I'll have a place for you and another Prairie Nell."

Sparr was not unduly perturbed. It was not the first time his canvas had covered a blood animal to which the title was insecure. He considered the Southern District in general owed him something in horse-flesh. An Arab creamy, cleverest beast ever purporting to come from the tents of the Ouled Nayl, had escaped from his grandfather's circus in Melbourne at the end of the forties, and it was rumoured that he lived thereafter in the direction of the Bulla Bulla Mountains near the New South Wales border, and had there raised the brumby lineage. Sparr said he wouldn't be surprised if Prairie Nell owed him something. Her quarters and staying powers and tight-tucked belly suggested it.

"That won't give you no claim to her with young Milly. All the country would take her side at onct."

"And that blotched brand wouldn't help you much, Broncho. It's no use having a decent swell girl like that against you," agreed Sparr. "Damn the women! They're a curse anyhow, but we can't get on without 'em. A pity that girl isn't the other sort. We could have made her an offer then, and she would be a big draw with her pony."

In the nineties, girls were still of several "sorts"; professional demi-mondaines and society amateurs had not yet formed a coalition.

❊   ❊   ❊   ❊   ❊

Milly settled herself in a ladies' carriage, where there were also two nuns. Larry could not intrude, so had to attend Romp and content himself till the morrow.

It was a peerless summer morning of the region, with sunlight glistening like bubbles over Queanbeyan and Canberra Plains as they set their faces towards the panorama running round the horizon, pinked out with the Tinderies and Tidbinbillies, blue as the sky against which they were outlined. Over the nearer rolling widths the spire of Canberra church came to view in its Plain, and Mount Ainslie. Beyond that rose the ramparts of the Murrumbidgee and Coolgarbilli ranges sentinelled at one end by black

Corroboree, and streaming on in another direction to the Bogongs, Michelagos, and Muniongs. They rode gaily, each with a splendid beast under, and Romp saucily trotting beside Milly at the end of a light halter. Milly would not entrust her pet to Larry, and her glances rested on her in pure idolatry. Larry laughed wholeheartedly at the perfection of the creature. Her crest, her croup, her carriage, the toss of her muzzle as she snuffed her native breezes rushing wide from old Monaro, were satisfying to the expert. Merrily their hoofs rang as they sped, with a saddle-bag of provisions, and a choice of sparkling streams for the billy-boiling. Larry was highly excited. He had determined that Milly should surrender and their engagement be announced as the culmination of this adventure.

Milly was thinking rather on the same lines, though not so happily; there was something of defeat in her attitude. Through the fall of Ronald she was suffering a mortal wound to her first conception of love. She had no experience at all to help her towards knowledge that such wounds heal somewhat with time, that men and women of ideals and sensibilities must reassemble their house that is built without hands, and that after each besiegement and resistance, though it may show its scars, it nevertheless becomes a more compact edifice. The shame of the disillusionment disrupted her, and with the headlong impetuosity of youth she wanted to hurl something into the breach. The only thing at hand to her unguided inexperience was Larry Healey. During the last months, never failing, never sparing himself, by sheer assiduity he had won her affection. Always at hand to help her with good nature and dash, in her stricken state, propinquity had had considerable effect. Teens could not conceive that five or even two years hence she would marvel that she could ever have been infatuated with Dice, or that the defection of a man so ordinary could have wounded so deeply. What she needed just then was an understanding friend to remove her to a change of mind and associates, whereas she was entirely alone.

Marriage was the natural end of women as Milly knew them. To be an old maid in that time and region was failure, and Milly was too strong and wholesome to accept that. This being her state of mind, Larry, she supposed, was as good as anyone. He would be something tangible heaped into the chasm of her disgrace in having placed her affections upon Ronald, her aunt's ... Milly knew no word to describe the vile and unmentionable relationship.

"You can nearly always hear the pheasants here," said Larry, when they were resting on the tussocks at Pheasant Creek, awaiting the billy for the tea. "I've sometimes seen half a dozen at a time." As he spoke a beautiful cock bird preceded by his lady passed down the sideling in spasmodic flight, and soon they heard the mimicked sound of chopping. Larry was trying to come to his point, but Milly held him off, talking about the shafts of sunlight hundreds of feet long flickering through the vaulted roof of gum-trees.

"Now, where are we going?" she inquired, as they got under way again. "I can't go back to Ten Creeks, as Uncle Jack is away. I'm supposed to be at Keba, but I don't like going there with Romp."

"No. We can't go there and have them gabbing like a lot of old magpies." Larry was not going to have Alistair Farquharson intruding upon his adventure. "Let's ride through to Wamgambril Springs and give Joanna a surprise. That will be all square for both of us."

"All right. Let's go there and see the new baby."

"Golly, it's fun to think of old Dan as a dad!"

"He can't be half as funny as old Alf Timson!"

This was a shivering thought to Larry. He sheered off.

"There will be a thundering dust-up when it leaks out what we've been up to."

"I don't care. Romp is mine. Flash Billy ought to be prosecuted for horse-stealing."

"It's not that so much, but you and me going away together that will make the bobbery. Every old woman from here to Goulburn will be wagging her head and her tongue."

"Let them!"

"I don't like to think how they will blame me for getting a slur cast upon you. Let's announce our engagement. That would choke 'em off. What do you say?"

Larry was agitated under his casual phrases. Milly responded so matter-of-factly as to indicate that she had pondered the question.

"I suppose I might marry you some day, but there is no hurry." She had been conventionally wise enough before choosing Larry as her partner in the undertaking to realize what it involved to her reputation, though she had never before shown the slightest sign of surrender. This was too much for Larry's equilibrium. He embraced her so violently that he nearly lifted her from her horse. Milly pulled herself free, clicked to Romp and Merrylegs, and went off at a smart gallop.

"This is too wonderful to be real," he shouted, coming up with her on a stiff sideling. Near at hand the birds sported among the shrubs of a creek. From below, the music of the Coolgarbilli amid its grey rocks, moss-carpeted, came up to them as it foamed on its way to old Mother of Waters.

"It won't be real if you act like that before I say you may," said Milly, and he saw that she was not merely inciting him to further demonstration.

"You must expect a fellow to go off his nut a bit under such good news as that."

"I only said I *supposed* I would some day. Lots of things have to be considered first."

"Let's consider 'em at once and get the thing done."

"What would we live on?"

"That's easy. Times must mend before long. I can get the management of one of the summer runs for a start, and from that work into a property of my own. With you to work for I could do as much as three ordinary men."

"That's the chief thing that Mother and Uncle Jack and the Uncles Saunders will think about."

Mention of the Saunders uncles made Larry uneasy. Could he count on their need to keep the scandal with Dot quiet to let him and Milly progress into matrimony unopposed? The thing was to make sure of Milly first. Possession! Possession that could not be revoked was what he needed.

"There's something I think a great deal more about than property," said Milly, after a pause.

"What is that?"

"Morals."

"Morals!" It fell like a whip-crack on the sunny afternoon, delicious under the pendent peppermint branches that Milly reached up and clutched now and again for the refreshing perfume and flavour of the grey-green leaves, like silken ribbons.

"What do you mean by morals?" he inquired, with a laugh, but inward confusion.

"I mean just morals—whether one has good morals or not."

"There's nothing up with your morals, Milly my queen, and I'll try to live up to them as well as I can, but it's not so easy for a man as a woman, you know."

"I don't see why. You all say that like a lot of weak-minded nincompoops."

"Not by long chalks; even the parsons know it's not so easy for a man as a woman."

"I still don't see why. It's just men's excuse so they don't have to behave themselves."

"You've only got to ask the doctors or read a medical book. Golly, if it wasn't so, the world's population . . ."

Milly intimated to her horses that she wanted a spurt, and with electrical response they raced down a gully into a streamlet, their hoofs splashing the water over the pursuing Larry, then up a rise, disturbing gyang-gyangs and black cockatoos. Milly was sickened by this reiterated bleat of the men. It was disgusting that the wonder of a lovely little baby of one's very own should rest upon such vulgar horror. Ugh! She would not marry at all, no matter what anyone said about old maids.

When it became necessary to pull rein, Larry returned to the theme. "I don't want to hear that," protested Milly. "It was something personal and special that I was thinking of."

"Let's get to the bottom of it."

"I hardly like mentioning it. It is so embarrassing, since one must never go upon mere gossip," said the earnest disciple of Uncle Bert.

"I never take any notice of anything I hear—lot of old magpies with the evil minds of crows, that's what most people are."

"But when it concerns my closest life, it is better to have it cleared up."

"What is it—that I got drunk with the crowd the night of Aileen's wedding?"

"I never heard that—you horrid dirty creature! No, it is something different."

To Larry it seemed that his heart was pounding as noisily as his horse's hoofs. Could she know anything about Dot? Surely not. Or had someone lumped him among those who visited Mrs Humphreys at Cherry Tree Hill? He was not going to supply further information of his misdeeds in groping round. Why couldn't he make her understand that the way he worshipped her made him feel like a god? Any previous mistakes through ignorance or boyish flashness were flooded away by what love of her revealed.

Milly nerved herself to the ugly thing. She looked straight between Merrylegs's beautifully shaped ears. "Is it true what—oh, what they say about you and Dot Saunders?"

The jolt was as severe as if his horse had slipped off the cattle-pad round the sideling and landed on a ledge lower down. Hell and blazes! Sulphur and damnation!

"Good God!" he ejaculated, a genuinely astounded utterance. The Dot affair, to the best of his belief, was unknown to SP-over-J or Dice, and yet Milly could bring it out to him on the cattle-tracks of the Murrumbidgee ranges. If it had reached her the country must be ringing with it, and he the only ostrich with his head in the mud. He jerked himself together. Milly could not know the facts. Some flirtation had come to her ears and she was *jealous*—flattering and reassuring conclusion.

"Dot is your own cousin, the jolly smartest and best-looking girl in the country, no matter what I am, surely no one could say anything about her unless they were liars, and mighty dirty ones to boot."

"People are liars, I know, and have no sense of delicacy, they don't feel about things as I do, but they would surely never dare to say such things about a woman like Dot unless there is some truth in them."

"Is it about Dot only, or about Dot and me?" inquired Larry, wary of putting his foot in a hole.

"If there is any truth in what has come to me, it would be a terrible thing for you to be trying to marry me: you ought to be married to Dot."

The gyang-gyangs rose in genteelish chorus, the black magpies made music with the button-birds, bower-birds, and a hundred others through the livelong afternoon, their notes ringing like an orchestra along the pillared aisles of the tree-clad ranges. Larry felt round for the right thing to say.

"That sounds devilish hard on Dot. Leaving me out of it for the present, I think it's pretty low down for anyone, I don't care who it is, to say such things. The Virgin Mary wouldn't be safe from tongues like that, and I don't know of anyone who could get hold of anything about Dot, she always seems to me as if she could jolly well take care of herself anywhere."

"I've tried to think like that, too. I hate to give credence to gossip, but it is a different thing when the question of picking a husband is concerned. I wouldn't touch any man belonging to anyone else, not even"—she nearly said, "even if I loved him," but she felt this ungracious, and it also took her thoughts to Ronald, whom she had loved despite his belonging to someone else and belonging dishonestly.

"You can be quite at ease about Dot as far as I'm concerned. She doesn't care a scrap for me, as I have reason to know. I buzzed round her a bit in a calf-love sort of way while you were growing up to take my breath away, and she gave me the cold shoulder the same as she did to ever so many others. Dot has had plenty of admirers ever since she put up her hair."

"This is different from that, too. It's this way, Larry, if it was true I wouldn't marry you even if it broke my heart and killed me not to; so now you understand how I feel."

"I think you ought to be pretty well sure on the face of it that such a thing about Dot wouldn't be true, whatever in thunder it is."

"I'm just thinking about the best way to proceed. If it is not true, as I was saying, I suppose, well, perhaps we might as well get married some day; but if it is true, of course I should think it terrible for you to have dared to ask me to marry you."

"I'm sure as anything that anything as terrible as that is not true, no matter what the devil it is, but how am I to prove it to you? The people who are ready to say things hop away like fleas if you try to bring them up to the scratch about their lies."

"It will be easy to settle," said Milly with a quietness that alarmed Larry.

"How?" he asked blankly.

"We'll get to Wamgambril Springs tonight, and tomorrow I'll ride straight to Saunders Plains and ask Dot to tell me the truth. I'll tell her the reason why; besides, she couldn't tell a lie about such a desperately serious matter."

Nemesis threatened Larry's day and made a ringing in his ears like the evil mess of crows croaking about a beast that had gone down in a gully at hand.

Here was a facer! Milly going to Dot in her straightforward, compelling way would be the end of the world for him. There was but slender hope of getting at Dot privately ahead of Milly. And supposing he threw himself upon Dot's mercy, would she relent, or would she consider it the greater mercy to save Milly from her repudiated partner in parenthood? To have the filling cup dashed from him robbed the adventure of its innocent glory, and Larry rode in stony silence for miles considering some expedient to secure Milly to him before Dot could confess the damaging truth. Passion overcame him. It was sixty miles from Queanbeyan to Dan's selection at Wamgambril Springs, and since early morning in the neighbourhood of Canberra they had ridden without meeting or overtaking a soul. Since ten o'clock they had not passed a habitation or gone through a fence. The world stretched away in rampart after rampart of rock and ridge, gully and spur of unbroken forest, with no human presence but their own. A full eighty miles away to the one side was Monaro and still thirty miles or more to Wamgambril or Goraig Flats. The shadows were lengthening as they left Jinninjinninbong and Ten Creeks to one side.

Larry's desperate determination hardened in the solitude. Milly had selected him voluntarily. The Milfords had suspected a planned rendezvous. Paddy Leary would spread the news up and down the River. If he held his tongue till he got out of Goulburn it would be as much as he could do. He would never pass Yass without knocking down what remained of his fiver and in the process blabbing as only Leary could. Larry had counted on all this in binding Milly to him, but she was quite capable of jettisoning scandal and defying convention after she had seen Dot. Fear of Dot grew to panic. When night fell they were still a long way from Joanna and Dan.

"You've taken the wrong track," exclaimed Milly, coming out on a little flat where a towering dead gum, killed by lightning, stretched a gallows-like silhouette against the darkening west. "We are right out on the way that Uncle Bert branches off to Curradoobidgee. We should have been there by now!"

"I was so happy about what you promised, I was not thinking about the way. Oh well, let's give the nags a spell and boil the billy at the old salt-shed before we push on."

"It will make us so ferociously late getting to Joanna."

"Never mind. Joanna and good old Dan won't scandalmonger on us."

"Others will, though."

"They won't know we have come all the way from Queanbeyan." Milly was hungry and agreed to stop. Larry's idea was to unsaddle the horses and have her in his power. Driven by his fever and his fears, he decided she was to be his before leaving the salt-shed. But he was only a tiro Tarquin lacking the technique to play with his subject till the propitious moment. In his nervousness he blundered. As the girl descended upon his shoulder he crushed her to him, devouring her with kisses. Milly, stiff, a trifle weary, was angered and repelled, and struggled from his grasp. She was not the least alarmed, only resentful that he should be guilty of such a breach of good taste and etiquette. In the course of moments it swept upon her that a demon had taken the place of her eager, pliant lover. This was no dream either but the reality of such a nightmare as occasionally tormented a girl of that period reared in the "complex" that most men were only kept from raids upon a maid's chastity by lack of opportunity. A spasm of horror shook her. Such a thing could not be.

Then Larry spoke. "Don't be frightened. I won't hurt you, and we're going to be married. We can ride straight away tomorrow to the parson before anyone can interfere. Dan and Joanna will help us."

His voice, proving that it was merely Larry, and not some monster substituted by the night, had an electrifying result. Had she spoken she would have said, "You will, will you!" but no sound came from her. She could have screamed like seven among rocks

222

and tree-trunks and nothing would have heard but the mopokes and curlews, the plovers and little wallabies. The kookaburras would have laughed and gone to sleep again. The marsupials, which had come out to feed in the dusk, sat up, arrested by the commotion, and hopped away. The only light was the crescent moon, going early to rest, and for the moment placed like an ornament in the locks of a big gum-tree. In an heroic moment fear and fatigue fell from Milly, and her being seemed to be transmuted into a white flame of rage that made the contest exhilarating.

Larry pinioned her arms and crushed her to him while she manfully kicked his shins. They trod round wildly in the underbrush, dry twigs cracking. With superior strength Larry wound her tighter and tighter till she felt she must suffocate. A movement to trip her feet with a thrust of his leg opened a few inches of space between them, and the girl tiptoed and bit with all her strength, catching Larry on the chin. He let go of her, startled and outraged; he tripped—in a wombat-hole probably—and floundered to gain his footing. Milly retained the reins and the halter of Romp, so now her toe found the stirrup, though high, and off she went, wildly, blindly, in the increasing darkness. Larry had to pick himself up and reach his horse to go in pursuit.

The single horse soon gained on the two, and the struggle began all over again in the darkness, on horseback this time and complicated by the rearing and turning of the animals. Larry's endeavour was to pull Milly into his arms, a simple matter when galloping from the rear and catching a girl off guard, but Milly's practised young knees were curled firmly round the horns and the horns were of the best workmanship. They strove together desperately, with no word to break the stillness of that far wild region. Not a splitter, nor a fossicker, nor a boundary-rider was within miles, except old Billy Heffernan, the dummy, whose hut was about two miles farther on.

Larry was no hardened Lothario, nor unhardened satyr. He was sensitive and of kindly disposition, really gentle underneath his inexperienced bravado. That inexplicable slip on Dot's part was to blame for his wild notion that he might succeed with Milly, but he was without the ruthlessness for such an outrage. He was too fond of Milly, too tender towards her, and his sudden wild impulse had passed immediately she resisted.

One cry broke from him, "Milly, don't panic, for no reason. I shan't hurt a hair of your head, I swear."

This increased Milly's excitement, and he knew that anything he could say would be taken only as part of his ruse to ruin her. Milly was now out of herself with rage and revulsion—virginal frenzy against violation. Larry had blundered so irretrievably that both retreat and advance were now fraught with danger of complete disaster. Horror at what he had brought on himself shook Larry, and he could have cried to heaven to return him to the *status quo* as it had been when he dismounted at Dead Tree salt-shed. He was in the dilemma of his life, loving Milly as he did, and knowing he had shut himself from paradise. His frantic necessity now was to recapture Milly without injuring her, to calm her and convince her that she had nothing to fear from him ever again in this world, and thus patch up normality between them to avoid public scandal.

He strove for Merrylegs's bridle-reins to render her rider helpless. Milly attempted to rush the mare at Larry, but all the animals were well-mannered saddle hacks, not cavalry chargers. She tried to hit Larry's horse with the end of the halter, but Larry easily countered that with the aid of his spurs. Suddenly Milly had an idea. She drew a pin from her hat and jabbed at Abracadabra. She caught him on the nose, and the spirited beast reared and backed madly.

The introduction of that silver hat-pin altered the course of their lives.

* * * * *

Billy Heffernan made money each season from wallaroo pelts. He used pits to trap them, baited with wild cherry, quinces, or damper, and cunningly covered with tea-tree. His biggest, deepest pit was two yards behind Abracadabra when Milly jabbed him, in the fairway used by certain marsupials as they came to browse on the little flats or to pilfer a lick of salt. The horse suddenly disappeared altogether. Merrylegs and Romp were too quick-witted to follow him.

There was a big catch in the pit and they could be heard scuffling and coughing. The horse plunged and snorted among them. Milly was rigid with fright, as she quieted her own trembling animals at a little distance. The slender moon was abed. There was no light but the high stars, which could not penetrate the dusk of the stately underbrush. No sound came from Larry. Milly's night sight came to her as she steadied herself; she saw the bait swinging above the pit and knew what had happened.

"Larry," she called. "Are you there?" No reply. She had no matches. She could not see into the black of the pit. She could hear that Abracadabra had settled down. Evidently he was not hurt; but what of the rider, was he crushed underneath? Was he dead, or silent only to entrap her?

"Larry! Larry! Tell me, are you hurt?"

No reply. Her terror grew painful. He was dead! She had killed him.

"Larry! Larry! If you are able to speak, please do. Don't just keep quiet and try to catch me. You won't have to go on fighting me. If you are alive, say so, and I'll . . . you can marry me if you want to as madly as that. Oh, Larry, do speak if you are alive!"

She felt about for a stick with which to probe, but found only upstanding wattle scrub, dead a year since by fire, tearing and tough as whalebone. There was no response from Larry. He must be dead! She could do nothing! She shivered with a sense of terrible disaster as she stood a minute or two lost in the dim pillared aisles of solitude through the rent of whose roof high overhead twinkled a star. She looked up and recognized one of the pointers of the Southern Cross—a treasured friend to one who knew and loved the night. Reason returned. The spring of action was released. She collected herself and made up her mind.

Watching minutely against another pit, she led her horses back as far as the salt-shed, and from there along the track by which they had come till she was certain of her whereabouts, and could see all the stars of the Cross. Then she changed saddle and bridle to Romp, who had run free all day, hugged and kissed her for comfort, climbed on her back, pulled Merrylegs's halter, and with calm desperation headed for Curradoobidgee eighty or ninety miles away.

CHAPTER 19

Dawn found the girl and her trusty friends many miles on their way. At sunrise she toiled up the passage of the Wamgambril for two miles or so by a precipitous track to the famous coolamon lying like a jewel at the base of the mighty rock, where the Wamgambril and the Coolgarbilli take their rise. Reaching the crest, she changed saddles again and let her beasts have a mouthful of grass while she breakfasted on the fruit of a wild raspberry vine. Then on and on again by gully and spur with never sight nor sound of man, not even a wisp of smoke above a distant chimney, the solitude to her not at all distressing. The familiar birds fluttered and made music round her all the way; even during the night the little wagtails had never left her, tweetering all the time, "Sweet pretty creature! Sweet pretty creature!" She knew too that Merrylegs was carrying her safely and directly homewards. It was the other thing that drove her unresting to Uncle Bert, the one of all who had sheltered her ever since she had been a passionate self-willed toddler. Uncle Bert, the great love of her infancy and girlhood, had never failed her spiritually, and would not cast her out now. Through the malhazard of his physical accident had resulted all that now dismayed her.

The sun rose high with blistering, irradiating heat tempered with zephyrs crisp and cool and of powerful sweep from Kosciusko, from Cootapatamba where the eagles drink the icy water, and from where the Snowy River rises to dash down to the lone and mighty Southern Seas to trade its song of mountain peak and ferny gully with that of the ceaseless winds that roam there with naught to say them nay for a thousand miles, bringing sou'-west stories from beyond Kerguelen or the Aleutian Deep, or sou'-easters freighted with the weird and frozen adventures of Antarctica from beyond the Bay of Whales, from beyond King Edward's Land, from beyond Haakon Seventh's Plateau, from beyond the South Pole, straight from eternity.

Merrylegs sweated and dried, and sweated and dried again, and did not go so lyrically as when she left Queanbeyan on Saturday morning. Milly changed once more to Romp, and she too sweated and dried again and somewhat steadied her gait.

The girl grew too tired to urge the animals. She dismounted, ate the sweets in her saddle-pocket, and, fastening the horses securely to her, reclined in the shade of a tree and slept. Merrylegs tugging to reach a farther tussock awakened her. She struggled up aghast to find the sun was sinking. Still heavy with sleep she climbed into the saddle and on without wavering, trusting entirely to the horses now.

Not only the ride from Queanbeyan to the Wamgambril salt-shed and thence at right angles to Monaro on one meal and a few sweets and raspberries had tired her, but the nights and days preceding had been full of excitement and short of sleep compared with her habit. The struggle with Larry had left her blue with bruises, and two eyes as desperately black as any maltreated wife of Sydney or London slums ever exhibited to a police magistrate.

To the fearless girl of robust physique, acquainted with the track and bred in the saddle, it was not such a stupendous journey, especially with a change of perfect horses and on their own beat. Her sleep had delayed her two or three hours, and she walked occasionally to relieve stiffness, but by midnight on Sunday, Merrylegs pricked her ears and mended her pace and Milly discerned by the light of the stars the stone fences marking the bald plains of Gowandale and Eueurunda, and knew she was on the buggy-roads that led from one to the other. Another ten miles to Curradoobidgee. She manipulated the different models of gates and slip-rails employed by Miss M'Eachern and the Pooles, and there at last was the song of Poole's Creek coming like the wind from Eaglehawk, and Merrylegs conducting her straight to the stable door of the old homestead.

She got stiffly down, feeling as if the bones had crumpled in her legs. Merrylegs stretched and shook herself thankfully. Her rider threw halter and reins over the horseshoes on the stable wall and sought Uncle Bert.

The commotion among the dogs had awakened him, and he always gave ear to the dogs since one night in his youth when he had ignored their warning and in the morning found his famous Black Belle mutilated.

Milly came timidly round the low old veranda encumbered by a motley collection of pot-plants, and darkened at the eaves by roses and other vines. Such a light step puzzled the listening man. It did not belong to any man he knew. Milly tapped lightly on his door. "Uncle Bert, oh, Uncle Bert, are you awake?"

Poole doubted his ears. "Just a minute! Is it really you, Milly, old chum, or a dream?"

He seized his crutches and, casting on a garment, hobbled to the door. Milly entered, distraught, disarrayed. Poole lit his famous lamp with the incandescent wick and was aghast at his young friend's appearance. Her habit was sweat-grey, muddy and torn, her hair wild, her face black and greenish round the eye-sockets and down to the cheek-bones, and stained with blood from Larry's chin. Only catastrophe could explain her arrival at such an hour in such a state.

"Is there anyone with you?" he asked gently, putting his arm about her and easing her into a chair.

"No."

"How far have you come?"

"From Queanbeyan to Wamgambril salt-shed and then on from there alone." Poole suppressed comment. He had removed her hat and was softly sponging her face.

"You had better rest a moment."

Milly became excited. "Oh, Uncle Bert, a terrible, terrible thing has happened. I have killed someone."

A serious accident, he estimated, but where—near enough to render speedy assistance? "An accident . . ."

"No. Not an accident exactly. It was, Uncle Bert—it was Larry Healey. Uncle Bert, I can't tell you! He tried to do something terrible, something he oughtn't, something worse than being killed, to me . . . Oh, Uncle Bert . . ." She looked at him mutely, nearly collapsing with fatigue and distress. He put his arm round her comfortingly, a glass of water to her lips.

"He only tried, he didn't succeed, did he?" said Uncle Bert, calmly, soothingly, as Charlotte, his sister investigating a family stomach-ache, but his thoughts bespoke no health to Larry Healey.

"I fought him, Uncle Bert. I fought and fought till I couldn't struggle any more . . . oh, I don't know, I got on to Merrylegs and got away and he came after me, and we fought again on horse-back, and I made his horse rear backwards, and suddenly he entirely disappeared."

"Good luck!" thought Poole, but he only gave her another sip of water and wiped her face.

"It was horrible in the dark. I got off and poked round and found he must have backed right into that monster wallaby-pit of Billy Heffernan's. There were sounds of all sorts of things, and I could hear Abracadabra, but no sound of Larry . . . I called and called to him and promised him everything . . . even to marry him as he wanted me to, if he'd only speak, but there was no sound, not even a groan. I couldn't find a stick in the dark, and it seemed so deep down . . . Oh, Uncle Bert!"

"You needn't worry about him. He's all right."

"Oh, but I've killed him!"

"Buckley's you have of killing a fellow like that with anything less than a charge of dynamite. 'I should smile!' as the Yankees say." Milly threw her arms round him, her weary head pressed tight against him.

"Uncle Bert, promise that you'll hide me here for ever and ever, and never let anyone see me or take me away to be hanged." She shuddered convulsively. "Don't let them drag me away where everyone will gape at me.... Promise me you'll shoot me yourself before you'll let them hang me."

"I promise that you will never be hanged for that, Milly, old chum. Larry is the only one in danger there." Oh, to take this sorely pressed young creature in his arms, to be his own, to keep and comfort and protect for ever! Ah, that youth had gone! He could never know its joys again.... But he still could be a protector. It was to him she had come all that way through day and night alone for refuge.

"But, Uncle Bert, you'll keep me always with you. This would never have happened if your foot hadn't been cut, and you could have come when I wanted you *ever* so badly."

"Hard luck that, all right, Milly, old pal. But we'll soon put the pieces back in their places, and things will be mended so that no one but you and me will know where the cracks were." Milly clung tighter about his neck, comfort in his presence. "Now, will you promise to do just what I tell you?"

"Oh yes, if you'll only keep me tight beside you all the time so no one else can get at me."

"Yes, you shall stay safely here; but mind, you must be as obedient as my old collie sheepdog. Do you promise—honour bright?"

"I promise, Uncle Bert."

"Well, you just rest a bit and get your wind, there's a brick!" He settled her in the chair and went to prepare a bath, etc. Returning in due time he handed a towel and one of his own garments. "There, now. You get into the hot water and then come back to bed to the room next door to me."

Milly obeyed, and when she returned found a light meal with a cup of cocoa awaiting her. Persuasion induced her to eat while Uncle Bert, unpractisedly, brushed her tangled locks. Tenderly, worshipfully, he recognized what a wonderful, what an exquisitely precious being a girl was. He too had been young once, young as Milly, but he remembered himself only as a big gawky animal very different from this delicate and fragrant embodiment of life. Youth, he pondered, so full of vague discontent and rest-lessness, what a royal thing it was! He insisted upon the cocoa, which had a stick in it.

"Now, when you wake, you'll find a letter under your pillow. You read that before you say a word to anyone—promise!"

"Promise—honour bright!"

"I may not be here in the morning."

"Oh, Uncle Bert, you are not going to leave me?"

"Only for a little. I want to get to that wallaby-pit ahead of anyone else. You see the sense of that, don't you?" Milly nodded. "You stay here quietly and say nothing. Spend a couple of days in bed. No one will know you are here, or why. You will be quite safe. You can say you ran against a tree to account for your black eyes. Here's one of the girl's dresses and you can go to Ma's room and forage in the big chest-of-drawers. Don't tell anyone what you told me about Larry—promise?"

"Promise—honour bright!"

"Fine! Now you just see how you can keep a shut mouth—no flies in or out—savvy? Good night! Sleep tight!"

He left her to the drowsiness perceptibly rising upon her. Finding Romp as well as Merrylegs in the stable-yard he knew there was an earlier chapter to this story. Automatically he felt the beasts' withers and legs. They were as fit as fiddles and a long way from knocked up. He awoke M'George, who, with his wife, had been secured to run the household since old Mrs Stepmother Poole's passing—as worthy and reliable a pair as ever came frae bonnie Scotland.

"Run in the Ace of Spades and Queen Anne and put my saddle on one and get my stepmother's saddle from the storeroom and put it on the other," was his surprising order to the sleepy man.

Mrs M'George was soon about too, and was instructed to fill tucker-bags, etc., while Poole dressed and applied himself to a couple of letters.

My Dear Little Milly,

Remember your promise to say nothing of what Larry attempted. Everything will be all right. Mrs M'George will do everything for you. Wait quietly where you are, you will be quite safe. Do nothing till you hear from me, no matter how long that may be. Don't worry. Miss Mac will keep you company.

Yours truly,

Uncle Bert.

He signed this, regretting that his years made any other role foolish for him.

Dear Friend Jessie,

I can depend on you, I know. Will you come straight back here and stay with Milly till my return? It is urgent and I know you will not fail me. An accident has happened which I have gone to clear up, and the less said the sooner mended, that is why I have sent for you to put the tin muzzle on all talk from the scratch. I shall explain when I come back. The quieter Milly is kept the better. I advise a couple of days in bed and squabash all curiosity about her if anyone comes round. You can rely upon the M'Georges.

Yours truly,

Bert Poole.

He put the first of these under Milly's pillow. She was sleeping soundly as he had often seen her sleep in childhood; many a time as a little thing she had had a nap on his waistcoat. Her head was bent, her long plaits spread across the pillow. He put her in a comfortable position, tenderly, reverently—ah, what an exquisite thing was youth! Only those that were young could meet it on an equality, or those who were mad or depraved seek to sully it. He laid her habit and hat tidily on a chair so that a disordered room should not discredit her; he extinguished the lamp and went out.

Mrs M'George had breakfast waiting while M'George had the fresh horses saddled and the two travellers washed down and turned into the orchard. It was plain to the pair that something out of the ordinary had happened, but they were too well trained to comment.

"M'George, take this letter to Miss M'Eachern at once. She will come back with you. I may be away four days or so. Tell anyone who inquires that you expect me any day. An accident has resulted in Miss Milly completing her journey alone, but don't worry her. She is only tired."

"Verra guid, sir."

Poole mounted with some difficulty and rode away under the stars. His foot was far from fit for a long session in the stirrup. He cursed to think how he had failed Milly, failed adventure, failed romance and his own reputation by two blunders excusable only in new-chums: one by being asleep about the beast killed at Gyang Gyang Gully, and again by disabling himself with an adze, he whose skill with the subtle instrument was acknowledged from Monaro to the coast. He must be getting bats in his belfry, he reflected.

He prepared for this journey with ingrained resourcefulness. The side-saddle and a sling made from a sheet were to rest

231

his wounded leg. Dawn found him well on his way. He looked round the sweeping plains and rolling uplands, khaki-coloured under the splendid summer sun, and away to the north-east over the ranges blue with distance, ridge on ridge, gully after gully like pleats, peak by peak, creek by creek, which he must conquer before another dawn. He set his teeth as his horse heaved and propped on some of the precipitous tracks, determined to reach the wallaby-pit with minimum delay. A generation had gone since he had turned his horses' heads that way with a sense of adventure sharing his saddle. Today that inspiriting colleague had returned. Never had she beckoned with more allure. Was he through age and accident to fail? Not if he knew it. It came to him in the stimulating morning air that vigour and joy of life were not entirely a matter of years but also a state of mind.

*   *   *   *   *

Miss M'Eachern read the note handed to her by M'George and said, "Go to the kitchen and have some breakfast and I'll ride back wi' ye."

She sat down to her own meal, remarking to her overseer, "Poole has some steers on Curradoobidgee that he wants me to look at. I might as well go straight back wi' his mon and you can carry on till I come back. Have the mare saddled."

She cantered away with M'George, leaving a curious employee. "She'd ride through hell to see a bargain, but there's something skew-whiff somewhere or she wouldn't scoot off like that with shearing half-cooked," he commented.

She arrived at Curradoobidgee while the forenoon was only half-blown, and Milly still soundly asleep.

"I've keeked in once or twice," reported Mrs M'George, "but the puir young leddy is verra tired."

A thin time loomed ahead of Jessie M'Eachern: she had brought no sewing, she never read a book, there was no one with whom to ha'e a crack, and shearing imminent back at Gowandale. She had, however, a true-blue understanding of friendship and buckled to its demands. After inspecting the house and premises she settled on the veranda with the *Sydney Morning Herald*, the *Town and Country Journal*, and the *Stock Breeders' Gazette*.

Milly in time awoke to the recollection of the tragedy hanging above her. Poole's instructions came back to her. She found the letter like a treasure. Uncle Bert would not fail. The mention of Miss M'Eachern worried her. Bother her, thought Milly, but Poole had requested her presence as a witness of the girl's condition in case of need.

Seeing her charge was awake, the good squatteress entered the room. "You're very tired. Stay there while I bring you a bite."

This startled Milly as almost indecent. She had never been ill a day in her life and had never seen a woman lie up except for childbirth or measles. "Oh no, Miss M'Eachern, I'm ashamed to be so lazy. I'll get up at once."

She twisted from under the bedclothes, finding herself almost too stiff to stand. Her bare legs astonished Miss M'Eachern by their bruises, black as if painted.

"Good gracious, lassie, but your legs are nothing to your face. You must have had a terrible fall."

Milly rolled up the blind and went to the little looking-glass. "I didn't know it was like that."

"It's a miracle you weren't killed."

Milly gave way to tears. "Oh, Miss M'Eachern, it was terrible! Larry Healey and I were bringing my horse home, the one that was lost, and it was dark, and an awful thing happened. Larry disappeared, horse and all, out of sight. I could hear the horse but not a sound from Larry, and I could not see in the dark, so I came straight on to Uncle Bert, and perhaps Larry is killed."

"Now, you mustn't get excited. If your Uncle Bert has gone to see, nothing can be done till we hear from him." She thought Milly must have hit a branching tree or fallen on her head, but wondered more what Mrs Saunders could mean to allow a young girl to roam the bush so far from home with a fellow like Larry Healey. It was plain that the girl herself was innocent. Lately, the Ten Creeks people had lost their child and had all the country in an uproar. Some folks were so feckless that they attracted calamities, reflected Miss Jessie, while others were called in to clear up the mess in spite of having concerns of their own demanding attention.

"We must bide a wee for Uncle Bert . . . How is the little boy who was lost?"

"Mother and Aunt Aileen have him in Sydney under the specialists."

"And who was looking after you?"

"Uncle Jack was there, only that he had to go to Riverina, and then Larry and I went for the pony."

"Ah!" commented Miss M'Eachern. Without doubt some people made their own troubles. She did not pursue the subject of where Larry and Milly had been when the accident occurred. She was more interested in Aileen and Ronald, seeing her connection with the old affair, since which she had heard whispers of scandal. After a few observations she astutely gauged that Milly was aware of the relations between her aunt and Dice and was filled with resentment, so decided that silence on all doubtful subjects was the safest course.

An hour or two and Milly had recovered sufficiently likewise to be suffering from inaction. She repaired and cleaned her habit, and at midday dinner made a suggestion, "Would you let me go back to Gowandale with you? You must be busy, and Uncle Bert can't possibly be home tomorrow or even the next day."

This was rescue to the business woman oppressed with idleness while the active affairs of her station were in full cry. "Are you fit to ride? What would anyone say if they saw your face?"

"I can comb my hair low and put on a thick veil and the ride will take the stiffness out of me."

Miss M'Eachern estimated that it would create less curiosity for her to have Milly at Gowandale than for both of them to be at Curradoobidgee at the busy time of the year, while Poole, bad leg and all, had gone on an unexplained journey. So long as Milly was not out of her care, her part would seem to be fulfilled. Soon they were skimming across the rolling plains swept with Kosciusko's zephyrs, little amiss with Romp or her mistress.

Poole, in another direction, progressed stubbornly and in grave discomfort if he left his foot in the stirrup for any length of time. To ride sideways and rest it in a sling was a relieving change, but the new and cramped position was painful to a man of his years, and he experienced the discomfort known to new-chums, but pushed on, hoping to reach the wallaby-pit in daylight.

*   *   *   *   *

The day that Milly and Larry left Queanbeyan, Billy Heffernan struggled back to his hut at Wamgambril Flats and slept all that day and Sunday. He had been away on one of his sprees by which he periodically leavened life. He generally started in one of the less pretentious hotels in Bool Bool, now a five-pub town, and when, for the general good, thrust out of this, retreated to a lonely shanty between Brennan's Gap and Melacmelac, where they had no scruples in topping off a pickled boozer with pain-killer or any other preservatives available at less expense than reputable alcohol.

On Monday he went round his traps, neglected for nearly a fortnight, and was astonished by the catch in the big pit near the salt-shed. It was thirty-six hours since Abracadabra and his rider had adventitiously hurtled in there to the dismay of the other captives. The horse was uninjured, for the sides of the pit were of clay, but he had unseated his rider and struck his forehead

234

and rendered him unconscious. Larry had fortunately been pitched into the corner of the pit, and the horse, in the way of his kind, did not step on him again, but after the first flurry among the wallabies settled down like a beast in a stall.

Larry returned to consciousness in time, but was in great pain with a head too bad to mount his steed and thence out of the pit, small effort to anyone in normal condition. He was in no state to speculate on what had become of Milly, but lay against the cool earth, taking no cognizance of time, dozing or semi-unconscious, till Heffernan had found him.

To drunkenness Heffernan attributed such a mishap to a bushman as familiar as a boundary-rider or brumby with every track of the area. He ascertained that Larry was alive, and set about getting him out, a neat little chore to a man as shickered as Heffernan, for Larry was helpless. He hoisted Larry on his (Heffernan's) head, and rolled him out on the bank. Larry groaned deeply. Heffernan then laid his patient on a bed of bracken and brought him water in his hat and left him to rest while he dug a slope so that Abracadabra could scramble up. During these operations he came upon a veil in shreds some yards away on the dead wattle shrubs, and, just at the edge of the pit, a lady's hat-pin in the design of a Scottish thistle.

Heffernan began to pleasure in his work. The hoof-prints squirmed round in rings near the mouth of the pit, that was clear by the trampled scrub. There had been no rain and no other travellers, the wallabies had been diverted from this beat for the moment and left the writing uncrossed upon the trail. Heffernan followed the tracks back to the salt-shed, where he found another piece of veil on a bush. The tracks of Abracadabra were upon the tracks of two smaller horses up to within three yards of the pit. There had been pursuit, overtaking, and a scuffle in which Larry's horse had gone over the edge; there was, too, a small footprint about the pit and tracks of two departing horses. There was a woman in it and two men—a fight over a female! It was as plain as a typed address to the bushman. What could be more enlivening to the unbroken solitude of Wamgambril swamps! Billy Heffernan's eyes glittered.

He gloated on the hat-pin and tattered veil, which would unravel the scandal. Had Larry been scratching about the Humphrey camp?—no, there would be no need of a scuffle about such a trull, and this was a swell hat-pin. It might have been two women fighting like cats over Larry. Billy dismissed that possibility with a guffaw. Larry had not the spondulics, and without it was not so blooming fascinating that the women would be scratching their eyes out over him. Now he thought he had it. Larry had his tongue lolling out after young Milly at Ten Creeks, and Dot at Saunders Plains had got hold of it and let fly: if what he heard of Dot had any stuffing in it, that is just what had happened. It would be easy to get the pieces to fit.

Billy, whose opportunities of vindicating his red-bloodedness had been restricted, was filled with obscene envy of a man who could undermine two young geebung females so that violence ensued. "Reckon these gewgaws will be worth a tenner at the least," he muttered, stowing them upon his person.

His plan was to deposit Larry with his sister Joanna about ten miles distant. Heffernan had no vehicle. Single-handed there was nothing but packing on horseback along the cattle-tracks. Abracadabra was too spirited for this, so Heffernan returned to his hut for a tame old pack-horse warranted to resent no burden from a dead beast to a hen-coop. He provided pillows for pommel and croup by filling two sugar-mats with tussock grass. Larry was not heavy and Heffernan a hardy, powerful old man. He lifted the groaning form on. The pain brought back consciousness. Larry complained of his head first. Heffernan soused that with cold water. Larry was in such agony that he could not lean forward even on the grass, and Heffernan had to abandon his own nag and walk at the stirrup and hold his injured man on.

It was tedious for Heffernan. It was torment for Larry, but, like many another pilgrimage where necessity dictated, it continued and ended at last. In good time really, Heffernan was calling for Spires to help him with his burden.

Dan was out on the selection. Joanna, not yet strong, had to do her part, while Susie, a Humphrey of more doubtful parentage even than usual, but a brave little pioneer bush maid in spite of her begetters, was dispatched on Billy's horse to bring the boss.

Joanna cut away her brother's clothing and Billy laid him on the only spare bed, the long home-made sofa in the front room, narrow and not very comfortable. Joanna washed some more of the clotted blood from his face and exposed the gash in his temple where the shoe of Abracadabra had caught him and left a brand till the end of Larry's days.

When Dan appeared Larry was again unconscious from pain and fatigue, and Joanna too alarmed to be left alone with him. Susie was therefore sent to fetch her old tyke of a mother, who had diverse uses in conditions so sparsely furnished with women. Heffernan volunteered to go for the doctor. His offer was accepted. Dan estimated that as he had just recovered from a spree he could be trusted to pass the Travellers' Rest going, if not returning. He had given Joanna an account of the finding of Larry suitably expurgated for a respectable female, the sister of the injured and with a young infant. He added a few more particulars to Dan, but slyly guarded evidence that might be profitable or entertaining only to himself.

*   *   *   *   *

After a weary and painful journey, Poole hove in sight of the bleak limbs of the big dead tree just about sundown. He had been compelled once or twice to soak his injured foot in cold water to relieve the nervous irritation set up by the pendent position. He was out of condition by long inactivity and nearly asleep from exhaustion.

The pit was empty but it was patent that Milly had not been hysterical nor had she lost her bearings in the dark. The tracks all about proved that the horse had been taken out of the pit, but not that Larry was safe. Where could he be?

Poole had made haste against darkness. Heffernan's tracks were fresh and he took them to the hut. The place was locked up, but Larry's horse was in the little brush paddock. It was now too dark to see whither Heffernan had gone. What to do? The kookaburras could not advise though they laughed like mad all round the horizon, and though the friendly willy-wagtails had been with him all the way, all that they could say was "Sweet pretty creature! Sweet pretty creature!"

Would they be missing Milly at Ten Creeks and raising the country? Would Heffernan have taken Larry to his sister? Every mile with the condition of his foot loomed like ten to Poole. He decided to go to Dan Spires first, and this happened to be also on the way to Bool Bool, and without major peaks to be scaled. Hearing a horseman coming towards him, he dropped his foot into normal position and met SP-over-J returning from Stanton's Plains.

"Good day, Bert, been to Ten Creeks?"

"Not yet."

"You wouldn't have found anyone at home. The Missus and Lucy are still in Sydney and I sent Milly to Keba till I go for her next Friday. Your foot all right again now? Have you heard of the accident?"

"What accident?"

"I met Billy Heffernan going for the doctor. Larry, horse and all, went into the wallaby-pit up this way and was there till Billy found him."

"No danger of his life, is there?"

"Billy wasn't too clear. Seems pretty badly smashed up. I'll come over tomorrow and see what the doctor says . . . I haven't seen you since you cut your foot, how is it?"

"Not well by long chalks, that's why I have the side-saddle. I had to get over to see you."

"Why didn't you send for me when your foot is like that?"

"There wasn't time. I say, Jack, Milly is not at Ten Creeks. I left her at Curradoobidgee."

"How in thunder did she get there? What's up?"

"It's part of this accident with Larry. I haven't got to the bottom of it myself yet, but they must have been somewhere and got the Young Whisker filly that was supposed to have fallen over the ledge at Mount Corroboree and in the dark Larry stumbled into the pit. Milly couldn't get a sound out of him and was frightened out of her wits, and, since you weren't home, she cut away to me."

"That was a thundering long way. She could have come to Stanton's Plains . . . only I told her I might be going to Turrill Turrill. Is there anything the matter with her?"

"No, only frightened—naturally."

"Her mother ought to look after her more."

"I came straight on to find you and see about Larry and not make any more talk than necessary."

"We had better go to Dan's straight away, then."

They rode silently. Poole was in such misery that he had to dismount and relieve his position again, so they boiled the billy and had the evening meal from their saddle-bags.

The doctor found several broken ribs and a smashed collar-bone to account for the intense pain Larry suffered, and it was necessary to put a stitch or two in his temple. The blow there had come within a fraction of an inch of being fatal. Mrs Humphreys had arrived to assist Joanna, and since he could be of no assistance, Poole said he would push on to the Travellers' Rest. He heard with immense relief that Larry was in no danger of his life.

"I don't know what Lucy will say about Milly," said her uncle. "You might send her down to Goulburn by train and she can pick her mother up there. They may be coming on Thursday."

"What about the horses?"

"She'll have to do without them and ride Flea Creek if she carries on like this—too much of a good thing, damn it!"

"A month or two on Monaro would do her good. Lots of young people up there among the Pooles and Timsons. She can have a flock of them at Curradoobidgee if she likes, and my housekeeper will take care of her. I can't take this ride again for a while, I can feel. Besides, it's shearing. Why don't you come up for a spell? I don't know when you were up last."

"Wait till Lucy hears of it! She'll put Milly's hat on straight for her, I expect. She's much too wild."

"You can't expect to tie young people up nowadays like when we were young. They won't stand it."

"Don't let Milly be a nuisance to you. She's not a child now, and ought to settle down."

"She'll never be a nuisance to me."

"Marriage would settle her."

"There is no one good enough for her. . . . If anyone is coming in to town tomorrow you might send me word how Larry is getting along. I'll be going up past Neangen and could let his family know. I'll be putting up at Three Rivers."

Poole's first care was a telegram worded to set Milly's heart at rest. His foot was so painful that a couple of days' complete rest was imperative. He spent these at Three Rivers with Charlotte and the old lady, who were glad to see him.

CHAPTER 20

POOLE PERSUADED Charlotte to return to Curradoobidgee with him for Christmas. In view of Milly's probable sojourn there he felt that his sister's presence would mean much in applying the brakes on what his years would make a foolishness.

For Charlotte to be absent from Three Rivers, where she had moved in with her family shortly following the death of Grandpa Mazere a quarter of a century before, created a mild sensation. Charlotte had always been there like a rock of refuge not only for the wide family circle but for many outside it. Others might bewail their misfortunes, Charlotte never. There was demur because it might be Great-grandma's last Christmas, but Poole pointed out her last Christmas had been expected for years. He believed she was good for a longer spin than Grandma Poole, and would have at least four or five years to play with yet. Such fears were not uttered in Great-grandma's hearing! She urged Charlotte to have a change and visit old haunts.

Poole borrowed a buggy-and-pair, and two days later he and his sister set out. Charlotte had to drive most of the way because Bert's foot was not fit for the brake. There was now a road cut round the sidelings of the Jenningningahama, up which horses could travel with less of old-time effort, and down which vehicles went comfortably with a tree attached to the back axle to relieve the strain on hocks and brakes and breeching.

There was more melancholy than pleasure to Charlotte Mazere in traversing that road on which she had not been farther than Bookaledgeree since, as a young wife, she had come a-horseback in winter by the hazardous bridle-tracks in the discomfort of impending motherhood.

They made to Neangen for midday and found Healey and his wife about to set out for Wamgambril Springs.

"Larry's so bashed about that it's going to be a long job," said his father. "So I'm taking the Missus over to help Joanna."

"He'll never be able to walk again, and the nursing of him is breaking Joanna down, very likely be the death of Joanna too." Mrs Healey set her voice in the key of a dirge. Like many ageing women of small mental capacity she revelled in disaster. It was to her what a spree is to an old man—an outlet.

"Julie is to keep house, I suppose," said Charlotte cheerfully.

"It is not right to leave her alone, but it can't be helped. I have more than my share of sorrow, first Aileen's baby is lost and now poor, poor Larry to be a cripple all his life."

"It was Aileen and Larry had the trouble, I should say," interposed Julie unsympathetically.

"Yes, the baby was found all right. Let us hope Larry's case will be equally wonderful," suggested Charlotte.

"Many a smash-up is not so bad as it seems when we set things together," said Poole; but it is impossible to stop an old woman when she starts on her woes. The only hope is to divert her, as Larry, sen., well knew.

"What I can't make out," he observed, "is how Larry came to ride into a wallaby-pit. He must know that track like the palm of his hand, unless, of course, he was drunk; even then his horse would have saved him."

"My Larry doesn't drink," said his stepmother loyally.

"He's mighty different from other people's Larry if he doesn't," muttered his pa.

"Accidents are like that," said Poole. "Take my foot—how I could have been such a new-chum I don't know. *I* wasn't drunk."

"Haw! Haw! Haw! There's no telling!" Any mention of alcohol was so enlivening that Poole needed to say no more to change the subject.

The Pooles reached the Timson pair by dark, and found them eager for the family news.

"I would have gone to help Joanna only Norah Alfreda is at the troublesome age and I have not been fit for much myself," said Norah.

Chores out of the way, the elders were free to appreciate this marvellous child, who could converse like a sage, according to the doting Alf. Norah said the child was so sensitive that the least excitement drove her off her food and sleep. She was a quaint little thing, as lively as a cricket, and seated upon the knee of the all-conquering Poole was soon fossicking for his watch. He never failed with children, right from tinies to those in their teens, reflected his sister. Such a pity he had none of his own, till now it was too late. It was to be hoped he would never go soft like old Jack Stanton and marry some young thing and have a repetition of Stanton's troubles.

"They are so delighted with that nipper, it's a pity they can't have half a dozen," remarked Poole, as they went on their way next day.

"One will be plenty. Poor Norah suffers a great deal."

"What's the matter? She's not usually a croaker."

"No. Something internal, she fears. I don't like her colour. She is like a corpse."

On reaching home they learnt that Milly was away at Gowandale and Miss M'Eachern was wiring into the shearing. Poole said he would bally well have to do likewise. However, owing to his accident, arrangements had been made to do all the shearing at his brother Jim's that season, and Bert's absence had not been so insane an aberration as it might otherwise have been accounted by family and neighbours. They simply thought he had grown tired of confinement and went off unannounced to prevent opposition. The M'Georges had "minded" their own business.

Milly's arrival at Gowandale was causing a good deal of excitement, and one young man after another appeared eager to borrow a wool-pack or a whetstone, or came on some such excuse. Miss M'Eachern had had no such cloud of callers since dear knows when, but what surprised that leal soul was Milly's depression. Even after the reassuring telegram she did not brighten to her wonted high-spirited self. Could she be in love with Larry Healey?

Charlotte wandered about the old place like a being returned from a planet. The house that she and Bert had been responsible for making the new house, when ambition had been stirred by contact with the Mazere clan upon Charlotte's marriage, was on its last legs, and the new house, built a good ten years later, and which Charlotte now saw for the first time, had a whiskered maturity. The face of nature was changed by the clearing and fencing, and there were two roofs within sight that made the station seem contracted. She found a few of the original fruit-trees, gnarled and beyond bearing, and the flower-beds before the old house retained the design in which she and Bert had dug them in their teens. Poole's Creek, as of old, came down by the back of the stables from Eaglehawk singing its immortal lullaby, only it, too, looked bald without the scrub. Willows and other aliens lifted their heads amid its tea-tree and blackthorn, but its curves were the same. Also unchanged were the contours of the ranges. They stretched away endlessly to the north-west just as when she had ridden into them on the morning after her marriage on a wedding trip to Mungee. Great-grandma Mazere—not then a grandmother—had been riding with her too, and not nearly so old then as Charlotte herself was today. How time had run!

The homestead was so forlornly empty. No one there but Bert. She gazed round the horizon towards Wombat Hill and Maryvale and Little River and Gowandale; of the Timsons, Gilberts, Healeys, M'Eacherns, and Pooles who had originally manned these holdings, not one now remained. The old place, parched and pallid in the summer sunlight, looked like an old dog that was sleeping before the door—too old to be of any further use and merely awaiting the end.

Bert came out on the veranda and joined her. It was great to have her there again at last. He wished they might ooze down into old age in peace together; but that was impossible. Too many vigorous younger lives of her own making claimed Charlotte, and there was still her husband; astonishing how he hung on in spite of drink.

"I'd like to go home as soon as possible," she said. "Forty-five years—too long to stay away without coming back—better not to come back at all than too late."

Bert saw that she was full of rare tears. He had been stupid not to realize what it would mean to come back to an empty nest after all the years. His heart smote him to fail his dear old Charlotte, who had never failed him. He should have planned a great welcome from all the younger tribe to fill the gap and keep sadness at bay. He must make up for it now, shearing or no shearing. Charlotte was more important than all the wool from Monaro to Muttama. He ordered the horses and set out for Gowandale to cheer her, and also dispatched M'George to Jim and Harry and Ada to announce the great surprise. They could be depended upon to respond in a heartening way.

Miss M'Eachern was surprised to see Charlotte and made her very welcome.

"Milly acts as if she had something on her mind," she confided to Poole. "Do you think she is infatuated with that young man and wants to go to him?"

"Oh no, she can't endure him," said Poole, so decidedly that Miss M'Eachern looked at him piercingly. She had seen amorous propensities last long into senility with men otherwise well balanced. "She's had a bit of a shock. She and Charlotte must be livened up with company. I'll expect you over immediately shearing is past."

Milly accompanied them home, and watching her closely Poole had to admit the truth of Miss M'Eachern's observation.

The family rallied to Charlotte, and Bert was content to see her first melancholy merge into quiet enjoyment of the Christmas festivities enlarged and specialized in her honour. Mrs Saunders permitted Milly to remain on Monaro without censure, and spoke of paying a visit at New Year to fetch her home.

Though Charlotte grew to enjoy her holiday, Milly's abstraction and uneasiness increased so that Charlotte, like Jessie, remarked, "Do you think she cares very much about Larry Healey, and is fretting about him, and would like to go to him?"

"Oh no, not at all. She'd as soon think of a gorilla in that respect."

"You never can tell what fancy a girl will have in the case of a man. She usually sees something in him that no one looking on can understand, and Larry is good-looking and taking."

"That's true sometimes, but there's nothing in Larry for Milly to see," he contended with finality, thinking there was no fool like an old fool, yet feeling in no wise old or foolish. "Milly will find her feet for herself presently if she is let alone."

* * * * *

Larry was painfully recovering at Wamgambril Springs, attended by his stepmother and sister. Mrs Healey was enlivened by the change and the importance she assumed. Larry, suffering pain and discomfort and with his mind in worse case than his body, was not an endearing patient. Seeing the door of delight closing upon him through the retribution of his act with Dot, he had sought to keep it open by violence, and thereby smashed the whole edifice. He was in a rash of curiosity to know what end and what face Milly had put on the escapade. That she must be alive and well somewhere was certain. The injury or illness of Milly Saunders would not be overlooked in that region. Strange that no one could mention Milly, though the infernal old wind-bags kept on and on for hours about everything else till he wished he could throw them a bait and relieve his aching head. They were as bad as the flies that buzzed during daylight.

He knew that Poole had been down and had taken his sister back with him, which was attributed to the leisure of his convalescence. Larry heard with genuine regret that Norah was not well. With unfailing kindness she had written to say that this was the reason she had not hurried to his assistance, and she invited him to come and rest with her and Alf as soon as he could travel. Of Dot he was likewise continually informed. Her movements appeared of interest to his womenfolk, probably because of Ronald Dice.

"Julie says that Ronald Dice is for everlasting at Saunders Plains now, but that Dot won't have anything to do with him."

"I'm sure!" ejaculated Joanna unbelievingly. "She was running after him for all to see while he was wanting Aileen; it is not likely she has changed so soon."

"They say she has changed so you wouldn't know her since that time in Sydney—goes nowhere, only looks after the old people, and she used to be such a one for flying round."

"Must have been someone in Sydney and it didn't come off. That's what is the matter."

"She'll be glad to take Ronald presently."

"The old people don't want her to leave them."

"Then he can live there. He doesn't seem to be much of a doer. Aileen must be thankful now when she sees the difference in the two men. I used to be anxious when I heard of Ronald being so much at Ten Creeks. You never noticed anything, did you, Joanna?"

"It was Milly he was spoony on there. Ronald is one of those light-weights with a rag on every bush, but Larry cut him out there, didn't you, Larry?"

Larry took his opportunity. "Where the deuce is Milly these days? She might have cantered over to ask how I am. And I wish to goodness you'd stop talking a bit."

He lay and puzzled about Milly. Surely the return of the Young Whisker filly would raise a buzz in the district.

Things were moving. That very evening little Tommy Roper, the unexcelled gatherer and disseminator of news from Riverina to Monaro, blew in to Dan's. He was working up the River to Monaro and had come by way of Cuppinbingle and Keba. At the former stronghold he had forgathered with Paddy Leary in mellow condition, and his share of the epic of rescuing Romp had been expounded with no minimizing of Milly's part.

Milly, while her mother and uncle were off the track, had bolted all the way to Goulburn, seized her own mare with no by-your-leave to judge or jury, nor permission of police nor benefit of clergy, and just travelled round the country with a young man and played Old Harry as she damned well thought fit! There was the hell of a fine snorting blood filly for you, if there never was another, and she barely eighteen! Milly had Paddy Leary's franchise enthusiastically.

"We'll hear of her marrying Larry next thing," commented Tommy.

"That's what Larry was —— well working for all right, and didn't she just have him on the go!" guffawed Paddy. "But there's many a slip 'twixt the cup and the lip, and if Larry got outside of himself a bit, I wouldn't be surprised if Milly gave him one over the ear and let him go tell his ma about it. She ain't got any of that sort of thing in her, it's plain to be seen by a wall-eyed bandicoot."

"She'll have to marry him after this or her goose would be cooked with anyone else," said Tommy, who had none of the Celt in him and appraised the escapade from a different mind.

"Miss Milly don't let anyone cook her goose as easy as they want to. She ain't one of the cowering crying females that flings up the sponge. I'll take a bet on that!"

Tommy Roper, progressing to the kitchen of Ten Creeks Run for his next night, was surprised to hear no word of the re-appearance of the filly, with which he expected the firmament to be humming. There was compensation in the boss item that Larry Healey on Abracadabra, a mountain-bred horse, had fallen into old Billy Heffernan's wallaby-traps at Wamgambril—a terrible crash, and was now at Dan Spires's.

"They say he'll never walk again, and his face is cut up like a Maori," Long Billy informed him. Tommy rubbed his hands with enjoyment. Stay in a place and nothing ever happened, but go away for the shortest spell and there were enough goings-on to fill a book.

"How the dooce did that happen?"

"Reckon he musta been soused, don't you? I reckon that he's taken to drink lately, an' young Milly's got hold of it an' that's why she cleared out suddent like."

"Has she cleared out?" Tommy's eyes fairly leapt.

"When the Missus and ole Lucy took the youngster to Sydney, Milly wuz here with ole Skinny Guts, an' all of a sudden he said he had business in Bool Bool, an' he sent Jane home so as we couldn't be doin' nothin' wrong with the pore innercent little girl," Billy put his thumb to his nose, "an' young Milly was to go down to Keba for a week. She went over the river for a night fust, takin' nothink but a little valise. That wuz all right, and then ole Skinny come back, an' we hear Larry is all busted up, an' nothink at all about young Milly comin' back at all; an' then nearly a week later ole Skinny comes to me with a parcel the size of a sugar-bag an' tells me to ketch the mailman at Keba with it, an' I see it was addressed to Milly at Curradoobidgee—must er been her duds, I reckon. Now I gotter ride over termorrer an' bring Jane home, so it looks as if the Missus an' youngster must be makin' tracks for this shanty. But don't you reckon Larry's been on the booze? There's been some kind of a bust-up among 'em, that's plain."

Nothing of the filly. Tommy was too skilled a news-gatherer to put his foot in the fabric. "What do you reckon Larry was doin'

246

poochin' about ole Billy's rat-traps—that ain't on the direk bridle-track from Keba to Ten Creeks?"

"That's why I reckon he was tanked up, an' young Milly belted off to Poole. She allers runs to him like as if he wuz her ma. I smell a rat somewhere, don't you?"

"You mean Larry was on the big brown outer that ole chestnut ole Larry used ter ride?" Long Billy nodded. "Well, it stan's to reason, if he wuz drunk, a mountain-bred horse like that would have took him home safe an' not been runnin' inter no wallaby-pit. An ole cab-horse rared on Sydney gas-jets would know enough fer that."

Tommy, agog to pursue this lively spoor, made Wamgambril Springs his next place of call, ostensibly to inquire after the new baby and Larry. The baby was pronounced a blue-ribboner and then he turned to inspect Larry.

"It's a life-saver to see you," said Larry. "How's the season down the river?"

"The seasons seem to have gone mad, but all the same it's not what you'd call *too* stinkin'. What the dooce have you been and gone and done to yourself? Been havin' no end of a birthday by the look er things."

"By golly, I don't know what happened till it did, and I wasn't drunk I might tell you—hadn't a taste of anything stronger than tea for a fortnight, but I might as well tell that to the grey magpies: so they can think what they flaming well like."

Deftest prospecting got nothing further from Larry, and left Tommy with whetted curiosity. He decided to inspect the pit and refused an invitation to stay the night. "Some other time, thanks, but a feller I know is in a hurry for skins so I'll drop in on ole Heffernan while I'm so near."

Though his opportunities were not so rich and his disposition more suspicious, Heffernan was Tommy's peer as a bush tele-graph. Roper rode to the hut prepared to do some news-trading. He took it upon himself to stay the night, volunteering to make flap-jacks. Afterwards, when pipes were going, he opened up. "I heerd furder down the river that Larry found that roan Young Whisker filly that was supposed to be dead that time we wuz all on the string hunting for her. You haven't seen her anywhere, have you?"

"Never heard anything about it," said Heffernan cautiously, but an inner light was exciting him.

"I had it from a man who seen him goin' by with the horse. He said he had someone with him, too. Do you reckon he an' someone had a fight over the filly, an' that's how he got smashed?"

"I don't reckon the fight was about a *horse*," said Heffernan, as if he knew much more.

"A female, eh?" Tommy winked dexterously.

"What female?"

"What female is most interested in young Larry?"

"Old Mother Humphreys?" Heffernan cackled at his own wit. The inner circles of ribaldry had a staple joke about Heffernan's rebuff by this practitioner.

"What female is most interested in the Young Whisker filly?"

Heffernan estimated that Tommy knew more than he did himself. He produced the hat-pin and tattered veil.

"Ever seen either of them things before?"

"I remember a hat-pin same as that."

"What do you reckon them gewgaws was doin' beside my wallaby-pit the mornin' I got Larry out?"

Roper whistled long and suggestively. Then he doffed guards and they put the pieces together with gusto. What Milly and Larry were doing at the salt-shed not directly on the track to anywhere some time between the Friday night, on which Paddy Leary said they left Goulburn, and the Monday morning when Billy went his rounds, was a matter for speculation. Familiarity with certain male propensities until that date unrealized by Milly aided them in their conclusions.

"What do you reckon we'll find out next?" said Roper.

"That Milly will —— well go to Sydney for a long stay like Dot." Heffernan winked as dexterously as Roper.

     *   *   *   *   *

Lucy, Aileen, and Lawrence John did not arrive at Stanton's Plains till time for the Christmas family gathering there. Lawrence was an object of interest. Maggots crawling into the ears had caused grave trouble, but the specialist was hopeful of recovery in time. His mother also was very well. She slept soundly, free from nightmares of snakes, and had a good appetite. She did not, however, recover her backbone, not that she had possessed a stiff one. She seemed to be lost without Lucy, who directed her far more firmly than she had dared to deal with Milly, since that young lady could hold her own spoon and bat in the eye those that crossed her will.

When the excitement of arrival subsided, SP-over-J had to inform Lucy how Milly had distinguished herself. Following Tommy Roper's peregrination, the country fairly palpitated from Yass and Queanbeyan to Goulburn and Turrill Turrill and back again to Bool Bool and Monaro. The family, the last to be informed of the scandalous element of the adventure, had at length to take notice. Some of the gossip reaching Stanton's ears was as infuriating as what he had overheard concerning himself the day that Towser was poisoned. He and Lucy had high words as the report proceeded.

"You ought to have kept Milly under a little more and this sort of thing wouldn't have happened."

"You might have taken care of her while I was away with the baby and his mother, who didn't look after *him*, or *that* mess wouldn't have been."

They tossed it back and forth till they came to the trite conclusion that nothing could be done by crying over spilt milk, and that the present problem must be handled.

"The whole country says that Larry will have to marry her," said SP-over-J.

"He was always pestering me to do that, but I don't like it. His prospects are not very bright, and if he's going to be a cripple it will be no joke." She dared not say that she hated the thought of any more Healeys. "Have you said anything to Larry about it, and asked him what he meant by acting that way with a young girl as soon as your back was turned; and do you know that she has really come to—to—you know, any real harm, or is it only scandalmongering?"

"I thought it better to lie low till you came home. Charlotte being at Curradoobidgee, it is the best place for Milly to be out of mischief for the present."

"Wonderful how Milly has always acted as if Bert was her father." Milly having rushed straight off to Poole was a saving element to her mother. SP-over-J grunted. He thought it was Lucy who wanted Poole as Milly's stepfather; as for Milly and Poole, he was blamed if he knew what they thought, but anything that hatched there would not upset SP-over-J.

"I'll have to go straight up to Monaro and talk seriously to Milly," said Lucy. Her brother gave a wizened grin, and said in that case Aileen had better stay at Stanton's Plains or go to Neangen to see her mother until Lucy returned. It was thus tacitly settled that in future Aileen was not fit to be mistress of her own household. This restored Lucy to a definite status with her brother.

CHAPTER 21

MILLY'S ABSTRACTION continued. In spite of her pluck and her repudiation of Larry she felt herself shamed and disgraced. Worse, in her young ignorance she was haunted by possible serious consequences. Sex knowledge had to come to girls in underhand whispers in her day, and in her excited state she had exaggerated possibilities out of all proportion till she was obsessed and robbed of sleep and peace.

Poole, watching closely, saw that she was losing weight, while her eyes had a sunken look that added years to her age. He felt it was time to intervene. Opportunity occurred one day when Milly with an attitude foreign to her had pleaded headache, and stayed mooning about the house while Charlotte went over to Jim's.

"Say, Milly, old pal, what is it?" he said, placing a kindly hand on her shoulder as they loitered in the drawing-room after dinner. "You haven't forgotten promising me that if ever you needed my help you'd ask for it." He swung her round to look deeply in her face. What he saw caused him to sit down and lift her on to his knee, as he had not done, for his own sake, for several years now.

"Is it Larry?"

"Yes."

"Do you care very much about him?" He tautly awaited her reply.

Milly started aghast. "I hate the sight of him. I loathe him! At first I was horrified that I had killed him, and now sometimes I'm sorry that he's alive, because it was his own fault. I didn't know the pit was there."

"It was entirely his own fault, all that happened to him as far as that is concerned, but for your sake it is much better that he is alive. If you don't like him, what is the worry?"

"Oh, Uncle Bert, can you help me; what am I to do? I'll die if you can't help me."

"That sounds terribly serious. Tell me all about it." Poole's quiet years had been rich in that experience which can become a key to the heart of groping, heady youth. He would never be guilty of phrases or quips such as had fallen from Potter and Dice to freeze confession or wither appeal for enlightenment. Under his calming kindness the girl's tortured distress tumbled forth. Nothing was withheld, not even what Milly would have died rather than discuss with her mother, who, though fine for lots of issues, had not her daughter's confidence in this field.

A delicate half-question here and there and Poole was able to restore his charge to harmonious sanity. She remained in his arms, her face against his heart, his chin resting on her wealth of bright locks. Her arms stole round his neck—tentatively. No response. The lowering of his head was the only yielding to temptation. Milly put her cheek against his.

"I'm never going to leave you again—*never*! If I had really been disgraced I was going to ask you to marry me to save me. You promised long, long ago when I was young to help me no matter how big a mess I was in, either that or I should have had to kill myself." Thus to inexperience loom desperate expedients.

Poole improved his embrace, the blood drumming in his ears with an excitation long forgotten but sweeter than ever, though this was madness—sheer madness. Presently he would wake from a dream into sanity, and the brakes of common sense and decency would have to be applied with a crash.

"In any case it could never, never have come to that while your old Bert was alive to save you."

"You would have saved me, even if . . . if . . ."

"Of course! You bet your life, mad with joy to have had the chance. It was all in the bargain we made, our old *compact*." Ah, he thought, what a privilege to help such fragrant youth to mend its broken shield!

"Oh, you darling, *darling*!" The strong young arms tightened round his neck. "Then do you remember that you are engaged to me, have been ever since the time of the bridge opening?"

"Do you remember too?"

"As if I could forget a *compact*! You said it was to be a secret engagement. It is time to make it public now."

This was surely delirium tremens; something from his injured foot had temporarily affected his brain, but ah, it was sweet while it lasted! "Milly, we have gone to sleep and are dreaming a lovely dream."

"Yes, and when we wake up we'll find it true."

"All right! Hush-a-bye baby, on the tree top," he said playfully, placing her more comfortably and falling silent in his grandly quiet way. No appropriate words came to him. Milly nestled blissfully on her rock of sympathetic understanding. Uncle Bert was always perfect. He never failed her and she was taking the only way of securing him for her very own, having grown to sufficient

251

understanding to marvel that she had not lost her chance long since. Relief flooded her harried soul. Her eyelids drooped. Bert looked down and caught a drowsy smile.

The old clock on the mantel ticked loudly. Queen Victoria in her girlish comeliness looked down upon them from above it, her consort by her side. A hen, feeling the moment auspicious, introduced her chicks to the flower-beds in the sunlight to be seen through the open doorway. She scratched like a hurricane undisturbed. Cocky, dozing on a rail near the geranium-pots, screeched at the vandalism, and, waddling across the boards, hopped down the steps to investigate. No one came at his call, so he relinquished police duty and joined in the looting. Farther afield could be heard the cackling of hens, bad housekeepers these, late at their duties. Occasionally the moo of a cow, the neigh of a horse, or the yap of a dog carried to the comfortable old room, arranged in bygone fashion, and a monument to the good taste of old Stepmother Poole. Such sounds embellished rather than disturbed the silence, and grew softer as the sparkling heat climbed towards 3 p.m.

Milly was sleeping easily, repose in every line.

Out through the open doorway was a wide rolling Monaro view, the road to Gowandale like an ivory ribbon running over a knoll, disappearing and reappearing and losing itself in the blue horizon of the ranges far away. As the silence widened in the peak of the afternoon the lullaby of Poole's Creek drifted in like a far sweet wind faintly borne from paradise, and to Poole, this moment irrespective of all that had been in his more than sixty years, in spite of all that could be in the twenty or so more coming to him, was paradise unqualified.

A man might well barter his soul for such a moment.

Cocky thought the silence called for examination. He climbed the steps with the aid of his beak, making guttural murmurs as he progressed across the veranda, and entered the drawing-room, a splendid gentleman in his snowy plumage. Seeing his master's occupation he raised his crest with magisterial air, his black beak very smart and his black tongue moving in it like an indiarubber ball.

"What's this?" he inquired.

"You might well ask, old man," whispered Poole, with a soft laugh of joy.

Cocky did not relish being ignored. He walked all round the peculiar pair, his claws making their own sound on the hardwood boards, uncovered but for a splendid skin here and there. Then he climbed Poole's knee. He was lifted away and set down at a distance. This annoyed him. He accepted attentions from Milly but would not be suppressed on her behalf. He established himself on Poole's shoulder and demanded, "Hullo! What's this?"

Receiving no answer, he began to scold the dog.

"You're no gentleman, Cocky," said Poole. "But perhaps you are bringing me to common sense."

Having wakened the sleeper he was ready to be agreeable.

"Cocky doesn't know what to make of us," said Poole.

"Ask him to be best man at our wedding. He looks like an old J.P.—pity he couldn't marry us now without fuss."

So! When awake and relieved of her fears she still meant it. Nevertheless it was madness, and if translated from the dream to actuality he would be culpable of something as reprehensible as the pressure SP-over-J had put upon Aileen Healey.

"I hear Mrs M'George coming with tea."

"I don't care," said Milly. But Poole, on guard for her, stood her on the floor and all was normal when the guid soul appeared.

"We'll have to tell everybody," Milly continued, when pouring tea.

"Do you think we'd better?"

"You don't mean you want to break our *compact*!"

"The whole tribe would want to give me a bait for such a thing, and I should deserve it. Surely you were old enough to remember something of what they thought of your Uncle Jack; and he was a year or two younger than I am now, and Aileen was a good many years older than you are, my lady."

"That was because he took her away from Ronald, and I was born older than poor Aunt Aileen will ever have the savvy to be."

"That's probably true. But still and all you're not as old as you'll be ten or twenty years hence, and if I took advantage of the whim of a young girl and you woke up to find yourself with a toothless old josser on your hands . . ."

"It's not you that's taking advantage of me. I'm taking advantage of you."

"I believe that's true, too. You are making a rattling fool of me. Aunt Charlotte will have to bring us back to reason. Don't you think it had better be the same old secret engagement just for you and me, till one day you'll come and tell me that you have picked a nice young chap? I promise never to sue you for breach of promise."

"Oh no! You are not going to leave me to get into more troubles with no-chop young men. You don't—what I mean is, don't you *want* me?" she demanded, looking deeply and earnestly into his eyes.

"Milly, that would be like refusing paradise. It is of you I am thinking."

"Well, then, we must tell Aunt Charlotte and make it secure as soon as possible, or someone else will be snapping you up."

Charlotte, in the judicious Poole way, said only that she was so astonished that she must have time to think. She spent a night of misgiving. She had long wished her brother to have a wife and children of his own, but this was a fantastic notion of this high-spirited girl, this child, young enough to be his granddaughter. It was unseemly. Oh, that he had chosen someone suitable to his years! But who was there? Jessie M'Eachern, but she was as rough as a man to look at, and old and set in her ways, and if they had not made a go of it long ago, it was sensible of them to know it was beyond them now. Everyone said Lucy Saunders was willing, a capable nice-looking woman and managing—too managing. Charlotte could not picture Bert comfortable, driven from his quiet easiness by her. There was Mrs Labosseer, his old flame at Coolooluk, near his own age, but fat and a grandmother—that was impossible. There were the Dice sisters, the Farquharsons, and other young women ready to capture Curradoobidgee Poole, but though they were more than ten years older than Milly they did not seem to fit, either.

Second thoughts of Milly were not so startling. There had always been a strong affinity between these two. It was possible that they could combine the relationship of daughter and wife, husband and father, and that it might work until that shoal ahead, such a little way ahead too, when Poole must become decrepit while Milly rose to her prime. But that shoal might never be reached. It would cause talk, but only a nine-days wonder, and Charlotte had known many in her time. It couldn't be any worse than the indecent talk forty-five years ago when Miss Mayborn, the English governess, to the astonishment of the whole district, had married her father, trimmed his beard and disciplined him, and remade life for the family.

"What is to be, will be," she murmured, and fell asleep.

Poole's own misgivings were more disquieting. In ten years he would have the real old man upon him, and Milly, twenty-eight, would be at the crest of youthful maturity. Would she loathe him then?

He lay awake all night wrestling with temptation, and with the dawn and the cool winds sweeping down from Eaglehawk, the spectre disappeared and he turned a face of deep happiness to the rising sun. He would take this gift. It should be Milly's to use him in accordance with her desire and her need. He would take this evening smile of nature for ten, five, or only three years. There was no doubt the child was happy with him now, and theirs was a long, steadily maturing friendship and understanding. When his senility should endanger their edifice built without hands— well, a man had only to die once; there were lots of simple accidents to a man of resource; and youthful widowhood was no bad thing.

*   *   *   *   *

Lucy Saunders and Stanton were informed before it was let go any further. Lucy was deeply chagrined and shocked. She said it was not to be thought of, and ordered Milly home. Stanton went up to Monaro to bring her away himself. He was cynical and sneering, but not dangerous, as he revelled in Poole's fall.

"I've come to rescue Milly. I've got all the advice you gave me without being asked, saved up for you, and you're older in the horn than I was five years ago, and Milly is younger than Aileen was."

"You can spare your breath," said Poole good-temperedly. "I've remembered it all, Jack, and you can't tell me anything I haven't thought."

"And are you going on?"

"If Milly doesn't change her mind, I am. There is one difference, if I might say it without offence—Milly is willing." He could have said that Milly had proposed, both now and earlier, but that secret he kept for himself.

"She is now, but perhaps later the regrets will be on her side. There's no fool like an old fool. *Don't you think, Bert, that you and I have left it so long that we had better leave marriage altogether now? Milly's a taking little girl, but rather a child.* Do you remember reeling that off to me?" Stanton laughed heartily.

"Yes, Jack. I know it all, but Milly is an exceptional child."

"Christ, that's good!" said SP-over-J, and rocked with rare enjoyment. *"It's none of my business, of course, only I hope you will be able to keep your noddle later if things don't turn out exactly paradise. It is sometimes better to squabash things in the egg stage."* Stanton would have been disappointed to find Poole could be deterred.

Milly, who had no misgivings, no reservations in her happiness, tackled her uncle, swinging upon his arm. "Uncle Jack, it's lovely and friendly of you to come as soon as you heard the news. I was bridesmaid for you, and you must give me away in return. And, Uncle Jack, don't you think you had better take me to Turrill Turrill and have me married from there? It will save a lot of talk." Stanton liked Milly swinging on his arm. She warmed his con-

255

stricted heart as so very few could. He remembered how she had stuck to him through his wedding, and all through his married life. He might lecture her mother about her behind her back, but his knees gave in her presence.

"Couldn't you find someone nearer the nephew age for me? It will look rather silly to have Bert calling me uncle, won't it?" He chuckled anew.

"I wish he was a bit younger," admitted Milly. "But that can't be helped. I'd rather have him a hundred and eighty than anyone else at any age."

"You'll have to face your mother."

"Let her stay at Ten Creeks and look after Aunt Aileen and you can do everything for me at Turrill Turrill."

"Why didn't you bolt and get it over that way?"

"As if I was ashamed! I want a real wedding with you helping me."

"I suppose I'll have to fork up a present. Do you want a very swell trousseau?"

"Uncle Jack, you know you are a scrumptious *darling*!"

No other called Jack Stanton such names. They went to his head or his heart. "You know, Milly, I'd like to see you happy," he said in accents of unwonted affection, "but in the course of nature Bert will have to leave you."

"I can't bear to think of that. Perhaps Aunt Aileen and I could keep each other company." There were tears on Milly's lashes. She was not engaging in repartee. Stanton forbore to continue the discussion in that direction.

"Well, if you can bring your mother round, I can't stop you from doing what you want."

❄   ❄   ❄   ❄   ❄

Poole pilgrimaged to his old friend Great-grandma Mazere. He wanted to tell her himself of Milly's affection for him. She took it wonderfully well, but, then, Poole did not seem so old to her.

"You have left it very late, my boy, and the girl is over-young for you. Do you think it is wise?"

"No, Mrs Mazere, I do not. I have had terrible misgivings. I am ready to release Milly."

"She was always very fond of you. She is not an unwilling bride. Her head is older than those on most young shoulders. The danger is that you may leave her with a young family, that is hard on a woman."

"That happens to those who have young husbands too sometimes."

"Quite true, and sometimes it would be easier to be left a widow than suffer what some wives do."

"I shall be able to provide for her comfortably."

"Well, my boy, if it is the Lord's will, He can settle all things. I hope you will be happy and that the Lord will bless you. You must be patient with youth."

"I shall, so help me God, if youth will be patient with me."

       ✦   ✦   ✦   ✦   ✦

The news was a blow to Larry. There had been moments of wild hope that the scandal would drive Milly to him, though underneath he knew her better than that. He had lost at the salt-shed for ever and must cover up defeat as best he could. He was not coming out of this as spiritually unscathed as he had from his other misdemeanour. When convalescent he gratefully accepted an invitation to go to Billy-go-Billy. Once there his shrinking from Norah Alfreda vanished. She was an engaging and sensitive chatterbox who delighted in her new subject and aroused a dormant love of children, which made him blossom in secret wonder and pride, in his share in the child's parentage.

His thoughts turned to Dot. Had she no interest in her child? Was she frightened of it as he had been; would personal contact alter that? —though in the nature of things she must have seen the infant. Was she an unnatural mother? How could she be otherwise in the circumstances—and they of his making? Larry was soft at the core, and the generous unselfish kindness of Norah and Alf showed him his own delinquencies. His sympathies awakened towards Dot. Formerly he had wished to hear of her disposed of as the wife of anyone: in view of his discovery of Norah Alfreda, he was relieved that Dot was still free. He wondered why. Did she care more for him than for Dice? He was pricked by that inner weakness, a conscience. The desire to make amends overtook him.

Dot, on the contrary, was increasingly embittered by what she had been through and continued to endure. She had no debilitating sense of her own shortcomings, and regarded Larry and a mad impulse as entirely responsible for her ignominious situation. She did not soften to Ronald, and was weary of her life. The hard possessive attitude and unrelaxing exactions of her mother were insupportable. Because of her daughter's fall, and her intervention with her husband, the old lady considered Dot her special property, and Dot lay awake many a night longing for a housemaid's job at the Wynyard Hotel in Sydney as an escape. Marriage was her only practicable opening and she had a vengeful notion to free herself from Saunders Plains by marrying Larry, but hardly expected him to approach her again.

The announcement of Milly's engagement naturally caused a freshet of gossip, following as it did upon the escapade with Larry Healey. In the talk that blew back and forth across the ranges Dot could not escape the assertions that Larry had been infatuated with Milly. Well! Ronald had been even wilder in pursuit of Aileen, yet here he was now moaning after herself. *Men!* thought Dot contemptuously.

The Poole nephews and nieces had always expected something like this to happen, but nevertheless had not believed Uncle Bert would be quite so silly as to allow himself to be fastened upon by an infant out of the cradle. They did not say much of this in Uncle Bert's hearing. He did not invite impertinence, he was so good-natured that it fell away from him, his record inspired respect and he was dearly loved. He looked so contented and well that his contemporaries thought the risk he was taking worth while, even if bliss could not last: and how many love affairs did last, when you took your coat off to them? said the worldly wise.

Great-grandma Mazere and Aunt Charlotte uttered no word of criticism, and among the youngsters Milly had always pursued an original path more among adults than those of her own years. Lucy Saunders tried to postpone the wedding till Milly was twenty-one. "Three more years on to Bert's age would probably cure her," she said, but Milly was no Aileen to be thwarted. Also Lucy's circle were more humorous than sympathetic to her, for they considered she was jealous herself not to be the bride. She felt that to let Milly have her way might be the lesser trouble. She would at least be provided for, and Lucy now had a *métier* with her brother, and so gave in. She urged a little delay for the promised year in society. Poole also recommended this, but Milly would not be deflected. So it was decided that the marriage should take place from Turrill Turrill in March and the family return there early for this.

Heffernan stuck the silver hat-pin in the rafter of his hut as a mascot. It had no commercial value. Paddy Leary was justified in his opinion and let it be known to Tommy Roper. "Sure, didn't I tell you that Miss Milly wouldn't let anyone cook her goose for her? Pulled right back an' broke the bridle, if I know anything! She wouldn't sit down under what a few old magpies said about her. Wonder what she saw in such an old feller though, an upstanding blood filly like that. Wasn't rared onder a hin, eh, Mick?"

"Sure, she knew a rale man whin she saw him, and didn't moind a bit of age. She knew at anny age he'd be bether than these flea-headed gomerils they're rarin' today—rared onder a hin, huh, they've been rared onder a bed-bug!"

Rebecca and Norah in the private parlour of the hotel had many a confabulation.

"Sure, wondhers will never cease! Oi'll not be surprised if I hear anny day of ould Great-granny Mazere herself walkin' off with a young feller half her age."

"There's plenty would do it for the property, if they could be sure it all went to her."

"It's Lucy Saunders is the disappointed woman."

"More suitable it would have been. Still an' all, Milly was always an odd child, and much more suited to being an old man's darling than a young man's slave. She's settled, at any rate. Poole has a good sound property and he will give it all to her—and the sort of man to have money in the bank as well, that is when the banks mend."

"Sure, he's betther than Ronald or Larry. There's something powerful quare and peculiar about what happened Larry. Milly could tell more of that than Larry'd loike annywan to know, by what Tommy Roper was hintin' in the bar."

"If all's true Stanton would have been within his rights to turn Aileen out, and then Ronald dropped her and took to Dot. Strange she won't have him now."

"They tell me whin Larry was goin' through from Dan Spires's he met Dot right in the road, and she pulled up and asked him how he was. The Stantons' servant told my Julia, and Dot said, 'You betther come an' see me whin you're well.' What do you make of it?"

"They'll get sorted out in the end. Tommy said the last Sunday he was at Keba, Ronald was there hanging round Rose Farquharson."

"Sure, a rose on ivery bush for Ronald."

"Milly is not going to show herself here till after the wedding. Little Ignez Milford is going to be the only bridesmaid. They're going to Monaro after the honeymoon and not show up here till the commotion has died down."

"There's wan thing you've never told me, phwat did Dot do with the choild?"

"It will come out in the wash presently. It's always facts that I tell you, isn't it?"

" 'Tis thrue, it is. Av coorse, I'd believe ye if ye said ould Mr Eustace Blenkinsop—the ould scut—was going to marry Mrs Labosseer at Coolooluk, and that Teddy O'Mara was chose for the next mimber of Parliament for Bool Bool. . . . But sure, Poole's more of an ould fool than I would have thought him. Left it till he's gone silly, an' picked a choild."

"Jacob says he's a lucky devil."

"Och, wouldn't ivery dhrivellin' ould great-gran'pa run off wid a little gurrul in short frocks if he could! Sure, they seem to lack aise entoirely in that rayspict, an' whin they settle down 'tis because some ould woman who can see through thim has a broomstick in pickle to intercept their capers."

CHAPTER 22

PHILIP MAZERE, third of the name, commonly known as Young Philip, went to the post-office with a bundle of telegrams.

GREAT-GRANDMA PASSED AWAY PEACEFULLY IN SLEEP 2 AM
FUNERAL SUNDAY WOULD LIKE YOU TO COME MAZERE

One of these went to Poole of Curradoobidgee, Monaro; another to Miss Jessie M'Eachern hard by; a third to Raymond Poole, Macquarie Chambers, Sydney; a fourth to John Stanton, Turrill Turrill, Riverina; others to names well known from Gundagai to Goulburn. A long message was addressed to Prendergast, a still longer one to Joseph Mazere to his last known address.

"By Jove, we'll all miss her!" observed the post-and-telegraph-master. "Bool Bool won't seem the same any more. She's always been there for everyone in the place. There isn't anyone left to remember Bool Bool before she came."

"There wasn't any Bool Bool before she came. She's the last of them all. There are only the M'Haffetys and Isaacs and Browning anywhere near her age that have been here from nearly the beginning."

"She'll have a great funeral."

"We're afraid of overlooking someone. If you think of anyone left out of that list, I'd be obliged if you would let me know."

"I see you have old Bill Prendergast."

"Yes. She reared his wife, and it was a promise that he'd take her for her last drive."

"I'll never forget her going to the bridge that day as spry as a girl under her parasol, and those four greys stepping so they wouldn't break an egg-shell. . . . I'll get these away at once."

Philip Mazere murmured a word of thanks and went up Stanton Street, which ran out of the township into a red road that topped a cleared foothill or two and disappeared into the blue ranges, still untouched of man towards Mungee and Coolooluk. He was a tall dark man in the forties, favouring his mother's people in appearance. He halted as he turned into Mazere's Lane and meditated on the panoramic view. It had changed little within his memory, and it was his birthplace. Most of the town had appeared in the gold-rush period of the late fifties and early sixties and since had dozed in arrested development. The valley in the ranges amid plentiful watercourses had been left very beautiful by the Creator and the aborigines, and though the settlers had done their best to tame it without substituting any worthy works of man, their efforts had so far been too puny to obliterate natural loveliness. The cottages devoid of architectural grace, set down where the timber had been indiscriminately extirpated, were the most disfiguring feature. The river, vocal as it circled the town, was still bordered by shrubs and ferns of unique species, and where these had been thinned the weeping willows added an alien feature like mermaids' tresses. Their long green ropes of young leaves shaded into the darker clover and rye on the rich river-banks. The willows away from the stream were cropped level as ballet skirts, and with the big acacia-trees gave a park-like beauty to the Mazere paddocks.

Philip progressed thoughtfully under an avenue of various trees, the early hop-leaves of some giant elms a miracle of loveliness against the sun. Yes, it would be strange to be without Greatgrandma—like the end of a dynasty. She had held so many of the family together in the cluster of homes. The disposition of the property would make a scatter inevitable. In the nature of things the old lady's death was due. A quarter of a century ago Grandpa Mazere had died, and every Christmas since, a bumper gathering had been rallied on the slogan "It might be Grandma's last." It was a family, nay a town, joke.

Philip looked away over the rich flats where the main street carried the road across the white bridge and hid it among the lanes high and wild with perfumed English hedge roses planted by the original Mazere's English gardener, Grubb. The road came to sight again round the foothills, and finally disappeared beyond Saunders Plains in the Nanda ranges, still little troubled of man. His glance circled to where Brennan's Gap let the Wamgambril through to Stanton's Plains, then on to the endless ramparts of the Bogongs and Muniongs Monarowards, whence his mother's people came. The settlers had scarcely made a scratch on that region yet.

Too much rain again promised too much grass, with smut in the wheat, the maize flattened, the fruit watery, aphides on the apples and peaches, bottle and fluke and foot-rot threatening the sheep, but the season was glorious at its inception. Surely the English meadows that Grandpa had talked so much about could not be more vivid than the valleys and foothills of Bool Bool? The pink of peach and almond blossom brightened the dark river foliage where seedlings had sprung up and laid a feast for possums and birds. From every backyard came the cackle of fecund hens, and many turkeys roamed the knolls amid the sheep of the Mazere runs, and contested the right of the town common where Stanton Street became the Mungee and Coolooluk road.

* * * * *

The Big House and New House and Young Philip's at Three Rivers homestead were crowded to every sofa, all but that portion comprising the dining-room and billiard-room, long known to the wits as the Town Hall of Bool Bool. Here the little old lady, a friend to all, known so long and known only as completely good, held her last reception in state. Her daughters and granddaughters and great-granddaughters had made a coverlet of purple violets adorned by a cross of white ones. Violets grew in every waste nook about the gardens, which had spread regardless of space. When a continent stretched round untouched, what need to consider the disposition of a few roods or acres? Never were such masses of English violets of such perfume as known to the valley of Bool Bool. Folks there could tread on violet carpets as in ordinary places they step on lawns.

Queen Victoria and her consort looked down upon Great-grandma resting upon her trestles. The royalties were flanked by some old steel engravings and by the popular Lord Carrington —very grand as to epaulets—and by his lady, very slim as to waist. A rich array of brass candlesticks still shared the high mantel and the old chiffonier with vases and cruets of twelve bottles each, though Three Rivers had been a pioneer with kerosene lamps with incandescent wicks. Grandpa's hunting prints and fowling-pieces enlivened the walls, and above the doorway instead of antlers were polished bullock horns and lyre-bird tails. The long hospitable dining-table and the billiard-table had been placed along the walls and piled with the overflow of flowers. The air was oppressive with violet and narcissus, and the odour of lilac and lemon blossoms came in through the windows.

Philip wondered why so many old people died in spring. Grandpa Mazere, the old Saunderses, Stantons, and Brennans had all passed in spring. The perfume of spring flowers was reminiscent of funerals to him. There was much to do and he turned from meditation to his duties as practising male head of the clan at Three Rivers; his father at sixty-six was so much the slave of alcohol that he could not be depended upon. His aunts, Isabel Stanton, Rachel Labosseer, Fannie Rankin, with his mother, took turns in sitting beside Great-grandma and in attending those who came to make a last call. Every hour saw fresh floral tributes and telegrams of condolence or new arrivals for the funeral.

M'Haffety's was full, and those whom the popular Mayor knew all became his guests. "Sure, am Oi a hucksther that Oi'd charge the frinds of her, me bist frind in the wurruld, more than me own mother iver was to me—comin' to see her put to her last sleep?"

Those anear were all accounted for. All the Labosseers and Mungee Stantons were there, attended by Teddy O'Mara and Mr Blenkinsop. Mr Blenkinsop had lost his standing at the Bool Bool Show some years before and was gradually sinking to a pathetic figure. It was left to Mrs Labosseer's sense of Christian charity and duty to do what his own class and family had shirked.

Jack Stanton wired from Turrill Turrill that he was coming; so did Ronald Dice, also down the river. Mrs Raymond Poole (*née* Mazere) was on the way with Raymond. Miss M'Eachern was coming with the Curradoobidgee Pooles and was to be accommodated at Three Rivers. Alf Timson and Norah and the Neangen Healeys were at M'Haffety's.

Grief cannot be so poignant for a lady of eighty-four as for a maiden of twenty-one. Emily, the affianced of Bert Poole, drowned over thirty years before, had been mourned with grief that startled. Great-grandma was paid a far-reaching tribute of affectionate respect. The sadness was more for the passing of an institution than for a person. People honoured themselves by honouring Mrs Mazere.

Mrs M'Haffety had her hands full but she took time on Saturday night to gossip for an hour with her old crony Rebecca.

"Oi'm wore out with it all. Sure, they're gathering up loike for a fair. An' whoi shouldn't they, too, when she niver missed seein' anny of thim off, with her flowers so noice, if 'twas only a poor lone shepherd or stockman, God bless her! 'Tis hersilf that has the rayspict of everywan."

"She deserves it. We'll never see her likes again."

"Isabel and Rachel are foine women but the ould lady was the rale thing. She never had to put on anny of this soide or excloosiveness as the Mrs Mazere of Three Rivers; sure, 'twas there to be seen, and she not the soize of three ha'pence set one atop of the other."

"Did you see Bert Poole and Milly ridin' by?"

"Sure, didn't they call in for a word. Poole was always quiet and frindly from a boy. There's wonderful little change in him. He'll see manny a young wan out yet, I'm thinkin'."

"What did Milly look like—happy?"

"Happy is no name for it. Her face beamed loike a young wan

that has her heart's desire shoinin' broight, and a look of peace and contintmint beyond her years."

"It's to be hoped it will last. Are there anny signs?"

"Divil a bit. She has a waist thinner than y'r neck, Rebecca, an' ye should see her horse standin' on its hoind legs, an' she as iligant as if 'twas a rockin'-chair, and Bert on another beauty."

"He might be givin' her a rest for the start."

"Sure, he's different from his koind if he is! Ould Miss Macorkaran, moighty thrim and thin, was there too. Sure, her face would cut meat—looks loike salt meat, too, rough as a man's it is. Not natural. That beloike is why she niver married after all. Strange how she threw over Hugh Mazere."

"Never could get Poole to look the same side of the road as her. That was the same year as poor Emily was drownded. *She* was a real beauty for you now, and no two opinions about it. Wonderful the change from youth to age. I remember Jessie at the ball on Emily's twenty-first birthday. Jessie ran Emily pretty close for good looks. They were both better-looking than Milly."

"Sure, wait till ye see Milly now. She ain't perhaps as pretty as Aileen at her age, but there is something that more stays with ye in the look of her—satisfying, that's what it is. She looks satisfied herself, and 'tis comfortin' to look at her."

"Poor old Norah Timson, is she as bad as they say?"

"Looks turr'ble bad. She is goin' on to see that specialist in Sydney again."

"What will she do with the little one?"

"It can go to its grandma and Julie at Neangen. Sure, there's a noice little thing, an' talk about praycocious!"

"Doesn't take after old Alf, then; he's a sleepy old lizard."

"But it's takin' to see how fond the little wan is of him."

"Poole is one that children liked. It is a pity if he is not to have a child of his own."

"Sure, give him toime. He! He! Haw! Haw!"

"He hasn't any time to waste if he wants to see it grow up a little."

"He must sometimes feel a fool starting mathrimony with a choild loike that, and all thim that he wint gallivantin' with, grandmothers."

"Did you see Aileen Stanton? I hardly knew her, she is growing so stout. It is taking all her good looks. Tommy Roper was saying that Dice has never been near Ten Creeks or Turrill Turrill since the baby was lost."

"He had a flea put in his ear beloike, and things have shaken down."

"Yes. And now Jacob tells me he wouldn't be surprised if Dot Saunders and Larry Healey don't wind up together. I saw some of it with me own eyes at that tea-fight to pay for the font in Mrs Mazere's church—bein' in business——"

"Sure, Oi wuz there meself, too. Wouldn't we all be wherever herself asked us, she wan of your rale Christians and no bigotry."

"That's true. Well, I was sittin' inside the tent where they had the flower-stalls and lollies, an' Dot came in there, too, to be alone I should think, by the style of her these days, never sayin' a word to anyone. Larry looked as if he had been follerin' her, for he came in after her an' stood a little shame-faced and said, 'Well, Dot, aren't you going to speak to me?'

"She looked as if she wanted to get away at first, but then she said, 'I might as well, I suppose. You've have a long spell of bad luck.' 'Just a little,' said he. 'How are you now?' she asked, just formal, nothing cordial. 'Not much,' says he. 'It's goin' to be a long job and it hurts like beggary.' Then he said almost against his will, 'I'm sorry you've been so terrible hurt.' And she turned away her head as if she was going to cry, and someone else came in and disturbed them and they slipped out by the side flap together. Now, what do you think they could have meant?"

"Some sweetheartin' or jealousy. He means beloike the scandal that was put upon her name through him. Young people whin they're runnin' after each other talks as if thimbles was wash-hand basins. An' sure, Rebecca, that scandal has been such a long toime comin' out in the wash that you must have been mistaken."

"There was something in it that never came out. That's what he meant by hurting her, most likely."

"Beloike it was. Sure, they'll all git sorted out in toime, an' thim that don't will have to put up with it."

"It will be very interesting to see all this crowd together."

"Sure, an' some of the most interesting things is thim that niver happened at all, loike Dot's baby," and with a downy wink Norah heaved her bulk on end and answered a call to business.

❋   ❋   ❋   ❋   ❋

At M'Haffety's later that night a few of the real old brigade sifted down into a review of the years. Prendergast had arrived with four blacks hitched to the new hearse of the leading undertaker in Goulburn, and hailed to Gundagai by telegram on the Southern Mail. His wife—Squinty Ellen that was—had preceded her husband in her own buggy driven by her son, and had gone to Three Rivers direct. The kindly creature wept copiously as she produced a wreath of lilac packed in moss and damp cloths. She had grown

266

closer to Three Rivers as the years passed and contemporaries thinned out. Time forces the dwindling remnants to close the ranks in protection of the affections. In the old days of his courting at Three Rivers, Prendergast had eaten with Ellen in the kitchen, but with time the Prendergasts and M'Haffetys progressed from inferiors to old friends, treasured members of the original brigade.

"I've taken a little of the froth outer them for termorrer," Bill explained of his four-in-hand. "I don't want them to be rarin' up on their tails, though it was a promise to the old lady that we were to swing along at a decent pace—no crawlin' like a snail—that was the promise between us."

"Poole is here with the bride," remarked Jacob Isaacs. "An' she still like an egg-boiler in the middle. It doesn't seem as if she can be constructed the same way as our old women."

"Sure, she'll come to it prisently if Poole lives long enough. There's a rale man for ye! Handsome and strong! Sound as a bell today, still able to hould his own with anny of thim. Remimber the noight whin he was a lad and shwung the ould lady into the boat, and the Yarrabongo near up to where the church is today."

"It doesn't seem as if we could have remembered right. Poole and Tim Brennan—pretty game they was all right! Tim looks fifteen years older than Bert now, but that rheumatism cripples him, an' he always did run to corpulence—a pot on him like a coolamon." This from Bill.

"You're not far off him yourself," grunted Isaacs. "Cornstalk you were in them days. Not much of the cornstalk about you now."

"You're dead right—more of the fatted alderman."

"Ah well." M'Haffety heaved a deep sigh. "Whin we've laid the little ould lady to rest, you'll see a great scatteration in the tribe of Mazere. She was the king pin. She was the queen bee too—you mark what I'm tellin' you."

"They're all trash beside her," said Isaacs.

"Yes, they reckoned because they had a flash start, they had a right to be cock of the walk without slogging for it. I reckon it does a man harm to have too good a start; he camps on it, and ten to one he never gets out of his own back-yard." William Prendergast, vaingloriously architect of his own fortunes, had in cordial agreement with him Isaacs the ex-hawker, and M'Haffety the retired butcher and ex-lag.

"No. There's not one of the men is worth the breed of the old cove and her we're buryin' termorrer. Young Philip is a steady plodder, but you can see the Poole sticking out in him a mile."

"That's bearin' out what I say. Old Boko Poole with his one eye, an' couldn't hardly write his name—an' look at Bert Poole beside the young Mazeres! Is there one of them could pick a young bride an' pull it off the way he has done today?"

"Sure, whin ye think of it, he is a man for ye, an' the ould buck his father ahead of him, shwingin' up this very street with a foive-in-hand and his missus and young Raymond—that come in by the coach today—as a kid in her arrums, droivin' loike hell. An' Bert Poole thin with hundreds and hundreds of pounds give him for clearin' out the bushrangers, an' all the girls woild for him in thim days. Sure, the beautiful gurruls there were thin!"

"The girls is still beautiful," said Prendergast. "What about Milly?"

"She has eyes and a nose in the roight place, but, och, she couldn't hould a handle to Rachel Mazere, the toime she married the big foreigner and wint to Monaro—she that's at Coolooluk now."

Since wives were out of hearing, Jacob chuckled, "There wasn't a man in the place wasn't dead soft on Rachel. If Labosseer had 'a' been drownded in the flood twenty young fellows were ready to jump into his shoes."

"Ye're roight! She was a propher hoigh-steppin' beauty for ye, if ever there was one!"

"And Jess Macorkaran ran her close."

"That queer-looking old bag of bones, with a long nose, and dried up like a piece of leather, could she ever have been pretty?" demanded Prendergast.

"Ah! wasn't she! Not many of the young ones today could have come near her. You must remember her the night of Emily's birth-day ball?"

"Emily's the one I remember."

"Sure, Jessie was all right, but Emily was lovelier—one of your lily-and-roses beauties, with a kind word for everybody. All the young min were mad afther her, but it never turned her head a bit."

"And the young fellows were men then. These pups today haven't any guts!"

"Sure, Jacob, the proof of that's to be seen in Bert Poole, still to have the young darlin's lovin' him."

"It's curious how some men is born to romance," agreed Isaacs.

"Sure, yes, and the rest of us git married young. Sure, we can't all have the luck to lose our sweethearts and live romantic, and then whin some of us is old and fat an' pot-bellied still to be slim an' run afther by the coming belle. Though there's thim that would run afther us now if we didn't keep our weather oi peeled."

"Yes, but they'd make us pay for it, Terry," said Bill. "Pay through the nose . . . Yes, the Mazeres remind me of a mess of rhubarb when it gets in-grown and you can hardly tell it from docks it's that thin and green. A scatterin' will do them good, an' to marry in with some good pushful stock that will think less of itself and for more reason."

"What do you reckon the family will do about the property—put it to auction or divide it upon valuation?" said Isaacs.

"Sure, there's seed for controversy there. They'll niver add to it, by the look of things, only sit down and waste it."

"It won't last long," said Isaacs. "Played out is what I reckon they are. These old early pioneers was all right as long as they had everything to theirselves. Some of these will scratch along like cockatoos on a piece of the property the old man got together for them, but they won't get rich at that, and the next generation will be working for others. You'll notice it's the coves from the city is the ones that has the foresight with property." Isaacs had graduated in a slum and reached Bool Bool in the early days on foot with a pack of drapery on his back.

"It seems as if thim who blazes the first thrack niver has much value of the completed road."

"It seems as if things works round in rings—one lot is up in the stirrups one generation and they take a turn padding the hoof next time. It'll all come out in the wash, I reckon. Ah well, Terry, I'll be round termorrer to see that the horses and carriage look all right. We'll do the last thing we can for her in the best style."

    ❋   ❋   ❋   ❋   ❋

At Three Rivers an honoured place among the guests was accorded Poole of Curradoobidgee and Miss M'Eachern of Gowandale. Also present were Hugh Mazere, the third son of the house, who had been engaged to Miss M'Eachern in '57, and Louisa, his wife, sister of Bert and Charlotte. The elders looked at them and wondered did Jessie regret her spinsterhood now, or Hugh regret Jessie and the loss of the Gowandale acres.

To some of the little ones this family gathering was to remain one of their earliest or most vivid recollections. It was considered the correct thing to show them Great-grandmamma in her last sleep, so that in future years they would be able to say they had seen her who had blessed them all and who meant so much to her circle. Awed and curious, the children saw a quiet face, lined with countless wrinkles, asleep, it seemed to them, under a wonderful counterpane of violets. Everywhere flowers were piled.

"Pretty! Pretty!" exclaimed the little ones. Molly Brennan was so small that she could only say, "Pitty! Pitty!" and Norah Alfreda wanted to pluck a bunch of the violets.

"Isn't she lovely! Doesn't she look peaceful!" said the elders as they say at all family funerals. "It would be wonderful if everyone could live as long as she did and do as much good."

The first great-grandson was given a little prominence. He was a double great-grandchild, being the son of Richard Mazere's eldest son and of Rachel Labosseer's eldest daughter. He was a thoughtful dreamy boy who remembered Great-granny well. He used to be brought from Nanda at Christmas or on Great-grandma's birthday to visit her. He would never forget going across to the Old House, piloted by Aunt Charlotte, to find Great-grandma sitting in a chair beside a table. On the table was a big cloth that reached to the floor, with heavy woollen fringe and a pattern of flowers. Great-grandma was always reading a big book—the Bible, of course—and her feet were on a fat heavy pillow covered with carpet, called a hassock. Dick liked the sound of that word *hassock*: it had grandeur in it. As a little fellow he would walk about after visiting Three Rivers and introduce the word into his play. Once he had taken the hassock and sat on it under the big round table and imagined wonderful things about animals, till his mother discovered and reproved him, but Great-grandma had said "Bless the child!" and cried "Bo-peep" at him and gave him sweets. They were peppermints that she kept in a little black velvet bag hanging on the knob of her chair.

The children looked at that bag when they entered the room. Like the cruse of oil, its supply was miraculously maintained. Dick remembered, too, the small brown wrinkled hands in mittens, even in summer, to guard them against rheumatism, and the black lace cap on her head covered with something mysterious, which long after he recalled as looped baby-ribbon. He liked better the caps of Grandma Labosseer, of cream lace with a velvet band near her curly hair—oh, caps of considerable elegance!

But he adored Three Rivers. It was a wonderful place. Like a town almost, of infinite resources. At home on Nanda on his father's back selection of his grandpa's run, the homestead was of the time-honoured bull-run design. When he came in the front door he could see straight through to the back-yard, but at Three Rivers—when he could escape from his mother, who was an artist at bilking adventure—he could wander round the endless verandas and peep at the bees working among the pot-plants, or peer through Great-grandpa's telescope. He always thought Great-grandpa must have gone out of the top end of it up to heaven. Great-grandpa had died a lifetime ago, but his presence remained so real at Three Rivers that Dick, an imaginative, fanciful child, of whom his mother said, "He'll have to have all that taken out of him or he'll never get on in the world," used to expect him to pay a visit from heaven by way of the grandfather clock or the stairs in the Big House. Those stairs were thrilling to Dick. Alone in the place, what a glorious time he could have had, but these visits were always so brief!

It was wonderful to have so many houses as Great-grandma. Other people had only one. At Three Rivers, counting the kitchens —but Dick could not in his early recollection count far enough. The gardens were similarly numerous and exciting. Near the Old House were lemon verbena bushes. He loved to fill his pockets with the leaves from these and smell them when no one was looking. Near the big white gates at the back was a thicket of shrubs where one could hide all day without being found—long after he found their name was lauristinus. And there were lilac and hawthorn bushes harbouring birds' nests, as well as lemon- and orange-trees, and beyond the orchard precincts, great weeping willows. He enjoyed pulling the long green ropes off them, they came down so easily, and the girls used them for skipping.

The actual house was even more delightful, if he could only escape from his mother into it. The billiard-room had a remarkable table in it, covered with a green cloth and with a little fence all round it and no one ever had dinner off it. The door-post near the dining-room had letters on it like his alphabet-book, only not so plain. His grandfather had lifted him up to see once, only his grandfather's letters were not there. Grandfather said he had not been there the day they were cut, but he particularly looked at his Aunt Emily's letters. Everyone used to look at them and say, "Poor dear Emily!" or "That was a long time ago," or "We were all a bit younger than we are today." Then there would be talk about a big flood, but it had not been big enough to wash the letters out, though it had tried to drown Great-grandma, but she had been too brave and got into a boat. Uncle Bert talked about this to old Mr Brennan.

They talked about it at the funeral. Dick crept up to Uncle Bert to listen. Mr Brennan was nursing his little granddaughter, Mollie, only two she was, but everybody made a great fuss of her and was always asking her to sing, and she sang, "Way down upon the 'onnee river", and everybody applauded and said she had a voice like a grown-up. Other songs were too hard for her to say the words, so she sang the words with goo-goo baby talk—silly, Dick thought it, but old Mr Brennan acted as if Molly were an angel. After singing she jumped off her grandfather's knee and held her face up for Dick to kiss, but he ran away. Her hair was a funny red colour; what had she done to make it nasty like that?

Dick, at the time of the funeral, was passing through a sub-pubescent phase which made him suffer acutely from these horrid little girls. There was another, worse than Molly Brennan. Her name was Norah Alfreda. She said she was nearly three, but Dick dismissed that as brag because she was not as big as Molly. Her father and mother made a silly fuss of her too. Dick puzzled why there should be this fuss over girls, who were obnoxious to him.

On Saturday morning Dick sat on the veranda by the Old House and coveted a bird's nest going on apace near by, and looked after Lawrence John and kept him from the bees. Lawrence John could not see so very well, and also suffered entotically be-cause he had been lost, and dingoes might have devoured him, only somehow they had not. Lawrence John did what he was told in a fascinating way alien to the girls, and had a little more size, and his guardian was content with him. Dick was old enough to meditate now, and fanciful—too fanciful to be healthy, his prac-tical elders considered. He was saying good-bye in his heart to every loved nook and object at Three Rivers, not alone because Great-grandma was dead but because his parents were leaving the district, and this was a farewell visit to Bool Bool. Dick's heart swelled with a romantic melancholy that he was poignantly enjoy-ing till round the corner came Grandma Labosseer and Norah Alfreda's mother with Norah Alfreda herself, at least that was her real name, but her mother called her "Pigeon Pie", and Norah Alfreda was so silly and little that she did not mind. The grown-ups were talking and Dick was unnoticed till that annoying Alfreda caught sight of him and began kicking up a bobbery. The grown-ups could not make out for a while what she wanted, but Dick had known instantly, and sat petrified.

"She wants a kiss—what a funny little girl—but where is Dick?" The awful little creature pointed straight at him.

"Oh, there he is! Come on, Dick, the little girl wants to kiss you." She ran to him holding up her face. Dick said he hated her. If no one had been looking he could have pinched that horrid little face held up in such a silly way.

"Kiss the dear little girl, Dick," commanded Grandma Labosseer.

Dick sat outraged, a hand tight pressed to the seat on either side as a brace against this unwarrantable attack. Norah Alfreda began to whimper.

"Never mind, Pigeon Pie. We'll go and see what Daddy has for us." But Norah Alfreda's wail increased in volume.

"Come on, Dick. Kiss the little girl at once. Surely you are man enough for that—a great fellow like you!" Grandma turned to Norah Alfreda's mother and nearly laughed, but not quite, because Great-grandma was dead, and said, "It won't be long before the trouble will be to keep him from kissing the girls." What could she mean by that? Did she anticipate total collapse of his manly fibre? But no one ever gainsaid Grandma Labosseer. Her pronouncements carried, and her phrase about being "man enough" put the thing on another basis.

"Run and kiss him. He won't bite," she advised Norah Alfreda. She obeyed, but when she neared Dick she changed her mind. He seemed big and uninviting. She looked up at him, thinking about it.

"I won't kiss you," she said quite plainly. "I don't like you. You are too big and nasty."

To be all taut to endure that horrid soft face slobbering on him and then coolly to be spurned as too nasty to kiss! Dick darted forward and implanted a rough mouthy kiss upon Norah Alfreda's nose. Her outraged howl startled her doting mother.

"What did you do to her?" demanded Grandma Labosseer.

"I only kissed her."

"You must have bitten her." Grandma had no high opinions of boys, though her own sons were held up as marvels of probity and capability.

"No I didn't," he maintained, and was renowned for truthfulness. When other villainies were thick as sheep ticks upon him, his unabashed confession generally proved mitigating with his Grandma Labosseer. She hated liars. "You can lock against a thief," she was wont to say, "but there is no protection against a liar!"

"He kissted me," howled Norah Alfreda, "and he's big and nasty and I don't like him."

"You mustn't be a silly little girl, crying for a thing and then not wanting it," soothed her mother. Norah Alfreda wanted to be carried, but her mother said she had such a pain in her side that this was beyond her.

"She'll not be the first of her sex who'll cry for getting too much of that sort of thing after wanting it," remarked Grandma Labosseer as they went round the corner.

Soon Dick's mother appeared and took him for one more look at Great-grandma, impressing upon him that she had gone to heaven and that he would never see her again. Dick felt he ought to cry, but he was too interested wondering what Great-grandma's soul was like, and imagining it shooting out of the telescope to Grandpa up among the stars where heaven was.

Poole went in to see his old friend last of all, and alone. The part of his life in which the old lady had been a leading figure had passed before his wife had been born. There were anomalies in the retrospect but Poole did not permit them to go deeper than wistfulness. Since he had taken his decision he had not wavered in serene purpose. All eyes were upon him and Milly, and all were agreed that there was no flaw in what they saw. There was a feeling that the marriage was a reward to Poole and a happy refuge to Milly. The radiance of Milly's face reflected her heart. Poole's visage, always the dial of mental machinery in which there was rarely a grain of sand, and of a comeliness not yet sadly impaired by age, showed visible rejuvenation as when inward harmony is leavened with adventure.

He went from the silence of his old friend into the night under the stars where thirty-seven years ago he had gone to find Emily on her twenty-first birthday. He recalled that night. The stars were ever the same—the stars and the song of the river as it foamed round the bend, its voice increased tonight by a spring freshet. This hour in the garden was for Emily, drowned long ago in Mungee Fish Hole, and for her mother, always his friend, on whom he had paid his last earthly call. He must put that part of his life away in the thankful memories of yesterday. Tomorrow would be for Milly. With her he would bask in this afterthought of sunlight tendered by a sunset held off beyond the appointed hour.

"No doubt they are happy now, but in the nature of things it can't last," Grandma Labosseer was remarking. But as for that, Poole had taken a decision, and—the gods have their favourites.

"Ah me, tomorrow afternoon," said Arthur Rankin to his wife Fannie (*née* Mazere), that night as he turned in. "She looked so peaceful, but all those flowers made my head ache. They have put them in milk-pans to keep them a bit fresh. That's the last of the old folks. No more tales of your mother coming up the country in the bullock-dray, and the blacks feeling her curls, and her going to help people at the risk of her life, or your papa reading the Riot Act and changing his will."

"No. They leave a great blank. It's the young people's turn now. . . . Did you notice our Rachel and Matt Dice?"

"I didn't. What's the matter?"

"They're much too thick. I don't favour this cousin business. It will be better for us to be a little cool."

"That would only help things along, Mother. Remember when

274

I was courting you and the old man flung that dipper of mustard of his in my face, yet here we are together in spite of it all, old girl. . . . I don't feel like throwing mustard at Matt."

"Her Aunt Rhoda might take her to Sydney for a change and let her see someone else."

"Humph!" Aunt Rhoda's hubby, Raymond Poole, was a successful barrister, Arthur only a country solicitor, and brother-in-law jealousy operated.

*   *   *   *   *

The sun shone radiantly for Great-grandma's last public function. Bill Prendergast felt her passing as deeply as did any of her sons and daughters as he and Terence M'Haffety wept unaffectedly together and inspected the funeral coach-and-four. The horses, with long-flowing tails superbly put on, arched their necks under the feathered tufts. Their hoofs were polished, not a speck was on their glossy hides, they moved like a poem with elastic stride, as good-tempered and well-mannered as well-born.

Cornstalk, true to his promise, and though preserving decorum, drove at a graceful pace. There were few to dote on the beauty of the team as they passed, with their light burden, for all were in the procession, but they saw the hearse as it dipped into the hollow and climbed again and swung into Stanton Street and out of that again at right angles for the church service; and *da capo* as they returned upon their tracks to the cemetery.

There was something gallant in the last ride of the little old lady, of late stiff with rheumatism and age, swinging along thus bravely in accordance with her wish, something equally gallant and affectionate in her old friend officiating for her.

The native violets, not yet extirpated, still grew in the graveyard and peeped into the grave.

Mrs Jacob Isaacs, looking round the gathering, felt sadness invading her marrow as she totted up the dates. Thirty-seven years since Emily Mazere had opened the new cemetery, and now it had a population as big as had walked the streets of the township then. What a lot were gone! The Mazere interments were specially clear in her mind.

To Poole they also came back vividly. He had had his sister Charlotte's arm in his on those former occasions of old Mazere's and Emily's making, while his brother-in-law, Philip, had stood by the old lady they were burying today. Relieved of this duty, he now clove unto his wife, as a man was enjoined to do. The place had not changed so much except for the ringbarking of the trees, taking with it the birds, though one or two old magpies still occupied the ungrubbed giants in the enclosure and were building their nests as of yore.

Prendergast could not trust his horses to stand and his heart was heavy, so after delivering his passenger he went back to M'Haffety's. While Poole listened to the clergyman, his gaze rested upon the horses as they swung along down into the hollow, where in the old days had been a slip-panel, but now was a culvert. They climbed the slope again, tossing their crested heads in the sunlight. Grace and beauty, strength and youth, health and happiness were in their message, as eternal as death and change and decay, so it seemed to Poole. Each was part of the weft of life, which went on and on for ever, even as the song of the river falling round the bend like a far sweet wind from paradise. Yes, there was youth and joy as well as tragedy and sorrow and old age, and would be for ever, each to be taken as it came with no backward glances of regret and melancholy. That, he felt, was the little old lady's unconscious message as he watched that lilting four-in-hand. She had never croaked, but met each happening with faith and courage. She gave all who had known her a lot to live up to.

The song of the river was a symbol of continuity and of peace—with its memories of yesterday. For tomorrow, the immediate tomorrow—he looked down at the soft flower-like young face and tenderly pressed the little hand on his arm.

Milly! Thank God!

INTERVAL